PLANNING FOR ESCAPE

PLANNING *for* ESCAPE

A NOVEL

SARA DILLON

GREEN WRITERS PRESS *Brattleboro, Vermont*

PUBLISHER'S NOTE: This is a work of fiction. Names, characters, places and incidents either are the product of the authors' imaginations or are used fictitiously, and any resemblance to actual persons, living or dead, events, or locales are entirely coincidental.

Printed in the United States

10 9 8 7 6 5 4 3 2 1

Green Writers Press is a Vermont-based publisher whose mission is to spread a message of hope and renewal through the words and images we publish. Throughout we will adhere to our commitment to preserving and protecting the natural resources of the earth. To that end, a percentage of our proceeds will be donated to environmental activist groups. Green Writers Press gratefully acknowledges support from individual donors, friends, and readers to help support the environment and our publishing initiative.

Giving Voice to Writers & Artists
Who Will Make the World a Better Place
Green Writers Press | Brattleboro, Vermont
www.greenwriterspress.com

ISBN: 978-0-9961357-4-0

PRINTED ON PAPER WITH PULP THAT COMES FROM FSC-CERTIFIED FORESTS, MANAGED FORESTS THAT GUARANTEE RESPONSIBLE ENVIRONMENTAL, SOCIAL, AND ECONOMIC PRACTICES BY LIGHTNING SOURCE ALL WOOD PRODUCT COMPONENTS USED IN BLACK & WHITE, STANDARD COLOR, OR SELECT COLOR PAPERBACK BOOKS, UTILIZING EITHER CREAM OR WHITE BOOKBLOCK PAPER, THAT ARE MANUFACTURED IN THE LAVERGNE, TENNESSEE PRODUCTION CENTER ARE SUSTAINABLE FORESTRY INITIATIVE® (SFI®) CERTIFIED SOURCING.

Book One

Greensboro; 2006

I have always planned for escape. Well, just that once I didn't, but that's a long time ago. Surprisingly long ago.

It was so cheap to rent a place in Greensboro in early September. All the summer people were gone, the cottages and even the houses on the main road were more or less empty. I didn't take a camp by the lake; that would have been too eerie and damp. Instead, I took a small white house in a field just outside the town, a kind of ideal really. I took my kids, Emmet and Madina, of course. Madina was confused about why she was leaving her school when the vacation season was already over. *Why are we going back up to Vermont*? she kept asking.

They played together in the front garden. I saw them sway back and forth on the old tire swing.

Madina is so tall now, I thought. I saw her passing by near the bushes and early fall flowers; she had Emmet by the hand. A car went by now and then. We could see the town from the front room; near enough and just nicely far away. Not like renting rooms right down on top of other people. This sort of location was what my sister Una and I would call *in but out*. We had company, but not too much.

The house had a phone number but I was darned if I could find the piece of paper it was written on. I'd never got around to buying a cell phone, and I didn't know if it would work here anyway.

The television was complicated. I tried to use the remote but it was too hard and I just gave up, sticking the contraption in a drawer.

Gramma's car looked funny in that particular front yard, the Buick that seemed to last forever, that never completely broke down, though we thought many times it might.

We called it Gramma car or Mumma car; my mother was Gramma, I was Mumma. Emmet would look for exact matches of that rare car type, the 1992 Buick Skylark, kicking his legs and calling out, *Mumma car, Mumma car,* whenever he saw one. It might be aqua blue or beige instead of our silver grey, sort of like a cousin to our car.

Emmet tumbled out of the tire swing. I heard Madina's voice shouting *Emmet, you drive me* ***crazy***. Then she was picking him up again and he let her scoop him this way and that.

I liked the windows, the curtains, everything. I liked the corner of lake I could see from the window, the edge of the general store, the stand of secretive trees and the dark green slope of a lawn with bushes all around. Clouds passed over the late afternoon sun. The phone didn't ring since I didn't know the number and so couldn't tell anyone what it was.

Emmet, Madina was telling him, *eat your num-nums, eat your num-nums*. She was making a gesture towards her mouth, which he imitated but still did not eat his num nums. There was a table set up outside the back door, for us to have supper there if we wanted, but it was September now, just barely, and already there was a chill in the air.

I had taught a few law school classes that August, and then I began to think. I knew somehow that it couldn't go on. I read some Hopkins. I rifled through my book collection, what was left of it. I've lost bunches of books with every move, though some I've enjoyed losing.

When we reached Hardwick on our way to Greensboro, we drove over the bridge where Daddy went to help with the flood of 1927. Everyone in my family is so old when they have kids that just a generation or two reaches back into the mists of time, skipping over the industrial revolution, and Daddy had been gone so long already. Madina and Emmet's little voices sounded so young and fresh in the back seat, it was amazing they could be my children, when it was my Daddy who had run away from the very house we were passing, to throw sandbags in the flood of 1927. It didn't make sense, really. I rarely tried to explain it to anyone.

The thing was, at some point, it just had to end. It was mid-August, and only law schools could begin in mid-August. August, of all the terrible and sacred times, the month of dog days and the death of summer and the death of the heart, the accumulated heat—August. Only people with no feeling at all, tiny bits of charcoal where feeling might be, would begin anything of the kind in mid-August. It's the time when we ought to be at the beach, staring at the changing light, watching the odd formations of sand as summer walks away once again. Instead, there I was standing up in front of a classroom, row upon row of faces, very bored faces, and I was talking about things I couldn't feel and didn't care about, and I knew it had to end, it just had to.

It was August, and I was muttering about global trade law and policy and the history of economic integration and the GATT evolving into the World Trade Organization; and on it went, the European Union, the postwar system of human rights and states reporting to intergovernmental and supranational organizations, and suddenly I saw systems of rules colliding like a series of Ferris wheels gone off their rails. Outside in the city, it was still August, the parks were withering, the sprinklers going full blast. The fretting in the room was palpable; the students utterly uninterested and nervous all at once. Maybe a few were fighting back feeling.

To do law requires that one pretend to have no feeling of any kind; so it was hard to tell how many might be fighting back feeling; maybe I was projecting.

No one could have any idea how funny it was, me at the podium, talking about law, pushing back the old lines of poetry and the memories of wine and cheese parties. Balance of payments and subsidies, and then, *Rescue me, calling out from the four corners of. . . .*

I would never finish that poem, no matter how much free time I might find, damn it. It is all gone, I kept thinking, all gone, not to sound too much like Gramma, but it is all gone.

Madina! Keep an eye on him, he could run into that road!

I will, Mom, I am, she answered in her new tone of annoyance and being put upon. *I* ***am*** *doing that, Mom.*

The exchange

I began to obsess on the landscape paintings that hung in the hallway of the law school, near the elevator banks. For one thing, I wondered how it would be to have your artwork end up decorating a law school's walls. *A law school, can you imagine,* you could tell others, detached, amused.

Ikitai, I kept whispering in Japanese as I stood staring down the soft and vague and indistinct lanes, the rows of trees in the dusk, *ikitai na, ikitai....* I want to go there. Then someone would come along and I would make a quick switch into rational mode. Things are going well, projects underway, I am dynamic and in demand. I may even get to present in the plenary session.

For quite a while since I hadn't expected any more new lives; I mean, even a cat runs out. And well, the cat knows. It is hard to admit, hard to say, but once you say it, it does get easier to realize—no more new lives. No more; sorry. Like, no more cookies before dinner, to bring it back to the family way. Lights out, all over, all gone. No more.

But I started to think, Well, at least I had been brave enough to see it, and maybe, at least, I had the right to go sit in a Morris chair, in the kind of place the elder Darcys all eventually died, and take in a Vermont evening, right? Wasn't that a fair trade? My idea of love, any version or vision of it, in exchange for just one day that would spin on and on.

Attitude, Madina, I hear that attitude starting again, I called.

She wasn't listening. I had become repetitious.

I'd always been repetitious. Natural selection, and this was my forté. A good thing science and the wheel did not depend upon me—nor the discovery of fire. I'd been on a search for feeling, nothing else. Well, that had been a flop. It was hard to know if I'd really given up. I was sneaky, stubborn, and there it would unexpectedly reappear, a fresh and pure gardenia hidden away in my pocket.

In the morning, we shopped at Willey's, where we could get everything we wanted, even decent wine. It was strange to be there out of season, so quiet. I'd only known it as crowded and with beach sand underfoot, people looking for plastic dinnerware and swimming tubes. It was a relief to be there when summer had finished, in the earliest part of the fall; the manageable twist of buildings, the bend of the road through town. I was careful to hold tightly to the kids' hands; it was a sharp corner even though the road had become largely empty of cars, and you never knew.

Up until now, at least for the last few years, it had all been the same pattern: coming to Greensboro with Una's family in early July, renting a house, poking around Willey's, the Miller's Thumb, going to look at Daddy's old house up the road in Hardwick, an outing to Crystal Lake; then back to Boston and another year of classes.

Now that I'd arrived back out of season, I could do some considering.

To be honest, my fall from grace had probably happened a long time ago. I'd always been so thrilled to be alive, if I can put it like that, as if I'd been promised some enormous present of happiness, just for me. Because I was the best, the greatest, the one with the most heart; and then swish, it just went quiet. Like, gone.

I understood Emmet. He'd learned within a few days of leaving the orphanage to raise his little hands in a gesture of bewilderment when I said, *All gone.* He would look around with a pained expression, like a little old man, inviting you to help search for what he had lost. *More*, he began to say, haltingly at first, *more*? It had a teeny whine in it, plaintive, *more*?

I kept furtively driving by Daddy's house, the well-kept red house in the flat part of Hardwick. It looked neat and prosperous and I kept thinking of Daddy and his sister playing in the yard as little children. It was like I had collapsed time by coming back here, especially out of vacation season. Daddy never knew my kids, he died long before I got them.

I felt his friendly and permanent presence up and down the street he was born on, his strange way of caring and not caring. Someone once accused me of talking about him like he was a saint, some awful date who was jealous, I think, but in fact he was as close to a saint as people come. In the sense that he had no malice. He also didn't give a darn about most things, just wanted to be left alone, to go out to coffee with Gramma and let the world go by.

The summer flowers had gone by, the clouds were rolling in. I drove past his house again and again, slowly and drinking it in each time. The kids were getting restless in the back. Madina wanted to know where she would be going to school.

I'm not sure, Madina, we'll talk about it soon, I said, trying to maintain that everything-is-all-right tone one affects with children, really out of mercy and because you don't want them to be upset.

I thought about all the new books I could order, buy them online, novels and poetry, stuff I never had a chance to read anymore. I'd been a failure, really. Once many years ago Yukito's sister had said to me that an artist had to be ruthless, not bothering about ordinary things or even people, only about art. I considered that an affectation at the time, that she didn't know what she was talking about. But maybe she'd been right after all; I had talent but not enough ambition, not enough backbone; too independent to have real contacts and too dependent to strike out on my own, an awful combination, even though I had once thought it quite marvelous.

I blew it, really.

Would I even sit down and try to write something up now, since I certainly couldn't say I didn't have time, that wouldn't wash, I had nothing but. I could blame it on the kids, just couldn't get down to it because they were calling me all the time. Or blame it on my worries, my tendency to lie awake and stew; but not on writer's block, I didn't like that one, the idea of a *block*, it seemed like a jinx to call it that.

The lake in Greensboro, Caspian, same name as the Caspian Sea, was steel blue and the grass was shining in the meadows. It had gone woodsy up here in recent years, but there was still a lot of meadow. It would last my lifetime anyway. That was thinking like an old person, wow, what was that all about. We went to the little beach and got out of the car. The kids started running down towards the rocky water they'd played in a few weeks earlier.

Wait for me, and *Don't go too far!* I called out almost automatically. No wonder they didn't listen. *Kids, not too far! Wait! Wait!*

Emmet paused when he saw the freshwater gulls wheeling about. He was still afraid of animals of all kinds, even birds. He turned towards me and started running in place to show how frightened he was.

Not afraid, I said soothingly; *it's not scary, not a scary gull.*

Goldengrove

I just had to get away from those lawyers. I had a right to. After all, I did. Even at my age, I caught myself thinking about things like taking off for the Aran Islands and trying to become as good at Irish as a native speaker. At certain crazy moments, it seemed it could still be done. It wasn't too late. Seek out the remnants, though maybe there were no remnants left. They disappeared so fast, the final firesides. At other times, I knew it was impossible, appropriate to my young self. I was beyond that, especially with kids in tow.

I'd always done everything that was asked of me—everything. I carried heavy bags and shoveled snow and sat through lectures and learned classical Japanese grammar and taught bills of lading and incoterms and even marine insurance, as implausible as that seemed. I kept on going.

I rented those weird apartments in Dublin and pretended to be a law lecturer. I even went in on Sundays to my office, driving in furtively, up the winding path to the castle that housed the law faculty, running down the corridors because I was afraid of the dark. It was a measure of my sense of being a fraud that I couldn't stay away from it. I spent every spare moment in guilty preparation of things I cared nothing about; The Sale of Goods Act, priority in liquidation, examination invigilators.

Twice or three times a year, at the end of my visits home from Dublin, my sister Una and her husband Sven—I guess he was her husband—would come to the Boston airport and say goodbye to me; either in the winter dark or the summer dusk, and I cried every single time. I left with the feeling of being forced to go, aware of it not making any sense, standing up in front of students who really just wanted to know how to get a job in a solicitor's office, talking from a small platform about goods passing a ship's rail. Worse yet, about charges on big-ticket items in a bankruptcy and what the silly old High Court might think of all this, the crux of the reasoning, the legal *bon mot.*

I attended faculty receptions like an idiot, nodding to the red faced judges who were of no interest to me nor I to them, talking to myself, silently repeating *a rat's ass*, I do not give a rat's ass about law or the legal profession, not a rat's ass about judges or three part tests or stare decisis. *Margaret are you grieving*, I would say to myself, laughing quietly as I headed for the Belfield bus, *over Goldengrove unleaving*, but no one was listening. It was all a cod, a fraud.

I did take an Irish language class, just me and a bunch of young European Erasmus students, singing *Mó Ghile Mear* in a depressing classroom with dull overhead lights. I told Gramma's cousin, Brother Clement, that I could escape when I knew enough Irish. I could teach it eventually. It wouldn't take me that long, I said. I was in the West then, at the monastery, smoking and drinking a brandy. The rain was beating on the window. *I'll get out of it*, I told him.

And he winked at me and said, *I'd say you will, I'd say you will.*

So back and forth I went. Dublin to Northeast Galway, wearing a hole in the road. I couldn't stop. *Will you be out this weekend, girl? Will you? Will you?* That was my cousin Bridie talking. But after I got Madina, at the very end of the 1990s, I called it.

That just had to end, too.

I escaped from Dublin and ended up first in New York, with more lectures and more lectures to write. I would wake up at four a.m. with the buzzing of the alarm, the lights of Manhattan barely a distraction in my anxiety to be ready for the day. Hoping to get in a few hours of reading, scribbling notes, sipping my coffee, vaguely aware of the ships passing by in the dark so close I could almost touch them. Then out would come little Madina, right away, as soon as I got up, whining, rubbing her eyes.

Mommy, me come too, me come too.
Mommy needs to work, Madina. You have to sleep, sleep.
No, no, me come too.

The nighttime temperature in Greensboro fell to the 30s. Sometimes I could pick up Vermont's NPR station and sometimes I couldn't. I kept thinking that Daddy would be proud; at least he wouldn't disapprove. *It's beautiful country, honey,* he might say in his vague, disinterested way.

I asked him at night, as I smelled the old wood and the apples deep in the wood and sawdust, Is it all right like this?

I would have to do something or other, I knew. But I could do something. If I could manage to lecture on contract prices ex factory or ship's rail, I could manage to find something near Greensboro; like, work in the IGA, or True Value, a mystery figure. *GED?* they'd ask. Well, actually, PhD, JD, lover of a Japanese rock star, lecturer in obscure points as to risk passage on the high seas. I can do this. Believe me, I can.

The phone

It was a nice little house we rented in Greensboro. The kitchen had stayed untouched for decades, but it hadn't gone ratty. It reminded me of Aunt Olive's kitchen in Hyde Park. Tidy white painted cupboards. I enjoyed lying awake at night, listening to the kids' breathing, and I would accuse myself of every kind of failure in the world.

I didn't like to sleep away from the kids; I didn't understand how people could sleep separately, in far-flung bedrooms, leaving it to chance that they would all ever meet again in the morning. Madina slept in a day-bed in the corner of my room; Emmet on the floor in a special bed made from quilts and comforters.

Your idiotic clairvoyance, I thought. Less like a talent in the modern sense and more like medieval hysterics—gazing out the window during a faculty meeting, closed up in silence like a tiny Sphinx, and looking for clues that the end of the world was at hand. That the ultimate had arrived.

Madina, be kind to him, he is a so much smaller than you, I heard my repetitious commands. She was wrapped in a beach towel, her bare feet sticking out at the bottom—she was never cold—while Emmet collected rocks.

Now wash the rocks, Emmet, I said, as this was one of his favorite things to do.

In Greensboro, it was odd to be able to decide everything myself—absolutely everything, to go to Willey's store whenever I liked, and buy what I liked. I knew I would have to phone Una. It was unthinkable what I had done. There were explanations you just couldn't make to my sister; she was merciless for the most part. Explanations such as, I was being inundated with excessive feeling and I had to follow its lead; or, I could clearly see my long pattern of submission and I knew that this was the only thing left.

I would have to tell her that I'd had a "breakdown;" or that I couldn't "deal with it" anymore. I feared breakdowns, though, and didn't like to use the word. It was Gramma's old word, and using it would leave a residue of contamination or a threat that victory would not, in fact, be mine in the end.

And perhaps I still believed in some corner of my soul, in the back bedroom of our old Galway homestead in Timard, that I would be, in some indefinable way, victorious.

I was afraid to phone Una. But it wasn't just that—I was also afraid of Una. I could never stand up for myself against her view; whatever she said I should do looked best at that moment. It was never until long after that I realized it was not at all what I wanted, that she had been advising me to be someone else entirely, and perhaps I'd been seeking advice on how to do just that. She sounded so right, so plausible, and every time I tried on my own to figure out where to go or what to do, I just saw pink lilac bushes or long porches in the dusk before my eyes—powerful and memorable, but without any possibility of translating this into a form that others could believe in. I thought in images, and it didn't hold up with her.

I decided to write her a note instead.

She had always made fun of these notes of mine. *You love scribbling these little messages,* she said, and she was correct. I hated to witness the reaction of others to myself, that was it. And jotting down a little note made it very unlikely that I would see how they took the contents. I would not have to *see* other people react to me, I mean. When next I ran into them, they would already have opened the note and read it and got out their raw reaction, had time to regroup and edit.

Una could be scathing.

I would never be forgiven at my law school job, no matter what reason was given. You just don't leave law classes in the lurch; it is unheard of. Everything is on a litigation model. From that point of view, to drop the ball and disappear has nothing to do with psychology. It's a professional lapse. I would have blown any chance of return by now. Once they knew I was alive and wandering around Greensboro, their concern would quickly, in a heartbeat, turn to exasperation.

And then within a week, they would be whispering in the hallway about how they should go about finding a replacement. Is subject matter really a consideration, or should we go for a deeper pool of candidates this time? In any event, I had been from the beginning a martian to them; the accidental choice. No matter how large a group of students I might actually have in a class, they continued to think my classes must be small, select, on the fringe. Had they really heard the last of me, they would wonder, or would I make some trouble, accuse them of some mistreatment?

Cooking up allegations, is she, trying to blame it all on being a woman? Or would she just go? This reminded me of standing in the law faculty tea room in Dublin, rain falling outside as it always seemed to be, the television on and Princess Diana speaking in one of her famous interviews, her eyes ringed round with kohl, explaining how the royals wanted to get rid of her. *But she won't go quiatly, that's the trouble, she won't go quiatly,* she repeated.

It might cross their minds to wonder if I would go quietly.

As the law school must have seen me, I was this shy woman who had spent years in Dublin; she did have those worrying holes in her résumé, the abrupt jumps, the unexplained shift from one subject to another, no clerkships, no demonstrated interest in the profession, hardly any practice, and she never explained it, just stared into space and said, yes, in that vague way.

And she was always complaining about something, but in a way that made it seem that there was really something else on her mind, something unspoken, wrong. Meet her in the law school hallway and she would start right in; how tired she was, the nagging tickle in her throat that made her run from meetings, the exhausting pickups at day care, her hands peeling from the cold outside and dry heat in, her mother's spine disintegrating. Conference attendance was tapering off, said she was getting phobic about planes.

It was true I could hardly think of getting on planes the way I used to. It had something to do with the kids—I wanted to protect them every minute and didn't want to risk leaving. I felt danger in the sky and wanted to stay with them, always with them.

At the next catered faculty lunch after my disappearance I would be the talk of the place—*You know, I never felt she was the right replacement for Ron to begin with, if only she doesn't make some diversity thing out of it. Is the Dean inclined to factor it into this year's hiring or what.* It had always been, well, funny, astonishing, incredible that I had shared space with them, that I had conversed with them; it was the anti-fate and I had endured mine.

I waited for Una to write back; I had not included the phone number to the house, though I had managed to locate it. I waited in fear; I was terrified of her, though I was the older one and she insisted up and down that she had grown up in my shadow. I couldn't decide anything for myself; couldn't drive properly, in the sense of never doing more than fifty even on the highway. Highway merging I considered a left hand turn. I couldn't buy furniture on my own; it was bound to be a mistake if I did. I'd always lived out of a suitcase, from apartment to apartment. That was in the days when I never stayed still. Now I didn't want to go anywhere. To pretend otherwise was too much, too much of a burden.

To do things over Una's objection was like walking and not leaving footprints.

The line between August and September was abrupt up there in Greensboro. September really meant something, despite the fact that winter was much less of an ordeal than it used to be, even compared to when I was young. There was serious mist on the fields in the morning. We saw deer. The car started hard. The stars at night were sharp as knives. The lights paused when they were turned on in early evening and, poof, lit up everything in strong contrast.

Emmet was confused; he wandered around the new house, looking behind chairs and under the bed. He'd only been with us a year, though, and had hardly had time to get used to anything. Madina and I rocked him to sleep; he would be a mommy's boy and a big sister's boy. He would take quickly to pouts and self-pity. Little tufts of pale brown hair had begun to sprout from his almost bald head; he no longer looked so teeny tiny. He tried to climb the stairs after Madina, and she obliged by hauling him up and down.

A mother cat with her kitten, that is what it looked like to me, Madina's strong little hands grabbing him by the shirt and pulling him forward.

When I'd brought him home the summer before, the doctors had told me to get as many calories into him as I could, and so I did. I would chase him around the kitchen with a spoonful of pudding and heap his high chair tray with a mismatched assortment of foods designed to fatten him up. Though he was nearly two and a half then, I gave him baby formula and snuck canola oil into his milk. At two, he had barely been the size of a small infant, but under the barrage of food, he was beginning to look chunky and it was harder by the day to pick him up. Gramma called him a bag of cement, or a stuffed turkey.

At night when he was asleep, I thought of him with his orphanage group, standing idly inside one of the miniature summer houses on the orphanage grounds, silent in the little dacha, twelve little boys and girls sucking on apples, the Central Asian summer sun beating down on towels spread across the windows.

Emmet and Madina, from the place where it snows every night in winter and swelters in 100 degree heat for a short summer. When they were asleep, I would go and smell the faint perfume from their hair, smile at their earnestness. *Where dreamland?* Emmet wanted to know.

I was starving, that was it.

I could see the boat leaving the shore—the boat is gone; the boat has left. *Le bateau est parti*, or would it be *s'est parti;* the grammar of various languages garbled together.

Teach me French and I'll teach you German, I remembered Miles Bradford in the hallway of the high school saying that to me. How daring, how unthinkable such a remark seems now. I had no idea at the time.

I was starving, and I would die soon. It was the last chance.

Now at least I could put my feet up and look out at the first twinges of red in the trees. Here I am, I thought.

Una

No one came back. Not one person from any of the many motifs came back.

They all left and never came back. My heart periodically turned to stone, a stone smaller and more useless all the time. In Greensboro, for the very first time, I was glad that no one could guess where I was or find me. Before, over years, I had imagined every day that someone would appear at the door, clothes streaked with mud, having tracked down my whereabouts, followed my trail, my e-mail, my anything.

I walked over to Madina's bed and watched her peaceful breathing. Her lovely black hair made a broad fan on the pillow; the heavy lines of her eyelids in perfect rest. I touched the coastline of baby hair beneath the more grown up hairline and she stirred in irritation. Emmet was sprawled out unceremoniously, his chubby hands outstretched as if to make sure he wouldn't miss anything, even in sleep.

The phone rang after nine—it felt very late. The cars had stopped passing and the stars were bright and sharp over the old Grange Hall building. I let it ring twice, three times. It was like being at Park Baun again, the overloud ringing of a phone in the quiet house. No one had the number yet, I was sure of that.

What the hell are you doing? I heard Una's voice. There was a moment of relief, as if now someone could tell me what to do.

Una, hi.

What the hell are you doing? I don't care about myself, but what about Gramma, what about your job?

I had a breakdown, I said. It seemed to work, even Una could respond to a breakdown, the old Irish appeal.

Don't be mad at me, please don't.

We thought you were dead or something.

No, you didn't. I left a voice message at Sven's office.

At first we did.

Una said she was coming up. *No,* I said, *please don't. Yes, I will,* she insisted. *I'll be up tomorrow. Not yet,* I pleaded. *We're just settling in.*

Settling in? she yelled into the phone. *Someone has to save this situation and I'm sorry to say that no one but me ever tries to deal with these things.*

We are settling in. I have a plan, I said. My plan was shattering, though, as I spoke. I was weak and Una was terribly strong, frighteningly strong, not beset by my sort of excessive brain waves, what I called the upside of OCD, trying in better times to make her laugh.

It's a nice house, I said, thinking that might appease her. Una loved real estate, and loved discussing buildings.

But you don't own it, she said.

She was right, of course. She always accused me, and her husband Sven, of being "risk averse." We didn't have the get up and go to leap on an opportunity, everything passed us by. *All Sven wants is a long weekend in a rental property*, she would jibe at him. *You're right*, Sven would reply, *I don't feel like fixing roofs.*

She tended to make pronouncements like, *I'm taking stock, things are going to change.* In the middle of every summer, she would say, *It's happening again, it's getting away from me, and I won't let that happen.*

Una, Una, my little sister, she was my baby and I would protect her. She always claimed to be an extra, an add on, an also ran, that Gramma hadn't liked her all that well, she came at the very end of four; as a small child she was strangely quiet, and, according to her, spaced out, everyone talked too much and she had nothing to say. She accused me especially of talking too much; I hogged the floor constantly, drowning her out.

If it was payback she wanted, she had more than accomplished this by now.

Una denied having any happy childhood memories. In fact, she often denied having any memories of herself as a small child. But I loved being a child, I loved our big stucco house in upstate New York, loved the yard, the street, the pond; I loved the Catholic school with its blue jumpers and blue shoes; a school built from old farm buildings. The kindergarten was the old greenhouse, the third grade was created out of the old barn. The twisting road into the school was lovely on rainy days, with rippling puddles and the smell of rain most intense as we went into the cloakroom. Winter was beautiful and early summer was overwhelming. We spent a lot of our time nursing baby birds that had fallen out of trees, and crying over their inevitable deaths.

Una might just have been getting back at me by saying she didn't remember anything. How could she not recall anything at all? Not even Daddy coming home from a business trip on a summer evening, and all of us running down the backyard walk to meet him? His white shirt was rumpled and wrinkled, but the starch still perfect in the collar and cuffs. He'd been on the road all week; how many hours? we would ask. Una was small then, but how could she say she remembered nothing, zero, none of it?

Daddy was handsome in a certain way; heavy-set in the wonderful manner of Jackie Gleason, solid, a graceful polka dancer for all that he had too much of what people in those days called a paunch.

Una became mine when our older sister Marie died. Marie was the oldest in the family, older than our brother Jack. Marie was the first born, Gramma's favorite. She had been born with a hole in her heart, that is how they explained it to us, and her lips turned blue when she tried to ride her bike.

I always wanted to chase after her when she went off with her friends, but Gramma stopped me. She protected Marie, and let her have secrets. Marie was thirteen when she had her operation. I remembered sitting in the car, looking up at the big bleak hospital; it was an early summer evening and everyone was scared. The doctor was not nice, he was not telling them anything. I had the feeling he was letting Marie die, maybe he even wanted her to die. And when Marie did die, I tried to tell Gramma that we were even now—two girls, even Steven, and she said, *But that's not what we wanted.* Gramma disappeared then; she was lying down for days. I knew she loved Marie in some way she would never love anyone else.

Gramma saw everything according to the way she imagined the feelings of others; the doctors who didn't value us enough, who ran away and hid as Marie lay dying. We were singled out for poor treatment; except by those people, like nuns, who singled us out for lovely treatment. It had to be one or the other, so cruel to us or so good to us. There were no random events or bureaucratic bungles, only the full intention of the universe playing around us like a spotlight at every turn.

And so it was that Una had to be mine, and I had to make sure she would never die.

They sent Una and me to peoples' houses; I didn't like people we didn't know very well giving us baths. Poor Una, she was mine by then. I decided I'd better protect her; she could be lost, gone, and I had to keep her. Being with her was like being with myself. I always held her hand and waited for her and looked for her. Though this did not seem to have registered with her—especially as she insisted much later that she didn't remember anything of it—not a thing; just nothing.

One hot evening, when everyone was sitting outside the way they used to back then, Una disappeared. She was probably around three years old at the time. She vanished, and for me the world seemed to be coming to an end. Gramma was afraid, too, I zcould see that. I raced up and down the street, calling her name. Finally I found her on the porch with three elderly unmarried ladies who lived in a house on the top of a little hill. Una was quietly eating cookies and looked unconcerned at my panic. A great relief, like life slowly coming back to me, a reprieve, filled my heart, and I guided Una down the hill and back home; my own little treasure.

In later years, Una always disapproved of everything I did. No, that was not right; she had disapproved of everything I wanted to do, and thus only some of what I actually did. I had bad taste in men, she said, and she was correct. She accused me of being too vague; too exaggerated; too impractical; too repetitious. She had to pick up the slack for everyone, she said. Una was taller than me, by quite a lot, and had reddish hair. This red hair marked her as Daddy's special favorite, against the odds. There were many family tales of how Daddy, otherwise in no sense a ladies' man, was partial to red-haired women.

Una talked me into going to law school, although she denied this. Before law school, when I wanted to ditch Japan—and it was true that I couldn't take any more of Japan—to go back to poetry, Una made up a mock poem that went like this:

You there in the light there
Grandfather there in the greenish light there

Is that what you want to spend the rest of your life doing? She asked. *Why don't you get out and help real people, do something real?*

Under this new scheme, I was to use my skills, whatever these might be; though I suspected full well and in advance that I would find I had none.

So I said goodbye to the white light, not *see you later,* but a real goodbye, to the absurdity that I admit I was; the excess, the exaggeration. I said, Goodbye, I will never be back again.

When next you see me, I will be someone else.

And I emerged after some years all alone, law school over and done, still just what I had been all along. I know she was very disappointed in me for that, for being unable to change.

She arrived mid-afternoon on a Saturday; the black Jetta pulled up tentatively. Greensboro is small, and I like giving very precise directions.

"Your Auntie Una," I said to the kids, and they began to hop up and down in front of the window.

I could see Una get out of the driver's seat; she was wearing a dark plaid jacket, like something we would have worn in high school.

"Auntie Woona, Auntie Woona," Emmet shrieked, as if his joy knew no bounds. The two kids clasped hands and went running down the front path; Emmet was still clumsy from his lack of exercise in the orphanage, all those days spent with ten or fifteen other children in a room, just looking at each other.

Una held out her arms to the kids. If you looked closely, it seemed a gesture of pity, but they didn't see that.

Well, she said as she reached the door, as if she'd agreed with herself not to fly off the handle.

How is Sven?

Okay I guess; I don't know, we don't talk. He never says.

It was the same old joke.

The extent to which that man can stay in his quiet place is amazing, she said.

She was already interested in the layout of the house, I could tell.

As I said, she really loved buildings; houses, especially farm houses, and meadows. Her eyes went automatically to the arrangement of the rooms in our rental house; the staircase, the possibility for expansion, the condition of the walls.

It smells like apples in here; the way Aunt Olive's garage used to.

It's wonderful, isn't it? Maybe Una could be persuaded.

It was a hell of a long drive, she said, complaining. *Especially after we were just up here a few weeks ago.*

Here it comes, I thought.

Your hair, she said.

I know, it's bad.

Kids seem okay, she observed, as if surprised. Una didn't like to dwell on the possible sadness of children. She believed that they would be happy if only they were let out enough to run around. Her son Hugh still had tantrums at eight, and whenever he was outside racing up and down, she would sigh and say, *This is just what he needs. Let him run, I always say that. Just let them get out of here and run.*

Whenever the talk turned to the past, she would say, *But weren't kids always allowed out more back then to run? They weren't cooped up all the time like they are now.*

The unpleasant side of this was the continual implication that if I exposed mine to a slightly higher level of physical danger, they would be happier. All indications of them having "issues" apparently stemmed from the fact that I was a nervous Nellie. On this, she and Sven presented a united front.

How's Hugh? asked Madina. They were nearly the same age and had been inseparable since Madina was adopted from Central Asia at the age of two. Madina hated missing out on anything, and the deep, beautiful folds of her eyelids clouded over as she asked Una.

Hughie's great; he misses you, Una said. She sat down in a Morris chair, patting the arms of it.

A Morris chair, she said. Our eyes met for a moment.

I don't have a lot of time, she said, *So let's sort this out. Somebody has to.*

I tried to tell her that we were all right. The kids loved it here, I could spend more time with them. I was looking for a job, something in Hardwick maybe. Emmet could go to family daycare; Madina would be starting school.

If you want to make insane decisions for yourself, that's one thing, Una said finally. *But what do I tell Gramma? What do I do about her?*

We'd begun to refer to our mother as Gramma, I guess after Hughie was born.

I'll take care of it. I'll call her.

Una clearly found this beneath contempt, not worth responding to. She stood and looked out the window.

Your job is history, you know that.

I thought of the ponderous hallways of the law school, the catered lunches, the steam off the pilaf.

Lally show sing, Emmet said brightly, taking Una's hand.

He wants to show you the swing on the tree, Madina explained. She was his translator, as I had been Una's when she was very small. No one had known what she was trying to say but me. *Of course, I had no practice talking, I couldn't get a word in edgewise,* Una always said.

I watched the three of them through the window. Una was pretending to run her fastest up and down the grass, as if she couldn't keep up with them. Emmet was hysterically joyful. I rapped on the old glass and waved.

I wanted to think about something immediate, like

food, about cutting vegetables, about lentils. I wanted to do my Saturday errands.

This weather was familiar to Una and me. We had moved to Vermont when I was twelve and Una only nine. Daddy's blood pressure was so high they told him he was "next door to shock," and they sent him up to run a plant in Vermont. He made less money and worried about being broke and sick. We left the big stucco house in Albany and lived on a mean little street and went with tough kids down to Lake Champlain to light beach fires. After we moved, it seemed Gramma and Daddy had no idea what we were doing. Gramma went to work in a big department store. Every Sunday we drove to Aunt Olive's in Hyde Park. The weather had been just like this. From September, there was no warmth left at all.

The leaves in the front garden and on down to Caspian Lake had begun to go yellow. Una came back inside, flushed and rubbing her hands together. I had the feeling she would not try and get it all sorted out. She had decided not to attempt that. She would punish me by leaving me to my own devices.

In fact, she didn't seem to want to talk to me any further.

I'll take the kids and pick up a few things. Is that farm stand still open?

Madina loved anything new. She waved goodbye and climbed into the back seat of the Jetta.

It was a funny thing. No one ever seemed to ask me if they could borrow my kids, move them, take them here or there. I always asked others, though, on the rare occasions I would make such a plan. There was something about me that made others consider me not someone you needed to ask. Just go ahead. She won't mind. It was my father's thing; that mark of diffidence that sent a silent message to others. But in Daddy's case, he enjoyed what this brought him, that is, being left alone to go driving for coffee and donuts with Gramma.

It still took a couple of hours to get Emmet to settle down and go to sleep. As he drifted, after crying himself into fatigue, I kissed his shallow little eyelids, his fingers. Madina was waiting, as she always had to now, for me to have time to say goodnight to her.

Are we staying here? Or will we go back? she whispered. It probably seemed to her that Una could order us to return.

I don't know, I said. *We can talk about it tomorrow.*

Oh; ohhhh, she whined at me. *You always say that.*

Don't wake him up, I said.

If it hadn't been too cold to sit out, it would have been just like the summer holidays: kids asleep at last, Una and I opening a bottle of wine and sitting together, wrapped in shawls, watching the car lights pass far away along the hills, trying to guess what other lights might be.

I can bring them home with me, she had said abruptly.

No! I said, uncharacteristically sharp. *They're mine. I need them.*

Just a thought, she said, raising her hands defensively. *It could give you time to chill out a little.*

It was a funny thing about Una, there was nothing you could say that she didn't get. She knew what this was all about, and yet held any statements about it at bay, substituted a false understanding of it for the real one. She knew poetry as well, she knew a great poem from a good one; she knew about the heart becoming a stone. She knew about me and Ireland, she knew about everything.

Chill out! I said, just on the edge of raising my voice.

Forget I said it then.

I couldn't afford to have her leave angry. I couldn't manage that.

I heard a funny sound and opened the door. It was foxes, laughing, just as I had heard them so often at Park Baun.

This reminded me again of coming back from the pub late on those merciless Irish nights, so terribly alone in my car, parking the Opel on the wet grass, leaving the headlights on until I got the front door open, running through the fog, certain that I would be killed imminently, slamming the door behind me. It was a new wooden door; the old one had gone rotten. Depending on the season, all sorts of creatures managed to squeeze through under the old one and get into the house. There were frogs and mice and bugs of all kinds. I could sit in the chair in the middle of the room and watch them sneaking in, tentatively at first, blinking their eyes in the light after they'd made it through.

Una had phoned me at Park Baun sometimes, the telephone sound echoing through the rooms with their stone walls. Una thought that everything I'd ever done was more or less stupid; that said, she claimed to admire me. Of course, she resented me for dominating our house with my incessant talk when we were little. In fact, though, she thought that everything in my past since then was also just stupid, even the things that were her ideas to begin with.

Maybe stupid isn't the right word. Rather, absurd. I was absurd when I had a sort of love affair with my high school history teacher, absurd when I left high school early and went to Ireland, getting so involved in the life of the countryside that it changed my accent; absurd when I went to St. Theo's, Daddy's college, and did drama, absurd in all the plays, absurd with my poetry, absurd with my piano playing in my college room (my abilities entirely overblown). Absurd to have got involved with an abusive and angry Indian exchange student, absurd to study Japanese, absurd to marry a Japanese man, absurd to leave him almost immediately (that was not quite as absurd); then absurd to believe myself to be in love with a Japanese singer.

Then, lost and disaffected, I was absurd to teach Japanese literature in a university. And with that, she encouraged me to go to law school. I would love to say she forced me, though it wasn't quite that. I was absurd to hate law school so much, with every ounce of my being; it cancelled me out, and very nearly killed me. There were lots of things that happened during that time I just couldn't remember. People later claimed to have seen me in New York, but I couldn't recall. All I could clearly remember was running and running at dawn on Riverside Drive; or writing late into the night and putting mountains of poems in a drawer, never to touch them.

After law school, I was absurd to meet Seanie Mannion in Roscommon, absurd to take up with him, absurd to move to Ireland again; absurd, absurd, absurd. She had a point, really.

Years back, Una's therapist told her I was psychotically delusional to think that that Japanese singer loved me, though everything I told Una had been true; strange and intense, granted, and in a sense he did love me, absurd though it surely was to want him that much. Of all the ill-considered things to want.

I don't think Una agreed with the therapist's suggestion, though she relayed this diagnosis to me to let me know how utterly absurd my love for that singer was.

The last I remember of the therapist was Una's story of how she chased Una around a bookstore demanding payment of an overdue therapy bill.

Una stayed the night after all, and woke up cheerily enough. She had decided, I saw, not to have it out with me. She bounced Emmet on her knee and said how much she would like to stay in Greensboro. We lined up to wave goodbye. Madina was wearing one of my old sweaters and looking forlorn. Una started backing out of the driveway, then paused and rolled down the window.

What am I going to say to Gramma? she asked, then rolled it back up without waiting for an answer.

I felt lost after her car disappeared up the hill, off into the yellowing trees, up the road to Hardwick, then back, back down to Boston, with all its angry drivers and highway exits.

It had been much easier before she came. I didn't feel able to keep on going after she'd left. I wanted to phone someone, to ask what to do. I felt cold; I suspected the heating system was defective, but didn't know what to do about it.

I felt all at once like I'd come back to die. My head was a jumble of places, Aix-en-Provence and Karaganda and Ogikubo and Roscommon. I felt like a disused encyclopedia, stuck on the shelf or at a yard sale. My mind turned quickly away from anything to do with law, the law, regulations, statutes, precedents, treaties, judicial opinions. At least there was no law here. The fields were fields again. The grass was brown, the leaves going red, the water dark blue green.

Get moving and write a book, a filmscript, Una had said to me many times. *Stop talking about it and do it. Do what you want. I'm sorry I ever gave you any advice.*

I thought with a shudder of the angry student who had come into my office after class, his eyes as he repeated, *If you don't want me asking questions, just tell me, say it straight out. I don't want to be the last to know, I don't want to be laughed at.*

How confused they were by the cuisinart of dicta, an arbitral clause here, a self-executing international agreement there, a future of debt and self-doubt. And then this petite woman pushing them around. Whereas in fact I was ridiculously polite to them, laughing at their jokes, nodding, Interesting, interesting, responsive to their slightest monosyllable.

I didn't think you'd be like that, he was saying. *But just tell me, because I'm really getting the feeling you don't want my questions.*

Goodbye, I thought. Gone fishing. Gone to a dentist appointment that will last forever.

I always avoided saying goodbye by telling people, *I never say goodbye, it's too hard.*

But in fact, I loved saying goodbye, shaking out the clothes, throwing them in the laundry. Goodbye, never see you again. White wine and pickles and the start of a new life, and no need to ever see you again.

Houses

I thought of selling the house at Park Baun, in East Galway, if it could be called a house. In the early 1990s, it seemed the empty houses needed me, and I picked one out. All that work I did on it, depleting my bank account every month, year after year. Did I phone Jimmy Meehan or Frank Dolan about the windows or the doors or fire-place or chimney; was the chimney cleaned, the birds have nested in it, I got smoked out of it last time, ring up Danny, he'll set you right. The walls were so cold, and thousands of bottles had been thrown into the back garden by the bachelor brothers over the years, all embedded in the dirt. I had ripped down the old back kitchen, barely a shell, and had a new one put up. I put in a bathroom and a fridge and a cooker and tiled the floors and still it felt like a barn. All the improvements had hardly made any difference. Left by itself for a few hours, it would return from whence it had come, go to ground, cold as a badger's lair.

Perhaps what they said about poured concrete was true; nothing to be done with it. Red rotten, knock the bastard. That's what they all told me.

I could sell that house and get some money, and then we would be all right, I thought. It had been standing empty since I came back to America, anyway. And then I reconsidered; I couldn't sell the house, with its sound of whoosh whoosh in the tall trees, the fox's hole with the feathers near it, the road with nothing on it. *I have just returned to the nineteenth century*, I would tell my co-conspirator in the Landscape Preservation Group, standing in the doorway with the blue telephone in my hand, smoking a cigarette. I never smoked in Dublin, but lit up as soon as I arrived at Park Baun. Sometimes it seemed to me I only went there to smoke.

I even kept a stash of ten on the wooden mantelpiece in the side bedroom.

Let me start at the beginning.

Please, let me start in the middle.

That was one reason only Vermont was left. Park Baun was the reason, I mean. They had ruined it, ruined Ireland. It was so utterly destroyed, my most feared thing had come true before my eyes. I had tried everything to stop it, but I couldn't. I had escaped back to Galway after law school and found that they were ruining it. I tried to save things, but it couldn't be done. *Would you have us live in hovels, Doctor whoever ye are?* I was shouted at in forums, so many of them, the speeches, the group meetings, plotting and planning against golf courses, roads and shopping centers.

I couldn't have imagined that it could just be taken away; it was a place, with rocks and a sky and water never far away. It had its own mad process, the loss of it. Not to personalize history too much, but things do have a way of slipping away from me and being destroyed. That was the fate piece.

I first saw Ireland when I was sixteen. My parents wanted me away for a while, that was part of it. Because of Miles Bradford. I went to Spain and spent time with my brother. It was during the Vietnam War and he was in the navy and lived in an apartment building that rose up on a cliff overlooking the beach. I left Andalusia after some weeks and went by train alone—first to Madrid, then to Paris, all alone. Then on a boat train to Dublin. My parents must have been out of their minds.

I went all by myself, my face pressed against the glass of the train windows. Everyone talked to me then, I suppose because I had young, lovely eyes. I was pretty, petite et sexy, *kogata bijin*. There were dozens of different motifs along the way; types of conversations and kisses and various forms of pretence. Then I was in Galway and it was grey and still and perfectly beautiful, its medieval boundaries still intelligible, countryside meeting the grey edge of the city with finality. The sky, the land and the walls all breathed together; inhaling and exhaling in unison.

Clement, Gramma's cousin and a Christian Brother, asked his supervisor to take the monastery car and fetch me. I was waiting in the Imperial Hotel in Galway at Eyre Square. Galway City was quiet then; it had its beginning and its end, you could hear the water lap lap against steel drums at the harbor. The matching click click of shoes on the grey stone.

Clement was filled with joy that I had come. He had arranged everything for me. He told me he had a motorbike for the fine weather and promised we would ride all over on it.

The houses were plain and stark then, each one surrounded by trees and vines. The houses were serious about their role in the countryside. I was told that people didn't dare knock down famine houses.

At the inn in the morning, I heard cattle bash into the wall downstairs that fronted the road, heard them as they passed from one pasture to another in the mist. I woke up to the sound of the mooing and the sticks whipped through the air to get them moving again.

More than twenty years later, in the 1990s, having no idea what else I should do, I accepted a post as they called it in the Law Faculty in Dublin. I bought an old grey Opel Kadett, and just as if I had brought bad luck or an ill wind with me, they started to take the country away from me. The whole thing. There was such determination to build all over it, huge houses in pink and white, with turrets and fairy tale staircases, as close to the road as they could, all lined up in a row, for mile after mile. They knocked down the ancient stone walls and stood about laughing, putting up concrete Dallas fences, whose posts would fall down after a few months, and stay dangling forever after.

There were more and more houses, larger and more preposterous, at the edge of every town, spilling out into the countryside, each one calling out for attention, six bedrooms, eight bedrooms, all ensuite. Some were modeled on Graceland, with huge gaping windows. The famine houses and the Land Commission houses began to be knocked down. I wanted to buy them all and save them, but finally settled on one at Park Baun. One day, as I drove into the nearby town of Turlough, I saw that all the trees and hedgerows had been ripped out, leaving fields of mud along the road. I ran into the hardware shop and demanded to know what was going on. *Tis the new Turlough greenbelt,* I was told.

No one seemed to know or care what I was talking about. With each trip to Turlough, there were more and more planning permission notices in the fields. *They know what they're doing,* Seanie's mother said to me, her eyes blazing.

Seanie. Well, that's another story.

I rented a flat in Dublin and went out to Galway every weekend, or nearly, for the first while taking the train as far as Roscommon, and then later driving in my old Opel Kadett, by way of Mullingar. After a while, the car knew the road so well, it more or less went on its own. It had its own personal track from Ranelagh to Park Baun, Park Baun where the trees sheltered the house and the garden sloped down into lower, wet ground and the old pine tree made a low pitched sighing noise. The fox hole was near the base of the pine tree, with white feathers stirring in the wind near the opening.

There was always a new threat of something—that all the foxes would be culled for eating the birds, that the badgers would be hunted down because of TB in cattle, that a thousand new houses would be going up in all directions, that the roads would be widened, or better yet that fifty new roads would be slipped into the County Development Plan, that the largest equestrian center ever seen would be built, that Turlough would be the new site for all of Europe's rock concerts. That Galway would be a place for cruise ships to call, that a million square feet of retail would be built. And still, for a long time, for years, I kept on going out.

At Park Baun, I would open the door and smell the must and the cold walls and the turf fire from the last time I'd been out. In one of the bedroom drawers, I had a collection of old religious pictures salvaged from now defunct and fallen in cottages, one copy of the Proclamation of the Irish Republic, and a framed postcard of Padraig Pearse and his company of revolutionaries, all seated around what looked like a picnic table, and as if they'd all just come from the barber shop.

If only they'd done it the way Michael Collins once imagined—everyone speaking real Irish, with the curses and blessings, not the *Ros na Rún* kind of language, and wearing Celtic dress for formal occasions. I would even have gone for a king and queen.

I kept asking people, why is it that when we think of the Irish past we get stuck with a portrait of a nineteenth century farm worker? What did Irish people look like at that moment in the murky middle ages, when they realized, Hey, we're cooked. It's all over. No more fire leaping.

I kept asking everyone I thought might have some clue about this; that is, why the visual blank? But then I gave up. No one seemed to have considered the looks on faces and the haircuts and such of the fourteenth or fifteenth century. Only the late nineteenth century fellow with a cap on his head and arms folded, or cycling off to mass.

I had wanted someone to agree that the loss of a nomad's life was a particular heart breaker; and that there might be analogies with the traveling people of the present time.

To say that no one showed any interest in such matters is quite the understatement. These were topics for Irish Americans, a laugh. In one of the legal writing program hypos constructed by my Law Faculty colleagues, a foreign lecturer came to Ireland to study bovine law, but found that she was forced to teach contracts instead. And who might that have been? The meanness of it.

I so wanted to do up that house at Park Baun. For a long time, I wasn't able to accomplish much but hang curtains and slap a coat of paint on the woodworm eaten table. I swept the concrete floor and huge clouds of dust arose. I ran my hands along the wooden mantle pieces in the bedrooms, hand-carved with archaic looking hearts and stars, and the heavily painted green metal grates.

I liked best to stand in the doorway, holding a cigarette. Or just to saunter around the house, on the concrete walkway, same as the ones that encircle all Irish houses of that type, kicking at the grass that tried to invade the cracks. The sun would disappear as quickly as it came, and sheets of rain move in in the blink of an eye—just as used to happen twenty or twenty-five years earlier.

The blue phone would ring almost as soon as I parked the car in the front garden and opened the door. As I talked, I saw the front gate, disused and tied together with string, at the end of the equally disused path, one vanishing point that ended in the road, and then somehow the raised green fields beyond.

But I was so scared at night, scared to death. I would leave my cousin Bridie home and drive back to Park Baun on my own. Despite all the local building, there hadn't been a dent made in the darkness on these back roads. The fog still swirled in and out at the edge of the car's headlights, and as I turned from the main road to the side road, to the dirt track leading to Park Baun, the likelihood of being attacked seemed greater by the second. I felt I was being watched as I opened the door. My hands shook. I had my last cig and a swig of red wine in the cold and dark and tried to relight all the fires. This could take until well into the middle of the night.

As I lay awake, I would hear cars approach, at ten or fifteen minute intervals. I'd creep over to the enormous front window, as old as the house and completely unrenovated, crouching down and watching the road so that I wouldn't be seen. Each car would slow on the bend; I'd think it was going to stop. This is it, I would think, the big one; I should have had that panic button installed after all. Then the car would drive on; these were only the cars of the half drunk, the curious, the locals taking a short cut.

Not infrequently, it took me until the first light of day at four or five to finally fall asleep; the first reddish streak over the trees was my signal and I would be in a deep sleep within seconds.

But when I was in Ireland at sixteen, that first time, I was never afraid of that pea soup darkness in the countryside. I would walk all night down bog roads by myself;

I would even hitchhike in the dead of night. But twenty years on from then, there were stories almost every day of women attacked in their houses in the West of Ireland, elderly women and divorcee artists alike, down roads just like the one to Park Baun. My neighbor, on her own for thirty years and counting, locked herself in her upstairs bedroom at night; she would come to see me when I arrived from Dublin and recite the prayer she always said at the top of her voice for protection before going to bed.

Maybe the protective spirits had gone, withdrawn.

The little people, leaping from one stone to another, holding tiny lights in their hands. They decided to go, to clear out.

All four houses in Park Baun got telephones at once. At least we could phone out now, we said. For a time I felt that I had brought some life back to the disappearing village. On the other hand, many of the stories of assaults had the culprits cutting the phone wires.

They would have to climb high up a tree or over the roof itself, but they might chance it; it was not out of the question

The piano; early 1970s

When I was fourteen, I said a kind of goodbye to the sordid surroundings of that public school in Vermont. When we left New York, we had to leave Catholic school as well, and the new public school was not only a shock, but ugly. I walked to school on the first day with new yellow knee socks held up by rubber rings, and a white corduroy jumper. Suddenly, in this new place, all the talk was of breasts and slam books; the books were ugly as well, set to color coded reading levels.

But at fourteen, I said goodbye to it; the smell of beer, parties in deserted cabins along the lake.

I am going to stay in, all the time, I announced to Gramma and Daddy. I started to teach myself piano. I had known a bit as a child, but now I became obsessed with the piano; sitting at the bench for hours every day. I listened to recordings of Rubenstein playing Chopin, over and over; rather as I now read the same books over and over, year after year. *The Sun Also Rises* every other spring. *Howard's End.*

To the Lighthouse and Lily Briscoe's unfinished painting.

Daddy came into the living room with his newspaper to listen. *I love to hear you, honey,* he said, so innocent, too generous. I did so well so fast, then couldn't improve beyond a certain point. That is so like me, a quick ride to something that seems like brilliance, then a fading away. No cashing in on anything, ever. I have never cashed in on a thing, in fact. I saw others spin straw into gold, routinely, but not me. No recognition. Why was that, how bizarre it was. There are no random patterns, Una would say, you must be making this happen. Maybe it was the mystical thing, but it did not seem to be a coincidental pattern; it was just something about me; zoom zoom zoom based on an obsession, then fading out of sight like a comet.

That summer when I was fourteen was like an old pathway down a backyard from my very young childhood, all lined with heavy peonies, pink and white. Piano in the evening, my job on the ferry boat serving hot dogs, and the beach at the lake when I could, baking in the feeble Vermont sun, dreaming of my great goodbye to all those who were beneath me.

I would go to high school and everyone I had known before would be gone or ignored. I would reinvent everything. I went to Aunt Olive's house with Gramma and Daddy every Sunday afternoon; an hour's drive to Hyde Park at the edge of the Northeast Kingdom. It was like a dream for them, as if I'd reverted to a small child, compliant and polite. Even Una had reached a stage when she would resist these Sunday trips, but I reveled in them.

Aunt Olive had never married, but had taught math for decades. As for marriage, *Those who would have me I wouldn't have,* she always said, and more tellingly, *but those I would have had wouldn't have me.*

I was all ready for high school; my clothes were all picked out. I was too hasty, as usual; I was dressed for the real cold when it was only early September, with work boots and a plaid jacket from the Johnson Woolen Mills. That was in keeping with the times; the days of the Vietnam War, and Burlington's City Hall Park packed with vagrant teenagers. They sat in circles, the girls with long dresses fanning in the breeze.

I signed up for some of the very hardest high school courses I could find; the most difficult and obscure English and writing and history. On the other hand, the math and science were just normal, ordinary. I hated the smell of the chemistry lab, all those silly numbers and letters to be memorized from that chart. I couldn't see the signs on the periodic table relating to any real objects; I only pretended to go along with it.

It was just how I pretended to learn swimming; I would obey instructions and appear to breathe as part of the stroke, but in fact I was just opening my mouth without drawing air. I'd wait until I couldn't stand it any longer and just stop swimming. I had no intention of learning to swim properly; I had no intention of understanding what it was the chemical formulae actually stood for.

It was Gramma who heard about a piano teacher, Madame Celeste; in fact, she met her at the department store, where Madame Celeste would breeze in and talk about gorgeous fabrics, and how women should never ever wear jeans. Madame came from France during the war, somehow lost her first husband, and had remarried a good-looking man who sold cars and drank too much. Madame Celeste told Gramma she would like to meet me; in fact, she eventually took some pleasure in planning my life for me. From time to time, Madame even introduced me to skinny teenage boys with European connections.

As well as that, more than thirty years on, I am still laughing at things Miles Bradford said.

It was Miles who made me think that I would have everything. Or, he confirmed my childhood idea that I would. He made it very plain to me: I would have everything I wanted. Not money or anything so crass. But I would ask for something and receive it, without question or struggle. It was, apparently, mine for the taking.

Miles Bradford was the teacher of my Western Civilization class, at the high school. After I had said goodbye to everyone and started learning the piano again, then studying with Madame Celeste.

When he entered the classroom that mild, early September afternoon, he was wearing a tie and a sweater, probably olive green. He walked slightly tilted to one side, as if his briefcase was terribly heavy. He was laughing to himself, at the tie, perhaps, or at the classroom.

He had the face of a Viking; wheat colored hair and a tidy beard, long grey eyes and a hint of freckles across the bridge of his nose.

He was smirking as he entered, that is a better way to put it, as if everything that was to happen, and that would ever happen, was terribly funny.

He made no attempt to conceal how uproarious it all was: the outfit, the briefcase (the briefcase was very old, where had he got it?), the room, the view, the blackboard.

And there I sat in my new work boots, chosen so carefully at a discount store.

I don't know if I was so pretty then; I suppose I was, though I was very small. I had always been the smallest in my class, but with some sort of charm; what can I call it? I always said that I could take a bath in the sink if need be. Actually, I never knew, then or long after, if I was the most beautiful creature on earth or terribly plan; it was, so to speak, a fluid sense of the self. For girls, there is the ball and chain of what they look like, beauty being the shorthand route to drama and excitement. Beauty was part of the lazy person's way of thinking.

I would never have asked anyone in any case; I could not stand to hear myself described in objective terms.

On the good side, I guess it depended on what my look seemed to elicit.

I don't know, I've never understood looks. I've never understood the humiliation or the limitation of being tied to one's looks.

Miles Bradford told us we would cover ancient Greece and Rome, the idea of empire, and all the major *isms.* There would be socialism, totalitarianism, nationalism;

and then he would make jokes by adding, say, defeatism. *As to word derivation, think it over,* he would say, *Autocracy, what could be easier, a self propelled cracy.*

His beat up leather briefcase was a bag full of historical events. But about many of these there was no laughing, as they were not funny. The holocaust, the Soviet gulag, refugees from the major wars. He showed us films of farmers burned out of their houses, their fields still smoldering, bodies left lying in the yard. Miles, or Mr. Bradford as I always referred to him, folded his arms and squinted out at the lake.

If I'm not mistaken, he even wore a jacket with patches on the sleeves. And with his brown corduroy trousers, yes, he wore a pair of work boots, too, though not as high up on the ankle as mine.

Of course, I had recently said goodbye to everything, the smell of beer and the talk of cars and dropping aspirins into coca cola; who was pregnant and who had nice legs; I would never again talk to or acknowledge those who wrote each other notes with bad spelling like, *yeah I love him to, Jennie.* Recall that I had just said goodbye. I was new in this large, sprawling high school. There was my writing seminar, there were tapes of Dylan Thomas reciting, there was Madame Celeste's house after school, and there was Western Civilization.

It was Miles who made me say long after, even more than thirty years after, that everything wonderful in my life was frontloaded. What happened that winter made me think that I could have everything, as I said. This notion lasted a very long time, and stood up against much evidence to the contrary.

He had just finished a Master's degree in history, something about the Puritan consciousness. He could only have been twenty-four at the most, it's not clear to me now, but he was young enough to be forgiven.

When I remember myself at that time, I see myself as I am now but he as he was then; it is bizarre how we can transpose ourselves, unchanging, though of course I must look so different, perhaps unrecognizable, though I cannot see the difference. I can't imagine that I was only fourteen, though then everything was before me and now pretty much everything is over and gone.

It was that fall that my brother Jack got married. Or should I say, had his first marriage. He was really too young to marry, and there was all the fuss of a 1970s wedding; the bridemaids with their hair in curls and matching clothes with an autumn motif. Una and I were bridesmaids. We looked ridiculous in wide brown cummerbunds and ankle length skirts. Jack, who had driven long distance buses rather than study during his first years in college, was joining the Navy in lieu of the Vietnam draft. Gramma was dead set against the marriage and took to her bed with headaches.

Jack always rather enjoyed that kind of opposition and went around asking us why our mother was against the marriage; could we believe she was doing this. He stomped, and hit one fist on the other palm. After the wedding was over, I had another bout of feverish longing for separation, determined to reign over only what I wanted, what was joyful. It was a theory, a pledge, and related to everything I did or thought. At least that's how I recall the coherence of the time.

I took out my notebook in study hall and wrote, *I know it could never happen; I could never have Mr. Bradford.* It's hard to know what I was asking for. Every walk down the path into the school became suffused with a sense of crisis and a kind of anticipation that made me wary of every car and every shadow. Seasonal forces were coming together; from fall to winter, a *passe-muraille.*

It seemed to me that Mr. Bradford had taken a long look down the sweep of history and come back with some great answer that made him laugh and laugh; a strange kind of laughter full of fatigue and compassion. He showed us grainy old film footage from World War I and World War II; the Russian Revolution, Lenin, and then Stalin, giving speeches and refugees everywhere on the move. He talked about *All Quiet on the Western Front* and *Quiet Flows the Don*. He knew so much, and he knew it so well. He knew it set to music.

Perhaps he was out of his mind, as they tried to convince me long afterwards, but even now at this remove I don't think so. I was almost fifteen and he was just twenty four, and he couldn't stop himself from looking for something in the pile of paperbacks on his desk, and in me, and in staring for long periods of time out the window with his long grey Viking eyes. You couldn't call it pleasurable, but that early winter had the unmistakable feel of the inevitable, and even then, I couldn't fail to recognize it as such.

I don't know which of the films it was. Undoubtedly, it had to do with the endless wars and the endless winters in early twentieth century Europe; the burnt villages and the summary executions. The class was over, and I wandered down the hallway and over the glass bridges linking one building of the high school with another. It was autumn, real autumn, late autumn. I got as far as the main lobby, alien territory, then turned around and walked quickly back up all the ramps, like climbing a mountain in stages.

As I re-entered the upper zone, I saw him walking towards me; the green sweater with a small hole near the shoulder. He was smiling in an angry, sad way, leaning slightly forward. We both stopped and looked at each other in the mid-day crush of students at the top of one of the complicated staircases.

I was looking for you. I had to find you, I said. It was daring, but I said it.

Mr. Bradford turned me around to walk me back with him towards the history wing at the top of the hill. He seemed to think something about me very amusing, as if he knew what I was going to say before I said it, and I was simply confirming what he already knew.

He said something like, I *was looking for you, too,* but not quite as clear as that, I think. *So here you are,* or *Yes, here we are.*

We walked all around the school for an hour or more, all the way to the end of each darkening corridor. We walked past unknown zones, banks of typewriters, the food preparation wing. We talked about the film, and even Jack's wedding. I told him about my piano lessons with Madame Celeste and he said he wanted to hear me play.

We had been looking for each other, clawing the air. Mr. Bradford and I were thoroughly lost, walking up and down the tiers and sections of the huge building with its bridges and sudden dead ends. We were probably thinking of the film we had seen, the pathetic wartime figures in black and white, stepping stiffly out of their real time, their villages razed and burnt, refugees on wagons, rural Ukrainians; Holocaust victims looking out through the fence at us.

I had to see you, I said.

Yes, Mr. Bradford was wearing his green sweater, the one with the moth hole at the elbow, and a button down shirt; and those corduroy trousers. It was fall, really fall now. In Vermont, that tipped quickly into winter. Spring and fall were short.

I want to hear you play the piano, he said.

We walked past the room, empty now, where I had my French classes. I thought of mentioning the *passe-muraille,* the story we had read in French class, though I didn't like straining after a metaphor like that, even back then. I knew better than to bring a metaphor into the conversation.

And so Mr. Bradford made me think that I could have anything I wanted. He confirmed my childhood belief that through some special blessing I was walking along a path ringed round with a kind of aura, an aura of white birches or maybe olive trees, depending on the motif. I would sit still and wish for everything, and everything would be mine.

It took a very long time for me to stop believing that. I did, though, eventually.

Mr. Bradford and I knew how to find each other in the hallway after that, on dark afternoons. It seemed to be telepathic, directed from somewhere over our heads.

In the mornings, I would often run into him on his way into school, carrying the heavy bag that made him veer sideways. He would ask me to come along to his office, where he brewed coffee straightaway. A few students were usually milling around, waiting to talk with him, wanting to run by him their ideas on the last days of the Romanovs, or Erich Fromm on Marx. I stayed for a few minutes and then left abruptly, without any explanation.

That was how I did things. I would always run into him later, even on days when I didn't have his class.

He assigned us each a book to analyze and report on; funny enough, mine was *The Puritan Dilemma*, a biography of John Winthrop, governor of the Massachusetts Bay Colony. On the day of my report, I remember him sitting riveted, staring at me as I said, *What the book makes me consider is the question John Winthrop wrestles with: How to do right in a world that does wrong.* Mr. Bradford took this up as a theme, the world that does wrong, and even told Gramma on parents' night what a splendid job I had done with my report.

One day after class he handed me a large, heavy envelope filled with typed pages.

Take it away with you and read it, he told me.

I went into my bedroom at home, sat on the brass bed that was so large it nearly took up the entire room, and opened what he had given me. There were so many pages they hardly fit in the envelope.

> *I am here in Saint Johnsbury, at my wife Alma's house. Her family is in the next room; I'm out on the porch in the cold with a blanket over my head. They keep asking me to come back in, but I can't go in. This is it, Catherine. Unequivocally it. It is up up up or downhill all the way.*

His letter went on in that manner, about how he got drunk on the day of his own wedding and passed out, remembering nothing. About going to the Democratic National Convention in 1968 and being beaten senseless, about Alma's paintings, and *Doctor Zhivago* (*Alma is Tanya*, he wrote).

Either it is up, he repeated, *or it is downhill all the way.*

And so Mr. Bradford in some way declared himself.

He was sitting alone, in Saint Johnsbury, not so far from where I was spending Sunday with my parents at Aunt Olive's in Hyde Park, with a blanket over his head, refusing to come out, hoarding the typewriter. Alma, exasperated, looking through the glass door at him.

He wasn't laughing as he handed me the letter. He turned away quickly, as if he wanted me to read it, but out of his sight and hearing, as soon as possible.

As the fall faded away, Mr. Bradford began to look scruffy. He wore the same green sweater for several days at a time. His straight, wheat colored hair hung down at a sharp angle on one side. He smelled of cigarettes and looked tired.

He wrote words all over the chalkboard.

He read to us on Blaise Pascal's wager and the leap of faith. He would begin to laugh and drop the chalk into its tray. The students waited patiently as Mr. Bradford leaned his back against the chalkboard and closed his eyes.

From November, it was the snow season. My mother bought me a coat at her department store that looked like a Russian army officer's, dark blue with grey trim at the cuffs and hem. I loved it, though I realize I could hardly pull off that look today. I might try, if tempted. On the day of the first big snowstorm, they closed the high school in the early afternoon.

It was rare for school to be called early. The Vermont kids spilled out of the doors, jackets hanging open, lighting up before they reached the end of the path. I walked back towards the corridor that went past our classroom; the lights were turned out now and the only brightness was from the falling snow outside the window.

Not surprisingly—in fact I was anticipating it— Mr. Bradford was walking toward me from the darker end of the corridor, smiling as if he had personally caused the snowstorm.

Even now, I can trust Mr. Bradford. From beyond the grave, his, I can trust him. He is there, walking toward me as expected.

He won't disappoint; he will not fail to appear.

We went into the empty classroom together. I sat in one of the desks and Mr. Bradford stood by the window.

Well, what are we going to do, Catherine? he asked.

The snow fell in that wonderful, endless way it can, when there is no thought for what happens when it stops, but rather you want it to fall all night, on and on until it causes ecological catastrophe.

We stayed in the classroom until everyone had left the school. Mr. Bradford pointed to a long white car. All on its own in the parking lot, slowly being covered with snow.

I've inherited that from my grandmother, he said. *It's a Cadillac. A 1960 Cadillac!* He began to laugh, and put his hands up to his eyes.

May I offer you a lift home, Catherine? I think he asked. As I recall, I hardly said anything. He asked me if I would call him Miles, and I said no, I couldn't do that.

Outside, the streetlamps threw down a yellow light into the parking lot. We could hear snowplows out on the road. I helped brush snow off the car and then climbed in next to him on the green plastic-coated front seat.

Can you believe I drive this? he said.

Driving was more like gliding that evening, or riding in a big slippery boat through the dark. I have no idea how the car moved forward; several times we nearly spun into snowdrifts on the side of the road.

Please don't bring me all the way home, I said to him.

Where do you want me to leave you?

Here, here is fine, anywhere, I said. I knew that I could handle any drifts of snow, however extreme, with ease.

He stopped the car, or it slid to a halt. No one else seemed to be out. He looked at me. I believe he reached out his hands to hold me.

I love you, Mr. Bradford, I said absurdly, then jumped out into the snow and started off for home as fast as I could.

We were used to snow up there; it was usual, familiar to be in deep snow back then. I knew that Mr. Bradford was turning his car around; I saw its lights disappear and the massive white boat of a car was gone.

At some point, I did begin to think of him as Miles, or perhaps Miles Bradford, but I really didn't call him by any particular name at all. For my birthday in late November, he gave me a copy of *Slaughterhouse Five*, inscribed, *With the best wishes and interests of a Chum.*

Come to my house, meet me there this afternoon, he said.

I took the bus downtown and found the apartment building he had described. It was almost right across from the department store my mother worked in. I ran up his block, up the desolate front steps and opened the front door with the spare key he had given me. It was silent inside, the most pervasive silence I had ever heard. It was a heavy old apartment, with grand sliding doors and large panes of glass. Alma's paintings were on the walls, tiny trees stuck in great fields of snow. She seemed to have a thing about sunsets. Sunsets on snow, not my cup of tea.

I saw her slippers in the corner. How quiet they were. Miles Bradford and Alma had a young son, Miles Jr, one apparent cause of their marriage. I saw his crib in a corner of the back room.

The grand piano Miles had told me about was in the living room, also inherited from his grandmother. *Make some coffee*, he had joked at school, but I actually did make some. The coffee maker hummed and buzzed. I could see the huge clock on the steeple of the Unitarian Church just outside the front window. Finally, Miles drove up to the house, looking unconcerned, even unaware that anyone was in his house.

I guess now I should say that something awful happened, that Miles frightened or hurt me, or that I ran from the house in horror, but nothing of the sort took place.

No such thing happened. They tried to make Miles out to be a madman, but at least with me, in those days, nothing of that kind happened.

Miles came in and stamped the snow from his shoes, smiled at me, and drank his coffee. And we played Mendelssohn's *Songs Without Words* on the piano. Miles played better than I did, to tell the truth, but he liked my playing, it made him smile almost to the point of laughing, another of those great private jokes of his as he watched and listened.

It grew late; I knew that Alma would be coming home from her job at the art supply store. Miles had to go and pick up Little Miles, Milesy I think they called him.

And then he reached out his arms and held me. He held my face down into his sweater, held me as the dark fell on the snow and the light rose up from the snow to meet it. He stood completely still in the room and held me, and that is all that happened.

That's all. Miles sat in one chair and I sat in another. It was beginning to get dark. Alma would be back. Alma was Tanya.

I had read Zhivago, but decided to read it again.

Miles put on his jacket; it looked like a bomber jacket, a little silly. I put on my Russian army officer's coat. We held each other in the middle of the big old room with its heavy doors, and then I was gone, leaving first, racing down the street, avoiding the store my mother worked in, hopping a bus on Church Street, one that would return me to the neighborhood of trivial little boxes, ours dark grey against the new snow.

My mother got me a job in the department store, gift wrapping for Christmas. She thought I would be thrilled, they always thought I wanted pocket money, or responsibility. In fact, I spent most of the time hiding in the back because people I knew came into the store with some frequency. I still remember the smell of the wrapping paper and the ribbons, new and Christmasy. I was clumsy at it; the customers pitied me.

Miles found out about the job and he would stand at the front door of the store, peering in, laughing at me. Twice or so he ventured in, walking past as if he didn't know me.

Mary Magdalene

It isn't clear when my parents began to hear what was going on; I think it was a teacher from the high school who came to find Gramma in the store and let her in on it. Just when they thought I was being perfect and good, it turned out I was spending a lot of time with my history teacher.

Your brother and sister are just humiliated. Gramma tried this approach; it was the one she knew best. *And imagine how I felt, hearing this from someone who cares about you so.*

Daddy didn't say much; he didn't like to get involved in such things. In his own way, he seemed sympathetic to me.

I didn't want them to know. I didn't want to crusade for Mr. Bradford. I didn't want to keep him and fight for him; there was no reaction that seemed right. I just wanted to meet him, and have no one know. On Sundays, I would still go to Aunt Olive's in Hyde Park with them. I didn't want to hear any weeping and wailing about Mr. Bradford, and what was I thinking.

The teacher who told my mother conceded that Mr. Bradford was charming, and very clever.

In the New Year, I kept meeting Miles at his house, but I felt myself in danger; I felt watched. It was risky to come home late. My mother could be set off at any moment about how well I was doing in my classes, and how shocked everyone was, and disappointed, and how embarrassed she was to see people.

My piano teacher, Madame Celeste, didn't know, and that was a relief. She continued to tell me never, ever to wear jeans, a subject on which I needed little convincing. *Wear velour,* she said, rubbing her hand down along her thigh. She said that I could be a concert pianist as she had wanted to be, but that her father forbade her, and then her first marriage came. She had to flee Paris during the war with her little son; she had lost everything at the railway station. But well, I couldn't imagine telling the person next to you on the platform, as she had, Mind this for a few moments, will you? Leaving the family jewels with a stranger when the whole world was going to hell? I mean, really. I listened to her as I ate one of her special mayonnaise sandwiches after my lesson. She told me how the same seagull visited her yard year after year, and she always made him lovely treats.

Oh, my dear, he is magnificent!

Sometimes Miles waited for me down the street from Madame Celeste's house, and he would drive me back home at dusk.

There were even days when Daddy would follow us in his car, a Maverick, the cheapest car he could get. Perhaps he'd been put up to trailing us by Gramma, as I can't think that Daddy would make much of a detective. If Miles and I drove out of town, we would leave Daddy behind; at some point I would turn around, and Daddy would not be following us any more.

Miles talked often of moving to the country, and as the winter turned to mud season, he began to take me for drives to towns all over northern Vermont. These were places I knew already and loved, so it was easy and natural to drive with him. As luck would have it, he had sold his grandmother's huge Cadillac and bought a zippy green MG. He hinted that he was asking me to join him in the country for some kind of new life, though he never said it in quite that way. We always visited a town as though we were shopping for a place to live.

Miles became less and less able to face the class; his clothes were sloppier. He passed out mimeographed sheets of paper from which he read aloud to us: *The heart has its reasons, which reason does not know.* He leaned against the classroom wall. *Le coeur a ses raisons.*

And in the early spring, that time in Vermont of endless mud and no warmth in the sun, he left Alma and Little Miles.

He moved to an apartment overlooking the wide valley that contained the city's principal dump. This fact made him laugh, of course. He told me that Little Miles was taking it badly, that Alma was worried, and that at some point he might have to go back home.

In the afternoon, I would wait for him in his rented place, high up as if on stilts, its ugly furniture included in the price, and no piano.

I think I started to want to leave Miles then. I didn't like the cheap kitchen, or watching out the window for his car to come up the unfamiliar and depressing street.

Within a couple of months, he did go back to Alma, but after that he sometimes stayed at the houses of teachers he was friendly with, on sofas and in extra rooms and breezeways. He occasionally stayed with an unmarried woman teacher named Liza, considered to be a "hot ticket," and probably in love with Miles. He told me about landing in on people unexpectedly. It was too chaotic for me.

I liked my brass bed; maybe I was selfish. I was tired of Gramma acting like I was fighting to the death for Miles, because I wasn't. I wanted to escape from Miles; I was afraid he would try and keep me, but for no actual purpose, just to keep me.

Once on a Sunday morning at dawn, I heard a tapping on my bedroom window. I got up and looked out, and there was Miles holding a black bicycle, looking exhausted, standing on the frozen lawn, laughing. He stayed clowning on the lawn and then took off up the street. No one but me ever knew that he had been there.

Hello.

Catherine?

Where are you?

Does it sound strange?

It's very noisy.

I'm at a party. In a closet.

You shouldn't call me at home. They're all here.

Someone's playing Jesus Christ Superstar on the stereo. You know, I was thinking, that Mary Magdalene had a hell of a voice.

Every chance she got, Gramma would start talking about Miles Bradford. She sat helplessly, pathetically, on a chair, repeating that my sister, my brother, were mortified and humiliated because of me. As Miles and I drove out of town in his new MG, I still now and then saw Daddy following behind us, unwillingly it seemed; hoping never to catch up with us. As before, he would invariably give up and turn back. We drove aimlessly to Montpelier, to Waterbury, not to scenic places but to the grittier towns where we could walk around and hold hands. Sometimes we stopped in rest areas to look at each other, even to kiss.

As spring came on, Miles came to class looking as if he'd just rolled out of bed. The spring light seemed not to suit him. When he met me in the hallway, he would make a gesture of biting the air, biting at something he couldn't reach, falling forward to get it, then he would laugh and turn me around quickly and steer us in the other direction.

And I began to plan my escape from Miles.

Miles never used expressions having to do with time, forever and so on; he never discussed staying together or being together. But then again he never spoke as if we would not, as if I would go anywhere else or have another phase of things. But for my part, I became preoccupied with how I could leave him.

I had two more years of high school. It was oppressive, frightening to think of seeing Miles in the hallways, going back and forth to his house for all that time. We couldn't survive this change in the weather. I found him more threatening in the sun.

One afternoon he told me he wanted to bring me to a friend's cabin, a crazy friend from his past. I can't remember what this friend did—pottery or glass blowing, a couple of German Shepherds in the yard. I didn't want to go; as a rule, I hate cabins in the woods, the flies, the mud, the lack of any vista, my fear of losing meadowlands. The visit was awkward and silly; I had nothing to say to his friend at all. He and Miles each had a beer, and we left the way we had come.

Miles and I went walking as far as the edge of the woods and entered a huge shimmering field. He put me up on his shoulders and walked down the hill as if into everything you could wish for or imagine. He danced in a wide arc, and I so loved him. We lay down on the rocks, those big Vermont rocks that poke up through the grassy fields, rocks that no farmer could ever get rid of. We shaded our eyes against the sun, and watched the trees, the branches moving, the clouds moving. Miles joked about it being a leafy cathedral, he could never lose any chance for a joke like that. Perhaps if he hadn't been so insistent on laughing all the time, it would have been better; though at certain moments, of course, he wasn't laughing.

Nevertheless, despite that day, I continued to plan how I would leave him.

I still went to Hyde Park on Sundays with my parents to see Aunt Olive; Daddy read the Sunday papers. In my own mind, I was already back with them, I had left Miles.

I don't remember exactly how Miles ended up in our living room; I don't know why Daddy finally got so riled he insisted Miles come over. Whether he had caught us together or whether Gramma egged him on, it's dim in my mind. I just remember that very warm late spring evening, sitting in the living room, waiting for Miles to arrive. I remember his green sports car pulled up at the curb, how out of place it looked, how strange it was to see him get out in front of our house. I went to the door, as if to keep him out, to ward off something.

Daddy wasn't good at being angry; I had scarcely ever seen him angry. He was incapable of being unkind, of making commands. He hated conflict, avoided it at all costs, and at a time like this was only trying to please my mother.

When Miles came in, I suppose Daddy said, *What do you think you are doing?* or *What's going on with all this?* I remember Miles, dressed in a shirt with a button down collar, looking almost pleased to be there. I think he shook Daddy's hand.

Mr. Darcy, I recall him saying, *I love your daughter.*

At this, my mother ran from the room, overcome. Daddy seemed to want to discuss it a bit, perhaps to show Miles the folly of the whole thing.

I love her, Miles repeated.

Daddy was excessively fair minded and uncritical. It was somewhat noble of Miles, after all, to put it that way, so plainly.

When Miles left—as it was clear nothing was going to be resolved then and there, that was obvious to everyone—I ran down the front path after him. Gramma reappeared to shout out the front door, *Get back in here this minute!* I stood on the front sidewalk, flapping my arms up and down, having no idea what to say or do. I didn't care for one side of my life peering in at the other like this.

Good night, I imagine I said.

And Miles was laughing again.

I did leave Miles. I told him, No more. I told him I would leave him and that was it, with no plans to be with him again, or stay in touch, or look each other up, or look into each other's eyes, or write letters or talk. I was going.

He dropped me off at my piano lesson at Madame Celeste's house. I was so rattled I couldn't play at all. When I came out, I saw him parked up the street, waiting for me. We walked to a field overlooking the mountains, and sat under a tree.

Miles began to cry. He said he didn't know what he would do, how he would go on. And I cried; I had never cried so much. I doubt I have ever cried so much since then.

Miles and I cried all through the afternoon, until the sun was low in the sky and it seemed strange to be there under a tree in the early evening. I could barely see. Miles drove me home. I felt as if I'd been ill for a long time.

I walked into the house and said, *Don't talk to me. I have told Mr. Bradford I'll never see him again.*

But Miles phoned that week and asked me to meet him in the garden of the Congregational Church. He was waiting for me, Little Milesy in tow. Miles handed me a letter and asked me to read it.

> *I pick up books and put them back. I lift up my arms and they are like dead weights. I don't know what to do with myself. I am not listening to my son. Why don't you come back to me, Catherine? You have to come back to me.*

I was comforting Miles, but I was cruel. There was a cold streak in what I felt towards him. I told him it would be all right.

He would leave me alone for a few days and then begin phoning again.

What should I tell people? he would ask me, *That I've lost my mind over a precocious high school student? And who do your parents want you to be with? A pimply-faced adolescent?*

I listened, but I was letting Miles go, letting go the string of the kite, watching the boat of Miles leave the shore, and ever so carefully, I turned my back and began walking away from the shore, walking in a way that would avoid attracting attention.

When the phone rang at night, we would all stop and listen. But Miles drifted away from us.

Gramma was entirely different towards me since she knew that I had told Miles it was all finished. *Why don't you graduate from high school early?* she suggested. *Leave this all behind you as soon as you can.*

She developed this idea over time; she wanted me to go to Ireland for a year, then come back and go to Daddy's college, Saint Theo's. Her cousin in East Galway, Brother Clement, would take care of me. They had written to each other on every religious and family occasion over the many years since they were very young. Their mothers had been sisters, and though my mother and Clement had never met face to face, each felt the other to be of the highest importance.

Will I write to Brother Clement about it? she asked persistently.

Miles drifted farther away. There was little danger that he would ever return.

But it's true, I am still laughing at Miles Bradford's jokes, decades later. I did see him again, over the course of the next few years; once when he followed me around and around the revolving door of a store, a chance meeting in winter.

Twenty-five years after I said goodbye to him, I saw a notice that Miles Bradford had died in France. I sat on Gramma's sofa in her little house on Cape Cod, where she and Daddy had retired, and wept. It was a very Cape Cod evening; the black birds were singing in the scrubby pine trees. Daddy was long dead by then. She asked me what was wrong.

Miles Bradford, he has died, I told her.

Her face went pale and she lashed out, *How can you*

cry for him? What do you think I've been through on my own all these years?

That made no sense, but it was plain I was not supposed to cry for Miles Bradford.

Rest area

Miles Bradford and I are hunched together in his little sports car. He is closer than close, his green jacket vivid and immediate. He shifts around to hold me. We look out the windshield, down across the hills, hills that used to have names but have lost them.

We are parked on the edge of the rest area, no one knows where we are. Miles wants to be with me in the little sports car, and I with him. It is wrong and it is right at the same time. Miles kisses me, and there is no kiss ever like that one. He holds me just comfortably close. I feel his jacket, his sweater, his tidy beard; his grey eyes are closed. There is a slight aftertaste of his cigarettes, but also the fresh air from the long, patient, anonymous hills in front of us. We kiss and we kiss. Our profiles are side by side as Miles puts his face into my hair and shares his breathing. We invented each other, and it worked.

Kids; 2006

It was Una who said that we were well past the stage of falling in love with the next person in line at 7-11.

Or, I might add, with someone coming up the stairs while we were coming down, as happened at the Budapest train station on that long ago trip, in 1989. The water engineer, Vincenzo, from Lago di Como, as a for instance.

Not a thing more was going to happen to me, nothing of that kind, ever. I saw that so clearly as August began, as I started getting together the syllabi, the handouts, the updates from the BBC relevant to my subjects. I half-heartedly bought some clothes—though nothing ever fit me right—and hunkered down as if hurtling through space, in the direction of the welcome back faculty lunch. The Dean would talk about why we should really be seen as in the third tier, not the fourth; the salmon would be brought out in silver dishes, and I would stare at my feet with their slight suggestion of hammer toes, indication of an ancient genetic blip. In the worst-case scenario, the faculty would form into teams by table, to answer the Dean's trivial pursuit type questions on a kind of bingo card. And there I would be, remembering myself in a white summer dress, all that time ago. I would think of summer as it had been on the Izu Peninsula, and of running along a summer road in Karuizawa. There were visions, urging me to save myself, not while there was still time, because I saw that in fact there was no more time. Simply to save myself, with no expectation of any restoration.

And then, two or three weeks later, I left.

Una always made fun of the many letters I wrote to everyone, going back decades. She would drag out the box and read aloud from letters sent in 1978, 1984, 1989, and for each one she would say, *Fast forward!* Because I wrote the same thing, more or less, year after year—how I was just about to turn everything around and remake everything. And so on. But more recently, I didn't write letters any more, to anyone. I had nothing more to analyze; this was it, and had long been it.

Meaning that at the very least, I could not sit down and write to her now. But I did want to explain that the real reason, the true and undeniable reason for coming to Greensboro was that I thought I had earned it, and was content not to ask for anything else. Only please, no more about the Supreme Court's docket. It was, as I said, a simple kind of a bargain.

But clearly, I would not fall in love with anyone coming through the door of The Stars and Moon Bookshop in Stannard, where I finally found a job that made a little bit of sense. There was the tactile pleasure of putting books that I knew away, in order, each one giving me a kind of timeless little smile in the process. I wish I could say that in my second week of employment, a slightly portly sixty something gentleman from Greece who had been hiding out in the Northeast Kingdom, mainly to paint, as well as to recover from several tragic losses, came through the door and we found each other in that unimaginably out of the way place.

But I have already said that nothing will ever happen to me again, or so it seems. At least nothing stupid will ever happen, as the cessation is categorical and absolute. I will not give out my phone number to friendly, even attractive customers of the shop, agree to lunch with the manager of the health food coop, or any other of a large number of possible doings all characterized by overwhelming stupidity.

Madina started the third grade at the local elementary school. She was an adaptable child, able to have chums anywhere, and except for her great jealousy of Emmet the interloper, she was more or less happy. I didn't bring work home any more, or bark at them to hurry and dress. All that had gone; the night teaching, the student evaluations, the fuming at not being understood. For God's sake, of course I wasn't understood.

At night we would hug all together before bed, and I would read stories too young for Madina and too old for Emmet, but they were both pleased that the books were not just right for either.

I looked at their clever, eager faces and thought, *This is the only thing I've done that was more or less what I wanted.* I would have defended them against everything, died for them in a heartbeat. I thought of how courageous they were, of the days and nights in those child care homes in Central Asia, so hot in the summer, and amazingly cold in winter, the long boring afternoons and the nights sleeping in a miniature bed, just one of many in the rows of little beds.

Tell Madina that you are sorry and that you love her.

Sorry, Dina. Lally wuv you.

I love you, too, Emmet, Madina said, sounding a little blasé.

Say that you will love each other forever, I said.

Luv ever.

I'll love you forever, too.

I found a family day care for Emmet in Stannard near the bookstore. The director was divorced with two children of her own. She had tried to fix up her house to look like a school, with bees and kittens festooned everywhere. Emmet was pretty eager to run in and grab hold of all the unfamiliar toys. He was good with other children; not aggressive or grumpy. He just wanted to make things go, to build tall towers. After he went to sleep at night, I would find patterns throughout the house—where he had put two yellow blocks, for instance, in every big truck and one green block in every small truck.

It hadn't been that long since his adoption, and I wanted to make sure he understood who Mommy was, that this wasn't some roller coaster ride of random grown ups, so I would repeat over and again as we drove over to day care: *Teachers are teachers and Mommy is Mommy. Teachers are our friends, but there is only one Mommy, and Mommy loves you more than anyone else in the whole world could.*

Who loves you most?

Mommy.

How much?

Emmet was trying to open the side door of a matchbox car.

So much.

Every single day?

He nodded his head, then covered his face, suddenly shy.

I hated leaving him there; he looked so trusting and so lost as he went running straight for the boxes of cars and train engines.

Look, mama, look, he would say, *Tay watchen me. Watchen me.*

At least in September we still walked in the evening, past the house I'd rented in July with Una, up as far as the now closed Lakeview Inn, its porch deserted. I thought of Aunt Olive and her weekly journey to Greensboro Bend from Hyde Park to teach. She always remembered the children in her class with a shake of her head, as if there were a few just completely beyond the pale. *Hard country living,* Daddy would say.

Emmet wore the grey green sweater Una had made him and Madina wore her Cape Cod sweatshirt. The dark came earlier. The radio mentioned frost on higher elevations.

I was never going to leave here. I would not do a PhD in Portuguese, rent a room over a courtyard in a small Portuguese seaside town, turning over another motif and finding a wall as white as the one Lily Briscoe so wanted to paint. The smell of fish, the games played in the evening by old men in the sandy dirt.

I wouldn't go anywhere, not a place. I would give this place to Emmet and Madina and hope it made them happy. From the time I came back from Ireland with Madina, I became agoraphobic, not about going outside, but about getting into planes and moving across different time zones. This despite being in international legal studies; oh, I guess it's my agoraphobia acting up again, I would joke, as if it were lumbago or rheumatism. I had always lived out of a suitcase, but now I was finished. They couldn't make me go anywhere.

Bears in woods? asked Emmet apprehensively.

No, Emmet, all the bears are gone away to the zoo.

Gone zoo?

Most of the houses around Greensboro were summer places now, so few lights were on; the rock gardens were drying up. The sky was renewed and dramatic, and darkness came down like the quickly folding wings of an angel.

At Aunt Olive's house in Hyde Park, Daddy had still seemed young, a boy, even at seventy.

Walking now in the fall dusk, down past Willey's and up the road towards the Greensboro Free Library and Grange Hall, with the first bats of the evening whipping past, it was as if nothing had ever happened. I hadn't traveled at all, Japan didn't exist, nor did Galway. I had never set foot inside a law school, and never read a statute. I was just starting out from here, and I would never go anywhere. It was a great relief.

I left it to Sven to sort it out with the law school. He was a lawyer who liked being a lawyer; liked the clean shirts and the secretary putting people on hold. He liked making accusations of negligence and demanding reimbursements, and listening to someone to see if they would make exactly the right slip of the tongue.

They gave me a year and a half's salary, and I promised not to blame my breakdown on them.

Madina ate everything on her plate, systematically, methodically; she slept soundly and ran fast across the grass. You could well imagine her riding a sturdy horse across the steppe. I sang Toora Loora, her request, and watched her drift into a deep healthy sleep, her cheeks a bright pink and her pretty mouth just slightly open.

God bless you to be safe forever, I said, signed the cross on her forehead, and left the room. I poured myself a glass of white wine and sat down to read Anita Brookner.

Emmet, more vigilant, cried out in his sleep. I went and tucked him in and he was off again, racing through his dream. My slightest touch was more directly magical than it had been with Madina. Mommy is here, I whispered, and I could see his small body relax all along its toddler length.

Down by the station
Early in the morning
See the little pufferbellies
All jub jub

That not how it goes.

See the little pufferbellies
All jibazhee

Not how it goes!

Emmet sucked on his bottle of pediasure and his shallow eyelids closed. Madina stirred in her sleep. I wished she would forgive me for bringing someone else into our house. How wildly jealous she had been of Emmet.

I was a little scared after dark in the rented house, but nothing like what it had been at Park Baun. The Hardwick police drove by every now and again; I remembered Una commenting that every year a contract dispute between Greensboro and the Hardwick police was being argued about on the front page of the Gazette. The contract appeared to be holding for now.

I picked up the Anita Brookner novel. I'd read so many of her stories, the plots ran together. There was always a flat, an old dark family flat, and an unmarried woman, getting involved with an odd married couple or a chronically sick person, deceived in the end and back to the flat to consider the whole mess. On the page I opened to, she had written:

I read the Blue Fairy Book, the Yellow Fairy Book, and the stories of Hans Andersen, the Brothers Grimm, and Charles Perrault. None of this was groundwork for success in worldly terms, for I was led to think, and indeed was minded to think, of the redeeming situation or presence which would put to rights the hardships and dilemmas under which the characters, and I myself, had been laboring. More dangerously, it seemed to me that I need make no decisions on my own behalf, for destiny or fate would always have the matter in hand.

Wow, I thought.

Although I was too sensible, even as a child, to believe in a fairy godmother I accepted as part of nature's plan that after a lifetime of sweeping the kitchen floor I would go to the ball, that the slipper would fit, and that I would marry the prince. Even the cruel ordeals undergone by the little match girl, or by Hansel and Gretel, would be reversed by that same principle of inevitable justice which oversaw all activities, which guided some even if it defeated others. I knew that some humans were favored—by whom? By the gods? (this evidence was undeniable)—but I was willing to believe in the redeeming feature, the redeeming presence that would justify all of one's vain striving, would dispel one's disappointments, would in some mysterious way present one with a solution in which one would have no part, so that all one had to do was wait, in a condition of sinless passivity, for the transformation that would surely take place.

This strikes me now as extremely dangerous, yet parts of this doctrine seemed overwhelmingly persuasive, principally because there were no stratagems to be undertaken. One had

> *simply to exist, in a state of dreamy in direction, for the plot to work itself out. This was a moral obligation on the part of the plot: there would be no place for calculation, for scheming, for the sort of behavior I was to observe in the few people we knew and which I found menacing. . . .*

Hmm. How bizarre; was this how I had gone about things? If so, how obvious a fallacy on my part, stubborn and conceited though I'd been. As if fate would bend to my essence; not even—which would have been more logical—to my will.

I had to remind myself that I wasn't asking for anything any more.

The first bats came out. The deer and the bears began to worry and sought out food closer to town. Foxes hurried past. The birds stopped singing. The last people cleared out of the cottages on the lake.

The first serious frost was announced, and I realized we had almost no warm clothes.

If I hadn't left when I did, I would surely have been diagnosed with something awful. Faced with a whole year of dragging myself in front of classes to talk about extraterritorial jurisdiction and treaties, my cells were clamoring, *Enough! There will be an end to this*, and there would have been, one way or the other. A few would have sent me get-well cards. I would have been telling Una, *Life was short, but nobody ever told me,* and she would be saying, *Don't blame me.* I would answer that I wasn't. *Oh, yes you are, in some way, you are*, she would counter, insisting. And there would be that little element of blaming her. I was stubborn, but had no real power of will; I was easy to convince on practical matters if not ever on the impractical ones.

A halt would have been called one way or the other.

It was stark; either I had to leave, or I was going to enter a steep decline, something I had dreaded ever since I was an adorable butterfly of a little girl. My hair would dry up, I would be confined to my bed, it would be time to say goodbye, a roundup. And I would have to lie there and consider how I had willfully wasted so much time; first one way, then another, as if just treading water until the end came.

While I was tidying up the shelves at The Stars and Moon, wiping the dust off the books and reordering the section with guides to the Long Trail, I also thought about who would have come to that last room to see me off, to whisper goodbye. I would have wanted Kido, to ask him why he never showed up, though I waited twenty years or more; Miles Bradford was dead and gone, so therefore off the list. However odd and out of character it might seem, he would not be appearing. Good old Miles, he had always been good for an appearance.

I so hated disappearing acts.

Yukito would not come; he would send an e-mail, a brief one. *I am so sorry to hear of your impending death. The doctor informs me that my cholesterol is very high and I am aware that I could also die at any time.* That would be Yukito, my former husband, as Gramma now and then reminded me. Calvin Pini from Saint Theo's might show up, amused, bringing flowers, not believing me when I told him that it would be fatal. But then again, I didn't think Calvin would come after all.

Una would come every day; it was hard to know whether she would be strict or indulgent with me. She might try to look on the bright side, and talk me into that as well. She would be wary of being blamed for having talked me into going to law school and thereby, once and for all, having ensured that I would never be happy.

The children I didn't like to consider saying goodbye to. I imagined Madina, her lovely angular face, her dark pony tail, and found it hard to proceed with the thought.

But undoubtedly, even one more day lecturing on GATT Article XX and it would have been all over. One more meeting to review résumés of job candidates for their strengths in practical experience and scholarly promise, and I would be visited by some malign disease from which there would be no turning back.

The highway to Vermont was nearly empty at that time in early September. It wasn't even a real highway. I remember Daddy telling me about awards it had won for its beauty. The long, long hills beside which the road meandered reminded me of him; cruising down down down into the beautiful valleys that pleased him so much.

It began to rain. I could be young again. On the first night in our rented house I had kissed the two children on their foreheads as they slept. I would never have to go anywhere again. There would be no slot for me at conferences. My house in East Galway would sink back into the earth and rot. Emmet and Madina would grow up in Vermont; they would know about snowshoes. I could go park the car and look at Daddy's house on Elm Street and no one could make me go anywhere else.

Book II

El Puerto de Santa Maria; early 1970s

You could say they sent me away, after all that business with Miles Bradford, but that would not be exactly true. I jumped on the idea; it became a project for my mother and me to plot and plan all that winter. I would go to Ireland to meet my mother's relatives, her many first cousins. Brother Clement would collect me and help me get set up. I would stay for most of the next year, then come back and go to Daddy's college.

For the most part, I guess I wanted to do things just that way. It had a perfection to it. I began to think about Galway constantly; the part about Daddy's college made me feel reassured. This was our creation; I would not venture out to where people were cold and dry and without the right feelings.

But before going to Galway, I added a plan to stop in Spain and visit Jack and his wife. He, of course, had enlisted in the Navy during the Vietnam War and the young pair lived in a stark white apartment building overlooking a beach in southern Spain. After spending a month or so with them, I would take a train, all by myself, up through Spain, through France, and on to Ireland, where Brother Clement would be waiting for me.

Clement would come and find me on a rainy night in Galway City, back when you could hear a pin drop there.

Well.

All that confirmed in me my view, started with the notes from Mr. Bradford, that I could have what I wanted, unquestionably. I don't like to put it in such terms as "I could have everything," as that sounds selfish or egotistical, and I don't believe I was confident enough or indifferent enough to be either. But I did see myself as singled out, inhabiting a zone of wonder and love. It seemed that anyone I wanted, would also want me.

It's hard to believe that it's the same life I now have, with a physical continuity, the same arms, the same face; that I am, that is, inhabiting the same self, as I now never really want anyone, and no one appears to especially long for me.

All this was in the latter days of General Franco, the early 1970s. I arrived at a chaotic Madrid airport, and instantly loved everything. It was all smoky then, and everyone wore sunglasses. People ran from airline desk to airline desk, frantically making arrangements, shouting over the din.

My parents must have been insane to let me go off by myself, not yet seventeen as I was, in a silly little dress that looked like it was made for a child, a high waist and short puffed sleeves. On the flight to Seville, a middle-aged man tried to teach me Spanish. *Barrrcoooo*, he said, pointing to a photo in his magazine. *A boat, a boat.*

It was an odd mish mash of US navy culture, plunked down in what was at that time a still rather unspoiled Andalusia. It must have been annoying to my brother and his wife, as I was constantly dashing about with either young American fellows from the naval base, or my friend Pilar, a Spanish girl who worked as a maid in the apartments. I kissed a man who looked like a very young version of Hemingway—I called him Ernest and that is what I remember him as. I drove with boys I barely remember now, up to mountain towns where, more than anything, you would want to get hold of the tiny bottles of coca cola, so hot and dry and bright it was.

At night, members of the Guardia Civil with their tri-cornio hats patrolled the beach. In the morning, I heard scissors grinders down below, and went to pull up the blinds. It was the most wonderful sight imaginable, the finest ever in my life, before or since; the beach far below, the view of distant Cádiz.

I loved the smell of fried fish, and the smell of life in Puerto de Santa Maria, home town, I am quite sure, of the poet Rafael Alberti. I recall all that he wrote about the angels; but zthere's nothing I can remember him having said about fish. I went there in the evenings with Pilar and danced on tables.

After several weeks, I went to the travel office on the base and booked my train ticket all the way through to Dublin. The young man who helped me was a blond Spaniard, quiet in all his gestures. I could see he liked the idea of sending me alone on this long journey by train, across days and nights, and sleeping on pull-out cots.

Somehow or other he got Jack's address; he found me and showed up one evening at the door of the apartment, standing in the dark hallway, asking for Miss Catherine. Jack was furious at me, glaring and striding around the apartment. I remember that it was dusk, with candles burning in the living room behind me.

If only I had known, I whispered to the visitor. *We have plans for this evening. I am so sorry.*

I'm not sure why my brother was so angry. I was annoying, I suppose. Now, by contrast, I am merely harmless. After the Spanish lad had left, Jack lit into me, accusing our parents of not treating him as well as they treated Una and me, despite all he had done for them.

I went out onto the nighttime balcony and watched the gauzy lights of Cádiz, imagined the little children up late in the side streets, clapping and shouting, the sound of their feet on stone. A few Civil Guards were going in and out of a small bar near the stairs that led to the beach. I was, I remember, wearing a blue and white striped terry cloth outfit, shorts and a top. I was leaving soon, and on to the next zone of wonder, according to plan and as I saw it.

As for that, they left me on my own as soon as the train pulled in.

The station was small; I could hear the electric lights buzzing. Grass was blowing softly and happily in the dark, whispery all up and down along the track. The train came; it stopped. I climbed the high steps, and almost immediately we were off again.

I probably waved heartlessly to my brother; I don't remember.

It was crowded, with Spanish soldiers mainly, and large families. I stood in the corridor by a window, not sure how the etiquette of finding a seat should work. One soldier with a comic tone of voice winked and nodded; disappeared for a moment, moving up and down the corridors until he found me a seat. Inside the compartment was an odd assortment of people; the lovers, the nun, the husband and wife with piles of provisions, bread, cheese and ham.

All through the night, they fed me and tried to explain things to me. We arrived in Madrid in the early part of the next day. I camped out alone in a corner of the massive train station. The sunlight filtered through the high windows, moving and changing color. The announcements echoed across the vast space. Moroccan families with small children sat on blankets and waited all day, as I did.

I met a young Frenchman with long fingernails, who criticized my French as being too formal. I even had a kiss from a Spanish man with glasses who, waiting for his regional train, tried to hurry up and tell me all about his life. He wrote his name and address on a piece of paper and implored me to contact him. He took me by the shoulders as he heard his train announced and kissed me on the cheek as if with an enormous sense of regret.

After crossing the Pyrenees on a wonderful blue pull-out bed, the train rocking me back and forth, lying on my stomach and watching the scenery, we finally arrived in Paris. A gendarme remarked on my *jolis yeux bleus* as I passed by.

And somehow I arrived in dark old Dublin, as it was then, where the dominant sound was of seagulls crying. And in turn, I took my last train, the one to Galway, moving out across the Irish midlands which were exactly as I had known they would be.

Calvin—This was your email address a few years ago—still the case?
Am writing from Greensboro, the Vermont one. Have quit law, not that you will care. Finally parted company, was about to die.

Have brought the kids, of course. Did I tell you about the second one, a little boy, also from Kazakhstan.
Hope you are well. Do you hear anything of John Merrill? It seems I am back in his state.
Am working in a bookshop—do we now have this in common? Believe it or not—also working on a screenplay called Once Upon a Time in Vermont. You will not like the title—you disapprove of all titles. Am also writing some poems—will send them to you. Wondered if you would have any ideas about me showing the screenplay around when I am done with it.
It's about the Viking—or sort of about him.
As ever (unchanging—don't you ever miss me?),
Catherine

I logged off the public library's computer, checked my name off the list and left the library. It had begun to drizzle several days before. The famed foliage season had turned into an endless light rain, but I loved it.

I remembered coming to the public library, the Greensboro Free, for a children's pajama party several years back, before Emmet. Madina had been so small, so naïve.

Fog hung over the Grange Hall and Willey's, over the Miller's Thumb and over the hills in the distance, over Wheelock, over Sheffield. Sheffield made me think of Galway Kinnell and my long ago poem about how he looked like he had been cutting his hair in the dark.

I didn't know if Calvin Pini was still running his antiquarian bookshop and art gallery in Rhode Island. Probably, it so suited him. He and his wife had split up, or so it seemed. But he hadn't stayed in touch. He had no mercy for me now, seemed to enjoy whatever misfortune I might describe. The last I saw of him was in a sheltered garden at the MFA in Boston, on a hot June day. Madina had been scolded by the museum staff for putting her hands in the fountain, out of fear of liability for germs, they really said that.

We'd had a drink in the museum café, then parted indecisively.

You look like your father, I called out when I first saw him.

And you look like your mother, he rejoined carelessly.

Did you hear that, Mommy? Madina had said to me excitedly. *He said you look like your mother, Gramma, right?* She put her hand over her mouth, laughing in delight.

But you see, what I really wanted to write to Calvin was actually something like:

> Calvin—
> Despite the magnificent stars we saw when we went outside the guesthouse on the Aran Islands back in the 1970s sometime, when they still swam horses and cattle out to the boats, despite all that you just let me be kidnapped later. I will never forgive you, it was your fault, all your poems meant nothing when it came right down to it. Everything that happened after was your fault, and Una's fault. You did not defend me, you did not rescue me.
> I was just used by everyone for a little inspiration, everyone was quite content to see me do a bit of suffering. You could have rescued me so easily, you who cared so much about my dog Roger who died.

But of course I did not write that; it would take being truly *in extremis* to write such things. And Calvin would not really reply even to that, or would reply at cross purposes, a cryptic poem about the fields, the birds, the navy blue sea.

On her grumpy days, Madina missed life in Cambridge; she moped and complained, and lamented her lost friends. There were no Asian kids in Greensboro, few adopted kids, no stores. I counted it a success when I put something on the table they liked and, with a small lamp burning, saw their faces light up with even a temporary joy, as the early dark set in.

Emmet had too much day care. Sometimes he acted as if he didn't know me, or he laughed at me when I got annoyed at him. He could laugh without any good reason for what felt like hours at a time. That is orphanage stuff, I told myself, as I marveled at his little blond duck tail of hair and his face the very map of south central Russia, where Europe melted into an endless steppe.

Snow comes early here, Madina.

Oh—oooh. I knew I would hate it.

I thought of the snow that fell each night in the Kazakh city where Madina came from. It always fell during the night, so that each morning the ground was covered with deeper drifts than the day before. The tree branches glittered and crosshatched like the brown and white pattern of a rug. Madina put her chin in her hand and thumbed through an American Girl magazine. She said she remembered nothing of her home town, except that glisteny brightness after snow. Whenever she saw the shimmer off new snow, she would say, *It's Kazakh light, I think.*

Una phoned every week or so. Sven told me that, as the law school saw it, I'd had a breakdown, and the administration was still afraid that I would blame it on the working conditions or the atmosphere. They were ready to settle with me and call it a day. So that would be it. I would never have to go back, never. I'd never even be allowed back in; they only grant you one breakdown. Locks changed, traces expunged from the student handbook. No more faculty meetings or sitting through the excruciating question-answer period that followed the talks of visiting scholars, no more receptions for judges. No more trade and the environment, product/process distinction or debates on the validity of the notion of comparative advantage in an age of capital mobility. Instead, I could see in the distance a door open, and there at the lighted table Anna Akhmatova and Randall Jarrell.

But how old I was, how unexpectedly old to be walking through that door. Emmet was lining up cars and trucks all around the room, front to back, front to back. Madina still asked for Toora Loora at bedtime, the way I always had. It was funny to think that I had lived with Madina in Ireland a whole year, driving out to Park Baun with her in the rain. If I had only done this twenty years ago, I thought; if I'd even done it ten years ago.

Later in the autumn, Una telephoned.

Gramma's had a fall, she told me; she was angry at me, saying that she'd been left all alone with Gramma again.

Is she all right?

Who knows? We're waiting to find out if she broke anything. What do you plan on doing?

I'm not sure what I can do.

Una sighed with vexation.

I wandered around the house after the kids were asleep. I remembered the house of our childhood in upstate New York, the green birdhouse in the tree outside my window, the sloping roof where I believed Santa Claus always landed. I thought of my mother's tidiness, her lovely May altars with the statue of Mary and the bowl overflowing with lilacs. She was still tidy, even as an old lady, the nice fresh bar of Sweetheart soap in the dish. Sven said that she raised two slobs, Una and me.

I should pack up the car and get back as soon as possible, I thought. I was afraid to leave the Northeast Kingdom, as if I'd go back into a zone where no one cared if I ever had another moment's happiness.

You are born in a bright field and die in a dark forest. Those Russians, what a proverb. The fields of snow in between the pine trees, Mother Russia as seen from the plane as I approached Moscow on my way to get Madina. *You are born in a bright field and die in a dark forest;* because, simply because you screw everything up. And you listen to everyone else and do things so abominably stupid your life becomes unrecognizable.

I thought of Miles Bradford biting the air near me, as if I were so delicious he couldn't contain himself, and then laughing his sardonic laugh.

It seemed that was what I was left with.

Someday you'll wish you'd stayed with old Mr. Bradford, he'd said at the end. *Just like Jane Eyre, you have been loved,* he said. But conceited as I was, his remark made barely a dent in my heart in those days. Right-oh, I might have replied.

The pub; early 1970s

The roads in East Galway used to bend and twist at will back then. At each curve, you could stop for a full enjoyment of the wind, the grass blowing dark green and light green. You could lean the Raleigh bike against a stone wall and listen to the low whistle that always ran along the ground.

East Galway was Gramma's home place, though she'd

been born and raised in Watertown. It was thoroughly and utterly her home country, and everyone I met knew her as if she'd been born and raised in Timard.

Eyre Square was silent on that evening in 1972, a rainy early summer's night, as Market Street had been silent all day, except for one accordion player and the creaking shut of heavy doors. Most of the upper windows and even the shop fronts were dark. I had arrived in the afternoon and walked around, carrying the canvas bag on my back. You could feel the raw sea air back then, the lanes and alleys still had their ancient cottages, the town was small and self-contained, and a dark grey brume hung over everything. I had tea and sausages at the café in Moon's Department Store. Lights were reflected in the wet of the pavement, and later there were no lights.

There is no such place to go to now; that Galway is utterly gone, demolished block by block, ringed around with roads and subdivisions; the link with the sea is broken.

Well.

Ireland was the next thing that made me think I could have anything.

It was the Midas touch, animating the fields and rain, my touch that brought things to life and sent them into orbit around me. I walked a path through the grey air, woke to the sound of bam and bang, sheep hitting the wall outside. The skittering of their feet—do you call them feet or something else, I cannot remember—when farmers changed animals from one place to another, twice a day every day. And I wore the same slightly too small green sweater, jumper I learned to call it, nearly every day, a white stripe around the neck of it.

You see, it turned into the opposite of the Midas touch as I grew older, that touch of mine that somehow came to switch even lively things to cinders, curled up weeds. And not unreasonably, it seemed to me I was being punished for something.

When I arrived in Galway, it was all of a piece, the talk and the weather and the maps and the roads and the ease of the frame to the road, gentle and not dangerous, no attacks on you in the night, the gaw of the big black-birds, seeing people you knew from a car window, they pedaling hard on their black Raleigh bikes, heads down in the rain. Going to the bank by bicycle, taking half the morning, just to withdraw five pounds.

You little womaneen you, look at the womaneen. You are scarier you are than an Alsatian dog. Now.

It was the contact of my fingers with the edge of the field that stirred something paradisal; it was all that, and even more. Of course, it had to go. There would be no revisiting the scene, because in short order it was no longer there. As completely as a world could vanish, it did.

I lived in a pub that year. At a crossroads, looking out over an undisturbed field, a huge field, with the old estate wall still standing here and there in places. There was a constant sound of wind, and no resistance by fields or houses to rain, no complaining about it, since it was so common, an every hour's occurrence. There was no such thing as a rainy day, just rain that came and went.

I arrived at the time of year when the sun doesn't really set; even midnight has a kind of expectant glow. By four in the morning, the sky is streaked with red and white; the animals are up, as has been the case for hundreds of years. Later in the season came the Celtic mugginess.

Back then, the sea was the sea and the roads ran through fields. You could hitchhike. The sea met the land and every building fit into its place on the land. The house doors were left open.

That first day, I walked past the jewelry shops in Galway City, with their Celtic earrings laid out in the display windows, straightforward into the dusk and the fog. The telephone was damp. What an effort the telephone was then, big coins jangling around, what a luxury to connect with the other end.

I phoned Brother Clement.

I heard the phone ring in the monastery, the muffled double bleat.

Kilke'n 94280.

Would Brother Clement be there?

He would indeed.

Stepping away on the cold tiles.

Catherine, are you there? Is it you?

I am. I'm in Galway.

We'll be there, Clement said, *in two shakes. Sit tight, we'll be there.*

The bar in the Imperial Hotel was quiet except for a few men murmuring to each other. The June night fell slowly, reluctantly, but everything was wet outside the window; Eyre Square under the yellow lights, the footpaths, the slate roofs. Summer as I had known it only existed there in the afternoon, never at night.

Brother Anthony brought him, as Clement didn't have the use of the monastery car. We left Galway City behind in minutes and the view gave way to long, flat fields and stone walls in the rain.

Brother Clement kept turning around and smiling enthusiastically at me.

So you've come, Catherine. You've come, as if he'd thought in the end I wouldn't.

Brother Anthony was heavy-set, good looking. He would be leaving at the end of the summer for Africa, for the missions.

The fields seemed to be slithering away down towards a low horizon point, like an uneven floor. There were sheep everywhere, stone walls in long, narrow rectangles. With each turn, the car brought us deeper into the country, where the walls were sometimes very high, left over from half crumbled estates, and there were so many empty houses, long deserted, left as they stood. Only seldom did we meet another car. A pale purplish light shimmered above and below the horizon. I smelled a sweet, acrid smoke.

Such as we are, Catherine, Clement smiled and nodded.

Out of two boreens, walking, carrying leather bags, one in East Galway, one in South Mayo, Gramma's parents came without turning around, so far back and long ago that the famine was a part of the memory of their parents. She walked straight, adaptable, practical; he was handsome and lost, dependent and stubbornly unable to get used to Boston. They both, unknown to each other, pitched in their Irish language, saving it only for the odd time when they didn't want the children to know what they were saying. Or for nursery rhymes that Gramma remembered into old age.

No other people thought like that, only the Irish, especially those from the West—that the language was no good for getting a job, letting it go just like that without a struggle, muttering that it was useless. So in the space of fifty years, every word of Irish except the place names receded from Galway East, never to return as the language of whispers, love and insults.

Clement, taken from home into the monastery at thirteen or fourteen on the grounds that he seemed to have a vocation, did all his subjects through Irish, even washed the monastery dishes through Irish, and really knew it, starting of course with the prayers, Christ before me, Christ at my side. Not that he had any real regard for the language as such. For him, it was linked with four a.m. masses in the winter, the cold bedrooms, and the sobbing of the other boys. But of all this, Clement said not a word, not for his whole life.

Catherine had come, things would go a bit wild, you could feel it. It was a year before Ireland was to enter the EEC, along with Britain, sure if they go, we have to go in as well. Many had left for New York, building and bartending. I was told the selection of young men was not up to the usual standard. It rained what seemed to be on the hour. Each piece was part of the whole; the trees grew into the walls, the houses were crumbling into the fields. There was some pledge I kept hearing of that people would never knock a famine house. The roads disappeared; the clouds moved past in rapid succession.

Of course, I couldn't have imagined that night, as we pulled up to the Crossroads Inn, how completely destroyed it would all be; how I would run away from it many years later, leaving my own house behind in Park Baun. Clement had arranged for me to stay at the Inn for nine pounds per week, meals included.

I must teach you all about Fianna Fail and Fine Gael, said Nell, *our political parties. You'll want to know their history, Cat, where they came from.* She held the Tuam paper in her hands, rubbing it smooth, newsprint coming off on her finger.

I had moved from the guest dining room to their own kitchen, Nell and Frank's kitchen, since I did not act or feel like a guest. We sat at the picture window at the crossroads, where each car had to pause before turning. Each pulled up slowly, then drove away again into the rain.

Tom Collins put his head in. *There's the little womaneen.*

In love with each field and each view and each day, in love with the little bar and the big bar and the mirrors that let you see into the different rooms from a clever angle, in love with the grumbly sound of voices at the bar. I could soon tell who had come in, even from up in my room, even without looking. I could tell by the tone, by the way they closed the outside door, by the sound and type of greeting from the other side.

I went miles to see all my mother's relatives, going slowly and deliberately on a borrowed bike, up lanes and asking directions, standing by the open doors and calling in, *It's me, are you in?* And inevitably they would greet me extravagantly, dragging out tea and biscuit, all varieties in the cupboard.

Catherine, are you called, and some do call you Cat? And you are here to stay with us, are you, for the year?

It was so unheard of a thing to do, coming in reverse, neither spending much nor making anything, living with Nell and Frank Lyons. *Clement set it up, did he? Clement is so good, so good to us all.* There were aging brothers and sisters living together, armies of the never married, pleasantly agoraphobic, just about able to accept a lift to church. They had complaints about their little hill being overrun with rabbits, with hares as they called them. And at the end of the visit, a wallop of whisky, without any sense of hesitation. Whisky meant something different then; it was presented like medicine or closer yet a vitamin drink. I would sit and sip and listen to the ticking of the clock and we would come around again to my mother, my mother's mother, to Clement, to Nell and Frank.

That was East Galway of the soury fragrance of milk.

How little clutter there was in the landscape then. Animals. Wet trees.

How can I say it except that I fell in love in high volume; the amount, the degree, the sheer numbers. And I was nuzzled and loved without hesitation in return. So you can see why I say that it was Ireland that was the next reason I came to believe that I would have everything I wanted.

I'd only been there a week or so and Clement brought me to the wedding of one of my many cousins. The reception was held in a hotel outside Galway city, one of a number built in a long string along the inner coast. Despite being June, the wind was whipping. I borrowed a long, tight fitting green dress, the silliest thing I had ever worn in public, but it didn't matter at all. I wore black patent leather shoes, purchased in Tuam.There was a madness I got into right away. I smelled it, saw it, held it like a rose made of frosting, put it to my lips.

There was a stream of baby chams that day, and dancing with Brother Anthony.

Oh, you are Catherine are you, I've heard about you. We know all about you, I heard over and again.

There was no resistance, no suspicion. It was being one of the tribe, that was it. Had I not been of the tribe, goodness know, but I was. I had only to intone a name or two and the name of a village, and all was square. Grand, sound as a bell.

The land and the sea came together in a kind of emptiness then, no mess, no grotesquerie.

As for the Tierneys, I fell in love with the whole family at once. It kept me busy, it actually did, going up to their house every day, twice a day. Leaving the crossroads and the Inn, turning left towards the lake, up the road, down the road, around a bend, and there was their house. It was a house like alzzl the houses then, small and white and added onto here and there, but not much changed from the original, with its scrub evergreens for shading and the black and white dog just outside the open door. The rooster, the hens, scrabbling around the garden.

It started when I met old Jerome in the bar; the small lounge that is, he never went into the big lounge, and no one dared take his seat in the small one. I was always up and down from my room to visit Frank and the girls who worked with him behind the bar; if there were messages to be done across the street, I would go with the girls. Otherwise, I would go down to be teased and look around and listen and then go back upstairs and read. People would come in to use the phone; the locals didn't have phones back then and you could hear them trying to get through to someone, yelling into the receiver.

Old Jerome was missing one hand, cut off in a turf

machine some years before. He was comical and proud, and fussy about the color of his pint and what he chased it down with. One of this and two of that, in particular order. *Proper order*, he said about everything and Nuala, his daughter in law, had picked that up, and said proper order about everything too. Back at their house, Nuala and I readied Jerome's lunch. The Angelus bell rang at noon. It rang again at tea time and I would head back to the Inn, the late sunlight on the road the most astonishing I had ever seen, everything lit up in excesses of gold and blue.

In the evening, I would poke my head in and Jerome would say, *Come sit with me, laady. Sit up here now and listen.*

Frank would come along from the other end of the bar, wiping his hands, laughing but a little concerned, was it all right with me, would I mind.

Now, Catherine, watch out for that one.

And what do you know about it, Jerome would fire back.

On his false hand was a fine leather glove, swish and fashionable in its way, not a hook or anything you'd have to look away from. In fact, he held this hand as if to better look at it, a kind of feature. Men came in and out in Wellington boots, their bicycles propped up on the wall outside.

Even back then, it had been some years since West of Ireland people held up their arms on entering a room and said, *God bless all here*, but in those days there was still a pause on all sides as men came in one by one, as if they wanted to say it, and we to hear it.

Now, laady, back when your mother was a little girleen, men were shot in that field over the way.

I sat close enough so I could feel the steam off Jerome's coat. When he smiled, he would run one hand, the one with the glove, back and forth in front of his mouth, as if repressing some funny idea.

Whether Nuala liked living in the house with Manus's family, I never knew. She didn't say. Jerome's wife had been killed in a terrible accident the same year Jerome lost his hand, so Nuala had to do everything; the animals, the land, the garden, the house, the lot. Nuala had gone to a girls' school in Galway City, and later worked at the bank in Tuam; she was tall and smart and knew everyone. She rarely answered Jerome directly when we sat down to meals; rather, she smiled a big smile, one that let you see her teeth and gums, and turned to me with a nod. *Now*, she seemed to be saying.

It had all started when Jerome had asked me, *Would you like to see a caaalf?* And I went off with him to the older house that served now as a barn, and we watched the new calves bumping their heads up and down on the wooden buckets. The Celtic mugginess of the afternoons had set in; the longest and fairest days of the year, and the midges were flying in swarms all around us. You could smell the sun on the mud and the dry grass. The cars then were mainly Morris minors, and the road was almost always empty and quiet.

Then he wanted to know would I help with the turf that year, and I went with the younger son Joseph, Manus's brother, and we walked the little old donkey down into the bog, where it stood, sullen and stamping its foot while we worked.

You wanted to do this, then, Da didn't con you? Joseph asked me. Joseph was terribly shy; he sounded like he'd hardly had any practice in talking at all.

Nuala and I made them tea in bottles at the house and walked it up the road to the bog. Joseph sat back and drank from the bottle. *Christ tis hot, Nuala,* he said, and they laughed. He was dressed in an old white shirt, a formal one, with the worn cuffs turned up. Manus worked for a builder and was always off in far flung places, following the work, so he missed out on all of this, was never there for calves or turf. It made things odd for Nuala, as if Manus was a kind of stranger she stayed with only when he came to town; otherwise, she took care of his dad and brother, saw to their needs.

It strikes me now that it was not far off the summer solstice when I arrived; and from that many other things follow. They put up a huge tent at the crossroads for a dance. I know now it was the beginning of the end of such events, but I couldn't have known it at the time. The band set up in the corner; the ladies stood behind the drinks stall. They had strewn sawdust around the edges; was it to spit on or to keep the dancers from falling, I wasn't sure. Jerome put out his arm with the missing hand, the leather glove, inviting me to dance with him, not an old time waltz but a whirling step of his own, his cap at the same angle on his head the whole time. I saw the ladies lined up, looking at us disapprovingly. I wasn't even seventeen yet and he was sixty; we whirled and he laughed and I saw the ladies' faces but didn't mind them. I didn't see Nuala watching, but later she smiled the same big smile with her gums showing and pushed back her glasses and said, *That was a lot of whirling and stomping you were doing, shaking a leg, Cat.*

Maybe it was that night I realized that the sky in June and into July never got completely dark there; it remained purple as if lit up from behind; expectant, refusing to sleep, no matter how tired. And I found out how very tough people in Galway were when it came to catching forty winks, then up again to move the cattle from one field to another.

Have you a key, Cat? Frank doesn't make you go up and in through the window, does he? Nuala's face was lit up by the bonfire. Joseph held my hand as we sat in the tall grass near the old deserted house that served as a barn; this was one time of year for bonfires, though there were other times as well, as in October.

She invited me to go with them, with Manus's sister Eileen and herself, out to Connemara where Manus was at work building a house. *It'll be good craic*, she promised, as casually as you please. We had a seat as far as Galway, but would have to thumb from there. In those days, Galway City came to a sudden end at its edge, and the grass sang a separate song as we left the grey streets and houses. Nuala pointed out where she had gone to school, and seemed completely at home and familiar with that place where the road parted company with the ordinary world.

As I remember it, the road changed abruptly; it seemed to be made of some other material, something that melted when looked at too closely.

And in fact, it was only after a few minutes walking out of the city that animals began to follow us. Animals seemed to come out of nowhere then; donkeys, sheep, cats and dogs. It was the donkeys that really tagged along with you, though. They were curious, and if they could have, would have been asking our names, where we came from and where we were going. They followed just behind, politely, with only the tiniest suggestion of mistrust. Their manes were shaggy; they were inured to weather, the rain falling or the Celtic sun fanning over them.

And just as you thought they would come the whole way with you, they disappeared without anyone calling them or making a fuss; they just ceased to be there behind you on the road, evaporating. Sheep were too lazy for all that; they would lie there looking aggrieved, watching you pass, faces turned crossly into the wind. Their favorite spot to lie down was right at the edge of the road, half in and half out of clumps of grass.

Nuala and Eileen and I sat on the back of an old wooden lorry, completely open in the back, swaying to and fro. Nuala was laughing and showing her gums; she loved using a bit of Irish and didn't often have the chance. The black and white sheep dogs understood only Irish. *Dia dhuit ar maidin.*

There were lots of famine houses there; in fields and on little roads leading nowhere, except down to the water. In houses where people were living, I smelled seaweed and milk. I heard an even louder whistle of wind, but Nuala was undaunted.

Every now and again it rained down on us, then the rain passed over and was gone.

It felt like no one from the outside had come there yet; we were the first ones. Voices were very loud. Things cost small amounts of money; a loaf of bread wrapped in paper; a wagonload of turf; the scalding smell of a fire in the grate; bacon.

It's in Carna, Cat, that they're building the house, said Nuala.

Although I hadn't, I felt as if I'd gone up to a very high altitude, and could barely manage to continue. Everything became rock; you wondered how people lived here; the deep grey clouds closed down over the earth, and then let go again. Nothing more than this was happening; only we were moving forward over the road.

Tis easy to take a boat to the Aran Islands, you know, Cat, Nuala told me. *If you don't mind getting seasick. Maybe next time.*

Nuala loved getting out of one car and waiting for the next; had no hesitation about getting in, and always held off telling the driver who she was or where she was coming from, would pepper him with many questions first.

I began to feel faint; the weather kept changing every few minutes, the sky went from dark to light, people appeared and disappeared. It felt as if we were down low and flat against the grass, but in the distance mountains rose up inexplicably. Nuala's conversations in Irish sounded like murmuring or a heartbeat, unintelligible yet familiar. The road was narrow, scarcely wide enough for two cars to pass at the same time. Something bracken brown yet bright played about at the horizon. Waves of air and salt and grass moved over us.

There was such a place then. I saw it. And on that day, on our way to Carna, I went inside it, as one had to do then.

You went through, and disappeared into the other side. Roads did, buses, cars, donkeys. Clouds and pools of water. Houses you thought were there.

At last we came to a crossroads where we heard the sound of hammers from inside a partly built house; the sun had come out, everything seemed more normal and calm. The sky was suddenly a boring blue. Manus looked out at us, put his hands on his hips and said, *It took ye long enough.* He and Nuala smiled at each other; his white shirt fanned out in the wind like a sail. Nuala lied and told him I was chatted up by a lorry driver.

That night, we all went out to the lounge in a small hotel nearby. I had never seen such darkness; summer must be coming to an end, I thought, or was it because of nearness to the sea, the road was so dark as we crossed it that you could not even tell where you were walking. As we entered the bar, we heard the hubbub common to every bar in Ireland, except that here the talking was mainly in Irish, though the speakers kept looking over, as if overly conscious of the difference in language. As I felt it, they were worried that someone from the outside would either want them or not want them to be speaking Irish, having been sent to check up on them.

Manus had the face of old Jerome, though nicer, and sad in a way Jerome was not. Like Joseph, he never mentioned his father, to speak either well or ill of him. We ranged ourselves around a table and Nuala ordered rum and cokes for the ladies.

The brown froth of the Guiness, which I could never like, and the brown coke in the rum and coke, after all the brown light and the brown trim of the hotel, the dark brown darkness, the dart board, the brownish sounds; the rum and coke went straight to my head. I met some French boys who had come on bicycles. I had had enough rum and coke to speak French with them and Nuala laughed, saying, *Cat, the way you rip through the French!*

I exchanged addresses with them, though even in that state I knew I would never write to them, ever, and they would never come to East Galway as they promised to do, to see the Inn. As we went off to bed, the three of us in one room at the end of the hallway, I began to call out, *I love Joseph, do you hear that, I love Joseph.*

It seemed to be the funniest thing Nuala ever heard. She and Eileen fell down laughing on the bed. I smelled the dampish linen, the dawn on its way, and I slept, invisible, in Carna.

So it was no wonder that Nuala leaned over me that night I stayed over at Jerome's place and whispered, *Which one do you really like the best, Cat?*

So began my unfortunate tendency to embrace motifs in volume, to link place and person, to go to excess in my wanting many at once, but only after a fashion and in the way I wanted.

It did become complicated, awkward after a while.

Brothers

To add to all this, after several months at Frank and Nell's, I began to listen for a particular voice, a particular sound, down below my room; the door from the outside would open, the other voices would stop, a drink would be ordered. I knew it was John Joe Gormley, who had been barred on many occasions, the worst thing that could happen to you there, barred, banned, exiled, banished. As was my tendency, I began to think most of all about Gormley, since he had the greatest effect not only on others—that wasn't it—but rather on the air around him.

He would come in with his brothers in tow, muttering and mumbling with them, in a close line as if they were part of a fence, a wall, moving in time with each other. *Brandy, Frank,* one of them might say, but they got nowhere. Everyone else would stop talking and Frank most times would refuse them service. Frank hated conflict, so would say under his breath, *Don't you know yourself, Gormley?*

I might pick just this time to go below and visit Jerome, sit by and watch as the regulars quietly took Frank's part, and waited until Gormley and his brothers left.

On one such night, John Joe came through the small lounge to use the gents or the telephone, passed us by and then turned, whirled around abruptly, and looked me straight in the eyes.

Frank lived in fear that I would bring a man up the stairs to my room, though I would hardly have had the courage to do that. He began to watch me closely in the evening, to see whether there were unexplained disappearances. The long windy days of summer came to an end, and I had the great luxury of not having to return to anything; no school, no anything, just riding my borrowed bike, stopping at every hillock and lake and watching the boggy land and the green fields change color as the clouds passed by overhead on their way to the sea. Some days it was too wet, and all I had to do was watch the rain hitting my window at a slant; unevenly, in fits and starts.

There was nothing I had to do, except to be in East Galway.

Clement called by for me many days, the ordinary days, and we went out on his motorbike visiting. He took me to more of my mother's relatives, the dark kitchens, the old delft brought out for showing. The dogs that had to be called out to and chastened before they would let us cross into the front garden. *Yeer, get out of that, you old bast'd ya.* Then the suspicious look at us, Clement who in some cases hadn't been seen for some years, and the young girl with him. Then adding turf to the fire, to make it blaze up, and the teapot, and the whiskey. Clement smiling with delight, as he managed to talk them around and get me into another cottage, *You can never know what to expect, Cat,* he would warn me, laughing.

Clement would drop me back at the Inn, his eyes shining with fun, unstrapping his helmet, refusing to come inside. He believed in me then, at the side of the road with the motorbike, and years later, on into time immemorial, I was beyond criticism, reproach, could never do wrong, could never be thought of in the same category with wrong. *Cat, Cat,* he jaggled my arm up and down. *Next time we'll go round to the old home place, your Gran would have talked about it.*

One particular evening, as I went inside I could feel that something had happened. I heard Frank's feet pounding back and forth on the wooden plank that ran behind the bar; he tried to smile at me but couldn't.

They've been in, Cat, he said. *The worst of the lot.*

Frank wanted to keep them out for good, but you couldn't do that unless there was some incident. He knew he couldn't completely count on my loyalty, though he wasn't sure what the disloyalty might entail.

Back are you, Cat? And how is our Clement? Good to you, was he?

There was this thing about the roads. You couldn't go anywhere without everyone knowing; and there was nothing that everyone didn't know. As you progressed down a road, those ahead of you knew you were coming. I could always manage to make someone pass by when I wanted them to pass by. As I said, this contributed to that unfortunate sense I had that I could have whatever I wanted. I became accustomed to magic.

I saw him one day; he passed me out, then stopped the car and pulled slowly back. It was a navy blue British car, not new, but unusual. He was dressed well that day as he generally was. You wouldn't know where he was coming from; I wasn't even sure what he did.

You're at the Inn, aren't you?

Yes.

And related to who was it?

I went through a litany list of cousins and relations.

May I offer you a lift back?

I hadn't taken the bicycle, so I was free to go, free to ride along next to him.

I told him I was hoping to go to the university in Galway.

It would be that, the uni, a smart girl like you, I remember him saying.

It was terribly wet on the road, though not quite raining. In between dark and light.

Do you know who I am? he asked.

Yes, I said again.

Who then?

Gormley, with brothers.

He laughed as if very pleased with my answer.

As the Inn came into sight, he pulled off the road and leaned into me, as if to smell me. He ran his hands over my hair.

Who did you say you were related to? he asked. He nuzzled my ears, the side of my head.

I hoped simply to duck into the side door and up the stairs, but Jerome was there, and Frank was standing, holding a glass, behind the bar. Neither spoke to me. There was no point in lying in Galway; and there were none of those handy remarks like, I was just busy, or just over the way, there was no such thing that you could be doing, and so everything had to be revealed. In this case, I knew they probably already knew. Jerome drank back his chaser. Frank was speechless for a moment.

Where's he gone, then? he asked at last. He glanced towards the stairs, as if wondering whether I would ever be that reckless.

The next morning, Frank did not open the bar on time. He was, well, missing. Frank was nowhere to be found. Old men on bicycles pulled up at the door, saw it closed, tried it once or twice and continued on their way. The rain started to fall and kept on for hours.

When Frank appeared later in the day, his eyes were red and shining; he was dripping wet and standing in his own bar as if lost, uncertain what to do next. *He's back on the drink,* whispered Mary, the girl who helped out in the bar and who'd come over to open up when she heard Frank was missing. As if it was necessary to say it.

He cannot drink, she said. *Just cannot; he goes mad.*

Ha, ha, Cat, Frank shouted. *How's my girl? And Mary, such a great girl you are.*

Nell took one look at him and left the house, off to her sister's in Castlerea, slamming the door behind her.

I remember driving in the car with Frank, through the rain that was falling mercilessly, up hill and down dale, to visit people he did not need to see, waving his arm to tell them I was in the car with him, with me waiting and watching out the window. Mary explained to me that Frank was one of those people who could not go near the drink, and that Nell kept him away from it constantly; though he worked in the bar, he pretended it was some other kind of business, always made a point of not smelling the glasses or bottles, and keeping up a big smile.

I'm fond of you, Cat, surely you know that? he said, staring straight ahead at the road as he drove. Darkness was falling; it was a failure of a day, a terrible day. Generally it rained a few times during the course of any day; on this one it rained with barely a moment's pause. When we got back to the yard at the Inn, there was quiet and darkness everywhere, as if word of the tragedy had spread, and people stayed away. Fog rolled in from the fields; the place to turn around cars was muddy.

Come up now to bed, Frank, Mary said, very professional. *No one's out tonight, sure they're not.* Frank was compliant, the drink wearing off, repentant, tired. He clung to me a moment, murmuring, *Darlin, darlin. That bad one could never have you.* After he'd gone up the stairs, Mary and I sat morosely in the lounge, she very wise. *Let's close up early,* she said.

Around nine, we saw Nell's car pass by the front window, and heard her enter the small lounge, tentatively, peering around, not knowing of course what she would find.

So where is he? she asked first thing. We didn't answer.

He must have been wild that I left; was he out looking for me? I had to teach him a lesson he wouldn't soon forget. My sister was firm about that.

Mary and I still stood foolishly, Mary pretending to clean the counter.

Did he come back at all, or was he out looking for me? The car's there, I see.

He's back, Mary ventured.

What did he say about me going? Nell asked.

At that point, there was a great thump from above; I thought Frank might have fallen out of bed. Nell looked up at the ceiling, then turned and headed for the stairs. We never saw another thing of either of them for twenty four hours. When they emerged, it was as if nothing had happened.

And you could say that after that it was a little awkward. I began to think about the piano; I hadn't looked at a piano since leaving home months before. Clement managed to set me up with a piano at the convent in Tuam; I could go there whenever I wanted, play to my heart's content. It was cold those days, and the room in the convent was unheated except for a big box of a space heater. The piano sounded tinny and ever so slightly out of tune. I took the bicycle whenever I couldn't get a lift, play for a few hours, then stroll around Tuam; the newsagent, the shoe shop, the home goods store. The young nun who scrubbed the stairs at the convent was always happy to see me; I was asked to come and play for the sisters.

I still wasn't that amazingly good. I was all right; I had the feel, I had the sound, but I did not really have the thing it was that made you go off on your own and play freely. I was stuck to the music books, I knew what I wanted to sound like, but I couldn't go head to head with someone who had a true musical gift. I didn't mention that, though I didn't hide it, either. I think that the nuns, sitting there listening, knew it.

It was just there, a fact.

But it was because of the piano that I left the Inn and left Galway.

I got it into my mind that I should go to Dublin and study music. Then it became, *Oh, Catherine and the music, the muuusic. That girleen and her music.* Funny enough, Frank and Nell took me to Dublin to audition.

Ah, twill do me good to get out of here and off to the big city for a couple of days, Frank said.

We stayed in what was then one of the newer hotels, with little fripperies of windows and a garish bar off the lobby.

Dublin in those days was damp and dark and you saw old men out on the street. There were newspaper hawkers and lottery ticket hawkers, and always the sound of the skinny sea gulls overhead. Dublin felt old then, and gritty, with yellow street lights, the burnt maple smell from the Guinness brewery, and the acrid smell of fires in tens of thousands of grates. The little alleyways hadn't been knocked down yet; there were still ponies and traps on the quays the odd time.

I auditioned at the school of music for a woman who had no interest in me or my playing and only talked about crotchets and quavers. It was decided I would move to Dublin and sign up for four lessons per week, on condition that I got myself a piano and learned my quavers.

Clement helped set me up in a hostel run by nuns on the near north side, catering to girls from the country. The hostel had once been a magnificent Georgian mansion, I wasn't sure whose. It had huge drafty vistas of balconies and stairs. We ate in the basement, where girls stood in line to get custard poured over everything. I would sit in my room at the very top of the hostel, looking out over the roofs of the north side, reading Rousseau, Tolstoy, Turgenev, Balzac, in no particular order but at voracious speed. After a while, they put a girl named Bernadette from County Clare in the room with me, and we soon decided to move out to our own flat.

How we survived that I don't know.

We moved into a one room flat in an eighteenth century building on Harcourt Street, long since demolished to make way for some mess, perhaps a bank.

The building itself was once the scene of great parties with lords and ladies, but had fallen into incredible and audacious disrepair. Each room was turned into a mishmashed apartment; IRA members were rumored to occupy digs on the upper floors. At night, the students from other flats would visit us and we'd have a sing along. I remember doing a solo:

I was born with the name Geraldine
With hair coal black as a raven
I traveled my life without a care
For all my love I was savin'.

You should hear the kid sing it! the English girl told the others enthusiastically. Thinking of it now, I am not sure how one could be born with the name of Geraldine.

And frankly, I am not much of a singer.

The rug was so wet you almost left footprints in walking across it. The only heat was a stinky gas heater that you had to light with a match; incredible that it never blew up. Everything we owned came to smell like gas cylinders; we could even taste it. Bernadette and I went off with the students to the films or to local jazz clubs; she had a job with the civil service, and I only had the classes at the Music Academy. Winter in Stephen's Green was bitter and spare; it was raw from the sea winds, no real snow, but lots of rain that went on for days and nights at a time. Bernadette and I came to a parting of the ways, and I moved on to a bedsitter off the South Circular Road, with lots of mice, so many mice you could hear them rustle and titter, and even watch them run past. I rented a piano that took up half the flat, and one of the other music students gave me ear training tests by making me close my eyes and guess what note he was playing. *Come on, come on, it's a b flat, surely you know that one.*

In company with what seemed to be the rest of Ireland, I went home on the weekends, leaving Friday night by train, then getting the bus to Tuam, then getting back to the Inn by hook or by crook, I could always find some way. I never had to ask Frank and Nell in advance, I would just appear.

Catherine, the very one! Frank would say, order restored. Jerome sat at his usual place in the corner of the small lounge; he would pat the seat next to him and say, *Come here, girl, and let me tell you all about it.* The tips of his fingers on the good hand were yellow as saffron from years of smoking; his cap was tilted rakishly to the side, but never ever taken off. Nuala came and grabbed my arm and whispered that Joseph had disappeared; he'd said he was going to take the exam for the Guards but had slipped off to Australia; loved it there, said he'd never come back.

In the distance, I could see Manus throwing darts, sad and brooding, his sleeves rolled up to the elbow.

In the morning, I slept in. Before Galway, I had never slept in in my life. It had been unheard of in our house, early rising being a sign of authenticity or anxiety in the appropriate degree, expectations fulfilled or otherwise, you had to get up. And it was not hard to; we just did. Up and out, ready to go. At the Inn, I slept, and the rain woke me as it had before, the animals hitting against the wall. A car, stopping, moving forward again. The sound of cattle, unchanged since the time of Queen Maeve.

As light as the summer had been, the winter was equally dark; combining the pea soup dark of the night and the wet, into a mix so bone chilling I could never have imagined it. One night after Christmas, Jerome and I left his house and walked towards the Inn. The wet grass seemed to shine in the dark, the starless, relentless night lay silently around us. No wonder people went out to the pubs at night, clawing their way along the dark roads, though this thing with pubs was relatively new, the last hundred years, less, and women never used to go, I was told. Those nights on the dark side of the year, the rain, the rattle of a bicycle, the sound of wellies on the floor, the loud voices on the telephone, Tuam 23568, Tuam 23568.

Jerome said he wanted to find ducks. I'd never heard him talk about ducks.

There were ducks down this way, he said, and I followed him down a boreen. My feet were wet and my face would have been cold to the touch.

There are ducks down this way, so there are, he said, and continued on, bent forward. The crossroads where the large tent had been put up that June night was in view, but made small, as if seen through the narrow end of a pop-open binocular set.

He wheeled around and held me to him, squashed me against his wet jacket. It was strange, as if pushed up against a scene already washed away by history, as if washed through the wall into another time, the wet grassy smell all around me and the scene of the crossroads visible but not accessible by ordinary walking. He continued to hold me, desperately tight until the direction of the wind was clear as a bell. I could have mapped it out precisely, by the angle of the rain falling against us.

After a time he let go and turned in the direction of the Inn.

In the time of your Gran, he said, *men were shot in this field, did I ever tell you?*

Sometime later, I told Nuala about the ducks, something even years later she never forgot, and the full details of which she could imagine without me saying a word.

The ducks, Cat, wasn't there something about ducks? And she would laugh, gums showing, until the laugh finished in her smoker's cough.

It ended in the early spring, the back and forth on the mail train; the mice, the piano, the organ lessons, pumping at the big pedals in the dampness. The bicycles, the whistle of the grass, the rain that came across the island and found nothing in its way.

Clement had taken me to the old home place, down a one-car-width-across boreen, a narrow rectangle of a house set kittycorner to the road, sharp glass set in the old concrete of the fence. Not pebble dash, but a much older house, hundreds of years old. More of my mother's cousins, a brother and sister, lived there now, passing out the cigarettes, huddled in cardigans. The sister looked like a grown up child, her cheeks fresh and red. The walls were kept painted dark red and green, the windows were so small they barely let in the light. Out of this road walked my mother's mother, carrying her bag, heading for Boston. And out of this same road Gramma got her ideas about body and mind.

I was in a jumble, a muddle as I left them, without any great goodbyes. I promised Clement I would be back.

Book III

Stannard; 2006-2007

The heating system in the Greensboro house was terribly noisy; it banged and shuddered, making Emmet cry. The landlord said there wasn't a thing wrong with it; the furnace was built to last. I never ventured into the basement; in fact, every night I checked to make sure the door going down into the dark was locked as tight as could be. I never liked finding myself in a house alone, especially after waking in the night. It reminded me of Park Baun every time; I've no idea how I survived that. Whatever was right or wrong with the heating would remain hearsay. The first snow fell in early November; November was a funny month for me. My birthday, the beginning of the winter holidays, the slow trail into the winter solstice.

Snow, snow, snow, said Madina, leaping up and down in front of the window. She hauled Emmet up like a puppy so he could see through the window. But in fact, Emmet was not so keen on the snow. As soon as it began to pile up, he wouldn't even try to walk through it, but would stand staring at it in outrage. I had to pick him up, snowsuit and all, and sort of drag him along the footpath.

> Should I congratulate you on being back in Vermont? Things are complicated with me, different, and I have no plans to return to Vermont, I assure you.
> Calvin

That didn't tell me much; Calvin was intent on not letting me in on any of his thoughts, though I pursued this goal—trying to find out what he might be thinking—in a half hearted way.

I liked the very boredom of it; the simple contours, the lack of choice, the same few loaves of bread for sale at Willey's. Madina liked her little school well enough; in the evening we did her homework, the beginning of times tables and fractions; cutting the pie into pieces, seeing her joy when she realized that a piece of it was a fourth or even an eighth. I felt old and tired as I saw where that road would run, all new to her, off into the distance where I would lose the ability to help her with advanced algebra, Geometry II and even calculus.

How clever you are, Madina, much smarter than I ever was.

She accepted this smilingly, knew it to be true.

And me, me smart? asked Emmet.

You too, you're the builder. He thought about this; was it as good a deal,

as big a prize?

Madina's face clouded over; she disliked the comparison.

I'm smarter, she muttered.

Nooo, Emmet rolled on the floor, as if in pain.

And so things went, as the days got shorter and people ran from their cars into buildings, grimacing in the wind.

The buses that passed through filled with foliage seekers disappeared, and I was left as I wanted to be.

Gramma has it in for you, Una told me.

Gramma hadn't broken anything this time. I wouldn't have to make a plan to bring the kids and go see her. Whenever I phoned her, she answered the phone as if she was at death's door, *Hello,* small, far away, breathless. *It's me,* I would say, and then silence. She wouldn't ask anything about where I was or what I was doing; she waited for me to speak.

I'm going to be teaching a course, I told her chirpily, *at Stannard State. Do you remember Stannard?*

Oh? she said, perhaps feigning disorientation.

Stannard, not so far from where Daddy was from in Hardwick, you remember.

She didn't answer. She didn't like my disappearance and I suppose even less the idea that I would make something permanent of it. Before I'd left, she used to comment on my fortitude, my getting dinner on the table for the kids every night, with all I had to do. Since I hadn't married an insurance salesman, this was the next best thing. Giving off my special aura of intractable aloneness, like Dolce Vita perfume, bringing the kids over weekly, in a predictable sequence, Emmet pulling everything out of her closet. *My, he can defy you,* she would say. But she genuinely liked children; that was what she had done best, taken care of children.

And it was lovely and safe and poetic, being a child in her world, at least while I was small and the world was oh so luminous; the May altars, the Italiante urns on the front steps. A chaise lounge on the back lawn, a library book, my arm around the neck of the collie from next door.

Calvin:
Just checking in, not that you want me to. You know I never lobby for anything, but when one of the deans from Stannard State came into the bookstore, I asked him about whether I could teach something and the upshot is I can do a comparative lit seminar in the spring. Remember when you and I went to Stannard for that poetry symposium, what was it called? I remember reading in the auditorium, and someone asked me why I wrote about houses so much. Probably thought I was nuts and was trying to be polite. What should I put in the course? What would you teach in a comp lit course? I can do some of my Japanese stuff.
C

Some of us from John Merrill's writing workshop at Saint Theo's had gone to Stannard that long ago winter day, to read our poems. I had had coffee with Calvin and looked out at a long, gloomy, snow covered slope reaching into some spindly trees; God forsaken. And I must have chosen to read some work of mine about houses. About houses, what did that mean?

I really wanted to get that course; I wanted to teach it, no matter how inconvenient. Comparative literature; it could be more or less anything I wanted, they said. Novel, desire and the novel, Japan and the novel, Ernest Hemingway and Europe, Ernest and his two bottles of wine for lunch, wrapped in cool white towels by the landlady. Or my dissertation topic, the Japanese writer Dazai Osamu, leaving his family in a cheap apartment at night, heading out to the bars, finally leaping into a river and drowning himself, a few fabulous photos of himself on bar stools left behind. The Japanese artist, self-denying, self-loathing, that was getting too close to my later things, and I wanted to go back to the original, so no to that. I wanted to be back in the workshop, with Calvin and Merrill and people telling me I was the super poet.

As the kids slept, I plotted and planned. I might have only five students, no one would take it, or if they did they would drop it. This worried me constantly over the years; what would I do if everyone dropped a class; could they be forced to stay and listen to me? Was there some clause that said a teacher could not be utterly abandoned by students? Things were cruel now, the teaching evaluations like slam books. I remembered the evaluation in New York that time. I was just a visitor, and one student had written, It makes me sick to see the way she runs out the door to go pick up her child.

Moustaki; late 1970s

Maybe in its own funny way Saint Theo's, even acknowledging its oddness, was the next reason I thought I could have everything. It was Daddy's college, his father had forced him to go there against his will at the start of the Great Depression, and Daddy had lived with Saint Theo's on his mind ever since. It was Daddy to perfection. Catholic, and lost in time, and intelligent without pretension and a little lefty in terms of sympathies.

Daddy had known all the old French Canadian priests who founded the college; remembered them all and visited them as one by one they proceeded into extreme old age and then passed on. Père Poulin, Père Gamache, Père Dulac. Daddy was an unassuming devotionalist. He liked to say grace in French. He knew about the elite world but it held no interest for him; it was too cold, treacherous, without the milk of human kindness without which nothing made sense to him. When I was in high school, he had quit his company job and started lecturing at St. Theo's; not only would I be going to his college, I would also be going for free. *It will make him so happy,* Gramma kept saying to me. *It will mean the world to him.* And so I didn't consider anything else, didn't so much as visit any other school. It was straight from Gramma's East Galway to Daddy's northern Vermont, with no stops or detours.

Yet I took to it right away. In a sense, anyway.

As for the students, the shrieking and the beer parties, well that was too preposterous. I walked around with my hands over my ears. I kept escaping from roommates. I would move in, and then decide I couldn't stand them, and get myself moved and be all gone— lock, stock, and barrel—before they came back from a weekend away. I wanted to get A's in everything; that made life easier. A's are the wallpaper; A's look nice, they keep you from having to explain anything. People leave you alone when you have lots of A's lined up in a row.

In the student plays, I didn't get the part of ingénue lead; sometimes I played a child with pony tails, sometimes a middle aged wife; most often the type of Mary Warren in *The Crucible.* As I saw it, my escape from being objectified under the proscenium was into the writing seminar; or the art studio, where I learned that one paints in oil from dark to light; or in yet one more foray into ponderous discussions of *La Symphonie Pastorale.*

And out into the snow at night; across the field from one campus to another, the stars whirling and blinking. It was suspended animation. I didn't come to Saint Theo's objectively, because I'd wanted to, but rather because in one way I had to, then in a different way wanted to, like an arranged marriage perhaps, always aware that it had nothing to do with me that I had shown up here.

I went home to Gramma and Daddy on weekends, even to Aunt Olive's on Sundays, and thus nothing had changed. There was a strange absence where East Galway had been, as if, which became so common for me, I had expended great effort learning something important in great detail, only to set it aside almost at once. I wasn't making plans to go back there, not even to find Clement, nor Nuala. As so often happened, I decided I would just consider it later.

Early on in my time at Saint Theo's, the first winter break I suppose, I was asked to go to Paris with a group of sociology students, as their translator no less, on the grounds that I was allegedly fluent in French. As with everything, I was so good that it first seemed to others I was great, but I was not that great. I could pick up a newspaper and read French with ease; I could chat and sound creditable; I could understand to some degree, though not slang. But something was missing, the follow through, the focus. *Teach me French and I'll teach you German,* Miles Bradford had said. But I never did more than a smattering of German; *Wie war's im Theatre? Ich muss mir eine neue Jacke kaufen.*

It was between semesters, that we went to France. I got a sore throat first thing, and had to go to bed when we arrived. I remember the quiet days in bed in the hostel in Clichy, the ladies who worked there, scrubbing down the stone floors. Their voices, speaking Portuguese and Arabic, echoed through the corridors. There were posters of Algerian revolutionaries in the common room; I remember strolling past the couscous restaurants in the evening. The students were interviewing immigrant workers in Paris, and I was to be the translator, meeting with local officials and workers' groups, young men who met us in doorways, petty officials in local administrative offices. I did my job, but tried to escape from the American students, left them to fend for themselves.

I wandered by myself in all the places you would expect: the Luxembourg Gardens, the Rodin museum, up and down the labyrinthine pathways of Fontainebleau. Even then, I was remembering and regretting; I recalled that Madame Celeste had wanted me to go to piano summer school at Fontainebleau, and felt her disappointment following me; I felt passive, felt a failure of sorts, though this was in its early stages. It was so much more natural for me to walk, observe and feel, simply feel. And there was the purchase of symbolic goods, in this case two French sweaters, one dark pink and the other bright green, too small and tight as was the fashion at that time. I wore them every day after that, I wore them as we made our communal spaghetti dinners.

I was proposed to by a singer with a voice like Georges Brassens.

Observe, feel, observe, feel, I was well versed in this even back then.

Without question, I got stuck in a time warp that dates to that trip; the lipstick, the bangs, the turtlenecks.

The discussions of what went wrong in '68, Danny le Rouge, Moustaki, Leo Ferré, my cold hand rummaging in books, books with clear, luminous prose. Imagining a two roomed *pied à terre*, ribbed tights. I saw Clichy by evening, and it was mine. I smelled the burnt sugar smell of the metro; I waited in line to eat at a famous, old and very cheap restaurant at Saint Denis. Part experience, part premonition, I stood and looked at boots in the shop windows. The boots were new to me, speaking a language I did not know, but believed I could master with ease. If only I tried; but perhaps I would try later. I would learn the language of the French boots later, later, later.

I had a secret admirer, though I was surprised and disappointed when I found out who it was. He left a white rose in my mailbox at Saint Theo's every day and sent me notes that said such things as, *Like Beatrice, conduct me.* The secret admirer is probably never the admirer you want.

By the second year, I had finagled my own room and moved in a piano from home. In his endless trust, Daddy thought this a great idea, and still believed I could be such a pianist, that one day he could sit and listen to me play wonderfully, his fondest dream. Even when he was very old, he would ask me with polite regret whether I wouldn't take it up again. I probably gave him the same sharp answer I gave him when he asked me if I didn't want to see my ex-husband Yukito ever again.

It was cruel to say, but no, and no again. Though I still felt a shiver of love for my Paderewski music editions, with their rough paper covers; the Nocturnes and the Mazurkas, most of which I never got to.

The students of Saint Theo's were mainly from the Italian and French Canadian middle classes; cozy and complacent, they drove banged up Toyotas and with whoops and war cries went home in groups at Thanksgiving to Maine, New Hampshire and New Jersey. I didn't know most of them, their names or their interests. I didn't much care; didn't attend their social gatherings. I was, as Una might have said, essentially spaced out. It was outside my abilities to share a room amicably or to quaff a beer in a dormitory corridor. I hurried away, always busy, always entranced with myself.

With my trace of an Irish accent, I was a chameleon; but not that much of one.

To that extent, I guess I was spared any unseemly involvement with the alien zones of ambition and calculation. I left no footprints, took no responsibility for my presence or even existence, which freed me up for higher matters.

Daddy would see me on the campus and race home to tell Gramma. *I saw her, she looked great, carrying her books, hurrying along,* he no doubt said.

Roger; 1974

As for who Calvin Pini was, well, he is the person above all who did not rescue me.

Even much later, while I was teaching at the law school, I would write to him, *Why are you still so elusive?* And he would answer with a poem or a cryptic comment. I thought in the end he would recall those days walking in the snowdrifts at Saint Theo's and with good humor and good will solve a few things for me. But he never did. He stubbornly nursed his grievance against me until he was bored with it, and then it wasn't even a grievance any more, but he did not want me to be too clear on this.

At that stage, especially after Japan, I had had enough of mysteries, and poetry is something that shouldn't rely on mystery *per se*. At least so I thought.

But as to who Calvin Pini was, it began at Saint Theo's with a dog.

Or more properly, it began in John Merrill's writing seminar. It began with John Merrill, and Calvin Pini, and my dog Roger.

It was when Roger died, on a late winter afternoon.

Calvin was such a gifted poet; he wrote boys' poetry, ships and sails and sand. He never wrote anything jarring or wrong, not audacious either, but just impeccable and true. Calvin was as tall as I was small; up to six foot four, I believe, but not slender, on the contrary, somewhat heavy set and he walked as if bending forward into a stiff wind. Calvin was from a world unknown to me; suburban Connecticut, parents divorced, real estate wealth and elaborate family battles. Calvin loved his Italian grandmother and vowed that he would stay with her forever and never leave her.

John Merrill had come to teach at Saint Theo's as a young man and was famous for his poems about lakes and rivers and gardens. I had gone to him early in my second year and told him that I actually thought in an odd way; in lines and waves of poetry. I told him that I tapped these out on my fingers and that all my ideas came to me in this way. Merrill, Mr. Merrill as we called him then, always sighed before he spoke, whether he was pleased or displeased, he stopped and sighed, as if he needed the time to think through what he would say. And so he sighed that day in his office, the air thick with pipe smoke, not only from him, rather all the men professors smoked pipes back then, the plumes of smoke trailing from their offices.

I see, he said, or something like it.

And perhaps John Merrill told me which workshop to sign up for; he was not sending me away, far from it, I had the sense of being believed. He seemed to know what I meant.

I went dancing and singing out of his office and across the huge grassy expanses of Saint Theo's. For you see, I resented everything about the place, and neither hating nor liking it, simply resented it as being a place I had not chosen. To that extent, I wasn't responsible for it. But I could daydream to my heart's content, and it was a pleasurable kind of resentment. I wrote and painted. Afternoons in the art studio, evenings in the theatre, late mornings in John Merrill's writing seminar, working out my attempts to impose the discipline of the sestina and other difficult forms on my tendency to simply talk too much.

How big he was, Merrill, in his red plaid shirt. Despite that touch of red and the old red van he drove, everything else around him was watercolor beige. He had the washed out Germanic coloring of the Midwest; he didn't speak at first, but raised an eyebrow and waited.

And he sighed.

As for the poetic sequences I told him about, I tried to explain that they had a self-generating organization to them. I thought in groups of words. This might be called, thinking in poetry.

Merrill wasn't one to say Wow, great, come on board. He regarded me soberly, and with a very slight but unmistakable degree of interest. As I ran from his office, I held my disorganized sheaf of work to my chest.

The students in his writing seminar talked of Merrill endlessly; his brood of children, his nature poetry, his likes and dislikes, which of the poets were his friends, his villanelle assignments, his propensity to listen to Mahler, reportedly in the middle of the night. We invented nicknames for him; we brought in copies of Merwin, Jarrell, Kinnell, asking him which he liked best and why.

He would sigh and look up at us, world-weary but never refusing to participate. His smile was a half smile, a quarter smile, usually a thrilling indication that Merrill was pleased.

It was in the seminar sophomore year that I met, among others, Calvin Pini, whose later failure to rescue me at a crucial moment would follow me around for many long years to come. I tried to make him repent for this, but he never did. I say that I met him, though in fact I had known who he was, from a required Bible history class.

Calvin proved to be an expert at disappearance and reappearance; for decades, each time he reemerged and looked back, there I was on his tail, faithful, ever vigilant, waiting for answers.

Calvin and I began sitting side by side in Merrill's poetry seminar. Calvin, you see, was a damned good poet.

To return to the beginning: I barely knew Calvin Pini, but he read nice poems about navy blue water and birds, lots of birds.

Looking back, there wasn't that about Calvin's poems that seemed to invite unlocking the ultimate door. That fact alone might have provided a premonition of things to come, had one only been able to see so far into the future, or even imagine its contours. My poems came much closer to that and in each case attempted it; I was unable to wish to conceal; a defect or weakness, though one of the higher order, something that also haunted me for decades after.

For whatever reason, I began to want a dog in some profound and overwhelming way. I really, truly longed to have a dog, maybe because my parents would so disapprove of it as a useless addition to things, and despite the fact of it being completely forbidden in the dormitory; I wanted a dog with a relentless determination that is hard now to explain, though I remember its demands on me.

And somehow or other, through someone's recommendation, I found myself gazing into a box of squirming puppies in an upstairs apartment in town, the hippie owners smiling down with peaceful approval. I chose a young brown nondescript male dog who was to be Roger, carrying him away inside my jacket, showering him with love.

It wasn't easy, hiding a puppy from the Resident Assistants in the dorm. I brought him in and out inside my clothes, on cold nights even sending him out the window on a kind of rope and pully system to go potty and then slowly raising him again. He was greatly loved, was Roger. He looked like all kinds of dogs in the world, a true mongrel, part Shepherd, but smaller, part this, part that, and without interest in anything except being a dog and running in the leaves, and then in the snow. In that impossible situation, I slept with him by my side every night, left him in my room every day to go to classes, then came back and managed to smuggle him out to run with me in the nearby woods and fields; nothing exotic or remote, just the fields around the campus, where at least spies for the Dean of Students would not see us.

He was good, was Roger. He didn't bark very much. He allowed himself to be hidden, as if realizing that his survival was at stake.

We walked out into the snow in the dark mornings; he slept in a box under my desk as I wrote. *Roger, Roger,*

Roger, I would sing to him; he was high-spirited, happy. My parents got wind of the fact that I had him and tried to quiz me on it. They didn't like me breaking the rules, but it was more than that. With Gramma, of course, she more or less opposed anything that involved change, truly anything—driving a car, taking a dance class, making a phone call. Her face would take on a particular look and she would quietly begin to oppose the plan.

Why on earth would you want a dog? she said. And then if the matter was important enough, there would be headaches and tears.

But Roger stayed, chewing my shoes and notebooks. I came back to my room some days and found shredded paper, cloth, towels, all over the floor. And despite the fact that I hated a mess, I forgave him. I don't remember even being vexed at him. I could not be angry at Roger.

I conned someone into minding him over the Christmas holidays; someone who couldn't leave the science lab, a boy with a crush on me, anxious to please. I would visit Roger when I could, joyous reunions in the snow fields, indulging his wish to run, rubbing his jaw along the ice as if laughing, something like a dolphin.

The only terrible thing that Roger did was to chew the edge of the piano Daddy had had delivered for me from home; the one that had belonged to my sister Marie who had died at thirteen. I managed to have the marks repaired by the same boy, the one with the crush on me, but I always looked at the spot nervously, out of the corner of my eye, trying to judge whether someone with no prior knowledge of the incident would notice it or not.

Winters were huge then, not like the tepid seasons we have now. Low hanging snow clouds, skating contests, Canadian television, the whole business. Daddy would lie on the floor of our living room watching hockey games, northern lights outside just beyond the horizon. Saint Theo's was a mere half hour or so from our house, so I could go home nearly every weekend.

There was an order in which I listened to music every morning before leaving the house or dorm, as if fortifying myself against reality—Concerto de Aranjuez, Swan Lake, Zeferelli's Romeo and Juliet.

Roger and I wandered out into those big winters, below the northern lights, rolling in the snow that never melted. Roger lived all that first winter of his, and he lived so well. Vermonters had a sense of different kinds of snow and slight changes of season, or they used to; the names of the months and the quality of the snow fit together like transparent puzzle pieces, and gave us something to do on the long, boring trek back to spring. That is probably not so any more; there isn't that kind of daily snow; winter has retreated.

To be fair, I never wrote poems about Roger while he lived, in praise of Roger, as it were. But I photographed Roger smiling, and Roger with his friends, as if he were a real child; Roger frolicking. And it was that wish to see him thoroughly enjoy himself that made me let him off the leash to run on the snow and ice of the end of winter; a March cover that must have a particular name. The idea was to catch him again at the end of the field, and put him back on his leash. Roger outsmarted me, though, and ran straight into the road. He never saw the van, and the van never slowed down. Roger lay dying in the March snow. Roger's spirit floated out and away into the grey white air, and I began to mourn in a way that lasted for days and weeks.

Classmates who saw me in the days after that thought that Daddy had passed on. Instead, they learned that it was Roger who had met an untimely end. There were a few more snowstorms right after that, I remember. I made my way through the drifts, hiding my face in a scarf, beside myself. And one day, I met Calvin Pini, jacket open carelessly to the elements, stalking through the snow near my dorm.

Jeez, Catherine, what happened? he asked me.

It's Roger, I said, *Roger is dead.*

Calvin stopped. He considered. He struck the air with his fist.

Damn, he said, *damn.*

That night, they called me to the telephone. Calvin was on the other end, and told me to listen, just listen. He began to read a poem about Roger in dog heaven, walking briskly along a river bank, meeting his pals. *Do you hear me, Catherine? Are you listening?*

Poor John Merrill; he had to hear all the poems about dogs and death in the snow. He sat back, puffed on his pipe, sighed. Another professor in the department complained that depth of feeling about dogs was becoming an acid test of human likeability. Yet, they were good poems. In particular, *For Roger* was about living through one long winter, only to die at the first moment of spring. Calvin and I lay side by side on my bed, stomach down, looking at the photo of Roger laughing, a huge smile, his feet dancing.

Good old Roger, said Calvin.

Yet, for all that, Calvin didn't save me when he could have. It's clear, I think, why I might have expected him to.

We began to go everywhere together, in Calvin's

ancient Peugeot. We listened to Astral Weeks, and spring came on in earnest, with such warm days. Roger wasn't able to know anything of this, of course; there was an odd, brooding quality to the new heat, the song of the grass uncovered. As for Vivaldi, it was his summer that was the saddest, not winter. This was the sort of thing I could tell Calvin. Just as there are things you can never forgive, the opposite is also true, that there are things of a gracious, indelible and beloved nature. Calvin telling me about dog heaven was just such a one as that.

And we even escaped, Calvin and I. It was rare for me to willingly bring anyone along on an escape. It might cut down on experiences, you know, or limit the process of storehousing impressions. But escape together we did, to Scotland. And, to a lesser extent, the West of Ireland, a place I knew a little about.

I had applied on my own to spend a semester in Glasgow; Glasgow of all places, in the 1970s. So Calvin applied for a place in Aberdeen. It was brave of him, I guess, and loyal. Once I had my place in Glasgow set up, a one room flat in an old house, cut up into pieces for rental, Calvin and I left to visit Ireland. I have the sense of having dragged him there. It had been a long time since I'd seen Clement and Nuala; I didn't plan to visit them, but wanted to bring Calvin to the West.

We sat side by side on a boat heading for Inis Mór. There were not so many tourists in those days; it was still a hidden place; it was as I remembered it. The boat rocked back and forth, back and forth, in a stomach churning way. A pair of twin brothers, with pointed noses and in contrasting stocking caps, went back and forth to the bar. The boat rocked up and down; the horizon was first above me, then below me. Someone, one of the brothers I think, vomited up whiskey. Calvin and I turned away; I put my head on his lap. The horizon spun up and then down, the sea eating the sky and back again.

On Inis Mór we walked to our B & B; there were German cyclists staying there. The landlady said her husband disliked speaking English; the girls working there joked in Irish using lots of dirty expressions they then translated for us. Calvin and I walked and walked in the huge puffs of air and grassy sunshine. We lay down at Dun Aengus with the rocks against our backs. *How deep is that ocean, how high is that sky,* Calvin sang, cabaret style, snapping his fingers and pretending to hold a microphone. During meals at the B & B, a lady teacher from England talked about the sensible waterproof jumpers of the children; Calvin and I put our heads down, trying not to laugh. I did sketches of Calvin, lying down, even sleeping. Calvin called my small feet in their blue shoes little hooves.

But after all, to describe small joys such as these is tiresome. As Tolstoy had it, recounting happiness is as difficult as it is predictable, and therefore perhaps does not require recounting. And even so, I wonder was it happiness. Even then, it is likely that I was planning my escape from Calvin, or if not from Calvin as such, my escape from this closeness, the leisurely mornings, the shared prospect of ancient navy blue and white waves, and angular rocks, and bright flowers in incongruous gardens.

We played gin rummy on trains going slowly across Britain. When Calvin had a winning hand, he would fan the cards out from his fingers and say, *Read 'em and weep.* He gave me books of poetry and wrote on the title pages things like, For you, who could raise small birds to a whisper.

He would arrive from Aberdeen on Friday evenings, getting off the bus that stopped right outside my window. The bus would pause, move on, and there was Calvin in his long leather coat, bought at a flea market in London. He would look up to the window, open his mouth and pretend to be a dog laughing. We would hide from my landlady, smoking in front of the electric fire. How damp it was, even colder and wetter than Galway. We would put on heavy sweaters and walk slowly around the university art gallery, talking about Augustus John. Calvin brought me small, beautiful presents.

We thought of spending the whole year, but decided to go back to Saint Theo's at Christmas.

Then there were wintertime parties at John Merrill's federalist house. His wife was an expert knitter and all the children wore elaborate knit sweaters. There was wool and yarn everywhere in their house. Merrill would stand in the passageway between the kitchen and living room, sighing, and rendering comments on poems that we brought him to look at.

You might just say it, well, from here on, he would say, his large hands running over the paper, bringing the lines to life. He was tolerant even of obvious mistakes and disharmonies. As midnight approached, he would put Mahler on the record player.

But yes, as with all such moments, they are tedious to recount, tedious to read about, only lovely in memory, that untranslatable place. Even Proust with his madeleine, well, I mean, an identification with that wonderful taste can take you just so far. And then, inevitably, you want to hear about unhappiness.

As far as that is concerned, well, I liked to kiss. Not more than kissing for the most part, just a lot of kisses. It has been said that my story lacks *eros*, and maybe it does; but I was a kiss expert. Which brings to mind Peggy Lipton, boasting that she was alone among women, as far as she knew, in having slept with both Paul McCartney and Elvis; an odd thing to want on your resumé, I would have thought. Rather, in my own more specialized sphere, I was intent on kissing men from many walks of life. And thus, the story of Calvin and Catherine becomes inevitably less of an idyll, and before too long.

How we came to have Louis (pronounced as Louie), the Brittany Spaniel, I cannot now recall. He was a wonder dog, he could sail over tall fences, swim for ages, look you in the eyes and tell your mood. This time, it was Calvin's attic room that hid the dog, but Louis demanded a good deal of racing around outside, the new focus of our drives to the country. Calvin would maneuver close to the small trees and bushes at the side of the road, and Louis would put his face out the window, letting the branches brush against his face.

We considered having him neutered, both to calm him down and because Louis had no need for a son and heir, but Calvin returned to campus after a short time, saying that he hadn't the heart to turn Louis into what he called "a creep." When Calvin went home to Connecticut in the summer to be with his Italian grandmother, he sent me photos of Louis smiling and enclosed new poems, mostly about birds. For some, it was angels; for Calvin, it was birds.

Merrill invited poets to come to Saint Theo's; he would herd us out onto the grass and let us read our work for them. The wind in the trees, the end of such long winters, my blouse with the high waist and my long wild hair, I do remember it, but to reach the scene in my heart takes more work than before. On the grass, holding my papers, doodling in the margins, and Merrill whispering to me, *What's the drawing of?*

This is Catherine, my super poet, he would announce. In retrospect, how I took it for granted, not in the way that sounds, but how I assumed some version of this would last a length of time that might as well be forever. *Now don't go all diffident on me, Catherine,* he would say.

Like other things, this time came to its end, though in a way that cannot be described with irony or in soft focus. This one came to an end like death, like the real end of all things. Probably because of kissing, my audacious wish to kiss.

Who can I blame for what happened next? It was Calvin, for not rescuing me. It was the notion, acquired over time, that there was no real danger in anyone and that nothing truly terrible could ever happen. It isn't clear to me if I have ever escaped from what came next.

On what is happy; 2006

I thought and thought about what to teach in the comparative literature seminar at Stannard. I had to be careful that I wasn't teaching Comparative Me. On the other hand, did it matter? Would they know the difference, catch the veiled references? The first thing that came to mind was René Girard. I don't know why his ideas stood out so clearly, when other theories, trendier, had fallen by the wayside. I remembered his vision of the novel, moving from descriptions of genuine desire through mediated desire. Mediated desire was something I had often thought about. It was part of my early plan that I would wage war against mediated desire—a phrase which meant, wanting something because others wanted it—and return the world, or at least myself, to a state of purity of wanting, just because, inexplicably and unalterably. The greater the mediation of desire, the stupider the person, that had always been my rule of thumb.

I thought again of teaching Dazai, *The Setting Sun—Shayō* in Japanese—the roadmap for destruction of the self. You had to be Japanese to enjoy that process fully and not see it as tragic; rather, to see it as inevitable.

And so I considered, at night, after Emmet and Medina were asleep, their healthy breathing regular and relaxed. The winter wind in the trees was comforting, the regularity of the way Greensboro's roads came together and went apart again was comforting.

Hello, she said, half a word, half a moan, sounding small and faraway and lost. I had to phone Gramma, I couldn't let that go.

What's wrong? It was the way I almost always started conversations with her.

What do you think is wrong? This was also familiar territory. She was referring, of course, to me.

Did Una tell you I was asked to teach at Stannard State? You remember Stannard? We used to go there with Daddy, remember? I felt my exhilaration waning; there was nothing to this teaching of a course.

How can you be happy when that is all so much less than what you had before? You were never happy with anything. Never.

She went on as if she had been waiting by the phone for this.

You married Yukito, you weren't happy. You went to Ireland to teach, you weren't happy. You didn't like law, didn't like anything.

She paused. *Don't you think everyone can see it? They can; they all see it.*

Who sees it? Who are you talking about?

It was far better not to argue at these times; I knew it well. Una said, *Be perky, be chipper, talk to her about table cloths or something.* Gramma moaned slightly at my remark.

What's the matter?

I am in such pain. Her bones were disintegrating, that was true. She was getting smaller and smaller; from a tall slender woman, she had become smaller than me, bent over.

What are you going to do with those children? she began again.

They are fine; they love it here. They always wanted to live in Vermont.

What a shame you ever got them, if you were going to do this. Didn't you know?

There was another long pause. *You did up that apartment so beautifully; oh, it was going to be great. Now Una's had to take it all apart.*

Well, I'm sorry about that, I said lamely.

I had so prayed that you would be happy this time. You didn't want to be in Ireland, wanted to come back, and then you didn't want that, didn't want law. Time after time, I have so prayed that you would be happy.

I wasn't sure if she'd hung up, or dropped the phone, or simply couldn't continue. Yes, looked at that way, it was madness. Una had been closing up our apartment in Cambridge; she reported from time to time that she was throwing things out, bags of old cards and letters. She loved bringing things to Goodwill, and always told how many bags she had managed to fit in her trunk. If the Goodwill store wasn't open, she would just pile the bags on the sidewalk and drive away. *I let them deal with it,* she would say, *I just make the donations.*

This was how I kept on losing things; when I left my husband Yukito, he cleaned out my things as well, and told me he couldn't pack it all up and send it on to me, it had to go. Years later, I continued to look for books and photographs that were nowhere to be found. I assumed they'd disappeared in a purge of this kind, now here was another. Una was especially hard on all the pink handbags and hair ribbons I'd bought for Madina when she was small. I could never throw those things away; they hummed quietly whenever I looked at them; it had been so easy to make her happy when she was small.

You open the boxes, everything is pink, Una said. *And all those postcards, what do you want them for?*

Una never tired of pointing out that, by contrast, I didn't own much of anything. It was true, I always wore the same thing, I never shopped for myself. *Why do you like black so much?* Madina would ask. *It's just that it likes me,* I would answer.

It took a while to recover from these conversations with Gramma.

It took until the empty hours of late evening or very early morning, when I could recover that sense of repetition, of thwarted anticipation, like sitting in a sauna of my own ideas, fully clothed.

There were things about Gramma that were actually wonderful. She would sometimes echo her own father and say, *Not funny, McGee.* She expressed herself with a surprising brand of violence whenever she caught sight of conservative politicians on television. *Old flannel mouth*, she would mutter.

This was a crisis, after all, and no one is at their best at such times.

But for Gramma there were no rules in the universe at all; nothing to speculate on or plan for. Rather, things just happened, out of the blue, all surprises. For that reason, while not irrational, she never said anything that could be said to be rational. People were either dear and darling, or inexplicably cruel and indifferent. Everything she knew came from East Galway, without the cunning that not infrequently crops up even there. We could never plan a path for ourselves, but only hope to run into something good, where, as Una I think said, we could fool people into being nice to us.

A cat; late 1970s

That time, almost thirty years ago, my parents liked it that I was at Saint Theo's, that I was the best of the best students, never anything less than an A. Well, what was not to like? They even liked Calvin after a fashion, laughed at the way he called out *Louis, Louis,* so loud it could be heard all over our neighborhood, as Louis came sailing over the backyard fence. Calvin could genuinely enjoy one of Daddy's ultra-sweet whiskey sours; Calvin was, they thought, a good sport. Gramma's ideal for me was that I would find someone who "understood" me. I never liked the sound of that.

Just as Daddy spoiled her, Gramma also spoiled him, and told me that I had made him so proud, so proud.

In my last year at Saint Theo's, I set up a kind of perfection.

I was ready to go; the seasons cooperated. I directed Molière, in French. I painted portraits of Calvin. I sat in the semi darkness with my complete Shakespeare. I found everything. And then Calvin gave me a cat.

It was a frightening cat, and I didn't want it; it was wild, feral, truly it was. It was tiny and white but very vicious, and it seemed to hate me, despite the fact that I tried to be very good to it. It would burrow down into the bed covers and attack my legs and arms. I went about with red scratches; just having the cat there troubled me; I asked Calvin if I could give it back. At first, I thought it was a girl and called it Feline. Then it seemed more boy and I switched to Felix.

I had been allotted a small, very old room of my own in what they called the Language House, where as I remember you were not supposed to speak English during the day, or some such rule. My view was out on the old polo grounds, and there were willow trees framing the long expanses of grass. I put my drawings up on the wall; a clear symbol, as I rarely, before or since, put anything up on my walls. I generally never move in. I am always ready to go.

There were bunkbeds, so I could choose whether I would sleep up or down on a particular night.

I wasn't sure what I would do when I left Saint Theo's; perhaps an MFA, maybe more travel. I applied for fellowships, half-heartedly, casually, not paying much attention to nice typing or clear statements of purpose. I wasn't worried. I was bothered by not being able to like the cat.

When Madina gets mad, she says, *I wish that was not in the world!*

And I too wish that Sandy had not been in the world. I don't like the chapter on Sandy. I don't like the story of Sandy. I wish that Sandy had not been in the world.

I wish that Calvin had not chosen that particular cat.

I wish I had stayed in my room in the Language House and then gone and done my MFA and never got that fellowship. I wish all that. And, yes, if wishes were horses.

Pattaya; 1976

I wondered where Sandy was from. That was my first mistake. In most cases, it was no problem to at least figure out generally where someone was from, but in his case I couldn't tell.

And thanks to Gramma, perhaps, I had no box into which to put experiences. I hadn't learned one thing worth knowing about life apart from myself; the sensory process of waking up and being surprised by new things, happening one by one in succession. I had no perspective, could not see people as part of a pattern, perhaps I had missed that part of schooling that makes children put the blocks and umbrellas and shapes in patterns of two one two, or three one three one two and so forth.

And I had that unfortunate thing about kissing.

And Calvin did not rescue me.

And there was the cat, Felix.

I had no immunity, no basis to understand what Sandy was saying. I'd never known anyone who spoke like that. It all backfired so completely, and there I was, with my silly little plan, all on my own.

I think I wrote him a note that said something like, *Where are you from?*

There was some complex scheme of go-betweens, some Libyan student whose task it was to bring a penciled reply on a saucer, or some such device. We spoke for the first time on one of the great porches overlooking the polo park.

I'm leaving here soon, yeah, said Sandy. He had come to Saint Theo's on an English language course.

Then we could live a year in a week, I said, stupidly, absurdly, having no idea what I was doing. It was meant to slot into my little comings and goings, my kiss thing, my motifs. But it certainly did not.

That Sandy didn't kill me, actually and in a manner of speaking, is quite astonishing, thinking of it now. It was a textbook process, but I simply knew nothing about it.

Sandy's family had fled the Punjab for Southeast Asia in the late 1940s, and bought a string of fabric shops in Thailand. Sandy had been pals with GIs during the Vietnam War, and spoke English like an American. He wore a black jacket; he smoked. He only wore a turban when with his family at home.

Sandy figured out in just a week or so how to make everything I had ever done or wanted seem small and sordid. You see, with good reason I don't like this story of Sandy.

Sandy visited my perfect room.

I tried to get Calvin to take back the cat; it became a bitter issue between us.

Sandy finished each of his sentences with the word yeah; *I went to see the guy, yeah.* Or, *I wrote to that dumb girl, yeah.*

According to Sandy, there was someone waiting for him in California, a girl from Hong Kong who was all ready to set him up with a car and an apartment.

Well, I said, *we can spend a week together, and I will remember you.*

Sandy went for that for a day or two, then scowled at me about it. *Well, that's talking like a prostitute, yeah,* he said.

And with one fell swoop, I was in Sandy's world.

He wrote to the girl in California, and told her that he would not be coming. He had a new love, in this cold place. That was me.

His first order of business was to prevent me from talking to Calvin. *I hate the look on that guy's face, yeah,* he said.

I saw Calvin from a distance and ran after him. *I'm not supposed to be talking to you,* I said. *Please help me, please do something.*

But Calvin, like everyone else, was cross at me for this new motif. Except that it wasn't merely that.

And then, I got the fellowship. It came through. I could spend a year studying literature as I chose. As to where, well, yes, Ireland. *I'll go there for you; I'll do everything for you,* Sandy said. *I'd die for you, yeah,* he said, and flipped the end of my hair, laughing. *My family will go wild, but I'll do it for you.* Friends from all over the world came in and out of his dorm room; the young men from Libya who said they were heading home to serve the Colonel, Thai guys in orange-lined parkas with fur around the hoods. Sandy remained stubbornly underdressed in his black jacket. He used lots of lotion on his face and hands. He strolled around his room in a silky bathrobe. *You'd look great in this, yeah,* he told me, referring to the robe. He hated the cat and told me to get rid of it, give it back to that damned guy, he told me.

Sandy was not a new motif. I was afraid of him. I didn't fully understand that I was afraid of him, but I was suddenly constrained and timid, and careful of what I said. Things were moving very quickly. Sandy was making plans, and telling me about the heartbreak of the dumb girl from Hong Kong who kept calling him.

Sandy had huge stacks of photographs. Photos of the now former girlfriend at a festival, photos of the family fabric shop in Pattaya, photos of his sister Gurmeet used for distribution to her marriage candidates. He told me all about his family, his nieces and nephews, their nicknames, how his sisters kept the weight down by running up and down stairs, how they played tricks like putting too much salt in the food when his oldest sister was serving a meal to her in-laws.

I'll take you there and dress you right, he said. *We'll pick out beautiful fabric with little flowers.* He held up his fingers and rubbed them together, as if to better see the flowers. *You'll look fine; we'll get rid of this stuff you wear, yeah.*

There seemed to be no way to make Sandy leave. If I told him that it had been nice, but he needed to go, he would accuse me of being a flirt, a phony. So I said nothing and thought that even if he stayed for a few more months, I could escape and move on. It was a bad ending to Saint Theo's; everyone was disappointed, they thought I was off chasing a motif, this time betraying everyone, upsetting mild-mannered Daddy just as I was about to walk away with every graduation award one could.

I handed Calvin back the cat, scratching and biting. I shed some tears, and part of my life was at that moment over.

It is not a good story, this one.

I brought Sandy home to meet my family. For some inexplicable reason, my mother found him to be what she called effeminate. Perhaps it was the brown silk shirt with the Nehru collar. He was already planning how we would spend the year in Ireland, but I convinced him that I couldn't tell my parents yet. I pretended to them that I was returning to Ireland to become a scholar of the Irish language, and that Sandy would be gone. *Don't worry,* I said, *it will all be over soon.* This cut down on hysterics.

But alas, it was not so.

Sandy followed me to what he called a God forsaken, terrible place, with no fancy hotels or good places to eat, or beautiful fabric shops, or cinemas showing Indian movies with gorgeous girls floating on rafts in Kashmir.

Funny enough, many years later Ireland became much more of a place Sandy would have liked.

To avoid Ireland, we went often to England. We wandered around London and shopped in the spice markets. We met old friends of his, and he told me joyfully that their families had decided to accept me. *My friends are all writing to me, asking how tall you are*, he said, laughing. *You lucky dog, they write to me. Dumb guys.*

In the oddest of ways, I'd been forced to escape with Sandy. Sandy had hatched an elaborate ruse, according to which he would enlist the help of the airline crew and I would meet him inside the plane, never telling my parents that he was coming with me.

I said goodbye to them on a hot night in Boston.

I am sick, I kept saying to them.

You'll be fine, they said. *You'll be just fine, you're always like this when you're nervous.*

I entered the plane and saw Sandy's head tilted sideways into the aisle of the plane. I felt some huge curtain come down in back of me, and I was hidden from everyone's view.

All I can say of that year is that I learned to make a very fine curry.

It was in London that he, of course, began to hit me.

No one took pity on me, or even thought of doing so. Who would pity the adventurer, for such I was considered, albeit in a circumscribed sort of way. I was thought to have all the luck, to be able to pick and choose, to be daring. I'd fallen into my own trap, but that might be good for the soul, and no one, but no one, thought to rescue me.

Dublin awaited like a stage set; in the country I had left some years before, then returned to with Calvin. It was there; the grey stone walls of Dublin, still unruined and undemolished, and then the train rides into the grassy green evenings, and then the West, the same, still unspoiled. Clement and I exchanged letters often, but I didn't tell him that I was going to Ireland; I didn't want to have to bring Sandy to meet them. I preserved all of them there, silent and separate from me, and did not approach.

Sandy accused me of flirting with men on the bus; on every bus trip, every stroll down the street, I was making eyes at men. His family wrote him letters, What are you doing, our dear Sandy, in that God forsaken place, you know what those places are like after the British leave, there is nothing, get yourself out of there, the girl is trying to fool you, our dear one, you are breaking our hearts.

I'm doing it all for you, yeah, he said to me again and again.

We rented a garden flat, and I became a prisoner on that suburban street, far away from anyone, so silent during the day. I watched the feet pass by at street level, now and again, forward and back. The late afternoon sun came briefly onto the navy carpet, then the sun was gone again. I never went out into the yard. When I went to the shops, it was always with Sandy.

He read all my letters before I did, and said that he suspected I was hearing from Calvin. *I remember the way that damned guy looked at you,* he said.

I cut tomatoes and potatoes at the sink. I learned about garam masala, dhania, jeera, haldi and paneer. The windows steamed up as I cooked. Sandy left and came back, left and came back.

It is a wonder Sandy did not kill me, as he came close enough.

I was supposed to be going to lectures at Trinity, supposed to be opening up the green world of the West, doing research on story telling. I went to class a few times, in my long homemade skirts, but then Sandy would hit me and I couldn't show my face outside.

Sandy is not a good story, and I would like to cut it short, very short.

He told me every day that if I left him, he couldn't get out of there, that dump, with no good hotels and no restaurants except those serving pot pies, couldn't rely on his pals in England, they would laugh at him, being taken in by this witch of an American. I would have to wait until the year was over, would have to wait until the end of the fellowship, he was counting on me, I'd made promises.

I kept promising I would marry him to make him stop trying to kill me; we would publish the banns in the back part of the paper; the blurry ad would appear, the details, let all object who might, and then just beforehand, I would somehow find a reason why it couldn't be that day. Sandy would fume and rage, and then we would start over again.

One day he told me he had flushed all my poems down the toilet; he attacked my typewriter with an umbrella until the keys were all mangled, the inexpensive light blue typewriter on which I'd written about Hamlet and John Donne.

I've stopped you from saving all that disgusting stuff, he said. *I want to get out of here and read something heavy, some philosophy, the Gita.*

Funny enough, when at last it was about to be over, I found the poems rolled up in a ball in the closet. He hadn't put them down the toilet; I wasn't sure why. But that day I thought it was all gone, John Merrill and Calvin and the poetry seminars. I lay in the back room, the bed clothes of unfamiliar fabric. I kept planning for escape, but my suitcase was under guard.

I divide it up into scenes, only several. That way I make it shorter, because this is not a story that can go on, who could bear it? It is *hors de narrative.*

Of all stupid things, I feared being asked to pay back the fellowship if I left; and I feared Sandy's family blaming me for leaving him in the lurch if I disappeared.

In those days, in the town of Clifden, you had to pay an extra fifty pence to take a bath in a B & B; there was nothing to buy but hats smelling of sheep. How Sandy hated it; it reminded him of depressing post-colonial locales in northern India. He made fun of everything, he lamented the hotels of Thailand, and his friend the Colonel with his stable of girls in the brothel. I moved out and went to stay in a room in a new Dublin suburb; Sandy lied his way into getting my number from Trinity, and phoned me every five minutes, until the landlady requested me to leave. He was waiting for me at the end of the drive.

Once I thought he had broken my rib, so I went to the doctor and told him I'd fallen off a bicycle.

At Christmastime, I secretly made my way to the airport and somehow got on a flight to Boston, and then eventually to Vermont. I arrived unannounced at the door, one holiday night, in the cold dark, walked through the garage, quiet, smelling of oil. Everything was the same; Daddy watching Canadian hockey on television, Gramma wringing her hands.

She never mentioned Sandy to me. Not a word.

I spent a week at home as if nothing had happened; no one mentioned my return to Dublin. One night before I was to go back, I held onto her and said, *Please, please don't make me go back. I'm scared; please, don't make me. Do something.*

She frowned and said, *But what about the scholarship, all that money you would have to pay them back?*

And so, I returned to Dublin. Sandy forgave me for leaving, at least for a few days.

To be fair to myself about it, no one had ever told me that anyone like Sandy existed. I just didn't know. The news had never reached me. For Grandma, men were good to their wives, she often described husbands of their acquaintance as being *so good to that girl,* the girl being the wife. Daddy if asked would have had a more worldly view, I feel sure now, but then again, probably assumed that I would never meet anyone like Sandy, or pay him the time of day if I did. But as for being trapped in a room, cowering in the corner, being accused of everything under the sun, a liar, a flirt, an unresponsive log, making a bloody fool of him, of such situations I'd not been told a word.

And somehow the months of intolerable Irish dampness passed into spring. I was invited to attend the grand finale of the fellowship year, in Bruges I think, picturesque Bruges, to meet all the other fellowship awardees. Sandy took the invitation as a secret code, designed with my complicity, to lock him out of the festivities. I wrote with Sandy looking over my shoulder, Could my fiancé attend the reception and events in Bruges; they wrote back rather coolly that if necessary he could be accommodated as well.

We found ourselves over there; I remember watching from the train window, an old man on a bicycle moving slowly, peacefully down the Flemish dawn, along an unpaved avenue lined with perfect poplars.

And we searched for a dress for me to wear to this event, a dress that Sandy would approve of. How he hated my clothes—the old sweaters, the tired looking boots. He told me constantly that one day we would go to his family's shop in Thailand, when he could trust me to meet them properly, and we would pick out fabrics with beautiful little blue flowers and they would make me so many dresses. Then I would be right.

He told me about his friend the GI who had married a Thai girl and how every night she knelt at his feet and said, I thank God for my husband. Sandy would laugh over it and take out their photographs; he always had new piles of photographs.

We looked in shop after shop for a dress. Nothing was quite right.

At last we found a long red dress with a bamboo pattern on the thigh. A ridiculous dress; not Chinese, not Thai; dark red cotton with short tight sleeves. This was the dress I was to wear to the fellowship event, and Sandy would be with me.

We went to a Flemish street fair, with rides and a Ferris wheel. It was honky tonk and unpleasant; the day was warm and chilly at the same time; papers blew down the street. We meandered through the crowd. Sandy wanted to go on the Ferris wheel, so we climbed aboard and were strapped into one of the little seats that swung back and forth in the air. The wheel began to move and we rose high above the town, the red brick and the steep-angled slates and the green countryside beyond. Higher and higher, until it wasn't apparent from all the way up there which century it was; birds we might have been, atop a roof in old Flanders.

Sandy moved his hand across to where the bar that held us in snapped into place.

I could open this and push you out, he said. *It would be worth it. They'd get me, but it would be worth it. That's what you deserve, damn you.*

We never went to the fellowship event.

We somehow went, by train and boat, back to Dublin and the garden flat, opening the door and finding the rooms silent and still. It was suddenly spring.

There were little outings; for spring, in the name of spring. The sun shone even into the recesses of the little garden flat. We walked out together, and one Sunday afternoon we took the train. I don't remember where we were going or why, but off we went to the outer suburbs on the train, along the seacoast. I was wearing a white jacket; Sandy sat opposite me. The train window was open and we were passing by row upon row of apartment blocks. Suddenly, the train seemed to lurch and I was falling sideways. There was blood everywhere. I thought the train had fallen off the track, had hit something, and I stood in the aisle calling out, *Am I dying?*

No, people told me, *you've been hit in the head with a brick. Those teenagers are at it again, throwing things into the train windows.* And there on the floor was a concrete block, with stones stuck jaggedly in the cement.

They stopped the train and an ambulance came to get me; I remember the stretcher and the hospital and the African doctor telling me everything would be all right.

My white jacket was streaked with blood.

Stay quiet for at least a week, they told me.

Sandy was told in no uncertain terms that I had to lie still, and could not do for myself. Improbably, he agreed to make me a bed on the floor.

I lay there through the spring afternoons. There was no longer any pretence that I would attend my lectures or do any more with the year, so I simply lay there thinking. I felt the period of time until the fellowship ended like a great ticking clock in the corner of the room. I lay silently, with the wound on my forehead that slowly faded behind a white scar; I watched the sun come into its own again; I watched the afternoons lengthen.

I waited, watching the clock. One day, when Sandy left the house, and I had seen him disappear at the end of the road, I got up out of bed, packed what I could easily carry, and walked all the way to a much busier street where I could hail a cab.

I went to the airport, got on the next plane I could, however I managed it, and went back home.

Sandy tried to phone me there, and I told him that if he didn't leave me alone we would do something awful to him.

I even asked Daddy to get on the phone. Daddy said, *Don't you ever call this number again*, and, miraculously, Sandy didn't.

Book IV

Stannard and Boston; late 2006

It might not sound like much, the chance to teach a comp lit seminar at Stannard State. As I drove up the winding road onto campus, still in Granmma's old Buick, it was oddly familiar. I saw Calvin and me as we'd been thirty years earlier, the day we'd been selected to read our poems, mine about houses and love, his about the navy blue ocean. It was the same endless winter and the bleak landscape, exactly the same then as now, the coffee and donuts smell that pervaded the campus buildings. Didn't Merrill come with us that day? I couldn't exactly recall.

I sat in the cafeteria, not feeling any older. I thought of that line from way back at Saint Theo's, was it Elizabeth Bishop, or some philosophical sort of poet like that, *In a dream you are never eighty*. No, it was Anne Sexton, everyone was reading those bells in bedlam poets then. I didn't like that poem too well, but in its way, it was useful. I sat and took in the glittery look of the slope, the straight dark trees, almost a Kazakh sort of a scene, the constantly replenished snow and the few adaptable birds.

I thought of course about the seminar and all that about the self; a Japanese self, a Russian self, a girl's self, a self like a big ridiculous suitcase, a self that says yes, one that says no, or no thank you, Lily Briscoe, Mr. Ramsay, and Dazai on his bar stool. Then the self that says yes and yes again, but to all the wrong things.

Maybe that was the Irish self, or a version of it.

I went to pick up Emmet and as soon as he saw me he ran to me, in the wildest kind of joy; then immediately said, *Have prize to me?*

No, Emmet, I said, *I can't bring presents every day.*

So he threw himself to the floor of the day care, surrounded by bees and butterflies, his little beige curls bobbing up and down tragically, his face red and wet with tears.

The woman on duty smiled sympathetically, but wearily; after all, she'd been with him all afternoon, and said, *Come on, now, Emmet, off you go with Mumma.*

And so I hauled him out to the car, mine, my prize as it were, strapped him in the car seat against his will; all this over the present that wasn't; maybe a matchbox car, but better yet something that made noise, like a rescue vehicle that barked, Out of the way! Out of the way!

We picked up Madina at her afterschool. I could see from the hallway that she was pouting, waiting for me so that she could unleash her dissatisfaction.

Where were you? She said without any greeting. *I was waiting forever.*

Emmet began to run in circles around the afterschool room, scattering papers as he went.

Dina, Dina, he chanted.

Wha-at, she said, standing, waiting for me to get her coat, her hat, gloves, everything.

They pulled and tugged on either side of me in the cold night, Emmet half crying and Madina moping.

Emmet had to be allowed to turn the key in the door,

had to turn on the lights, off, on, off, on, as well as the radio.

Play restaurant, he said.

It was hard to get him to wash his hands; I had to warn him of germs and sickness. Sometimes I'd turn around quickly to find Madina giving him a little shove.

But as the evening went on, they told their little stories; they ate their chickey and rice. I reminded Emmet how he used to call my dinners caa-ca, and they both laughed.

At bedtime, Emmet tried to get one more book than the number I had said. If I told him three, he demanded four, *Peees, peees,* he insisted.

He tried to shove as many cars, trucks, and stuffed animals under the bedclothes as would possibly fit. After a while, when he couldn't fight it any longer, his little Tatar eyes would close, he would stop talking mid-sentence, and a great peace and quiet would settle over the room.

*Cuddle with **me** now*, Madina would say petulantly, clinging to my bathrobe, sometimes holding my head down. *Stay with **me**.*

There was nothing I could do about the approach of Christmas; I remembered that movie from my childhood, and the sonorous warning: *Christmas is not coming this year.* How it made us cringe and hold our hands to our faces in fear and dread. Who could be so cruel as to steal our Christmas?

But so it continued to come; as in the time of the Grinch, it came just the same. We got Vermont presents for everyone, and packed up the car. I could not avoid it. For the first time since my escape, I contemplated return, a very brief return, though one that endangered my survival as surely as a wild and low-tech return from space into earth's atmosphere, brushing past the sun on my left, the cold emptiness of space on my right.

There was an invisible net that fell from the sky around mid-New Hampshire; cross through it and you were in the Boston zone.

I couldn't do much about Christmas. Probably only once or twice in my life had I missed going home for it. Gramma had been the Queen of Christmas when we were little, in the big beautiful house, before everything went wrong. Holly and strings of lights and snow made of cotton balls, even on the top of the manger. The French doors mysteriously closed to keep us out; the smell of the tree, the silence of six a.m. mass. It was then that heaven and earth intersected, and it had all been her doing. Even this Una says she doesn't remember. But how could she not?

And I guess this made us Gramma's little Christmas angels.

I suffered from this sense of disappointed perfection, of almost perfection, in odd and unaccountable ways. So many aspects of life were affronts to this sense of perfection; unfair, inexplicably snatched away at the point of completion.

It all seemed somehow related.

We arrived at Una's door, and for a few moments, it appeared no one was home. It was always colder in South Boston; a good ten degrees colder than Cambridge, which I had been used to. From the minute she bought the towering old house in Southie, Una hated it and vowed to put it on the market. Ten years later, there they were, with the house in varying stages of restoration, its five stories tall and skinny as what you'd find canal side in Amsterdam; the staircases going straight up, as if into the sky itself.

We stood and we stood and I began to think there really was no one home. They'd forgotten; they'd gone out. Hugh had a sports event of some kind, a hockey game perhaps. Emmet pounded on the door. And then Una appeared, smiled, opened the several doors leading to the inside of the great, mid-nineteenth century house, one that climbed precariously into the sky.

So much had happened in that house—it was the place I'd first brought Madina back to, it was where so many repetitious Thanksgivings and Christmases had taken place.

Oh, Lord, Una said, looking down at Emmet. *I hope he's not out of control.*

Where's Sven? I asked. Sven was good for a party any time; cracking open a bottle or two of wine. I didn't know if he and Una really liked each other; it was impossible to tell. Yet they stayed together, so perhaps they did after all.

I didn't want to be back. I felt myself weakening. I felt the pull, the undertow of the repetition. There was the untrimmed tree in the corner of the cavernous living room. I had the urge to turn and go, and yet there I was, taking off my coat and hanging it on the familiar hook. There was Emmet on all fours, heading up the steep staircase to look for toys. Madina stayed quietly by my side, wanting to eavesdrop.

Sven appeared from down in the kitchen (there were two floors below where we sat), carrying a tall green bottle of Alsace wine.

Hi, hon, he said genially, hugging me and Madina in turn. *How you doing?* Sven took things in stride, including my recent disappearance from the law school scene, an event in which he had even gone so far as to take on my case. *How's Greensboro?*

He had already absorbed the information; we lived in Greensboro now. Maybe later we wouldn't. Or would. Whatever. To that extent, Sven was not one of us, always second guessing each other and taking pot shots at any and all decisions made.

Well, I said, *it's complicated.*

How so? he asked, pouring me a glass. *Madina, Hughie's upstairs and really wants to see you,* he went on. Madina left reluctantly.

We've got to deal with Gramma, Una said, as if it could be dealt with that minute.

In what sense?

She's struggling, she said ominously. Una had special terms for certain observable psychological states; *struggling,* or *out of control,* or at the worst of times, *really bad. Something's going on* was another favorite. And *down in the dumps.*

Is she weaker?

Well, sure, she's not getting younger. And she's bored. This was the equivalent of Una's belief that kids needed mainly to run around outside. Grandma, she believed, needed to be taken out shopping, to CVS or better yet the Christmas Tree Shop.

But I knew that this was a reference to me; that I had caused this new phase, the downward spiral.

I cannot move back here.

And no one is saying you should.

Fill 'er up? Sven suggested cheerfully.

As we always did for "sleepovers," as the kids called them, Emmet and I cuddled together in the tiny half bedroom at the front of the house. The streetlights shone through the icy tree branches; we were directly above the street and all night I heard people talking as they passed by, some swearing in the Southie dialect, liberally peppered with exotic profanities. Emmet's eager, anxious face was transformed in sleep, into a calm, placid mask, happy in his dreams, contented and satisfied in a way the daytime could never provide. The radiator hissed; it was the warmest room in the house, Una always said, though that wouldn't have been hard. Madina had chosen to sleep in Hughie's bottom bunk, and, unusually, the territorial Hughie had allowed this.

Hughie always carried a book with him, even at mealtime, and when tired of the conversation, simply turned to his book, slumping sideways, slowly and deliberately turning the pages no matter what was going on around him. When asked a question, he seemed to be emerging from a deep sleep, or another world. He would look up and say, *Huh?*, answer perfunctorily and then return to his book.

I watched light appear over the steep roofs. Emmet stirred and held out his hands.

Go Gamma 'day? he whispered, and of course he had it right. He was always taking inventory. We would be visiting Gramma.

Her little white apartment in the assisted living facility was as neat and tidy as ever. She always placed things just so, even the soap. The towels were folded just so, the magazines stacked up just so. Her clothes always matched, right down to the hankie and pin. Emmet burst in with a great whoop and ran to give her a hug.

And there she was, smaller than before, but bright and lively in her wheelchair, perched in a corner of the room with a thick novel by her side. Gramma was a great reader, and a fast one. She could read a huge novel in a matter of hours. Since she'd gone into the assisted living, she had stopped listening to her Irish music; it was as if she thought she had to, as if she wasn't allowed music any more. She'd also stopped taking a brandy before bed. Yet she still read large and difficult and romantic novels. I wondered what she thought as she read them.

She lay against the back of her wheelchair and looked around, as if confused.

How did you get here? she asked.

We took a taxi from Harvard.

You didn't have to, she said, but it wasn't clear whether we didn't have to take a taxi, or didn't have to come at all.

It was easy, I said. *Only a few minutes.*

Of course it's not a few minutes.

Una's coming later.

Oh? And Sven? Gramma liked to have the men show up.

I don't know.

It doesn't matter. She leaned back again and closed her eyes.

What's wrong? I asked. It came out with an edge, though I'd not intended that.

You know what's wrong, she said, eyes still closed. *Oh, my eyes bother me so much.*

Is something the matter with your eyes?

It's the same thing I've always had; you know.

Why don't you see the eye doctor?

They don't have any doctors over there. You can't get an eye doctor, just that same one, and he's so clipped.

Madina asked if they could watch cartoons. *I hate cartoons, Madina,* I said, my voice rising, *what do you need cartoons for?*

But she took the remote and switched the television on anyway, just as if I hadn't said anything. *Oh, Madina.* She looked sideways at me, but didn't reply.

Oh, you've gotten so big, Gramma said to her. *I hope you're not fresh.* Madina, who hated criticism, flicked her hair and turned away.

Gramma closed her eyes again and ran her hands along the arms of the chair.

Please tell me what's wrong, I said. It sounded childish, petulant.

Stop torturing me, she said. *Of course you know what's wrong.*

What, what?

What you did; you know what you did.

What did I do? It was so pointless, yet I couldn't stop myself.

How will you be able to take care of these children now? she asked.

What do you mean? That's ridiculous.

Oh, it is not ridiculous. Then she waved her hand as if to shoo me away.

I told you about the course I'm going to teach.

I knew when you said you wanted to do law that you wouldn't be happy, but you went into it with your eyes open.

People can change, I said. It sounded so silly.

Jack and Meg were going to come on for Christmas, but I begged him not to.

Why did you do that?

Why would they want to come home to this?

To what? What have I done?

Oh, honey, please, she said, as if giving up, putting her hand to her stomach to ward off some unnamed pain. Jack of course was my elder brother, who had recently remarried and moved to a golfing community in the mountains of Virginia.

Jack's been married about a thousand times, and moved houses to match. People can change, I can change; why can he move whenever he wants?

It's completely different, Grandma whispered wearily.

How beautiful she had been; tall and charming. She had loved cars and dancing and had been engaged by her own admission at least three times. Daddy had doted on her, adored her, through every crisis had waited on her and enjoyed it. I never thought she would survive without him, but here she was, well dressed in her wheelchair, and over ninety.

On Christmas afternoon, Una, Sven and I brought over a cake and a bottle of wine. The kids played tag in the hallway and we toasted. Nothing was said about Vermont. Not a word. For that day, it disappeared. *Keep it light with her,* Una had always warned me. *Don't tell her what you are really thinking. You always feel you have to prove something, to have a showdown. Just tell her what she wants to hear.*

In fact, the week passed and Gramma said no more about where I was living or what would happen when I left. This had always happened, about everything I did. The resistance, then the long silence, the pause button pushed, for how long one never knew. I spent time in the bookshops, trawling for things to teach in the seminar.

Una was always very generous, and gave the kids

beautiful gifts. By contrast, I hadn't done nearly as much for Hughie, though in my defense, Hughie was very picky about presents. For Sven, I'd merely got a stainless steel flask for taking nips in the great outdoors. *Great for ice fishing,* he quipped. For Una, a purple wool scarf. They'd given Emmet a huge yellow crane and he spent hours cranking the hook up and down, up and down. Madina had a new handbag and lovely books.

As for the seminar, about which I kept trying to talk, Una said, *It might work out fine for you, but I'm not holding my breath.*

What Daddy had always said was true. When you crossed the Vermont border, things really did look different.

Stannard, 2007; Yukito, 1979 and beyond

I'm not sure why it was that getting ready to teach one lone seminar in comp lit should have brought me to see the sad and sorry ruin that was my life; apart from the kids, at least. I thought first about introducing a post-modern note and quickly realized that I was in fact not even modern; alas, I was pre-modern. I had lived for love, and love had not done an awful lot for me.

Living for love, I had put myself in the least likely places to find it. Were I a lady writer of two centuries ago, I would put it down to something like *She had self-regard and self-punishment in equal measure.* But most clearly, self-punishment had the upper hand.

Why had I gone where I did and why done what I did; there was no easy answer. I had been as little Emmet was in the orphanage—alone in his crib, waiting to be picked up and told he was wonderful. Why above all I'd turned to law; enough there to keep me busy a lifetime, an eternity of endeavor. Enough to completely ruin me; and chosen it seems by me.

The seminar could be on Courtly Love and Beyond; Love as Buried Treasure; Love as Culture; Love as Deep Dark Secret. Love as Tragedy, Love as Silence; Love as Enemy, but that was getting too post-modern. It was all self-serving, and of course that was why I was so suddenly happy. I hadn't merely escaped, but had been asked, yes, been asked to consider my self. I scribbled into little notebooks, the ones I'd bought everywhere I went, but left empty. I wrote notes to myself in the kitchen. In my slipper socks and LL Bean pajamas, there I was, taking notes on mediated desire, on Dazai and the almost there, on, well, me. I didn't want to be Lily Briscoe, too quaint, or Grandma Moses, paintbrush and bun; but I did allow myself to write little notes that came out so well. I was surprised to see I could still pull something up; a thought, a still life with plums. Mauve plums on a violet cloth.

So then there I was; washed up on the beach at Stannard State. I was standing in front of the students. I had never liked teaching, truth be told. I hated being looked at. Maybe the sort of class where you all sit around the table might do. I liked being a student; not a teacher. As a student, I could be clever, wise, ironic, off the cuff; rebalancing the talk, introducing a bit of madness. But as the teacher, I knew that I was at the other end of a lightning rod of various unknown complexes and neuroses; it was too frightening. They hated you or admired you, despised you for your clothes and your car, made assumptions about your life. God, it was horrifying. More so in the law school, so many people watching, and I was rowing away from everything they wanted to be. They hated me for it, couldn't wait to get their hands on a slam book and denounce me.

I couldn't help remembering the student evaluation from Brooklyn, the angry young man who had written, It makes me sick to see the way she runs out of the building to pick up her child. What clearer threat could there be, a death wish against me.

Yet at Stannard, I could just about enjoy the small classroom. I didn't even have an office, so no need to feel guilty about my chronic failure to hang pictures on the wall. I had to meet students outside of class in a cubby in the library, being shushed by people reading. It was wonderfully contingent and strange. Underfunded and unadorned, Stannard in the woods, timeless.

I found myself laughing quietly in the little cubby.

I thought of the twinkling little poem I had chased all along, like a stream or river that followed the road.

I thought about the days when I had had to write about law. I couldn't quite swing it with the tone, and ended up sounding like this.

> *Dear Editor: I enclose for your perusal an article recently finished on the subject of various heinous outrages upon the souls of humankind. This article will expose law generally as a fraudulent activity, a makework scheme, professionalized obstruction, all designed to forestall awareness of murder, mayhem and disappointment. Yours in outrage, etc., etc . . . .*

Or,

> *Dear Indifferent Sir: Long Have I struggled in vain against the cross currents of our time; I have written up, in haste and with footnotes incomplete, a chronicle of misspent determination, for, as you will see, I*

did attempt to turn back several tides of staggering proportions.

That sort of thing.

And now, here I was, the big event of the day was to buy a new Vermont key ring. Instant coffee, a pack of blue envelopes. A 40-watt light bulb to cast a softer light. The kids and I went upstairs in Willey's when it was open, to see how they had cleverly rearranged the hats, gloves and rain boots. I would not ever succeed in forcing a redefinition of the international war crime. I had checked out. I must go pick up a good-bye card.

But oh yes, there was the seminar; it was all new to me again, entry level, ingénue.

The Self: Love, Art and All of the Above

It sounded like *The Sword in the Stone*, but this was Stannard after all. *Eva Trout*, my favorite book, one I had never understood but felt some rare affinity for. *The Sun Also Rises. The Setting Sun*. Remember, I was pre-modern. But I was pre-modern living in the post-modern; that was the difference. I'd no intention of doing *Moll Flanders*; wrong self. I needed something Russian and felt myself at a loss. I kept coming back to *Uncle Vanya* and *Quiet Flows the Don*. What if I could ask Miles Bradford, I thought incongruously, long dead as he was.

How could I be so exuberant about a cubby in the unrenovated end of the library at Stannard State? I felt, irrationally, that I had come home. I was home. Hey, I'm home! Though anyone who might have hoped to hear my footsteps coming up the drive was gone at this stage. There was no one to greet me; only strangers.

The class, as I had predicted, was small. Maybe eight or nine, not a disaster. After class, I strolled into Stannard for coffee. I knew every change in the light. I remembered everything. I had taken it with me; I had treasured it. A hapless, hangdog young Russian named Sasha took to stopping by my cubby at office hours, running his hands though his hair and telling me about his family troubles. He wanted to know more about the Japanese. When conversation lagged, we sat and looked out into the trees. I had never, ever liked winter so well.

At the law school, I would never discuss Japan or Japanese, not really. I would wave my hand in the air and say, *Oh, that's another world*, or *Another life, he de ha, funny me,* thus avoiding any talk of the place. *In the eighties I always thought, well, I used to say, I was Japanese, I mean, I felt I was, but then you get to a point, you know, um.*

What's that, Catherine?

Oh, nothing. Nothing.

It became as remote and artificial as a Japanese calendar hanging on my office wall. Full stop. No more to be said about Japan than that. I refused to speak nonsense, though. I never used clichés; that was absolute. I refused to chat about corporate governance, or problems of gender equality. Better to leave the mere impression, if such there was, of something tragic, subtle, light sensitive.

Well, Japan too, or especially, made me think that I could have everything I wanted. Even before that night I arrived in the early 1980s, the summer night when I stepped out into the warm, humid air and saw the sun setting like a huge red disk over the city, I knew Japan well. Knew it before seeing it. Arrived, and was completely at home.

Here I am, and stepped off into the maze of trains and tunnels and escalators, perfectly fine and content, the smell of tea in baskets in the heat, the summer markets, the beautiful mornings and precious evenings.

As it happened, I had spent the summer at my parents' house; the summer after I left Sandy. A fellowship came through from one of the big midwestern universities; I would go and start a PhD in English; start again, move again, pretend I had not spent any time in that garden flat with Sandy. It was never mentioned by my family. I arrived in Chicago by train; then onto a bus, across the alien farmland, the red barns, the open landscape without any definition of the kind I was used to.

And then, well, soon after, I started another escape.

I took a Japanese language class, in addition to my English literature classes. Just because I wanted to. I saw from day one it suited me so well. So neurotic, so exaggerated, so emotional. So vague, so full of hints. *I am so, so sorry, but I must bother you and then run away to just over there . . . . Please forgive me for writing to you like this, I know you are so busy, and perhaps you do not even recall our conversation, how sorry I am to make you recall it . . . . On these hot and uncomfortable days, are you taking care?*

Amid the Chaucer, the Henry James, shibboleths and narrative dissonance, I also learned the language of girls drawing baths for customers at postwar *ryōkan.*

Lay out the futon.

Right away, of course . . . .

And into this mix, poor Yukito walked. I don't envy him having met me.

I was introduced to him at a dinner party, a young professor of applied mathematics, shiny hair like a seal.

He revealed that he wore special contact lenses, but had terrible vision even with them, nearsighted, farsighted, almost blind. He'd grown up wealthy and privileged in Shibuya; now he ran marathons, and lived alone in his modern house in a midwestern subdivision. Mismatched as we were, Yukito and I found some peculiar form of common cause; I needed not to feel so much, while he needed to feel more.

Something, that is. He needed to feel something.

He was in his way a good-hearted sort. He was helpful. When I met him, he had a saying that went: no wife, no plants, no pets. He was reserved and secretive, critical, but with happy memories of touch football with his rich Tokyo friends.

You could say that we had not one slightest clue about the other, and it would be true. Yet, reader, I married him.

I was not good to Yukito. He managed to pay me back for my misdeeds, I suppose, but still, it left a bitter taste, and I couldn't help but feel extremes of guilt over it.

Though he wouldn't have agreed, I saw that Yukito was so like his mother; she a small, elegant *Edokko*, quiet and sarcastic. When he was young, she would phone ahead to every place she knew he was on his way to; he would arrive at the bookshop, and be hailed with, *Oh, is it you? Your mother has phoned, she needs you to phone her right away.* And, phoning back, Yukito would be given commissions of things to buy and look up. In her quiet way, she kept busy buying up property; small office buildings and restaurants, apartments. His father never revealed just where he came from; he made his fortune during the war, ferrying goods and raw materials across to the Japanese army in continental Asia. Then after the war, he filled his suitcases with household products and went to sell them in the Middle East. Yukito's mother made his dad respectable; his father made his mother rich.

They liked me. This was their mistake and misjudgment.

His father thought I was sweet, and cute, and charming, but I was not. I was devious and confused, and nothing at all like what they were looking for on behalf of their only son. Yukito had a sister Miyako who believed she could become an opera singer through force of will; she locked herself up in her apartment in San Francisco and sang along to records.

Yukito was oddly pleased that his family liked me. But in fact it was mainly because their view of Americans was that they were mostly big and wore sweatshirts; because I wasn't and didn't, they saw me as trim and stylish and appealing. I was also studying Japanese. My accent, despite the short time I'd been studying, was bordering on native. I oddly meshed with the language and this led Yukito's father to send me cartloads of books geared to helping small children learn *kanji.* I practiced and practiced; stroke order right, *kanji* tilted slightly backwards, as if running away on the page.

I used to be certain it mattered, mattered enormously about Kido, the singer, but now I don't know. That first night Yukito and I went out, out into the Midwestern college town where neither of us belonged, he said, *I have some Japanese music I think you might like to hear; you might find it interesting.* And back we went to his modern townhouse in his tidy subdivision, to hear this music.

And you could say I found it most interesting.

We listened to Kido, Kido Ansé, though most Japanese seemed to call him by just his first name, Ansé. Kido was a genius; that I knew instantly, knew through my meager Japanese, knew through his combination of traditional longing and poetic surprises; there was a good deal I knew about Kido after just a few moments of listening.

It's hard to look back from here, from not wanting or expecting anything, to those days when I expected everything, believed there was a promise made in the stars to me. Poor Yukito, who assumed it was just nice music, of interest to this girl who liked Japanese and had a strange affinity for it.

That first album was named just Ansé, with an accent mark. Kido was standing in a field, I don't know what kind of field, wearing a jean jacket too small for him. His hair was wild, curly and wild, he had tiny eyes that looked embarrassed. He sang about riding his bike on hot nights in a small Japanese town, and about the sound of the barrier that comes down when a train is about to pass. He sang about things that would never happen. And if it provides any hint of what is to come, Kido Ansé was the one thing from which I actually did not, as far as I know, wish to escape.

Never mind Kido.

I don't know if I ever managed to escape from him. But, never mind.

Una did not like my Japan motif. She resisted it as family members resist bad boyfriends, or the wrong house purchased. She wanted me to ditch that motif; it did not interest her. But at the time I was busy escaping my PhD in English; ditching the perfect fellowship, requesting to convert it to a Master's degree instead, complaining vociferously about the boring midwestern town, about the concrete buildings, the lakes with their joggers. Yet everything I did or wrote created such a stir, the PhD would have been easy. The professors adored every word I produced; small assignments were done brilliantly; I was needed in medieval studies; I was needed by the Edwardians; I was needed by journals that sought out work on narrative disjunctions and dislocations.

But there I was, fast away as greased lightning, at the picnics and potlucks with other students in the Japanese classes, plotting and planning and becoming Japanese.

Oh, dear; poor Yukito. I was not good to him. He was distant and secretive, but overall kind, complimentary. He did not require someone like me, but then again, perhaps I changed things for the better, humiliating though it must have been.

So we listened to Kido, and read Japanese books. We went to restaurants, and even on occasion rode out into the midwestern countryside. I complained about my program and about the boring town. The long winter slowly passed, and I made plans to go to Japan to teach in the spring, when the Master's exams would be over. Yukito disapproved because I'd accepted an offer to teach in a country town and would develop a provincial accent, something his family could not bear. Through some strange complications, the school in question turned out not to be as good as the director had advertised; Yukito got on the phone with him and berated him for deceiving an American girl. He was pleased that it had fallen through; I would not be going away, I would not be going to the south of Japan and developing what he and his mother insisted was a terrible accent. I would not be a mere English teacher. But from my point of view, I would not be meeting Kido any time soon.

So, Master's all done, and no plans, I hung about in Yukito's modern house, with its beige Japanese colors and lines. Yukito liked to cook and bake, so we ate and ate, cold noodles and puff pastries. And then we decided, rather foolishly and precipitously, and with no anticipation of pleasure, to get married. I would take classes to prepare me for a PhD in Japanese literature, and I would be married to Yukito.

We drove out to the farmland and Yukito parked the car. He looked at me, and in many ways he appeared to me as a stranger.

You will hate being married to me, he said. He was clever, and fairly honest.

Yes, probably, I replied.

Yet, impelled by some force we could not have named, we went ahead and got married. Once secretly, and once with the knowledge of our families.

Marriage

What do you need to marry him for? Una shouted at me. I had no answer for her. It was true, I didn't need to.

I do not to this day care for married people; I don't like the way they band together and find a common interest against others. I don't like talking to a married couple, and then imagining what they say to each other when they are alone. They may not like one another, but their common interest requires that they dislike others. At least, that is usually the case.

And even Yukito and I, for all our oddity as a unit, had a certain loyalty to one another, a certain desire to oppose the world, a certain commitment to seeing the other one recognized by outsiders.

Yukito's father, Papa as we called him, showered me with gifts.

Ano ko, suki da kara ne, he would say. *Because I like that girl.*

Yes, he liked me. He liked to talk to me about strange and funny things in the reading of Japanese characters, and long French novels, and wood block prints.

And amazingly enough, a mere three weeks into my marriage, I completely lost my marbles. I fell apart as if from one moment to the next; the earth opened up as if in an earthquake and I fell down through, unable to see myself as myself. I lost everything at once.

I was no longer moving forward. I would not have everything. I was terrified; I was obsessive; I was dying.

I had been next to Yukito, walking along the aisles in the grocery store. The Midwestern summer was hot; I was lost. There was no Catherine, no past, no promises. The jig was up, and I was dying.

Yukito went on a trip, to a conference, to some vague place in the South. I walked around the house in the early evening heat, wearing a bathrobe. I spoke with him on the phone, and then it was like falling off a cliff or being dropped through a trap door. I couldn't think of any rescuers.

I went on living, but it didn't quite feel like that. Our plan to move to Germany for a year went forward; Yukito would be a visiting professor. I packed, I spoke.

In Germany, we rented a funny little apartment on the side of a hill. The landlord and his wife were very nervous and clearly were not sure about their decision to let us have the place. The landlord liked to come into the flat and open all the windows, pointing at the corners of the room, fretting about the possibility of mold, I think. The trees on the hilly street were bright and wild and frothy. We took the bus back and forth to the forbidding town, all built after the war, as the old town center had been bombed into nothing.

The aesthetic of that hill was soothing, luminous. I began to write in Japanese, a method I called *shiteki chokuyaku*, or direct poetic translation. From my mind to a certain set of sad poems.

Poor Yukito; he helped set me up with Japanese classes at the university in Bochum, another sterile set of buildings in a nondescript town. But how pleased I was to take off by myself in the early morning dark, in my loden green coat, carrying books and papers. I hadn't recovered, not yet; I was suffering in a silent, secretive way. Since my German was skimpy at best, I could only take a course offered completely in Japanese, and this brings us, well, to Herr Murata, patches on his sleeves, thick glasses, at ease in German and Russian. Yukito called him a "typical teacher type", which sounded quite insulting in Japanese, *tenkeiteki na kyōshi*; one got the sense of a pipe and slippers, a genial bicycle ride each morning to the local station.

Yet, how happy I was to go through the Bochum library's maze, asking where I might find Herr Murata, ready for class, all prepared.

Whenever I am asked how long I was married for, I invariably say, *A couple of weeks.* For so it felt. Poor Yukito, how embarrassing it all must have been for him.

My little affair with Murata, walking through the snow, meeting in cafes, was like drinking a lovely draught of medicine. I began to feel that I would live after all; I was less frightened. I even felt less wacky. It had taken weeks and months, but I was decidedly less mad.

Murata showed me photos of his family, his heavy set Austrian wife left behind in Vienna, his two children with their regulation straw hats on in summer. And I didn't even care; that is, it didn't bother me. As Murata helped me on with my coat, I stood, eyes closed, ready to be kissed, and so he obliged.

Yukito, I said a week or so later. He sat with his face turned towards the ceiling, thinking through a math problem. *Herr Murata and I have become close friends. I want to move out on my own for a while.*

It was utter folly; the idea of being Murata's friend, the idea of leaving one German apartment for another. But leave I did, and rented a three room flat in a working class neighborhood. I remember washing the floor and listening to the BBC World Service, the reassuring voices that said all was right with the world.

Nonsensical though it was, the entire concoction did go down like a big bottle of tonic marked Murata, three times a week for a month or two. In that way, I knew I would ultimately recover.

Murata was my wooden footbridge over a distant and dreaded river rushing below; a gravel path into the trees.

I broke it off with Murata in some way or another. Then, inevitably, Murata was gone, back for his Austrian summer. Yukito moved in turn over to my flat in the working class part of town, and then together we, naturally enough, went back home to the Midwest.

In the meantime, Daddy and Gramma had retired to a little shingled house on Cape Cod, so we stopped there to visit. Yukito and I bobbed in the warm waves, while my parents sat in beach chairs right at the water's edge.

Suddenly and somehow, I could speak Japanese, really speak. Perhaps thanks to Murata.

In our beige house in the Midwest that year, both Yukito and I were making plans, thought quietly separate ones.

I began to phone Calvin Pini; sometimes he would take the call and sometimes not. When he did come on, he was mocking, cryptic. *So, how's your marriage working out?* he would say.

Calvin, do you really remember me? Can you rescue me this time?

You got yourself into it.

We did, though, talk about John Merrill and Roger and Louis (Louis had died since, Calvin told me); and the drives in Vermont in spring, when Louis would put his head out the window and leaves would brush his muzzle.

It all runs together: the odd loyalties, the residues of that particular madness, the dissimulation and the planning. I studied demurely, diligently, Heian, Tokugawa, Edo, Meiji. Blossoms scattered, not really my thing, the fragile flowers, office workers and *hanami*, but Prince Genji pursued his adventures, hardly more complicated than my own, if rather more linked to his volition.

I applied to PhD programs, and told Yukito I would be moving to northern California. Just for a while, I said, to see how it goes, using the merciful Japanese tendency to fog and vagueness. I didn't mention divorce, or even separation. The move was merely a fact, a regrettable necessity.

In Japanese, you are supposed to guess why the other person is doing what they are doing; an approach to things that was sometimes kind and sometimes cruel.

For his part, Yukito accepted an academic post at his old university in Tokyo. His parents kept asking him if things were over between us, but Yukito, of course, did not provide an answer, one assumes on the same theory of vagueness and guessing.

Ano ko, suki datta kedo ne, said Papa. Meaning something like, darn it, I really liked that girl.

Shibuya; 1980s

On the first day of my California program, once I'd settled into the bare, stone-walled dorm room, I ran across the campus, past the flowers still such a deep red, and always, as it turned out, in bloom, past the fountains with their perpetual rushing and rustling, into the courtyard, up the stairs and into the offices of the Japanese professors, bowing and shouting out, *I am Catherine! I am starting my PhD in Japanese! I will be looking forward to your help and guidance!*

They looked embarrassed, as well they might—it was not such a glorious prospect for them—but pleased, for exactly the same reason. This one would be a live wire; nice Japanese she spoke, too.

I bought a secondhand bicycle and rode everywhere. The weather was hypnotically bright, cool and deeply warm at once, with that constant rustling of the water in the fountains and the slow motion of a too- dazzling sun across the sky.

There were wine and cheese parties with both the Japanese and Chinese sides of the department, boisterous arguments over the status of Taiwan, and where Japan would have been had it not borrowed writing from

China. Evening stole down over the idyllic campus; lights went on in offices around the courtyard. Fall moved forward with no discernible changes in temperature or light.

Yukito and I kept in touch by letters. He was happy to be back in a place where he was not only real, but a familiar figure, flesh and blood. Yukito was as Tokyo as Tokyo could be, as his mother had been. For him, all of Japan was in fact Tokyo, or more accurately, Tokyo was all of Japan. He said that he remembered the Midwest with a shudder, and that he would never go back.

Then there was my first trip to Japan. The evening sun, the chock-a-block beauty of the city, the lack of a horizon, the motion and noise of each and every street corner. I was right at home, too; it was precisely and exactly as I knew it would be.

Thus began a summer of sleeping on Yukito's sofa, teaching private students English and having Yukito take photos of me, hundreds of them: climbing Mount Fuji, visiting the Izu Peninsula, wandering in a temple yard in a crowded neighborhood. This is the photo I still display on my own desk, the one in the urban temple grounds, turning to look at the camera, swinging around to see who is there.

We went out together and explored. We were peaceful, friendly, warm towards one another. I was not forgiven; nor unforgiven. We never mentioned it.

I began to run, all over Tokyo, as much as ten miles a day. I ran mainly in the early morning before people were up, before the intense heat. I ran along the small rivers, I watched the old folks open their doors and look at the sky. I ran and ran in my white shorts and top. I developed a way of running that Yukito called the flying fish, close to the ground and remarkably fast.

And in July I wrote a letter to Kido, the genius singer, the greatest romantic of all time, the poet. *If I meet you once, I know that we will stay together. I know that we will love each other.* I sent the letter to his record company; I heard nothing, and the summer drew, slowly and beautifully, towards an end.

In early August, Yukito and I went to his family's summer place at Karuizawa. It's awful to recount, but over that year, one by one, all of Yukito's family had died: Papa, then Mama, followed quickly by Miyako. In an oddly Irish way, Yukito believed that Mama had come to snatch Miyako and take her along soon after Mama herself had died. In any case, they all went, so quickly and inexplicably, of mysterious cancers of the blood and stomach. Yukito kept remarking that he was the last, the only one left.

We went to Karuizawa and ran together around the artificial lake. The heat was intense; the sound of the cicadas amazing. Everything was completely Japanese style, with no exceptions: the fragrant tatami, the view up the grassy hill, the tall weeds bending, whispering, as in an Ozu film. Papa's paintbrushes were there in a basket in the corner. His expensive book collection; Mama's special kitchen utensils. We sat on the mats and ate *edamame* beans. Yukito never drank beer or wine; he seemed to have an allergy. I had sometimes asked him to drink just a small glass to see what would happen, and in minutes his face would flush a brilliant red and he would lie down, defeated.

Una hated my Japan motif, as I have said; within my Japan motif, she especially hated the Kido motif, if motif it was. I have my doubts.

Kido. Kido, Kido. Despite what I might have anticipated, it has remained a great silence, a blank I have been left to fill in myself. Years later, at different times of the year and depending on the time of day, I might present it to myself in very different ways.

In Greensboro, that was one more task I felt myself finished with.

Yukito and I were back in Tokyo; there was a mere two weeks left, and I would be returning to California. We walked around the city, stopped at restaurants, went shopping together, since, for the first time in my life, everything I tried on fit me. We did not talk about marriage or divorce; we were like two close pals, loyal to one another, but without saying a word about it.

How handy it could be to be Japanese, in that sense.

But one night in August, the phone rang. Yukito was in the other room of his flat, getting ready, as we had plans to go out. I picked up the phone, though this was unusual. I rarely picked up his phone; it was just that he was busy and had looked out and made a sort of gesture, as if to say, Would you get that? And so I did.

Catherine, is this? asked in Japanese.

Yes.

I knew it was Kido; I knew his voice from interviews, I knew that voice well.

What a letter that was, he said, or something to that effect. *I really wanted to phone, once I saw it.*

Yukito was looking at me. *It's Kido Ansé*, I mouthed to him. He looked at me, aghast, no doubt, at my duplicity.

I'm going out, Yukito muttered, stomping past, slamming the door.

I arranged to meet Kido in Shibuya that evening. I put on my favorite black dress with the small white dots, and high-heeled brown shoes. I remember walking up the long slope, away from Shibuya station. I had never been prettier, lovelier, never felt more comfortable with the warm air, my hair riding the waves of a summer wind, my brown shoes taking step after happy step.

Kido Ansé was waiting for me, sitting simply and quietly on a railing near the street. I didn't care for the way he looked or sounded; he'd grown heavier since the early photos, he was used to being spoiled, but not by happiness, and that made for something unpleasant, almost corrupt, in his manner of speaking.

Kido took me to a modest little apartment and we, well, we talked. He sang songs for me. He asked me why I wrote, where I got this idea of my love for him. Most wonderful of all, Kido certainly believed me, as clearly I was speaking his language in the letter. There was the absolute, the ultimate, the unchanging that both Kido and I had given so much thought to, and for so long. Either one did or didn't, when it came to such things, and Kido and I both did, however much we might try to hide it from others.

I am certain he didn't doubt me, after meeting me and spending that evening.

Indeed, Kido called the next two weeks Catherine's time to destroy Kido. He was afraid of being tricked, of having the Japanese paparazzi hop out of the bushes, of being lied to. But not I; if nothing else I was pure and honest. This was Kido's flaw: having been spoiled, though constrained, by the absurd and thuggish world of Japanese pop music, he worried most about the risk to himself, and did not consider the risk to me. As everyone had always thought, he also assumed me to be fine, just fine, needing nothing.

We spent afternoons and evenings together, in hotel

bars and walking in summer-dark parks. It was sad, that early time. It's a hard word to use properly; it was truly sad. We rather, well, loved each other, I do think so. But Kido liked being loved more than he intended to love; this was a problem, as it made me important to him, but not important in the right way.

How disgusted Yukito was with me; he barely spoke. He wasn't one to anger, but he threatened to send on all the things I might leave behind to Kido's; my red shoes, my books. Of course he was appalled; how terrible for him.

I knew that Kido was married, but it didn't register with me. He had been married once when he was young to a home-town girl, but then divorced when he got in some obscure trouble with the law. The entertainment world rehabilitated him when he might have lost everything, and he remarried, someone not right for him at all. I knew that and so it did not register. It did not matter.

I suppose it did matter, but it didn't matter to me.

I assumed he would leave her, and come to me. I believed that because of the language we spoke and the way we thought. I knew he had children, little children, though I didn't know that it was three, and that they were very, very young. Even so, he would leave them and we would be together; it was so inevitable, it was so clear. Kido needed to be purified and restored; I did not want to escape from Kido.

I wanted the whole thing; marriage with its messes and unhappiness. I wanted the complexity of being with him and being annoyed and dissatisfied. I wanted to marry Kido. It is the only time I have ever wanted to marry.

Kido wore his sunglasses all the time; so when he wanted to go incognito, he simply took them off, and no one noticed him. We wandered the warm evenings, sat side by side in small restaurants, me holding my chopsticks in the air, hardly able to eat. We made love on the floor of his apartment, though what I remember best is stroking the back of his head, the familiar, wiry hair. I didn't know what name to use, so decided on whispering Kido-san.

And so those two weeks passed, and I was about to go back to California.

On the last night we wandered all around Tokyo in the warm darkness, ending up on a high hill overlooking the city lights. When we said goodbye, I watched Kido run away up a sloping street, under trees that bent over as if to touch his hair. Goodbye, no resolution, no plan, nothing, just the darkness holding Kido's shadow where he had been, and a sad, tired return to Yukito's to face the next day.

I returned to my program, of course. This short phase had outlived its usefulness, and something else had to happen.

It was then that Kido changed, made a comeback as the magazines might say. He began to write wonderful love songs; the words seemed to be taken from everything we had talked about.

Could that be explained to anyone? Well, imagine it. How did it sound, saying that this singer's words came from our conversations; that I believed he loved me, but had no real proof, and that I was waiting for him.

Una was appalled; I was cut off from mentioning this at all. Should I happen to raise the topic, she would wave her hand in the air and say, *You've got to get off this. Okay, he has a nice voice.* Then one day she told me her therapist said I was a psychopath, believing that a rock star was singing to me, delusional, mad as a March hare.

Well, I was many things, but not delusional.

It was bizarre, though, to be living in this parallel universe; I didn't like the implication of star gazing, which I'd never done. I had no interest in Kido for his fame; if anything, that was the silly part.

And while I say that this was the one time I did not want to escape, there was no way of testing this. Perhaps I would have, eventually.

Secrets; 1980s

I soon made plans to spend a whole year in Japan; Una opposed it, as did Gramma, but I relentlessly put this in motion. Yukito helped me rent a small apartment near an exhausted looking river in a near suburb of Tokyo. I had classes to go to; even a seminar at Tokyo University on the subject of *the house in Japanese literature*, of all things.

I wrote to Kido and told him where I was. He phoned in early fall, and we met at a station not far from where I was living. We walked together in the park that evening. We continued our agonized conversation about inevitability, he saying that Japan was not like that, that my idea was too American, and I insisting that this was what must be. There was no resolution; we met and parted, met and parted.

He would phone me at odd times and odd hours; the phone would ring once or twice, then ring again and it would be Kido.

Sugoi na, kimi, he would say. You are something. I spoke with extravagance: always, never, we must, we shall.

I also met Yukito every week or so, generally in some wonderful new restaurant he had found. He did not want to hear about Kido and me, or my plans. He placed his own particular limits on our conversations.

It was a bitter winter that year, unusual for Tokyo, which was generally so mild. I made my tofu and bean sprout dishes, the days and nights passed. I wandered about the city, and began to write prose in Japanese.

The first of the two novellas was about an American falling in love with a has- been Japanese actor; the second was about an American falling in love with a Japanese cello player who had true genius, but no belief in himself and no courage. I wrote away sitting in *kissaten,* and at the tiny desk in my tiny apartment near the river.

I dressed in the same way every day that year; black stretch pants and a white painter's shirt. When it was cold, a black cardigan and coat. But never any deviation—the ankle pants, the white shirt. It became a kind of uniform and lasted for years afterward.

Kido asked me to tell him about my life, about America, about Vermont; he asked me what I thought of certain things, what about John Lennon, what about Japanese artists. We should have met before, long before, I should have known him when he was very young and I even younger; we should not have gone through those months and those ambiguous conversations. The absolute and the uncertain sat uneasily side by side; the spring came, *hanami*, then the rainy season, and Kido seemed to disappear again.

He knew that I was leaving on a certain date in August. August is so intense in Tokyo; the smell of baskets filled with hot tea leaves, the stalls and shoe sales, the crowded streets, the mercifully air-conditioned train cars, with shades pulled low, families with straw hats, heading out, out to festivals and the seashore. I saw from the ads that Kido, shy Kido, was to give a televised end of summer concert several days before my departure.

Well.

Kido, who had over the years become so bitter, so hidden, stood in front of thousands of people and sang of love in a way that astounded even me.

The city was hot, dark and muggy around the stadium; I sat in my apartment and watched on my tiny screen. Kido looked into the sky and sang of love in such a way.

It must sound absurd. Of course it sounds absurd. Yet it happened.

It seemed clear to me that Kido had decided to come to me. He would leave Japan and its restraints and its frightening entertainment world and he would come to me. And we would be free, and we would not escape again, not ever.

We could go to Paris; make a small home in Tokyo.

Una kept hanging up the phone on me. She not only refused to listen to anything about Kido, but also anything about Japan, at all, anything.

I went back to California after that. I ran and ran, white sneakers and white shirt, morning and evening, I ran everywhere. I even ran inside my student apartment, up and down. I worked on my dissertation, on the subject of Dazai Osamu, the twisted, lyrical, confused and thwarted Japanese writer who committed suicide after the war. I wrote about how he mocked himself, how there was a non-Japanese artist, proud of himself and lionized by a different tradition, inside the constrained and failed Japanese artist who could not be a team player and could only describe himself as "weak." He could conceive of being loved, but knew himself to be a phantom. And at the place where I parted company, and knew myself not to be Japanese, Dazai actually enjoyed the sickness and sadness of this.

I suspected that Kido did as well. I mean that Kido probably enjoyed such a sickness and sadness.

The drama of Japan was in secrets, wondering what the other person was thinking, across the city or across the world. Secrets could go on for years, for decades. Though I had once believed myself to be Japanese, whether in a former life or not, everything about it familiar, everything my own, in the end I was not Japanese.

In the end, I wanted Kido to appear at the door. But he did not.

Soon after I got back to California, Kido released a strange little group of songs in English, strongly implying that he was in love and would be leaving Japan. His English was strongly accented, touching, artificial. Still, I appreciated the effort. I listened over and again, riding my bike in the dark around the campus.

I remember the sound of the fountains in the dark, and the sense of intolerable repetition.

After even a short while of this, I knew that wallowing in secrets was not for me. Listening to songs with hints and messages was not for me. There was too much of Dazai and the weak, lazy artist who sits on bar stools and laments the failures of love and the demands of Japan.

Then it all went dark.

Kido came out with a new album, called, quaintly, *No No No*—looming across the cover in English. The theme seemed to be, They won't let me go, they won't let me love. I had written to him asking, *Why why why won't you tell me?—Doo shite Doo shite*—one song was called, of course, Why why why. It actually was. And so it went.

You see how it was. On the cover, Kido was dressed in traditional Japanese garb, the ironic message being, I am Japanese and they will not let me go.

Well, after that, I didn't want to study Dazai and the self and the failed Japanese artist. I was not going to defeat those forces, and, frankly, decided to be done with it all.

I had left my novellas with Yukito, who found a publisher for them. I went over on a little book tour. On the inside of the book jacket, I had written up a kind of farewell to Japan.

And there I was, at last with my PhD, one that I didn't want any more, and an expertise in a Japanese literature I did not want to think about any more. I took a job teaching at a major university; it was a plumb academic job, or so they said, but to me it was torture. At a dinner party, someone asked me to tell them about garden imagery in Japanese literature and it was then it struck me: I had to get out of this. I had to leave.

There were two ways I could have gone; how I wish I had gone back north, gone to some college, taught writing, gone to sit like a cat in the window and refashioned and reconfigured what had gone wrong.

But no. I did not do that.

Laugh though one may, after all this, I placed myself in the most alien and forbidding place imaginable. I went, incredibly, to law school.

Una says that I blame her for this; perhaps I do.

Book V

Mr. Merrill; 2007

I asked Sasha about the Russian proverb, the one about being born in a bright field and dying in a dark forest. He frowned and said he had never heard of it; I was slightly disappointed, but it wasn't his fault. I had hoped it was better known than this. He tried to find something to say about it, though, and suggested that Russians are really into forests.

I'd been reading *Eva Trout*, again, when Sasha showed up at my office hour in the little library cubby. Why did I like the book so much? Probably its, for me, familiar take on self-imposed, expectant isolation. *Resignation is not experienced; it is undergone.*

Sasha looked over and asked what I was reading. As it was too hard to explain, and too unlikely to resonate with Sasha, I scarcely replied.

Just something I used to like, I said.

From Sasha's point of view, I was a much older woman, probably close to his mother's age. He liked to tell me his troubles; money, and being stopped for driving after just two glasses of wine. Like other Russians I'd met, he enjoyed hearing about me going to Kazakhstan to adopt the children. I always got on well with Russians; I loved the way they complained, as an amusement, the way the Irish do. I really did not know how to live, and certainly did not know how to bond, without complaining.

But I was happy; I enjoyed stirring the coffee in the cup, enjoyed watching the snow fall from the trees.

It had not turned out as I thought, but at least it could still be something of a story.

At night I sang the kids the Barney song, *I love you, you love me.*

And in March I even wrote to John Merrill. I found him on the Saint Theo's website, still there, still in his poetry seminars, older, thinner, but determined and completely recognizable, always sporting some different sort of hat.

> Dear JM:
> How I think of you! You will be surprised; I am back in Vermont, even teaching a seminar at Stannard State.
> How are you?
> What are you doing now?
> Catherine Darcy

I didn't hear back for a while, though I waited. I tried to think how old he would be now; what he might be like heading into old age. One afternoon, I saw his name come up on the e-mail and felt woozy with delight.

> Catherine—Misplaced your email address, then found it, and still not sure this is the right one; doesn't look familiar. So you are back; welcome back.
> I am in my mid seventies, and not writing much. Not sure what to do, as this is all I've ever done and no poems seem to be there now.

Do you stay in touch with anyone from our seminar?
Those were different times.
John

He was still there, in one sense still mine, still JM, still himself, cross and grumbling, but with the old, inexplicable gentleness. He was still there. I put my head down on the desk and cried.

I wrote and told Calvin the news that I'd heard from Merrill; that he was still there. *I'd like to find someplace like that, not Saint Theo's exactly, but something of Saint Theo's as it was for us then,* I wrote to him.

God, he wrote simply, *are you still longing for the time when you were batting your eyelashes at everyone?* And then, *Not I, thanks. I've moved on.*

It was hard for me to tell whether Calvin meant this. Had he really moved on that successfully? Una was convinced both that Calvin was dissatisfied with his life and work, and that he was pursuing younger women. As for being an antique book dealer, it sounded all right to me. As to the younger women, I had no way of knowing, but Una mentioned it every time Calvin's name came up.

I'm sure he's dating a younger woman now, she said, totally confident on this score. Maybe this was to help me see Calvin as disloyal, detached from our past, likely contemptuous of me as I was now.

I thought about what stories from the past John Merrill might like to hear. I wrote and reminded him of the young man who said in class that women like to do to men what they do to their hair. It hadn't made sense, but lasted unscathed in my memory through all these years nonetheless.

It was a thrill, an honor, to report to Merrill on where I was, to exchange words with him again. It was like I'd come through a war, bloodied and roughed up, but still recognizable to him.

As I said and had predicted, the Stannard seminar was very small, less than ten students. Sasha among them, of course; most of the others seemed to consider me as somewhat haywire. I had settled on Geography, Self and Narrative. Imagine how that would raise eyebrows as it went out on student transcripts.

And why on earth shouldn't I have my narratives; that is, without having to be an antiquarian? Why should they be forcefully removed, in the name of living in one's time? Narrative with its astonishing coincidences, its unified and unifying icons and appearances, narrative that rejects acts of madness, narrative that tells you what to do far better than family, for instance, could.

> Catherine, it's good to remember that group of poets in your class, especially at the age I am. I will be going in for back surgery when this semester ends.
> I don't want to force myself to write, don't want to be Robert Frost.

I wanted to cradle John Merrill's head in my arms, to shower him with thanks for remembering who I was and writing to me. Calvin I would continue to leave and return to, leave and return to, mostly as he would have it.

And then, the small seminar and the part-time position and the cubby at Stannard State, where I didn't even have an office, and mainly chatting with Sasha during office hours—it seemed I would be allowed to rejoice over it.

Calvin would ask if I was teaching pirate literature—the part about geography—but that also didn't matter.

I would not be angry at Calvin, and doubted he was pursuing younger women. After all, he had once read to me from Alberti's *Concerning the Angels*, despite his own preference for birds. I would forgive Calvin a lot for that alone.

Forgiveness

There were those, the vast majority, who chose to be taken by something. They met, and, even the very hard to please and full of themselves, married. They lived with an I love you sorta, don't love you sorta, set of circumstances; they went to bed and conceived, they moved on into phases and either split or didn't. They had a story, they had ups and downs, they expected this and knew it when they saw it. Their spouses were either surprisingly attractive or unattractive to others when brought along in tow to public events. Each decision they made carved out a certain period of their allotted time.

No such thing for me, of course. I resisted tooth and nail from my earliest childhood, no such small beer for me.

No such life for me.

There were those who might have been a good bet, if I could have brought myself to pause and consider.

We were in the Central Station in Budapest, Una and I. In our younger days, we made quite the duo, and more than one man agonized over which of us he liked best, or indeed whether he could only like us as a duo. We were walking down the stairs, in 1989, not so long before the fall of Communism, and arguing, we were of course arguing, about what I can't recall.

As we walked down the stairs, a young man was coming in the opposite direction, from the top. At least I think so, though at times I ask whether I can be sure that it wasn't the case that we were walking down and he walking up.

Whichever it was, he turned on a dime to walk in our direction, quickly and deftly catching me by the arm and telling me, *Oh, it is not worth it to argue!*

How funny he was, Vincenzo from Lake Como, in his trenchcoat and jaggedy hair. He was what you would think of as a family man, or would have been, a good one. He was acceptable to look at, sweet to hear speak, charming and dedicated.

We exchanged addresses, and I did write to him. He was, of all things, a water engineer. He invited me to come and meet his parents.

A water engineer! Una shouted. *What would you do with a water engineer? Forget about it!*

And so Vincenzo was relegated to my rather long list of persons encountered in railway stations, though he actually would have fit in another category for me: a husband. Not the glorious marriage to Kido that was the one I wanted, but a more modest marriage that sliced up time into pieces of bread, rubbed in oil, a dash of garlic.

Cambridge; 2007

We always came to the same hospital; one corner of it seemed to be Gramma's own wing, at this stage. We knew all the waiting areas, the food on the cafeteria menu.

Una had phoned, and informed me in rushed and staccato tones that Gramma had pneumonia and was completely dehydrated. She tried to talk to Gramma and found her "loopy"; she was still loopy now, not doing well.

They don't know if she'll pull through this time. You never know, but this time she doesn't look good.

Does she know what's going on? I asked.

She's in and out.

The kids were behind me in the corridor, armed with "activity bags" filled with unused crayons, drawing paper and legos. I stood at the doorway and felt relief that at least it was a private room. She looked so small, lying there, apparently asleep, in between one world and another. She was as small as a child, unequal to the task of recovering, dressed in the kind of hospital gown she hated.

She had been really tall; tall and thin, a great dancer. She followed the dances all through the war, laughing with the GIs, spinning and spinning. She met Cardinal Cushing for tea, and had her photo taken with him, wearing a black veil over her hair.

How teeny she was now, fallen sideways against the edge of the bed. Her mouth was quivering the way it did when she was unhappy. I sat on the side of the bed and took her hand, something I almost never dared do. I rubbed the skin on her hand and felt that this time, she needed just silent comfort. She had done a good job without Daddy.

She may well be crazy as a loon most times, I thought, but she had done her best.

It was Una who had always longed for a different sort of mother; a mother who joined country clubs and ran meetings of women devoted to high-minded charities. In fact, Una would have taken most anything: a mother who skiied, a mother who went on foreign holidays. What she was embarrassed, dissatisfied, by was a mother who sat and stewed, complained and brooded. But for me, at least that aspect of things was all right.

Gramma, I said. I had taken to calling her Gramma all the time. It would have felt strange to resurrect the childish Mom, let alone Mommy, at this stage.

Are you here? she asked. She looked extremely, amazingly old, although I was familiar with that trick her illnesses played. She could seem to be on death's door, only to rally and get back home a few weeks later, dressed in matching pants and sweater, neat and fresh.

I'm here with the kids, I said. Madina and Emmet were intimidated by the hospital surroundings, and held back at the door. Emmet kept wanting to run his cars up and down the corridor floor, eliciting a sharp tug on his arm from Madina.

How did you get here? she whispered, off the point in a sense. After all these years, she still believed I couldn't drive.

We have to get you better, I said.

She shook her head. *Not this time. No good,* she said. It was one of her doom phrases, saved for situations *in extremis*, grief or severe sickness.

You always pull through, I said.

Can't God just take me? she asked.

I don't think he wants you, I replied, but I could see she wasn't ready for humor yet. The hospital staff always liked Gramma; they would stroke her cheek and say, *Beautiful lady,* as if they could see in her what one could often not see in old people, the lovely young person she had been, favorite of her father, wildly popular with the boys.

We stayed with Una for over a week, going back and forth to Cambridge Hospital. Una and I took turns, she the morning shift and I the afternoon or vice versa. Gramma seemed to be making no progress, but as always, impossible though it seemed, she began to come back to life in tiny increments, maddeningly slow but unmistakable. She would never admit it, or God forbid enjoy it; both directions were bad and undesirable from her point of view, recovery or lack of recovery. Her sodium levels stayed low; her body resisted rehydration. She said she wanted to go forward and finally to stop, but my suspicion was that she wanted to get back home and catch up on the gossip in her assisted living, though she had almost no strength.

I knew she was getting better when she tried to engage me in conversation about why I had to go back to Vermont.

Some evenings, I would leave her feeling fine and resting peaceably. The next morning, there would be a message on my cell phone from Una, telling me that Gramma was depressed, unresponsive, wanting to die.

What happened? I would grump at Una. *She was great when I left her last night.*

The repetition was as unbearable as it had ever been, the up and down rhythm of the days and nights, as

Gramma forced us to will her to live again, but with precious little input from the lady herself.

Gramma didn't want books or magazines, wouldn't turn on the television news, wouldn't pull the cord for the help of nurses. She just lay there and thought, impossibly distant but always holding us in her incomparable grip. Of course, she didn't want me to go back; one more reason to postpone getting better.

I would try to bring her up to speed on everyone's plans; that Una and I would take turns visiting, that I needed to get the kids back to school, that I would go back to Vermont, but could return if needed and so forth. As soon as I mentioned these details, Gramma would look away and wave her hand, as if refusing an unappetizing meal.

Why do you keep trying to tell her all that? Una said to me. *She doesn't need to know all that.*

When I saw Grandma sleeping, I had the impulse to wake her and thank her for the green birdhouse, the snow on the roof of the manger, the obsessive approach to life she had taught us. Who was to say that wasn't the better part? When other people were worried about what tennis camp to get their children into, she had the old values of East Galway, knees turned to the fire, witty, resentful, terribly circumscribed.

For Gramma, the worst thing a person could be was "sure of herself." There were no points made with Gramma for pursuing success. Indeed, every investment in personal glory became part and parcel of a later lament: what a shame you did it at all, if it was going to turn out this way. Gramma sought out the tragic, and in the tragic she could truly enjoy herself.

And once more, she pulled it off. They got her back in

her tidy apartment, the shamrock and the African violet, the Quimper teapot. *Why didn't you just let me go?* she complained. But God help you if you let an afternoon go by without checking in. My brother Jack phoned and said to us in hushed tones, *This time she really wants to go. Wouldn't it be better just to let her?*

But what the dickens did he know about it?

I looked up from grading research papers and saw Sasha standing there.

Thank you for a wonderful seminar, Professor, he said. *It looks like we will have you back in the fall.*

Yes, I'll be teaching two courses, I said, without elaboration. I wrote to Calvin, asking what books he would teach in such a case. I didn't hear back. Summer was coming again.

New York; 1990s

It wasn't that I ever wanted to be a lawyer—what a thought! Or that I even knew what a lawyer was or did. It was that I wanted to repent.

I would repent for my self-absorption and conceit. I would repent for not being a good enough person. I would repent for the fact that I wanted praise and recognition and told lies to others on my way to Kido. I would repent for wanting Kido to the exclusion of everything else. I would repent for vanity and self-love.

Law school would be a means of redoing everything, a great I'm sorry written in the stars, if I would be allowed to consider stars.

Knowing that Kido would not be coming, I finished up my PhD. Towards the end, I had wandered around

Europe, even wandered around Ireland, again. I had half-heartedly indulged myself with short-term admirers, from Taiwan, Jamaica, Korea. I went out on Friday nights and danced, improbably, to calypso music. I had a job teaching Japanese literature, but felt nothing for it. I floundered around in the past, and could not imagine the shape of the future. I had identified an ultimate and then had no vocabulary left with which to proceed.

I joined anti-apartheid networks, international women's groups working for peace. I got the idea of being a public interest advocate, defender, activist. I abruptly, in an act of madness, quit my university teaching job, and made plans to go to law school. I had never moved into that university office, either. The unpacked boxes just followed me around from place to place.

It was so hot in New York that August. I had to share an apartment with a graduate student in genetics; she studied mice and stayed up all night making calculations. It was so brutally hot outside, but inside the law school it was like an icebox. The massive law school classrooms had no windows. Everyone was frightened. Frightened of the professors, of the assignments, of the huge heavy books with their disjointed tales of people being hit in the head with tennis balls or trying to get redress for arms cut off in train accidents.

As with the story of Sandy, I want to make short work of this one. One thing about going to Greensboro, I would not have to think about those days in New York again. I would not have to spin out that legacy, do something with it, as Una might say. I could simply forget it, pretend it had never happened, wake up as a modern day Rip Van Winkle, rubbing my eyes and wondering where all those years had gone to.

I hated the talk, the look, the smell, the men in suits, the crowded elevators. I hated it with all my might for three long years. I hated my summer jobs, however worthy these might have been, running around courthouse corridors trying to get landlords to stipulate to the extermination of roaches; then a summer of death penalty work in Alabama, reading through trial transcripts of atrocities and mayhem, hotel clerks being shot at point blank range, extended families in trailer parks, and at the end of the hot days wandering the quiet streets of Montgomery in the dark.

It took a great deal of work to hate anything that much. I did not register meeting people, but moved forward like a drone or a robot to memorize details that meant nothing to me. My classmates were like radioactive aliens; I was not only distant from them, but revolted in their presence. I could not hear their voices or see them without mortal dread and terror; I was left for dead.

At night I began to write poems; I wrote cycles and collections and put them in a drawer, unused and unseen. They were long, elaborate, I think even ambitious. I'm not sure where they are now.

I might have gone to do an MFA in writing; I had been offered a teaching fellowship. It was Una who asked me why I wanted to go back to all that, but I know it's absurd to blame Una. All I had to do was say, Yes, in fact I do. Simple. But I couldn't. I was stubborn and cowed at the same time. No one had taught me anything about resistance, only submission, aches and pains.

When I finished law school, I asked Una and Jack to come and get me, to bring me away from New York. We packed up a UHaul truck, and I remember seeing the Upper West Side pass by in a blur; the sound of horns receded until it was quiet, and the city sat far away on the horizon. I was finished with it. I had the impulse to duck down, as if I were running away, fleeing the city, a fugitive.

I did not become a public interest lawyer. The very idea of representing others was completely unfamiliar to me. I didn't want to be the conduit for other people's problems. I didn't want to represent anyone. I only wanted to flee from New York as quickly as I could.

I landed on my feet in a small town in Western Massachusetts.

After dark, I ran along a small lake, beneath the trees, listening to Van Morrison, *Poetic Champions Compose.*

I tried to unthink the law I had learned, but it continued to weigh on me, as if I was forcibly bound to it. Looking back, I realize I was free to pretend I had never gone, never heard of law school, but it didn't seem that way to me then. I was hired to teach law to college students, another office I would never really move into, an apartment I would never move into, suitcases ready to go at a moment's notice.

Neither crimes nor divorces nor treaties moved me.

I considered various roads back and forward. I wish I had gone then to see John Merrill; he would have known what to do.

But as always, no one I knew or spoke to had any notion of where I might go next.

Hajimemashite, Sara desu. No, there was no Japan. No Ochanomizu station on a hot summer afternoon, no Kagurazaka neighborhood in the evening.

Not surprisingly, I made a quick search of the soul for a particular place. I had to see the West of Ireland again.

A motif; Seanie, 1993

God, of all the motifs in all the world.

It wasn't the first time during those years I had gone back, riding my bike in East Galway, wondering who I might meet along the road. I had visited now and again during those years; I had gone back whenever I had the chance, especially after Japan.

But this time, the summer after law school, the beginning of the 90s, it had a particular ferocity.

I was staying alone in a B & B above a pub in the town of Turlough. God knows why I thought Seanie Mannion looked like Peter O'Toole; recalling it now, there was no resemblance whatsoever. Well, he was lanky and slightly bent forward, if that qualifies. And he had that certain washed out look, and a ready roguish smile, if that qualifies.

I was sitting at a corner table on my own, one late afternoon. Seanie was sitting at the bar. An older man at the bar began to ask me questions; this made Seanie laugh. He asked where I was from; I answered, but he made as if he couldn't hear me. He put his hand to his ear and moved down nearer to me.

I could tell immediately that he had a hesitation in his speech, a mild impediment, an unwelcome halting in midsentence. *Mammy said my thoughts ran ahead of my talk,* he told me later, though in retrospect that seems doubtful.

What do you do yourself? he asked me. My desire to simplify things is surely understandable.

You've more degrees than Mary Robinson so, he laughed when I had told him. Still, he was game.

It's astonishing that I found him attractive, witty, a kind of romantic pal. I remember phoning Una to tell her I'd met a dead ringer for O'Toole as he once was, and wondering aloud what he would look like in a Panama hat.

It puts me in mind of that old television show, *The Millionaire.* The elderly gent, off camera, would hand his minion an envelope with someone's name in it and say, *Our next millionaire, Mike.* Well, Seanie was, let's say, in the right place at the right time.

I would move to Galway, the home place, for good, that was it. That was my next bright idea.

Seanie and I spent the next three weeks knocking around the place, wandering through fields and graveyards, sitting in his parked car of an evening and remarking how the sky never went truly dark on an Irish summer night.

It seemed a very long audition for a part in *Playboy of the Western World.*

It wasn't the first time I'd gone looking to East Galway. I'd always said I wanted to be buried there, though long after I changed my mind on that.

Several years prior to meeting Seanie, soon after I realized Kido would not be coming, I went over to try and find Jerome, to be young and carefree again, to sit in the small lounge and listen to his tall tales. Instead, I found Manus, Nuala's husband, in Jerome's old seat in the corner.

Cat, my father's dead, he said. *You missed him by a few months.* Then Manus and I cried together.

How imposing, how handsome, Manus seemed then. We made an elaborate plan to evade Nuala and meet on the road to Newbridge. We drove into the bog and kissed with total regret for everything one could think of. Manus had odd memories that came as a complete surprise to me; of being annoyed at me back when I was sixteen; racing around the countryside with boyfriends as I was.

The night before I was to leave we all sat together in the small lounge. Nuala was there as well. They had recently put televisions in the bars, and, oddly congruous, the movie *Elvira Madigan* was playing on one of the stations.

After law school, I'm not even sure I was in my right mind. At least I can say that Seanie was utterly free and unfettered, and ready to play at being the salt of the earth. The locals were surprised, it must be admitted. *Who's with Seanie?* they'd ask, and get the land of their lives when they heard, or so I was told.

When I went back to my teaching job in western Massachusetts after the summer holiday in Galway, I spoke of Seanie all the time. My sweetheart, I called him. I wore a small locket he had given me; we spoke by phone every other day. I could always tell who it was when I lifted the receiver, as I heard only a swishing and swirling sound as Seanie attempted to speak and was met by his own hesitation.

He even wrote letters, with old-fashioned writing slanting down the page, filled with predictable sentiments. When will you be coming back to me, pet? he would write.

But in fact Seanie came to visit me in Massachusetts that Christmas. Sven and I met him at the airport; he approached us looking confused and woozy and I realized that, of course, he'd never really been away from home before. We went off through the lightly falling snow and met Una in a bar in Cambridge. She greeted Seanie joyfully, with a great hug and full approval. The first major pronouncement from Seanie, after he was asked by the young woman tending bar what he would like, was along the lines of *I find that girl such a turn-off.*

And so it went that Christmas, rescuing Seanie from bars, not being able to trust him to read a map and find his way back. It was the last Christmas Daddy was alive, and in all the photos he looks tired and ill, but smiling and genial as he struggled to figure Seanie out.

I can't understand a word the boy is saying, he confessed to Gramma.

Still, Seanie at his best was good fun, and perfect in a crowd. Sven, Una, Seanie and I drove to the Cape Cod beaches, cold and deserted in the dead of winter, listening to Van Morrison, very faddish at the time, and stopping at warm and charming hotels for a quick brandy. Like Seanie or not—and I could never say I actually liked him—he lived up entirely to the designated motif.

After Seanie went back home, I continued to get his phone calls. It was like being phoned up by the West Wind, a breathy interval in which I would wait for him to say, *Hello, darling.* I turned towards East Galway like a sea turtle making the long, cold journey back to its original beach.

I set to work trying to find something I could do in Ireland. I would move to Galway, and that would be it. Or I could work in Dublin, or Cork—not Limerick, I couldn't take it that far—and then go to Galway on weekends, and things would be settled for me. I would stand at attention again when they played the national anthem, *A Soldier's Song,* after the last number in the pubs on a Saturday night. I would stand for the good old ways.

I heard there were international law teaching jobs on offer for the next fall in Dublin, and decided to give it a whirl. *It isn't likely,* I told Seanie, *but it's no harm to try, is it?*

No harm at all, peteen, Seanie agreed genially.

As it happened, I was called over for an interview. The news arriving on official stationary with green seal, I was amazed to see that, for no reason that I understood, I had made it into the top list of candidates, and that I was being asked to appear before the academic hiring committee on such and such a date. I had no idea what to prepare, so I didn't try. Seanie said he was *over the moon* about it.

The interview board was composed entirely of middle-aged men. They sat in a row on the opposite side of the table from me, in dark blue or pearl grey suits, pleasant enough to me, which should have acted as a tip-off that I was their girl, their choice. I had no clue what purpose I might serve for them, but that didn't mean I wouldn't serve any.

We don't need any family lawyers, you know, one silver-haired professor said. *We have plenty of those.*

Great stuff, was the gist of my reply. I do just about anything.

Back in Roscommon, I told Seanie that there was no chance in hell I would be offered that job. I didn't know them; they didn't know me; what had it all been about?

Never mind, pet, Seanie said, intending to comfort me.

And yet, astonishingly, the letter arrived in due course, informing me that I was the first choice of the committee, and announcing the terms of the position, and would I let them know by such and such a date whether I intended to accept.

1912; 1990s

I had been hearing something strange, in the months leading up to it. The faint noise woke me in the night; it sounded like a truck passing on a faraway highway, except that there was no highway near enough for me to hear. When I put my ear to the wall, it was even louder. A train, a car on the highway, the sad whistle of something moving in the night, but outside the town, across the valley, distinct, annoying, unending. I heard it every night, and it woke me every night.

After Daddy died, the sound stopped.

He woke one spring morning, a Monday, walked out to the kitchen in full expectation of things to come. He asked Gramma, *What shall we do today, Ma?* Then he fell sideways, and simply died. He died lying peacefully against the wall of the little Cape Cod house, with Gramma trying to say goodbye to him.

She phoned me first. *Dad's just gone, he's gone*, she said.

He hadn't wanted any of us to die first. My sister Marie had done that, but apart from her, he was determined none of the rest of us would.

You'll be fine without me, he used to say to Gramma.

When Jack wished him many happy returns on his last birthday, he had said, *No, not for me, Jack.*

He wrote me, quoting Jefferson on death, like a summer shower, not to be feared and yet not to be wished for.

The night he died there was a terrible thunderstorm; the lightning lit up the house, the rain fell horribly across the lawns.

I want to get drunk, I said, and Gramma didn't even

mind. It was a sensible response. I poured everyone brandy, out of one of Daddy's decanters.

I had asked him to tape the story of his life, and after he died, I found the blank tape and the tape recorder on the table by his favorite chair, all ready to go.

Airports; 1994

I told Seanie when I'd be arriving.

Already, I dreaded the job and the Law Faculty building; dreaded meeting my new colleagues, having no idea what they wanted or expected from me. I still imagined that I would be going out every weekend to Galway to spend time with Seanie, to hang out in Turlough, to start over again in the rainy fields.

I need to ease into it; I want to be in the West a while before I head to Dublin.

Whatever you need, pet, Seanie whispered into the phone, ready for all eventualities.

I thought he knew I was coming into Shannon; I'd made it so plain, *I will be in the West first,* I'd said, over and again. *I couldn't face Dublin right off the bat, I'll be in Turlough,* I had said.

I arrived as one does, into the surprise of an abrupt change in the weather, the light, the lingo, pushing my cart full of bags, as after all, I was planning to stay until my Christmas visit home. I looked around tentatively, wondering which direction Seanie would come bounding out from. I pushed, then stopped, and looked, and wondered. But Seanie was nowhere to be seen. The crowds quickly scattered and dispersed, floated away into the early morning mist. I stood with my mountain of bags, looking around with a bit more annoyance in evidence now, looking at my watch, checking it against the airport clock, making a face, I have no doubt.

And so the first hour passed, and the second.

I went through all possible scenarios for Seanie being this late. I was inherently disorganized; had I given him the wrong date? But we had just spoken several days ago; there was little chance he had got the date mixed up. He wasn't that terribly busy; the idea of an emergency or an unexpected obligation didn't ring true.

At some point, however much I disliked the telephone, I would have to phone Seanie's house and find out where on earth he was.

The airport had lost its early morning buzz and mystery. It had gone quiet, workaday. A few planes came in from English cities; the airport staff passed by, gossiping and laughing.

He-llo? Seanie's mother answered, her voice on the telephone sounding far away, fearful.

It's Catherine, Mrs. Mannion. I was wondering where Seanie might be.

Well, isn't he with you? He left to get you last night.

Last night? It wasn't making sense to me.

He went off to Dublin, to meet you, she said, vaguely accusatory.

Of all the incredible, moronic things. I looked at the bags piled high on my cart; the clock on the wall; and thought of my letter on official letterhead, telling me that I was the first choice of the committee, and what my salary as a newly minted Irish civil servant would be.

Holy God, I managed. *If he phones, tell him I am at Shannon, and will he phone and page me there?*

Hours passed before I heard from him. I had wandered around, in and out of newsstands, in and out of the restroom, in and out of the open plan restaurant. The planes from England came and left again. I knew clearly that I couldn't stand Seanie, absolutely could not stand him and never wanted to see him again.

Yet there I was, waiting for him to page me.

What the hell happened? was my opener to him.

Ah, pet, I couldn't believe it. Since you were going to work in Dublin, I just thought.

Well, do you have the car? Can you come and get me? It would take several hours, but at least it would be progress.

I didn't bring the car at all. Mammy thought my tires might get slashed. Sure, I took the bus.

So where did you think I was?

I wasn't sure.

He asked me could I get to Dublin on my own. I pushed my bags around from counter to counter until I found someone who could tell me the bus schedules. I remember pulling and tugging my huge bags onto busses, changing, waiting, standing in line.

I had told Seanie I would meet him at Heuston Station at such and such a time, and eventually, after the various busses and cabs, I was dropped off at the appointed locale overlooking the grey Liffey, me and my mountain of bags and my letter of approval.

I sat on the biggest of the bags and put my head in my hands. I wasn't sure where Seanie would be, or why I was meeting him. Some drunks walked past and made remarks: *You need someone to carry your things, love*, or the like.

Pretend you do not see me, I shouted at them. *Pretend I am not here, I am invisible to you!*

Somehow or other, I found him, at the end of that ridiculous day. He told me he had got us a guest house to stay in, lovely and clean. But it was gloomy and depressing, and I told him I wanted to go back to Turlough and spend some time sorting myself out before looking for a flat in Dublin. So we made our way to the Turlough scene with whatever fortitude I could salvage, the country bands, the after-hours chipper.

My tone had become hectoring with him, more or less overnight. I could see the madness of it unfolding before me; would I stay a year, or three? Would I move here, would I bring him around to my cousins? He still lived with his Mammy on the farm, and went off to his job most days. He told me that Mammy would turn the farm over to him in due course; that his brother Eamon had moved into town with his family ages ago and had no designs on it. Mammy was tall and tough as nails, and wore flowered dresses very youthful for her.

She would set out the tea with lettuce, and sliced tomato and salad cream.

This is our culture, Catherine, now, she would tell me, poking the air with her fork, a reference to the teatime cuisine.

The castle; 1990s

Up the winding road I went to the Law Faculty; then back down again, walking always, in the rain, early, late, in the constant rain.

I sat at the Dean's enormous desk in the front room of

the restored castle, overlooking the rest of the university, most of it designed as it happened by a Polish architect during the Cold War—what about that for a choice?—and asked him, *But what do you want me to teach?*

Perhaps it didn't matter to him. I was to teach something or other. Something international; something about Japan, New York, about being a citizen of the world. A bit hard to prepare for that.

Well, now, Dr. Darcy, Catherine, why don't you read the GATT with them?

I fell to my task with a mad devotion. I sat on the bed in the student room I was renting until I could find a flat, turning the pages of the General Agreement on Tariffs and Trade, making notes, copious notes, turning the back shelves of the library inside out in my insistence on finding every scrap I could, as the days ticked down towards the starting line. GATT, GATT and more GATT. And thus began my international trade career, born in terror.

On weekends I took the train to Roscommon where Seanie would collect me. There was a distinct chill from the direction of my former Galway friends as they sought to show their disapproval of Seanie. Seanie's Mammy, Mrs. Mannion, occasionally put me up in a spare room in their house. On Saturday evenings we would all sit about and listen to *Fáilte Isteach* and then Seanie and I would take to the roads, out and about in Turlough and environs, listening to country music.

All I really want you to do is teach me to jive, I told Seanie. Jiving was the swinging style of country western dance they did in East Galway, all of them experts at it from an early age. I had never learned it properly in the old days; I was merely faking it when I tried. I asked him, repeatedly, and in that hectoring way I used with him. Yet he resisted. He would try to jive with me, but not teach me. *Just follow your feet*, he would say, meaninglessly. *Swing now, and now*, with emphasis.

Seanie was good at it, jiving. They all were. They learned with sisters and cousins, in sitting rooms and kitchens, from the time they were little, until it was second nature, like walking. The fact that Seanie wouldn't teach me to jive, systematically, until I had mastered it, was placed on the ever-growing list of grievances I had against him.

I never missed a weekend in visiting Clement. He was still in the old monastery that overlooked the exact place he'd been born, the very house. I never went out to Turlough without phoning him, without getting someone to drop me over, and he would have out on a little table in the parlor a small glass of brandy and an ashtray. Rain or shine, he met me at the door with the same look of delight. It had come as a real surprise to him that I had come back to Ireland to live and work.

As for Seanie, Clement only said, probably without meaning it for a moment, *He seems a nice lad, Cat.* He amused me with his imitations of each of our cousins, as well as the other locals and even the superior of the order; for instance, your man who went to America on a Chuesday and returned on a Tuesday. He pitched his voice high and blinked to make me laugh.

I told him that I hated law, hated it with a passion, and that I would learn Irish; somehow I would master it.

I'd say you will, he would say, agreeing with me, giving me the benefit of any doubt.

It wasn't as if I'd lost contact with him over the years; I managed to sneak over now and again during vacations, being struck each time at how good it was to see our boys in thick wooly jumpers park the cars at Shannon, the salt wind in their hair. I even brought Gramma and Daddy a few times, sometimes went on my own, and I would see Clement without fail, he with a broad smile on his face, welcoming, ironic, arms out to catch me. *Cat, Cat,* he would murmur, as if in heaven to see me again.

And each time we had to say goodbye, he would walk out onto the high garden, the black dog running after him, and wave his hand up high, navy blue sweater over his habit, smiling and shouting, *Next year in Timard, Turlough!*

Over and again, week after week, I would walk up the gravel path of the monastery and ring the bell. The outer vestibule was tiled in chilly black and white; the sun would appear and disappear through the slotted glass.

There you are, he would say, laughing under his breath, *And how are you getting on in Dublin, Cat?*

It was a familiar enough question, as so many went to Dublin for work; but as applied to me, how odd and unexpected. Had he ever imagined I would live there, or be so much talked about again?

But things in Dublin were cold and nasty. Some in the Faculty referred to me as an "exotic;" others hardly spoke. I was given tutorials on the English Sale of Goods Act. I went into my office even on weekends, walking up the hill to the castle, opening the great door, up the deserted stairs. The ivy grew thick and fast, covering over my windows in short order. I wrote up reams of notes, on the passing of the title as the goods cross the ship's rail, on marine insurance, on bankruptcies and thwarted international purchases, letters of credit that moved forward with the power of a freight train.

I found a flat, of which I used only one room, scrunched up on the side of my bed alone, still in all my valor trying to start over and forget, reading *Dubliners* and *Portrait of the Artist*, right from the moo cow and Dante's velvet hairbrushes, one green and one maroon.

Elmore; 2007

I remembered it and yet was in it at the same time; rather like being in Galway in that sense. I remembered everything; the way Daddy became animated, child-like whenever he came back to the Northeast Kingdom; the wildflowers we called paintbrush; the sound of the waterfalls in the woods. I had never liked waterfalls, as unwelcoming as a cold shower, could never understand why people travelled so far to see them.

Back came the warmth after all that snow and cold, all in a rush across our yard, the children saw it, too, the sun returning and the wildflowers springing up as far as you could see.

I sat at the computer in the public library in my usual way, and after a long silence, saw another message from John Merrill. It was like one of those impossibly wonderful dreams, where you are flying or being kissed by a prince.

I wrote to Calvin:

> Merrill tells me he is going to have back surgery. I would like to go see him, maybe after he is better. Do you ever think of going? Do you ever think of those days? Are you hiding, or something else? Maybe it is time to tell me. The kids are well; we survived a winter.

This sounded a bit too much like *Little House on the Prairie*. But in fact this summer, I wouldn't have to dread the season's progress, fret about my age and the passing of the long days into the shorter days. I could linger over the New Fiction table at the bookshop and, even dismissing much of it as junk, I could take up what I wanted, I could bring home my books in a bag, I could get one for Emmet about a truck, one for Madina about a heroic girl in history.

It's true, as Lily Briscoe thought, that it is terrible to want and want and not to have, and certainly I wanted and wanted and did not have. But it was better than wanting and wanting and not having, and also having to be a lawyer.

Nothing new, no coast of Cornwall, no unspoiled Greek island, just Elmore and its Moose Crossing signs. Elmore where you could lie on your back in a field on a summer's night and look up and see a million stars, shooting, twirling. I had written a poem about *Venus Over Wheelock* and thought I would send it to John Merrill. He would still like it; he was still there, miraculous as it was, he was still there.

Park Baun; 1990s

After I decided to move to Ireland in the early 90s, I literally went shopping on the back roads, and that was how I found it. I had a savings bond Daddy had given me years back, worth eight thousand dollars. Una had come over to Galway for a visit and we drove together up and down the back roads, and I stood admiring the way the fields ran off down towards the far off sea, maybe suggesting that one day it would all be gone, returned to the water, but for now, the hedgerows and vistas hid their little deserted houses. Una pulled up the car in front of the empty house at Park Baun, and sighed. How she loved buildings.

It's fabulous, she said. It was drowning in gnarled bushes and brambles and piles of old turf. No one had lived in it for years, that was certain. We wandered inside, and were struck by the smell of old concrete and long dead fires. In some rooms, the floorboards had either rotted or been pulled out, and there was simply dirt where the floor used to be. It was dead silent within; only the strong sense of an earlier form of life, its moments of high drama flattened out by time.

It was the sort of house where you should always, in fine weather, leave the door ajar.

We could see a good long way out through the hedgerows, the grass sliding off into an artificial plantation of evergreen, animals in the distance, cattle, horses; for whatever reason, we had the sense that we were being watched or soon would be.

I felt I had to have this house at Park Baun, and sent Seanie off on a mission to make my case. There were no secrets in East Galway, so as soon as Seanie entered the farmer's parlor that evening, saying in his whispery, convoluted way that an American lady wanted the house, it was understood far and wide with the immediacy with which news is snatched and sent forth, that Seanie's girlfriend wanted to buy it. It was assumed that Seanie would fix it up and the two of us would live there.

That was not, of course, my assumption.

The farmer agreed to sell it to me, through Seanie, for the amount of the bond Daddy had given me, the equivalent of around five thousand old Irish punts.

Una, who had gone back home to Boston, was totally on board with this news. She, of course, adored buildings, walls, rooms, chimneys. She promised that she and Sven would come and help me fix it up; they would paint, they would garden.

The sun shone through the cracked windows, and in Park Baun, a settlement of six houses, two of them completely deserted, a settlement that used to have ten or more crowded, lively households, it was the nineteenth century.

And so it started. I got hold of local workmen, and they arrived in haphazard fashion, first a drywall in one room, floor tiles in another. I stood with them and gazed at the hand carved mantelpieces; they assumed I was mad when they heard I cared about these obsolete items, as I'd instructed them never to interfere with an original feature. There was as much chat as work being done. Old fixtures from country bathrooms were hauled in, installed as well as could be, a hot press, a newish window where the old one could not be salvaged.

The moths came, and the mice, the frogs and even the foxes. Badgers were always invisible; they were said to be everywhere but managed never to be seen, even in the headlights of a car at night. Every Friday evening I drove from Dublin in the rain, arriving and starting a fire by myself, running back and forth between the enormous turf pile in the front garden, into the safety and silence of the house. The widow next door would appear as soon as smoke started up my chimney.

Tis good to have you here again, Cat. It does get lonely and I am saying my prayers all the time, she said.

Seanie brought me a sofa, dragging it behind his car on a sort of makeshift trailer. Still, it was months before

I could bring myself to stay there all night. I generally got a room over one of the nicer of the pubs in Turlough instead. Seanie and I would sit in the crowded bar, and I would give out about Dublin and the Law Faculty, and Seanie would laugh, *Ah, pet, I don't know how you do it.*

Back across another kind of rain on Sunday afternoon, after having got through my cousin Bridie's dinners, past Athlone, into the midlands, and back up the quays. In my small apartment off Morehampton Road, I realized that I smelled of turf smoke and was as tired as if I'd stayed up all weekend. In the Law Faculty, my image became inextricable from the idea of a West of Ireland cottage and a fixation on country culture. This meant that I'd be no threat; merely an unwelcome American eccentricity of the Dean's. I woke early every morning. I walked through and around Dublin constantly; the center was small and easy to cover in a short time.

In Dublin, there were building sites everywhere in those days. Bricks were falling, green glass walls going up.

Each Friday afternoon on the way to Park Baun, I'd stop outside Mullingar and buy my pack of ten cigarettes. I never smoked in the car, only when I pulled into the house at Park Baun, opened the old front door and looked around. I would light up and look out at the long crooked path into the nineteenth century.

Lady Brett; always

It was one of those dreams of which Una would have roundly disapproved. After some university event, perhaps the screening of a human rights film, Sasha and I found ourselves on a quiet path, walking and talking. In this dream, Sasha turned to me and said, hesitatingly, *I know I should not ask you this, Professor, but could I kiss you once? Just once? Please, may I?*

It seems I did not answer; as, even in a dream, what answer would be the right one? No—a certain end to the story. Yes—too suggestive and certainly too far off from my real life behavior.

Sasha, so the dream went, took my face in his hands and kissed me—how to describe it?—thoroughly. There was a vivid fragrance off his face and hair.

I woke up feeling not guilt, but only a mild surprise and pleasure at seeing my story writing skills had survived intact.

Thinking it over, as I could not help doing, this dream seemed to contain all the sad, sweet moments, existing in their strange hierarchy of importance understood only by me. As for Sasha, he was a bit too much the ski bum type for me, wandering the lodges and slopes of Eastern Europe.

Yet it was his capacity for sad passion, as revealed in the dream, his hesitancy, his apologetic approach, asking just one kiss and no more, that gave him this part to play.

I wrote to Calvin, though he only seldom replied.

> Am re-reading Hemingway, Gods know why, I just have to take him up again year after year. I know he is a sexist, though a quirky one. Just took out The Sun Also Rises, a good book for springtime, makes you feel you are about to go to Spain and that it won't even be too crowded, that you will bump into people you know. The way Jake runs into Brett everywhere; Brett and the matador, I get that. It used to be that way, if you put it into the **it's all about me** category.

I could survive on just this slender thread of communication.

I must have been endowed with some great gift of endurance; strength others had for the cold, I had for longing and deprivation. Madina and Emmet bickering in the back seat, I could continue to do everything, and so persistently, get them into the car, out of the car, through the town, perhaps a stop at Willey's, though you had to watch Emmet every second, up the hill, out of the car, hands to be washed, vegetables to be peeled, beds to be made up, warmed, comforted.

NPR was so familiar and so boring, year after year, the same news. If the world was coming to an end, NPR would try to make it sound like a routine event, a few interviews on the scene with unknowns.

How many thousands of dollars you have, Mommy? Emmet's language had improved immensely.

Oh, I don't know, enough I guess.

How many? Twenny dollars?

More than that.

'finity dollars?

Less than that.

How old are you? One hundred?

Not as much as that.

How old you really? Emmet put his hands together in supplication and fell on the floor, arching his back and repeating *pleeeease.*

Siteen? Seventy? Twelve?

I don't like to talk about my age, I said. *Go build a castle.*

Now and again I thought of Sasha and the dream. Pondering it was a minor pleasure, essentially spectral, like that glass of wine I'd have after the kids had gone to bed. Likable Sasha with his funny stories at least brought me clippings about Russian poets and ballet dancers. Skaters as well, as he knew figure skating was a weakness of mine. I had wanted to be a skater, never was anyone made more perfectly for skating.

That had been the frightening part about teaching at the law school in Boston; no spark of any kind, no looks exchanged and no one with whom I would have exchanged them, no symbolic pictures on the wall. My empty office, that looked like I had not moved in even after years, and never would move in, the messy desk attesting to nerves and overpreparation. No one to watch for at the door, no surprises, no rainy evenings or revelations, just endurance, a grim, head-down, self-punishing endurance. And thus into the dream came Sasha, or should I say skied in, smiling, admiring, pockets overflowing with bits of poems and proverbs, looking me in the face, guiltily but with joy, May I kiss you, Professor, just once, but thoroughly?

Drifting apart; 1995

It was that phrase I couldn't stand. *Winnie in the pub asked me how was it going for us, me and you, and I told her, ah well, sure, we drifted apart.*

I nearly lunged at him.

Not drifted apart, I shouted at Seanie. *That had nothing to do with it.*

And so, in what was really no time at all, Seanie was banished from Park Baun, never to return. Such was our fundamental dislike of one another that, once we had, well, parted, we would have hated like poison ever to meet again face to face.

I had tried to convince him of the utter and absolute beauty of the high ditches on either side of the dirt road leading to Park Baun. In winter, the grass turned the palest yellow, almost white, and the sound of the wind was several notches louder than usual. There was a rare frost, a cold rain, clouds outlined in black, racing across the sky.

Sure, pet, I know, he'd said, though quite unconvinced in manner. He didn't want to work on the old kip, as he saw it, not a bit of comfort in it, sure, knock the bastard anyway.

One evening as we got ready to head out on the town of Turlough, with Seanie all set to go and the deep dark pea soup night outside his mother's door, she'd banged her fist on the table and said to me, *I'm turning the farm over to his brother 'cause sure, isn't Seanie's place with you now in Park Baun?*

Hold on now, this was a new twist on things. Never since I'd met him had I been more eager to turn him back to his Mam, and never had I less intention of taking him on or bringing him into Park Baun with me. I'd rather spend a thousand nights scared out of my mind than to gain protection in that way.

Well, that is certainly not decided, not the way I see it, I said, frightened of her in one sense, but certain I would not let this be put over on me this way. *And as for the farm, don't let me change anyone's plans.* His mother huffed and turned away, because it certainly did change her plans. I'd provided the perfect cover for ditching Seanie and giving the thirty or forty odd acres to his brother as she'd always wanted to.

I left the house and went out into the brumy dark, never a deep dry cold, just Celtic mugginess even in the dead of winter, the sense of being low down, crouching near the sea.

What the hell did you tell her, Seanie? I fumed at him.

What was she on about at all? he asked back, evasively.

And thus by morning, the entire town and environs knew that any thought they'd ever had that Catherine and Seanie would be married and living in Park Baun was up in smoke.

But yes, the only downside to this was that each night I spent at Park Baun I was doomed to lie awake until morning light, wide awake in the intolerable dampness, waiting for cars to pass, wondering if one might stop, what I would do if I heard footsteps, a parting of grass in the front garden, no one to hear me or save me.

It was the nineteenth century down my road, and especially at night, an Ireland less hospitable by the year to spirits and fairies was preserved, though uneasily, down the road to Park Baun.

Truth to tell, I'd lost a bit of my old local luster by virtue of going about with Seanie, and as a consequence no one asked me what had happened to him. They took his presence on the scene as a brief bit of madness on my part, and accepted his departure— though in point of fact he'd gone nowhere, geographically speaking—with a slightly embarrassed nod of satisfaction.

The fiasco had left behind a series of lovely photographs, though, taken by Una at various local castles and even on the beach at Cape Cod. Seanie photographed well, especially in bad weather, had that Peter O'Toole look of world-weariness that did especially nicely in black and white. Seanie was forever about to quit the smoking and never quite got there; that indecision and in-between quality showed in the photos, weary and in between drinks, gazing out to sea, about to be banished, but good fun on a road trip in the meantime.

Motifs

If I knew anything, it was that we were compelled to create something of manageable size; and hence, the motifs. Not to be able to settle on one with any consistency was somewhat anomalous, but not contrary to the general theory. At its worst, the need for this self-limitation became agoraphobia; mirror, mirror on the wall in the company of just one; even worse, though, was the opposite prospect of some indistinct and anonymous wandering.

Tuscan cooking, Civil War obsessions; organic farming, arranged marriage, self sacrifice, Park Baun, Caspian Lake, the building of igloos and yurts, the particular blue of window shutters in Provence, sealing wax, Corgie breeding; all these resulted from said requirement of situating oneself in a motif.

And then a feature as yet undiscovered and unexplained by scientists, the kernel of unyielding loyalty to one's own way of liking and disliking, marking territory, the desperate embrace of *me, me, me,* incredible, strong beyond belief, like the well-known matter of snowflakes being each one different from all others, falling and falling according to the rule established by that absurd and apparently useless fact, but there it was.

And so I found myself, windshield wipers taking on rain from Lanesboro onward, pulling onto the grass at Park Baun, opening the door, hearing the echo as the empty rooms received a visitor, the cold dust settled in every corner and the wood lice pleasantly surprised at company. Here I am, no idea why or recollection of how, but I am back, collecting turf into a big bag out in the wind and rain, running back in, cigarette box awaiting me on the mantelpiece.

It was a project that could never be completed, a house that could never be made warm, the bathroom cold as a barn, grounds that could never be tamed, grass and hedge rows and half size trees in a knot of mess all around the place; never to be brought to heel without a massive investment and marshalling of machines that would entirely remove the point of it.

I had my collections; the old dishes, some left behind by the family that had lived there for decades, dying one by one, tea mugs with stripes; other pieces brought from thrift shops on Cape Cod, across the sea in a plane, gravy boats and dinner plates. I had my collection of religious pictures that had hung on the walls of cottages in an earlier age, the age just ending as I had first arrived, way back when.

I had my old sweaters, changing into either of the same one or two whenever I arrived out. They could get dirty with turf or stone dust, it didn't matter. To go to church one needed only to cover it up with a coat, a pair of spiffy old boots, and it was just fine, intriguing.

My share of old friends and even a couple of former lovers showed up from time to time in the early evenings, greeting this strange lady with her falling down estate in the trees of Park Baun.

As time wasters go, it wasn't bad.

I could fritter away a fierce amount of time. Perhaps if I'd put it to better use, with less day dreaming, there would have been more to show for myself. I was only a stone's throw there from the places where Gramma's people had come from to leave and go away, rarely to be heard from again, arriving in America, the fuss, asking for jobs, the sounds of the horses and carts, the train whistles. And then here I was back, standing in the crumbling doorway at Park Baun, looking out at the deserted fields, no more EU heddage payments for sheep, hardly a horse, the equestrian only a hobby now, and cattle only stragglers in the global food chain. Thinking of Queen Maeve and the ancient lowing of cattle, must have another look at that, confirm a theory of dying culture, look up a set of verses that showed conclusively the formerly sacred nature of the land.

Groups of people seemed to have these tendencies as well, more or less like the kernel of the unalterable individual, and among the Irish, there was an urge to head out of the house, to drink and to speak, a lot, an awful lot.

Some days out there I'd have a burst of optimism; I could make the house tidy and bright, banish the frightful nights of pea soup darkness. I stood on painted chairs, painting the walls brighter and brighter whites, playing the radio, a traditional music program from Roscommon or Ballina. The unimaginably tall pine tree moved always back and forth, back and forth in the wind that lived in the land and would never leave it. I avoided certain of the rooms as too dark and damp. I kept the fire going. I painted all the old chairs, the old table, painted right over the evidence of woodworm past and present.

From there to here, funny things are everywhere

I could not have explained, let alone to John Merrill, how I went from being that star young lady, so clever, small, pretty, tad wild, tad timid, game for everything, to the craven creature I'd become, desperate for an e-mail telling me I was remembered.

It would be unwelcome news, in any case. *Oh, that one,* the folks in Turlough insisted, *she's her money made.* And from Saint Theo's, *She's gone into law,* and other dreaded phrases.

As I dragged the kids in and out of cars in Boston and Cambridge, up and down escalators, dropped them at school, hauled them out of bed, arriving at my law school office to hear a talk on intellectual property licenses, the blood draining from my face, eyes turned towards the door, panicking, needing to escape from the room, the power points, the quips, leaping from my seat, looking quick for the recycle bin to drop my plate in with a crash and head for the noisy set of doors, out into the air, away from them, away from them all. My heartbeat whooshed in my ears, an epic struggle twixt life and death, Joan of Arc, I'm going, going, tis a far better thing I do, get out with your life, abandon ship, get out, out if you can.

So you didn't like it, then? It wasn't a story anyone especially wanted to hear.

You are not banished, Catherine, Merrill had said to me during my time in Dublin. That was the rare jewel in my pocket, the simple and generous promise of some future restoration. And so I often wrote for Merrill, self-consciously, assuming that he knew it all, and didn't especially wonder or balk at how I could so screw things up. Of course, he didn't enter into my motifs; in other words, could not be expected to share my taste in motifs. He had his own, though they tended more towards hobbies than dramatic, life-changing events. I liked that notion, though I'd never achieved it: the living room filled with evidence of motifs explored, but always the living room dominating the motif.

I by contrast had been taken over by my motifs, had gambled more, despite my innate personal caution and dislike of chaos. I had gambled at a level of daring that surely qualified me for the blackjack tables at Monte Carlo.

For Merrill, it was say Mexican art, maybe veering off in the direction of textiles; one hoped there would be no obsession with serapes. I might have done the same with Rodin water colors; too 1970s, perhaps, and not surprising enough. I had that predictable vein, too, though, and didn't go in for anything of questionable aesthetics.

The fireplace, shelves of chosen items, a glass of brown spirits with unmelted ice cube; winter vacation, oversized books. It might have been like that, but, for me, it wasn't.

And despite all that moving about, I'd come down to earth in the strangest of places. *Isn't that your field of law?* they would ask, that incomprehensible notion, *What exactly is your field?*

Lady Brett; 2007

COULD YOU COME HOTEL MONTANA MADRID
AM RATHER IN TROUBLE
BRETT

It was in just that way I wanted to write to Calvin. But for Brett Jake did arrive in a taxi; how quickly he had moved when he received the telegram, stopping to consider the implications of literal translations of Spanish to English, and having found her at the end of the long dark corridor; good enough, Jake was, to make sure she was dusted off and sitting up on a hotel stool drinking a good and cold martini in very short order.

She'd had that affair with the matador, the perfect matador, a mere nineteen years old, the madness of it, and yet how expected. *Oh, darling,* she'd say, *I can't help myself, I can't help anything.*

Come please, am rather in trouble, and Jake appeared, Spanish fluent enough to banter and dicker with the proprietor of the Hotel Montana.

I would troop over to the Greensboro Public, up the little hill to sign in to use the computer. I could have written to Calvin, Come please, am rather in trouble, or not that exactly, but something to that effect, am rather in trouble as nothing happens to me any more, do you remember me?

Hemingway and his two bottles of wine with lunch, or three, more if there was a small crowd. How could anyone drink like that and still speak, let alone have a sense of irony and be able to translate that well? Always able to do things, really do things, order food correctly, tie flies, chill the wine in the river, speak any and every language idiomatically, an *aficionado* always. He seemed not to read much poetry, rather the newspapers, two or three at a time, even when the news was essentially the same in each.

ARRIVING SUD EXPRESS TOMORROW LOVE JAKE

Let's never talk about it, Brett kept saying to him, though that would not have been my approach. Let's never talk of it, don't let's ever. Of the young matador who wanted to marry her. *There were some funny things, though*, Lady Brett said to Jake. I liked that phrase, it worked for me. There were some funny things, though. And then their olives in the martini glass, the understanding bartender. They got away with all that.

There were some funny things, though.

Montrose; 1990s

It became a thing in Turlough that I was sometimes on the television, commenting on the Clinton visit to Ireland, hanging about in the television studio, dropping in off the cuff remarks about American politics.

There you are, up in Donnybrook with all the big noises, I'd hear as I walked through a pub door in Turlough. *Our own star of stage and screen.*

Clement would hear all the news from the lady who cooked and cleaned in the monastery. They were all talking about me being on the television. *She asked me what age you'd be,* he said, laughing quietly. *And I told her, around the thirty mark.*

Everywhere I went, from the hardware store to a walk up the Park Baun road, it was the first thing mentioned. *Last Sat'day, there you were with the high ups and our own Martina Cuniffe on a quiz program the same night. By Jayz, we were well represented.*

Back and forth I went, and it always seemed to rain on Sunday afternoon as I headed back to Dublin. As I dreaded the deep dark nights in Park Baun, I was glad to get back, though there was little point in the return either. I was suspended in fog and cloud, driving and driving, walking up the aisles of shops with a basket over my arm.

I wrote pieces on the imminent destruction of Ireland, the folly of road building, the death of culture, the disappearance of the landscape.

Once before a meeting of preservationists in an ancient house on the Dublin quays, one of the few left amid the cheap and tawdry apartment blocks, I climbed a ladder in a half renovated attic and looked out on the roofs of the city; how much it still looked, at least from that height, as it did from the window of my room at the northside hostel when I was sixteen. And I felt how small and hard my heart had become, like a tiny stone. I would not be able to save the old houses brick by brick, I would not succeed in saving the fields of North Galway. I saw the rooftops and felt how timid, how false, how terribly hidden I was.

Aix; 1999

Little squares with dry combed sand in the evening; the breath of the South; the generous roses. There could have been no place lovelier than Aix-en-Provence in late April, nor any greater contrast with the muddy, ravaged landscape of Turlough. The little apartment I stayed in in Aix was not lovely, but apart from that virtually everything, right down to the shop selling shampoo, was lovely once I stepped out the front door onto the street. I heard the little rushing sound of water as it passed down through the mouths of fountains. Old men sat and talked in the cool evening, though it was not yet truly hot even in the day. It was a place I should have come to long before.

Except for having seen too much of reproduced Cézanne all my life, the real thing in his actual town was marvelous. Right down to the color of shutters on the windows of country villas, each thing in that part of the world was seen to with care. The vats of wine at the side of the road, pouring a glassful from the little spouts, trying it, as it cost almost nothing, citrus, tart, and cold. The bright low bushes, the calm of the South, the beige stone, a startling blue against dry and muted green.

But God, what I was there for! To lecture on international trade matters. I couldn't manage that sort of subject in French, though I did launch into some half-remembered phrases by way of self introduction to the class. *You see, she can speak!* they whispered to one another, as if this showed some treachery on my part—but to then subject them to hearing about trade law in English! Good Lord, who could endure that, and why should we?

There, in Provence, to speak on trade, on trade! On industrial subsidies, on anti-dumping, all the while apologizing for the fact that I just could not handle that sort of thing in French. Surely they could appreciate that? But they were no longer listening—in fact, they had only listened for the first half hour or so and then put down their pens, indifferent, this would gain them nothing, and began to talk and laugh among themselves. What a bore! What a drag! Trade law in English!

Oh, they need the language practice, it will be fine, the course director had said, perfunctorily, it meant nothing to her either. I was there to provide some practical knowledge on how the world worked, maybe to aid their careers. If that was not the case, well, *huh, tant pis.*

Wait, don't misunderstand me, I am one of you, I wish I could have said. Instead, I continued with my notes, as dramatic a reading as I could make of it, page after page, painstakingly gone over at dawn, the WTO, *OMC to you,* I conceded, this got an upward glance from some, Oh that, sure, yeah, then back to something interesting, dates, intrigues, where to have lunch, ouch, it is so crowded everywhere.

Mais, ce que vous pouvez dire, vous dites bien, said the Aix Dean, charming and urbane. It was easier and certainly nicer to over-attribute, to assume the very best. And what he said was true of me always, as a matter of fact. That which I could say, I said well; it wasn't much of an achievement, but always true. I was picky about what I said, even the smallest thing. No clichés. No idiocies. I would give myself that one. But then again to be lecturing on a business law course; and about trade, trade!

The generous flowers of the sloping park, the tall gate, the tree-lined road with a casino at one end, restaurants up one side and down the other. The sun set late and pale cardigans came out; the shops drew their shutters.

My clothes were all wrong for the place. April in the Mediterranean world was not April in the West of Ireland. I had on dark tights—wrong, all wrong. A dark skirt—the wrong fabric, uncomfortable, frumpy shoes. My hair—a fright. Lipstick—too dark. My French; look, I had not really spoken French since high school, apart from the Molière plays at Saint Theo's, so what was I to do? I had oversold my French, and then was expected to shoot the breeze about trade policy—it was unfair. My jacket—too bulky, slung over the back of a restaurant chair; I wished that I could lose it, never to see it again. I normally went to great lengths to recover lost items, putting in phone calls to train stations, detailed verbal identification of how the sleeves had been hemmed, but this lot I would gladly have walked away from. *Alors, Aix, my gift to you.*

I was poorly dressed and it was awkward. Think summer, opening up into the mountains and the sea with such promise. If only I'd done Mediterranean studies, a PhD in the Mediterranean world, Phoenician aesthetics, stone iconography, inner sea and outer sea, wine red sunset. If only there is one life, why couldn't I have done Mediterranean studies? But of course, I had not. And here I was lecturing on you know, trade, trade rules, subsidies, dumping, dispute settlement. *Madame, ce que vous dites, vous le dites bien.*

It was a small city; I walked its circuit every evening. And then on the outskirts, an abrupt departure into the literal world of Cézanne. Trees lined the roads with perfect posture, grace and calm; the little villas held wine and olive parties; small terraced parts of houses jutting out over shimmering dry green.

I was poorly dressed, and nothing could hide it. A scruffy raincoat, dark heavy socks. I had shoved everything into my suitcase, not paying attention because there was little choice in the matter. I didn't have much by way of clothes. I didn't shop for clothes, nothing ever fit.

I needed a dress, needed to have my hair done, clipped away into some sort of shape, the tousled mane look would not make it here.

I visited a town that seemed to be carved all out of one block of stone, the houses all connected, the church, the town hall. The breezes at the top of the hill were tremendous, dry and sloughing, the world far below, the hot inland behind me, the crowded, overly desirable and seductive sea in front. Why, why such a waste, when I could have been setting out olives, tomatoes, bread and oil. Somehow it was all forbidden to me; a door marked do not enter; the beauty itself designed to pain, not please. Microfibre black trousers, a black sweater. Families stopped at the lookout point, tumbling out, pre-divorce, post-divorce, happy after a fashion, chic, pleasantly fatigued.

At the weekend, I saw the outdoor markets in Aix, saw them setting up and setting out all the shining blue kitchen ware, the bolts of cloth, the crisp emblems stamped across shining white. Mountains of fruit, scent of coffee. At the corner café, the coffee I would have invented in a dream, the steaming milk, the wide bowl.

More than would have been the case when I was young—it would have been quite the opposite—I saw in the sky over Aix, in perfect lettering, the simple message, *Non.*

The worst moment came at a faculty dinner held at a painfully quiet restaurant several miles from the town. My French, as the Dean had indicated, sounded good, but was soon dismissed as inadequate for discussing architecture or the true origin of the Ligurians. After a while, I could not get away with such remarks as: Oh, tell me more about that, or, I had not thought of it that way! At the end of what seemed the longest meal ever endured, the Dean turned to me and asked if I would kindly order the cheese for all. My God, it was meant as a kindness! The cheese! At a table of mistralian academics! I crumbled in despair, waved my hands. It had gone too far. Cheese! What was I to say, That white one here, that yellowy one there? Impossible, the cheese!

On the next to the last day, the teachers in the business law program took me to lunch at one of the student eateries. We sat in the sun, the gentle wind tickling at the crowd, the plastic table cloths, the stunted trees. One of the teachers, I cannot recall her name, was dressed impeccably in matching grey and pink, grey suit and pink accessories, pink hairband and smooth hair. She took out photos of her husband and baby, having to hold onto them carefully in the wind. She seemed to have no interest in the business law end of things, which was to her credit, and didn't mention the OMC or European antitrust. Rather, there in her perfect late spring ensemble, she showed us her baby and smiled indulgently at the photo.

She looked up at me; how serious I felt, how impossible to explain the least thing about myself, where I was from, why and how I had arrived there, what I had thought of the place. How much work it would have been, and how little will on anyone's part to bring about that kind of knowing. I hadn't the optimism or the lightheartedness that allows for instant friendships, phone numbers exchanged, husbands encouraged to bond in a game of squash or over a beer. And oh, my dark clothes.

And you, she asked, all brightness and good cheer, *and you, do you have children, Madame?*

My first thought was that no, I wasn't allowed to. Mommy said I couldn't.

No kids for me, I had to stay a little girl myself, or else someone might be mad at me.

You see how it is?

No, I replied to the perky, perfect young teacher who had much more and better things to think about than world trade and European business. *I don't have children, I'm afraid.*

Would it have seemed absurd at my age to add, not yet?

I hated leaving it on that note of tragedy, regret, *I'm afraid that*, as if something unkind had interfered, and here I was, in my bad clothes, no photos to show. As if I were inviting their sympathy.

It reminded me of the time I went to a midlands wedding with Seanie, when in the course of the ceremony the priest asked the couple, *And will you accept and raise all the children that the Lord might send to you?* I leaned over to Seanie and asked, *How old are they?* as they certainly did not look young. *Somewhere in the forties,* he said, with no sense that anything was amiss in the dialogue.

She no doubt expected me to say, Yes, I've two college age, all grown up, and here I was thinking, Not yet. No, not yet!

And it was then, at that moment, in Aix-en-Provence, that I decided I would never answer that question in that way again. I would be able to answer, *Yes, I do; I do, too.*

Air East; end of 1999

All through the night we had waited at the airport in Moscow; we couldn't understand the flight announcements, and there were no chairs. Stray cats roamed about. Finally, panicked about missing our flight, an announcement was made and we jumped up and started to follow another group down a dark corridor toward the outside door. A kindly man stopped us and gestured to us to go back.

Going to Uzbekistan, he said emphatically, *Uzbekistan.*

When our flight was finally called, at around two in the morning, we walked out into a cold that I had never felt before, not even in Vermont in my young days. We had to get across the sweeping tarmac ourselves, and climb the stairs of a plane that sat, dark and deserted, in the middle of the frozen asphalt. The night was clear, deep marine blue and prickly with cold. After a long wait, a kind of giant Bunsen burner removed the ice from the wings and off we went, a peaceful and calm flight across Central Asia.

In the morning, I looked down and saw nothing but white, with here and there some tall grass sticking up from the drifts. Animals moved about; were they dogs or horses, I wasn't sure. Then there were the tops of small houses, and we landed. The airport was dark, no lights turned on yet. We filled out customs forms in the dark, filling in answers for Russian questions we couldn't read. The bus that came to meet us had broken windows. It was the early days, perhaps the worst days, of the Central Asian post-Soviet transition; it was bleak but vast; grim but sparkling. I was going to get Madina.

How bright and hopeful she looked in the little grey photo; looking up at something, a faint smile on her face. Why had she spent so long in the orphanage; I wasn't sure. She was a big two year old, sturdy and strong. You could well imagine her learning to ride a horse, braving a snowstorm.

From my first step inside the orphanage, I could smell the cooking, the soup, the potatoes and cabbage on the boil for hours. There were heavy-set ladies in white coats, their faces a mélange of East and West, Asian women in Russian-style make up and rubber-soled shoes. The windows were large, and looked out onto bright stars of snow, bare trees, apartment buildings set in sparkling courtyards. It seemed that little shoveling was ever done, except at hotels and public buildings, and I would come to find out that it snowed nearly every night. Sometimes the planes flew in, and sometimes not. Sometimes the trains ran, and sometimes not.

I heard Madina before I saw her; of all the children they brought in to meet families, only she was wailing. They told me that the several words she kept shouting meant, *I don't want to, I don't want to.* She was dressed up in a fancy skirt and shoes too tight, a large bow on top of her head. How hardy she looked, how sturdy. They put her on my lap and she lay still, cautious, wary. She began to play with my pen, clicking it open and shut. I clicked it back at her and she laughed. The tears had disappeared. She looked up at me; I seemed all right. She seemed to have concluded that, and began to rummage in my pockets.

They brought me back to see her later in the day. She was getting ready for the long, long naptime the children had every afternoon. She spotted me from far away and, sitting up on her little bed, in a row of many other little beds, she smiled her biggest smile and waved as hard as she could.

The hotel was big and cavernous; apart from the other families traveling with me, there were few guests. They told us that this was the hotel the cosmonauts stayed at when in Kazakhstan. Every morning the trees were covered with bright bluish-white snow; we bought bread and cookies from the baker in the tall hat. Ice and snow built up on the walkways between buildings and it was hard to keep from falling. Outside it was routinely zero to ten below. Even so, elderly ladies sold hot items from little braziers at the side of the road; some kind of nuts perhaps. They put their hands out over the bit of fire and waited for customers.

Day after day, morning and afternoon, I visited Madina in the orphanage. While the other children played ball and blew bubbles, Madina wanted only two things: my wallet full of cards and my makeup case. She would rub the cream all over her cheeks, and then move busily on to the credit cards, spilling them out to look at each in turn. She walked with one arm hitched up at her side, swinging comically back and forth. Her dull black hair was cut in orphanage regulation style, up and around her ears; her clothes looked small for her.

One day her group was putting on a little dance we were meant to attend. We arrived late, and all the other children were up and dancing to the Russian tune being played on the piano, but not Madina. She sat in her navy sailor pinafore, a great white bow in her hair, crying her eyes out and shaking her head no. When she saw me, she jumped up, smiling through her tears, and held out her arms. I picked her up and danced among the other children, holding her high off the floor.

During regular visits to the room where her *grupa* stayed, the other children would gather around, lifting their arms up in the air, begging to be held. Madina would push them down and away from us, like a soldier defending a fort; their faces would remain turned up, hopeful, tear stained. When it was time for me to go, Madina would turn wild, kicking her legs and rolling on the ground.

And then at times she hardly seemed to know me or care; she would run after other adults, hedging her bets.

She had been in that building for almost three years, after all, through long winters and hot summers. How could she really know who I was? On the good side, whenever she got her hands dirty, she would come to me with them held up in front of her, asking me silently to clean them. She knew her way all around the orphanage, and would take me by the hand, tugging me after her, up the staircase past the cartoon mural. I held her up to the window to look out at the snow. It was familiar to her; she knew about snow.

From that time forward, Madina and I spent five years together every moment, on planes and in apartments, at Park Baun and Boston, always together, Mutt and Jeff, me carrying her until she was nearly as big as I was. For five years, it was everything Madina wanted, every minute; until, that is, I went to get Emmet.

On her first night out of the orphanage, Madina got quietly out of bed and dressed herself. She found her coat, put her boots on the wrong feet and stood by the door, waiting patiently to be let out. She must have thought she should return to the orphanage. When I tried to get her back to bed, she stiffened up and cried, not knowing where she was or where she was going.

Several days later, she stepped through the metal detector at the airport in her provincial home town, and danced out into the light that came through the plate glass window, with bright snow spread out before her. She hopped back and forth in her red coat, pointing. It was fun to be naughty, she realized. From then on, for five years, it was all Madina's way.

I often said later that with Emmet you could not get him into a stroller, and with Madina you could not get her out. She liked to get a ride, all around the city, into shops, up hill and down dale. But when it came time to jump out and play ball or roll down a hill, she pouted, digging in her heels and pointing to the stroller. She loved her ride; quiet, peaceful, looking around. I would let her choose the hair clips for the day, and she wanted lots of them; kips, she called them, all colors and shapes.

On her first day of preschool back in Dublin, we walked together into the old brick building. I had been telling her about "school;" she would be going to school and wouldn't that be fun. We packed her a bag, and along she came. As we stepped inside the door, she got the scent of children, groups of children; the milk, the food, the spills, the diapers. As soon as she smelled it, she began to howl. She raced for the door and covered her face, kicking, resisting any attempt to turn her around to look. It was a smell she knew very well, the kind of place she remembered.

I managed to leave her there in any case. By the time I got back in late afternoon, she had positioned herself with a big box of toys, sitting at a table with her arms linked possessively around it. She saw me and seemed surprised; maybe she'd thought I wasn't coming back. Maybe she had decided that this would be it, and she looked up at me from a long way off and shook her head resolutely. Mine, she seemed to be saying. My box.

I sat on the rocks at Sandymount, looking out over the bay. Madina dug in the sand with her new shovel, bright green. She was deathly afraid of dogs, and would climb right up onto my head when one came near her. She wore her dark yellow sweatshirt with the zip and hood; her sturdy shoes were caked with wet sand; the shovel went up and down, not very convincingly. It was hard sand, packed down flat and hard all along the narrow beach.

I spoiled her, I guess; it was just the two of us, after all. I felt it keenly when she was cross and when she was happy. I marveled over her every new word and every drawing. I held her hand and walked her from room to room. We went on trips together, down to West Cork, where she ate her lunch on the brow of a hill overlooking the sea, squinting into the sun. Madina was never to be left uncomforted, or lonely. Still, there was something in her, a sadness that moved slowly, always hidden from view, a reluctance.

Mama, Tubby Tubbies is on, she cried, running from the television and back to me. *Tubby Tubbies! Tubby Tubbies!*

Her love for Dipsy, or was it La La, was fierce and intense, unshakable and relentless. When the Teletubbies appeared on the television, she could hardly believe her good luck.

One day she tapped her hand on the wall of the apartment, then on a side table.

Dis is Dina house, she said in wonder. Then she tapped her hand on me. *Dis is Dina mama.*

The road; 2007

They drive fast, Vermonters. Una always said so, and Una was right. They drove like wildfire up and down the road that went past the Lakeview Inn. The Inn had been closed for a couple of years; it troubled me. I worried about it. In years gone by, during our week or two up here, we used to go get our coffee inside the Inn and then sit on the porch, half pretending to be residents. I often went with Sven, who was always up for an outing like that, especially one that involved escaping for a few minutes from the kids.

Why didn't anyone buy it, I kept wondering. Una had joked that we should buy it and run it, but God, could you imagine. Guests from Montreal or Indiana throwing up in the bedrooms, domestic quarrels, fussing about bills, trying to keep the restaurant stocked with food. I had enough trouble remembering to buy Cascade for the dishwasher.

Still, some people like those things; why didn't anyone drive by, see that long, long and utterly wonderful view of the lake from the road as you enter Greensboro and say, By George, we'll take it and run it! Such things happened all the time; or was that the case only in poorly written novels, where a plot conceit is urgently needed?

It seemed the Miller's Thumb, the gift shop where we spent so much time, and so little actual money, every summer, was also to close. Only Willey's would be left, but Willey's at least would never close. And the little post office. It was a short drive to Hardwick, to a book store and the diner. Still, it wasn't nice to think of Greensboro as, well, going out of business. There was the ice cream place; the kids loved that, though it was strictly seasonal. There was the Greensboro Free Library, where Hughie and Madina used to go to pajama parties during vacation weeks when they were little, and where I now gravitated to check out the internet and see who if anyone had written to me.

The same houses were on the market; a funny thing was that they could be on the market for years on end, yet no one ever dropped a price.

The paint was peeling a bit on our house; the owner really needed to do something with it; the front porch, the door frame. Madina always wanted to open the door herself, but it was a difficult lock and it stuck. She would give up and hand the key back to me, cross and pouting.

I liked being up high; that was why I had always liked this house, even before, when I could not have imagined we would be living in it. It looked down over the Grange Hall and the lake, the meadows. I would get depressed in a house down too low or too flat; there had to be something going on in the landscape that had me moving along with it; there had to be motion, activity, a rise, a vista. I hated to see houses built in the trees, especially in a valley. A brown log house in the brown trees on the brown dirt; nothing would make me want to get away from folks enough to make that attractive.

In our white house with the peeling paint we sat in the front window where I had moved the table; we sat and ate our dinner. If you asked Emmet his favorite food, he would tell you, *Tofu.*

Madina; 2000

She never knew that it was even going on; I fibbed to her about it from the beginning, as I couldn't bear to have her worry.

It was the blood test that showed the Irish doctors something was wrong, but nothing they could figure out. My view of Irish doctors was that, without touching you at all, they simply asked you what was wrong and what you thought it might be yourself. There were two approaches to being Irish and dealing with the medical men: see them ridiculously often, or hardly at all, maybe just for the odd sore throat, go get a Lemsip recommended. I was in the latter category; my mother and her cousins in Ireland in the former.

She may have a disease of the liver, the young doctor at the children's hospital was saying; the color was no doubt draining from my face. She was sick, strong little Madina was sick and it could be serious. Strong like a young pony or a camel, Madina was sick and we needed to find out what it really was.

Back and forth to doctors and clinics we went; sending blood samples through the post to England, writing to foundations, reading up on symptoms. The young specialist hemmed and hawed; he wasn't sure.

I pretended that everyone got this many blood tests; see, Mommy got them too, and ouch they did hurt. How she cried, Madina, her round face red, her mouth open wide in misery. The doctor urged me to take her out of the preschool, to place her in private care until we got to the bottom of things. Poor Madina, strong Madina in her red coat, singing along with all the songs at her school, making the gestures so nicely for *Wheels on the Bus, round and round, swish, swish, swish.* I drove her all around the city in the rain, trying to find out what was wrong. She sat so patiently in her plaid car seat, looking out at the changing scene, growing sleepy, her head falling sideways until she was fast asleep.

Madina liked to go to Park Baun. I put her to bed in the room with the small hand- carved mantelpiece and stone fireplace. I would make a lovely fire before putting her to bed, and lie down to trick her into thinking it was my bedtime then, too. As she slept, the firelight played on her face and hands. The wind was noisy in the tall evergreen tree that stood near the gate at the road.

The young specialist did not know what was wrong

with Madina, but there was something worse than that about it. He really didn't care much. Not to sound like Gramma, but in fact he did not care. For him, it was a bit of a nuisance, this child plucked from another part of the world and brought to him for some kind of insight.

Were they related, her parents? he asked me off handedly.

What do you mean?

There could be some genetic link, you know, carriers. Were they of the same family?

Instead of lab reports, the doctors sent letters, typed by their assistants, round to one another. Doctor such and such feels that it is not such and such, it is more likely to be such and such; the like of that. Had they looked at the labs and cut out the letterhead, we might have found out a bit faster what on earth it was about.

I heard of an opening from an American lecturer I knew at Trinity. He'd been offered a visitorship at a law school in New York, then had to call it off, and would I be interested by any chance. It would start in just a few weeks, but he would put in a good word for me if I wanted. I was already packing my bags, sorting and tossing. After seven years I was going back.

Health insurance, does health insurance go along with it? I was asking their personnel department. *Will I have coverage for my child?*

Yes, they assured me I would.

Completely, no carve outs, no exceptions? I asked them again and again.

Yes, they repeated, everything, no exceptions.

I arranged for a Dublin solicitor to cover my courses, and told the Dean I wanted a leave of absence. After six or seven years of teaching in the castle, I knew I would not be back. I didn't care what I would have to teach in New York, or whether American casebooks were familiar any more. I had to get Madina to America, I had to find out what was wrong.

We arrived in Brooklyn in a huge snow storm. From our apartment, we could see the Statue of Liberty. Enormous barges passed by right under our windows. Across the way was the Manhattan skyline. I would teach something, something or other, European Union, Trade, International Business Law, anything, just so long as Madina would be well.

New York City; 2001

After every visit to the hospital, we got off the subway mid journey to stop at a toy store. I let Madina pick out anything she wanted. We would trundle back onto the train, carrying in turn a plush horsie on a stick, a big plastic doll house, a Madeline doll with a real blue boat and straw hat.

The American doctors had figured out in twenty four hours what was wrong; it wasn't good, but we could live with it. Madina would have to be monitored. She had no idea, of course; I told her we were checking her tummy to make sure that something she'd had as a baby was all better.

Meanwhile, I had to teach American law students. I had only days to get ready; I hadn't taught from those chopped up casebooks before, and I'd forgotten the system. I'd also forgotten how in your face the American law students were, how demanding, how skeptical. I got out of bed as quietly as I could at four a.m., setting out my books and notes on the kitchen table that overlooked the river and the Statute of Liberty, and began the long slog that was the start of the story of the rest of my life. Details and more details, cases and more cases. And out would come Madina, rubbing her eyes and whimpering, *Me come too.*

What did anyone mean when they said they loved it; loved it, of all things? To love law teaching, love a law school; have you hugged a law school today? Whatever about lecturing in the castle, fearing that all the students would drop my course at once and I'd be left talking to an empty room, compared to this that had been easy as pie, reading from my notes, sometimes funny, sometimes impassioned, sometimes outright boring, as what could you do with the Sale of Goods Act? But this was something different, the anger in the room and the silent accusations, the awful smell of ironed white shirts after a full day of wear in an office. It's for you, Madina, I am walking into the classroom like a robot, my past is gone and I am not really here, I am a lost soul, but I will continue to do it, just for you.

I could still hear Alberti, faintly.

What leaves and never returns:
Wind that in shadow
Dies down and flares up.
Look for me in the snow.

I didn't think or write a word, there was no room for anything but to read on in the casebook, read ahead, make notes on the issues, ask questions upon questions, What about, and did you consider, and what if? That was the worst one of all, What if, what if the case had been brought in such and such a place, what if the plaintiff had actually told them such and such a thing, God I don't know, I've enough trouble with the this is, never mind the feckin' what ifs, but I had to pretend that I loved it, loved the what ifs.

There came the one I wanted,
The one I called for.

Was I dreaming it, that I sent out a few letters, half-heartedly, without any real hope of escape, to say that I wished to reenter an old orbit, that I was seeking a position as a, well, combination poet thinker lover of art and writer of verse, ancient and young, wise and foolish, ready to teach on a light schedule, not too much wear and tear on the psyche if you please, shall teach readily and upon your application anything from the theory of courtly love to the self negation of the Japanese artistic will, narrative and sanity, highways of the soul, if that does not make up a course as you would like to see it appear on your course catalogue, make me an offer and we can always discuss it, I am easy, easier than you could ever imagine. In short, I can and will teach anything at all, anything; anti-narrative surrealism, *Eva Trout*, John Donne (shall try), goodness but only if I truly have to Edgar Allen Poe.

A couple of professors wrote back, as I had only sent out a few and far too hesitantly, that I was just the sort of person the world should be seeking out and seeking out with a vengeance; I could not agree with you more, I thought, but alas, it is not turning out that way. The world should be beating down your door, one wrote. Indeed. As for the job ads, all I could come up with were notices for applicants for the position of, say, Visiting Assistant

Professor of Acupuncture; Associate Dean of Budget and Accounts; Adjunct Lecturer in Bacterial Science.

I prayed for Madina and she got well; miraculously and suddenly well. Her illness blew away on a sweet breeze. As we were checking into a New York hospital for her treatment, the doctor came rushing into the room.

Hold on! he cried. *The blood tests are normal; everything has fallen back into normal range; she is fine, you can go.*

I had convinced her that the hospital stay was going to be great fun, a real lark, and so she was a little miffed at not seeing the clown. I hustled her out to the taxi stand on an Upper East Side street, and held her close as we drove down, down across Manhattan. Sturdy little Madina, made to ride horses on the steppe; we had been touched by divine kindness.

The Red Line; 2001

I came to earth with a thud somewhere in Boston; they hired me to teach trade and European things and international transactions; it sounded awful, the word transactions. I would have said they wanted me to, but whether they wanted me at all remained an open question. Who were they looking for when they found me? They always spoke in terms of "pools" of people, a deep pool or a shallow pool, how superior or inferior the pool, whether few or many had applied and whether they had enough "comparison" and choice.

It seemed funny to think of people that way, résumés and pools, great for us if we can compare them one to the other, woe betide if we have too few to put one next to the other, as in a line up. It made no sense to me, but then, I likely made none to them either. Couldn't you remember those you'd met before, and just quietly compare in your own mind, the way we tend to do anyway when meeting people in any other context, put them in the basket of other memories of people, how they look and talk. This was something else, the references and numerical evaluations telling whether they'd scored a 3 or a 5 when observers were asked, *Would you recommend this person to others?* for God's sake.

And what about that one from Ireland, hardly a bit of teaching in an ABA-accredited institution, no clerkships, no practice experience even; what has she done with the international bar? Will she bring in conferences, moot court teams, foot traffic generally to the law school? Alas, no, my principal impulse was to hide beneath my desk.

I wonder why I worried so much about survival. It was a character flaw that would dog me every step of the way, though it wasn't part of my conscious life in my younger days. Back then, I would have spent hundreds on a phone bill without blinking an eye, or headed off to the airport with a wad of bills and sorted out where I might go once I got there. As time went on, maybe I developed the Swedish hostage syndrome or whatever it was called; the sense of identifying with my own captivity. But that is too hard on me; I would have left it, if I had seen anything beckoning. I did write letters, if half heartedly, as I said. Reading about those *transactions* was hard, though. God, I'd already spent so much time on that kind of stuff.

Madina and I went everywhere together. At her insistence, I carried her about in my arms, even when she was a big kindergarten girl. She would help out by sort of hopping up on me and making herself lighter. We went to the pizza shop at the end of our street in Cambridge; we spent endless hours in the playground where she tried again and again to go all the way across on the monkey bars. Our third floor apartment would get roasting hot on a warm day; the roof baked in the sun and even our floors were hot to the touch, but she never complained. She was spoiled, she was happy. She drew pictures and played with her Barbie furniture on the floor in the corner.

Often she would wheel over her empty baby stroller and say, *Bye bye Mommy, I am going to Kazakhstan to get a baby now*, and off she would go into her room, returning a few minutes later with one of her little dolls all wrapped up. It was easy to make her happy in those days in Cambridge.

I didn't so much live through the seasons as worry through them; I was getting older, my spirits rose when the birds began to sing again after the long winter; I treasured the first snow; the first autumn breeze, the first day of summer, Memorial Day, Labor Day, all were occasions to lament the passing of time, and yet I actually enjoyed nothing. I hated every day for what it was and treasured every day for what I knew it could be but stayed separate from me in some dazzling other world behind a pale curtain.

Madina, you are pushing too many times with your foot, push off once and then glide the scooter, glide and glide the scooter, that's what it's for, I told her. Still, in frustration, she worked the scooter forward, pushing her foot once, twice, three times, and almost falling sideways.

The very day after Thanksgiving started the Christmas season; we decorated the attic apartment, putting white lights all around every window. Madina wanted to be the very first to buy a tree at the corner stand. I would carry it home over my shoulder and haul it up the two long flights of stairs.

I dreaded each appearance in the classroom, and hated the words *jurisdiction, countertrade*, and *doctrinal. Decanal* was another word I couldn't stand. Just as in law school I had hated *eggshell plaintiff* and *pareto optimality*. I hated to hear people say they *loved teaching;* hated being expected to say it myself. To love the classroom, love being the boss, the one up front talking about confirmed letter of credit; were they mad? All I wanted, after all, was rescue, adoration, revelation and transcendent, possessive joy. September rain chased the heat of summer, then on to the deep fall and into winter, summer, winter, summer, the people on the T a throwback to Czarist Russia, sullen and down-trodden.

I'd never felt especially American, God knows, let alone in a crowd of lawyers. I thought of the tigers Madina and I had seen at the Franklin Park Zoo, white tigers with pale stripes, pacing, pacing back and forth at the wall, first to the right and then to the left. Did the tigers expect something to happen, or was it just habit, or was there just no choice but to continue pacing?

Between Daddy's notion of kindness and Gramma's brandy on a rainy afternoon, nothing had prepared me for this utter emptiness, the desert of sounds and concepts. When the very first birds returned in the spring and began to sing at four or four thirty, I cried with gratitude to them. I thought of the long winter and the silence without them. I remembered the long green lawn at our pale stucco house in upstate New York and my summer dress; I had never known how to turn that vision into a life in the day to day. I had no idea still.

And if you get hit with a tennis ball, who may you sue and how many days do you have and what if the tennis ball is made in Liberia but got a stamp on it in Taiwan, who can you sue now and same facts what if the phone rings and the assistant picks it up but there is a defect in the phone and the notice is given but never heard, do you see analogies with the tree falling in the forest, then who is liable. Who can you sue if you drop your briefcase with all your papers in the street then someone finds them and doesn't return them but you intended to live another life but didn't.

The mockingbird; 2007

Calvin—I know you don't answer me much and there are various theories as to why—as between Una and myself. Are you threatened or are you just bored or have you gone into some other zone where it doesn't matter? Didn't you write me a poem about birds once, that I could raise birds to a whisper or some such? I am bowled over by the birds this spring—as if I never heard them before. They work so hard at it; they sing from 4:30 on; the world is filled with this birdsong. Madina drew a picture of birds and wrote Te Te Te for tweet. By the way, I am teaching at Stannard again in the fall and getting ready with what I will give them to read—my idea is to make it about narrative and sanity—I had this idea and it explains everything—deviation from or coming in nearer to the desired narrative as the measure of joy—it really makes everything clear; I can explain it to you some time.

Calvin wrote back that he could hang in there without having narrative and sanity explained to him, but in fact it did make everything clear for me.

I could get Emmet interested in the birds. In the early morning, I would whisper, *Who is calling you?* And he would say, his shallow eyelids still cloudy with sleep, *Birdies.*

Had they always started in so early, in years gone by? I had no recollection of such an extraordinary thing; what were they doing up at that hour. There had to be a story and it was according to the story that we chose or rejected things; we feared counter narrative and fought against it. Some had a small, narrow sense of narrative; maybe it was just that they had a boring narrative; and others were nearly overwhelmed by the strength of one.

As for the mockingbird, it seemed to me that I could talk to it. There was a mockingbird that sang the first two bars of *All Around the Mulberry Bush,* over and over, starting at dawn and sometimes on into the dusk, *All Around, whoop whoop.* I began to answer him, *The Monkey Chased the Weasel whoop whoop.* I sat on the little front porch with my coffee and chatted back and forth to the mockingbird.

At least I imagined it was a mockingbird; perhaps I was wrong on this. I'd read that mockingbirds were mimics and they seemed to have some ability to connect with people and play tricks on them. Maybe they did no such thing; maybe someone wrote that after too many bourbons, I've no idea. I couldn't see any actual bird, as they stayed well hidden in the trees.

At Park Baun, the birds were incomparable, the trees had been lush with them, teeming. Hence the fox hole and the feathers that festooned the grassy place in the ground where the fox's world went underground. An endless supply, I suppose he thought. The farmers hated both foxes and badgers, the last vestiges of wild life in

Ireland, pretty much everything truly wild long gone, gone for several hundred years, all those people crowded in, trying to get as much out of every square patch of ground as they could; what could thrive? But the birds; they must have sailed high, forgiving, enjoying the scenery as much as ever a person did.

It was resilient, the narrative, the story line.

It could get by without much in the way of substance, but what it couldn't brook was real opposition in the way of facts on the ground, a contrary story line. I mean, you could endure endless hours of boredom and emptiness, holding onto your tattered narrative like a child going to preschool clutching a beloved rag doll; but let the wrong person so much as breathe on you or lay a hand on your arm and horrors, that was an intolerable thing.

I had to wear my same boring clothes, black, white, white, black, odd times the slightest hint of navy blue, back to black, white, beige, black. My hair was parted the same way, as far back as college, high school even, the same hair do, the same black slacks. And lipstick, even when spending the evening with just myself.

Mommy, you have lipstick on? asked Emmet, who disliked sticky things.

No, I would lie.

Then he, not believing, would run his finger along my lip and stare, investigative, unsure and suspicious.

My favorite thing as a child was to go to bed on a summer's evening, too light to really sleep, imagining the birds, at one with them in the second floor room I shared with Una.

When my mother had said goodnight and Una had probably drifted off; faded flowers on the wallpaper, darkening at last. I could last through a lot; but I would not let anything *hors de narrative* touch me.

Tokyo at a distance; still there, 2007

The Greensboro Free library could get awfully quiet of an afternoon. I hadn't yet invested in a computer for the house; I had something against screens, how they pulled you in. But I could spend a few minutes at the computer in the library and find out what was going on from Galway to Ulaan Bataar. I could even spend some time back in Tokyo, though I feared remembering most of that, me in a white dress on the platform at Ochanomizu on a hot day, an unbearably hot day, the smell of tea literally baking in the heat of the station market. The crowded streets, the kissaten. It was a mental excursion I could not allow myself often.

It is a funny thing, the internet. What you can find there.

I hadn't sought him out in any way, and we had parted company one cold and dreary winter's day in Tokyo; whether he had made a silent promise to return would remain a mystery, and it is imperative that at some point you lose interest in solving such a mystery. It was demeaning to want to know too much. What's more, or on the other hand, there was always a grave danger of assuming the wrong things, and trusting too much to one's intuition.

It was a different take on things, what I found about Kido on the internet.

The children were off at school and day care and I was free to wander around the town, listen to the radio, work on my poetry cycle. And, maybe due to that self-destructive character flaw, I went to the Greensboro Free and had a look to see what Kido had been up to in recent years.

Elizabeth Bowen I think it was wrote that with respect to the young war dead, they didn't simply die, as we always had the sense of living out their time along with our own; that we were aware of the time they ought to have had but didn't. Thinking of Kido was like that for me; I had assumed something was broken off between us, unresolved cruelly, forcibly. I had assumed that this reinforced his earlier sense of tragedy and frustration. Even as I gravitated to thoughts of Kido, I avoided him.

I assumed all the while that Kido loved me.

And then I checked off the years for him and for me; his children were growing up, then grew up, and still no Kido. A few years, then more years, a decade, two decades, and still no Kido.

Maybe he was too old and tired and worn down or maybe simply the desire of that time had disappeared, though I wasn't sure what that would feel like for him. I didn't ponder it too much, as that would be demeaning. Degrading to wonder, impossible not to wonder.

And then there, on the computer, there they were, his family, his wife's blog, his own photos and silly interviews and it was as if, after all these years, Kido died at last for me. Right there in the Greensboro Free Library.

Maybe I'd just given him ideas for a few great songs way back when, more profit for the production company.

It was his wife's blog that did it first. A blog; how did I stumble on it?

As unlikely as it would have been to have Kido turn up at the front door now, with the bloom of youth more or less entirely faded, still I had no idea things were this bad.

These days, he was apparently making songs and selling them along with cosmetic products.

Una had often said, *When a man wants something, he will step over his own grandmother to get it.* I'd made a million excuses for him on this score: the Japanese sense of obligation, Japanese repression of the artist, the fear of condemnation, the fear of losing everything, the tyrannical record companies, the refusal of the wife to divorce, the fact that he would not see his children if he left them, on and on, so on and so forth. When in fact, Una had it right, and I hated to admit it now, when I had less to fall back on than ever before. Una with her less noble vision had it right: If Kido had really wanted to, he could have come to get me. We could have married. He would have been at my door decades ago; he would have done more than used my letters as a basis for a hit song or two.

Now, as he got older, he seemed to be writing songs that doubled as jingles for face powder and lipstick.

On this ultimate point at least, Una had been correct.

I'd never thought much about Kido's wife, having decided early on that she was irrelevant to Kido and me and that somehow that marriage of his had happened, but was not something to spend time contemplating. Well, she more than made up for this by writing about virtually everything she did, every day, on her blog.

A blog, a blog about your own daily life, can you imagine. In her case, it seemed a good move, I had to admit. Going to the spa, drinking carrot juice, flashing around bills for hotel facials and bath salts, new shoes, designer sunglasses. And not just that—still clips from foreign movies, fashion shows, photo shoots featuring herself—and she was not young any longer; she was older than me.

There was frequent mention of the "great Kido-san," her dear husband. There were links to interviews in which she wept over how wonderful it was to have been born Japanese. There was something deeply maudlin about it; resounding praise for various singers and actors, how marvelous they were, how she loved and adored them; profound thanks for all they had done, how she loved loved loved them; happiness sublime that they could all see each other and share profound moments of mutual thanks and such like.

Yikes. Waiting twenty-five years and more had perhaps been unwise.

In interviews, she told of how she'd fallen ill several years before, and how Kido had rushed to her side and spent every day in the hospital, watching her for signs of recovery. Her dear children, her dear husband.

Kido, as I remembered him disappearing under the heavy trees on a hot Tokyo night, and my own thought that I would somehow marry him and we would have all the messy troublesome stuff that went with it; I had been ready. I hadn't wanted to escape from Kido, it was the one time I had not wanted to escape.

But then again, I never had the option, and who knows.

After years of being kept in the shadows, Kido's wife was blogging away, photos of herself at various luxury *onsen* resorts, going to rock concerts, attending receptions put on by fashion companies. Which brand of sunglasses, which brand of sneakers, was best.

Well, whatever.

More power to her, I guess.

I left the Greensboro Free in a daze.

Kido had died at last.

Kido was gone. There was no red thread of destiny, there was no aura or sense of shared genius. Well, I had waited more than twenty years at my peril.

No promises broken, as he hadn't made any. Not even the courage or dash to be a cad. I gave him ideas for a few wonderful songs; I had believed as I watched him sing them that he loved me in an irreplaceable way. Well, that was twenty years ago, more.

His children were grown up, in the entertainment business in their own right, his wife was out and about, wearing a great reddish wig, net gloves like a teenager might wear. More power to you, *Okusama*. Una had been right. A man would step over his own grandmother to get what he truly wanted.

All my theories on Japanese life seemed very long past and more or less useless; the lack of necessary oppositions in that life; such as, artist versus non-artist, men versus women, groups and clubs as against the courageous seeker of absolute love, the pair of us standing, as it had been in my Japanese tale, on the bridge in Paris.

He liked the very first love letter I wrote to him, way back then, when my ex- husband Yukito, poor man, had not answered his own phone, but rather I did, and with the duplicity and sneakiness of which I was so capable then, I'd answered instead and said, *Yes, I am Catherine, I wrote to you, yes.*

So we met, and kissed, and touched in that particular life-changing way. I won't make any grand statements about how I know that much to be true, but something was, surely. I won't go as far as Yukito or Una and say that it was all just rubbish and nonsense.

Yet stay at home Kido did, subjecting himself to those

awful Japanese interviews, where the interviewer says, *And what do you like for breakfast,* and the interviewee pauses and laughs nervously and replies at last, *Well, I do like a bit of miso soup,* and the interviewer—or maybe two or three of them—falls over with surprise and says, *Hey, wow, is that right, my my, whoa...*

And oh, Kido-san, you wouldn't be the type who could, well, make it yourself...?

Hmm, perhaps I could...

And more oohs and ahhs and feigned shock and amazement by the interviewers. He stayed for that and must in some way have liked it, the attention, the fawning, the basement bars in Tokyo where he would slither in, wearing sunglasses all the time, day or night, seeing his fellow travelers in the "entertainment world."

And Lord, while I was on it, why did I choose Japan of all places? It could have been France, where love and rebellion went hand in hand; poetry and street demonstrations, Leo Ferré singing *Avec Le Temps.* No, I had to choose Japan, with its salary men dying of overwork, its artists hopping in rivers to make sure that no untoward behavior could erupt from the soul or psyche. And not only that, to have in the back of my mind for twenty-five years that I might, in my silent way, overcome it all, by the very power of my self.

In most Japanese dramas the only plot element was a secret, and only about fifty words were used in an entire ten-part series—*How are you, Hmm, It's a little sad, but well, How are you, let's try hard, let's.*

It could have been Greece, Sardinia, Corsica or Lake Como—but no, it was Japan. Enduring the rainy season, dazzled by summer, short, sweet and over so quickly, I chose the greatest genius and then over time, silently and without apparent reference to me at all, watched the almost wordless connection unravel.

What a fool you've been, Gramma would have said, as she would have to anyone who'd had an affair that went nowhere, except that this was not even an affair properly so called, but something infinitely more bizarre and more about my own unvarying inability to trick joy out of silence.

And if we had been together, Kido and I. What did I want it for, what had I been thinking of?

Well, it went something along the line of messages. I thought that there were unspoken messages one could not send *unless*; unless he had been a great genius and in desperate need of uniting the imagined with the real, he could not have written and sung what he did. I don't think that notion was naïve; it was probably factual. But as for the distortions caused by little Japan, the groupism, I don't know. Perhaps I was trying to make excuses again.

There have been brave and rebellious Japanese.

But I thought he would come to me and it would be like a dream of flying; not daily delight but something complex and deep and infinitely satisfying. Rooms in a Tokyo apartment, overlooking the endless roofs. The bright summer night lights of the city; the smell of fresh straw and carpet.

Would he have slept in his sunglasses, fearful of being wakened in the night without his disguise? No more silly than me in my lipstick when no one was there to see, I suppose. Only a bit more extreme.

I thought we would travel and only be in Japan once a year or so; I thought that he wanted to be elsewhere, to be free of having to go on stage and strum and sing the old tunes.

Funny thing about the internet; I saw that he was doing more concerts than he ever did in his youth; calling together teenage choruses, he with a big unfamiliar smile who had rarely smiled, at least who rarely smiled without it looking like a great strain. I didn't know what he was doing; I guess I would have to consult the blog; family barbeque, taking photos of the family cat with a cell phone.

Well, see you guys. Bye bye.

And so it was like Kido died; it had the same effect as an announcement that he had died in some abrupt, far away way, invisible to me. He was gone. It wasn't even tragic, and barely even sad. He was meeting and greeting his fans, holding court in the green room, taking bouquets of flowers, a frozen smile.

I left the Greensboro Free and headed down the lawn; I had to get the kids, they would be waiting.

I thought of Kido saying goodbye and leaving me, walking away into the heavy trees. I had thought he would come back, I felt him longing and dissatisfied, but Una, with her pithier approach to things, had a point.

Wherever he was, he wasn't coming to me.

Next year in Park Baun; 2004

It was cruel the way I heard about it.

Months before I'd left Boston and the law school, a letter came from my cousin Bridie; I could always tell the writing; barely legible, a scrawling hand with several letters either left out or at best scarcely there, sometimes written in pencil.

Well, Clement passed away a fortnight ago. Too bad, but listen he was a good age.

Oh, it was hard, standing there with the little slip of a letter, the pencil scrawl, the friend of my whole life slipping away.

They had sent him off to Galway City to the retirement home for brothers. I could only imagine the traffic noise and congestion, something of which Clement would never complain, as, like other country people from the West of Ireland, traffic noise equated to prosperity and should never be complained of. He fell ill and came back to the old monastery, recently turned into a nursing home. They allowed him back in his old room, the one that overlooked his boyhood home. In the night, he simply died, not a word to anyone.

He had written to me just a few weeks before, *Will write to you, Cat, in the New Year, DV.* No hint that he would be leaving, no hint that this was the last of his narrow angular script that I would see in this life.

He had befriended Gramma back when she was a lovely young girl, writing to her regularly, to her and to her mother from East Galway, with whom she lived, back in a lost world of dances and soldiers on Gramma's side; old people down overgrown boreens on his.

He didn't have much of a life, did he? Gramma said incongruously when I told her, though I'm not at all sure he would have seen it like that. Into the Brothers at twelve or thirteen, on the pretence that he had a vocation, washing dishes, doing the accounts.

He had taken me in, sight unseen, back in the seventies, and never had anything but the sweetest words to me from that moment on. We would ride on his motor bike, through the countryside, past the fairy mounds and old gravesites, the abandoned famine houses and disappearing lakes. He didn't evaluate or criticize, but only waited to hear and then brought out the brandy and the ashtray, the packet of ten cigs, the space heater flipped on in the corner.

How many old houses of our cousins he had brought me to, most of them empty or knocked down now, approaching first as if on a scouting party, turning back to me and laughing in his strange and slightly mad way, *This way, Cat, nothing will hurt you.*

Some wrote that Hidden Ireland died in the fifteenth century, some the eighteenth, still more the nineteenth with the Famine; as far as I could see, it began its final death march just in the seventies, when those who knew the stories and the fun and the long warm summer evenings began to be lost.

But Clement had lived on, and stuck with me, in thick and thin, he thought I was the best.

Back then, he must have heard from others what I was doing at all times, out late, at the dance halls. He not only thought it was delightful, but that I was embracing the place, into it completely. Be it Tony, be it Tom, it was all the same to Clement, who loved me unreservedly no matter what I did.

He seemed to be there right from my earliest childhood, with his mysterious giftz of plastic encased shamrocks every March 17th, still smelling faintly of sod and water. My mother would open these carefully, separate the roots as if loathe to harm them. The card always showed

Saint Patrick himself, holding his great shield and staff; I assumed he was a great character from far over the sea, like one in a book.

Then Clement took me in, met me in a dark and dripping square in Galway and off across the Galway night, such a night as no longer existed. Under a sky such as no longer existed, into the rumbly talk of a pub such as no longer existed, familiar and warm, no worries, the old men in their wellies perched on stools.

All my best to your mother, Cat, he wrote, and then within days, he simply left. Had he thought I was never coming back to see him? Was there anything he would have said to me if he could? Or did he want to leave it like that, ready to go, a catch in the heart valve, but they say I've a bit left in me yet, he'd insisted.

There was no one to lament with, no one who would have got it; wasn't that true and getting truer. The news came as I slogged my way through the law school lunches, meetings on the grading curve and whether First Year Contracts should be four credits or three.

Maybe I had intended never to go back to Galway. I had lost the ability to plan, to see ahead, had lost the wish to do anything that involved clear moves forward or back.

He had met Madina when she was small, called her a darling little girl, offered her a lemonade, but didn't miss a beat just the same. The brandy and ashtray were set out for me just the same, the same mad giggle. I don't expect he believed I would learn Irish, and escape for good and all towards the West, if such a place could be found. Others criticized me for trying to block new houses, it was even written up in the Tuam Herald; how she had formed a group and was going to object to the planning applications.

Big houses, aren't they, Cat? he had laughed, gazing into my face. If I thought it was a good cause, there must be something in it.

How awful all the extended family members could be to each other, the Irish genius for cursing in full flight: *that greedy feck, rotten full of himself, never a thought for us,* yet Clement could smooth the waters for each of them, bringing one to the other, leading some down the road and up the pathway into a zhouse with an open door, understanding that the old one with bad legs couldn't make it up out of the chair, we'd expect no such thing, and sitting quietly in the corner, brightly smiling to see everyone talking on, peaceful as can be. My going there made it a new place for him, and he made it a place for me to go to, to enter through a magic door.

I remembered him talking to the young policeman when I had just arrived and needed to register with them and attest that I would be there all the year, and make no trouble. *Yes, Guard, no, Guard,* he said, polite as you please, but under it that wish to burst into quiet laugher. I could see him arriving on his motorbike, removing his helmet outside the pub's plate glass window, gentle with the rain, nonjudgmental about it.

Will we go for a spin, Cat?

Brother, how are you keeping, Frank would welcome him.

It wasn't so much that Clement lamented I had gone and would not come back. People came and went from America, that was part of the order of things, the way of the world. But just as I did, he missed our meetings at the monastery door on a brilliant summer's day, the monastery dog loping back and forth, the valley below us. He liked it best when I cycled over, confirming for him again that I was still a great girl, I was always a great girl.

Once in a great while, as I was leaving, heading out into what he thought was a great adventure, a summer's evening almost unbearable in its beauty, he would whisper in my ear, *Love you, love you, Cat.* It was his one chance in life to say these words.

Book VI

Fish

Raphael Alberti was born in Puerto de Santa Maria; so Calvin had told me, and it turned out to be true. The town where I danced on tables, where the sweet smell of fish came in on every summer night breeze. I liked seeing photos of Alberti, though I never truly got the point of surrealism, what its underlying obsessions were about. I was stubborn; I never tried to understand what didn't suit me. But Alberti followed me everywhere, his books were never lost or stashed away out of reach in a damp cardboard box.

Say it's so,
compañera,
marinera,
say it's so.

He followed me through various forms of boredom, including walking to the office in the rain in Dublin, plotting my next move for the salvation of the Irish landscape. The sweet smell of the fish pier, the thick air of a summer night.

Tell me I must see the sea,
that I must want you in the sea.

I had an endless capacity for producing things that went nowhere; reams of poems and stories in particular. Perhaps they were invisible, but fine if I did say so myself. I had always kept on producing these items for an invisible audience. During law school, in the loud and unsettled New York nights, I would stay up—and I was no night owl—just to keep writing poems and novellas, only to stick them in a drawer and take out my exam outlines, the dead and icy principles of law, endorsements of paperwork, matters of intestacy.

Remember me on the high seas
My love, when you leave

Alberti was born in Puerto de Santa Maria. It was a non-translatable, virtually unusable fact, but a question of high importance to me. *When you leave and never return. When a storm drives a spear into the sail.* I left Andalusia and boarded a train. *When the captain on watch doesn't move. When the wireless no longer understands.*

There were long periods of boredom, but I had endless patience.

Poor John Merrill. When I lived in Dublin, I conceived of a cycle of poems, epic in nature, meant to capture the Ireland of way back when, the Ireland of Sandy, the Ireland of plotting and planning to save the place; I packed it up in sections and units, like a house that could be carted off in pieces, and sent it to him in aesthetically pleasing envelopes. I inserted cover letters, saying that I feared I was forgotten, banished. I never said by whom, but this did not seem to faze Merrill.

His letters took a while to come, but they always did. *Catherine,* his oversized handwriting across the page, *you are not forgotten, or banished. Read your cycle of poems. Send me final version when in hand, and I will show them around.* Just suppose I had written, *Dreary here, am coping on innate insanity and an occasional dip into Alberti,* similarly he would not have minded or been fazed.

The dreary, dirty boredom of the double decker buses and the rain that blurred the edges between the seasons; the walking back and forth; the meetings in half restored Georgian houses.

No one could keep track of my addresses. I was always changing, every year most typically, every two at the outset. Yet my new addresses must have been noted and kept at least long enough to send me off a letter. *Catherine, good to hear from you.* Not overdone, just right.

The cycle would bear the title, *The Happiest Night of Your Life.* It was a good title. And a subtitle, also good, *Or, Carna, Mon Amour.* I had thought of *Hiroshima, Mon Amour*, a strange film I always liked; and then I substituted Carna for Hiroshima, a touch of madness that equally, as is clear by now, also did not faze Merrill.

I had walked a good deal in the rain, in both the boring rainy seasons and more unexpected showers. I had passed the time in transport public and private, airplanes and trains and occasionally taxis. I carried my notebook, something I'd picked up all the way back from *Harriet the Spy.*

When the foremast finally
Is swallowed by the waves.

When you are a siren
At the bottom of the sea.

I doubt that Merrill wrote back reluctantly. What he thought of my zanier affairs I couldn't be sure, but I doubt he thought about them that way. I had a great power of sound, and only required an occasional airmail letter to confirm it was still intact.

Stannard; 2007

It was the sort of thing either Calvin or Una would have called me out for, my agitated planning for the next comp lit seminar; at least they would have made a derisive remark or two. Sasha did admire me. But for God's sake, even I needed to talk to someone, and most of the time it was just Madina and Emmet.

Sasha had no idea, of course, as to why I chose the books I did for the seminar. But he listened and made suggestions, almost like a research assistant. No doubt he was not crazy about being at Stannard, and had wanted to attend a more prestigious college. His parents could hardly wait for him to graduate and get to work, so that he could help bail them out of their often harebrained business ventures. But Sasha liked hanging out and talking about books, liked the book covers and names of authors and had interesting tidbits of information from their biographies. He did strike me as a ski instructor manqué, but he could be good company on those long late spring afternoons as I got ready for my upcoming

Stannard seminar. Solzhenitsyn sounded as ancient to him as Tolstoy did to me; poor fellow, he said innocently that it was "neat" I was thinking of including Japanese novels in the mix.

Little did he know on that score.

Maybe it was a mistake to dredge this up again, on the pretence that I wanted to include some books from out of my former "expertise." I had already done it to death. The nights in California, love sick, riding my bike under the stars and listening to Barber's Adagio, parsing and analyzing *The Setting Sun,* Dazai's *Shayō;* my dissertation with its manic quality, brought to life by my own persistent wish to triumph over Japan. Poor dear Sasha; yes, it was neat all right.

I was to have a little office of my own. I'd bought a small boom box, and on a really fine day might listen softly to Françoise Hardy or Leo Ferré, even the theme song from the movie *Un home et une femme.* Maybe it was time to bone up on French literature, Spanish literature, and the one I wished all along I'd done, Portuguese.

The problems of Dazai and his alter ego of the forlorn Japanese family man did not have to be my concern any more.

Yes, but Japanese literature is just a subculture; it has its own themes that are hard to convey.

Sasha thought I was talking about some other kind of obscurity than what I was. I felt like I was doing Dazai a favor at this stage.

It was long ago, in California, that I worked for up to seventeen hours a day, going through Dazai line by line for evidence of what I knew to be true: Dazai imagined himself as a great artistic hero, but enjoyed seeing himself pulled down by those around him who completely failed to get it. Enjoyed may not be the right word, but there was a certain cruel delight in describing that process of death by misunderstanding. And in those days, I gave myself over to Dazai, and by extension to Kido. I didn't have to do that anymore.

> Dear Calvin:
> You will not believe what I have pulled off. I can hardly take it in. I am staying here, at Stannard, and I can teach whatever I want. I am living like Eva Trout, but what's new? What do you think of this? Will you come to Greensboro? I would love to show you our house. I have a swish little office now at Stannard; do you remember the day long ago we came here to read our poetry, and they asked me about houses and I had no idea what I was writing or what it meant. Kids are good, a bit nutty. Come see us soon; it is spring. The meadows are so overgrown, compared to what they used to be.

Calvin wrote nice poems, even sometimes great poems, about navy blue water and the waves running smooth against the side of the sailboat. He knew about most everything. However off base it might make me seem, I couldn't get over the idea that Calvin and I were on a team, and that I should periodically prove to him that I was still alive.

Calvin would have agreed with me that it was time for Dazai to shove off; that his problems were not my problems any more. Even if Dazai was restrained, repressed and his life distorted, what had that to do with me? It had caused enough trouble.

Madina and Emmet were happier now that mud season was over. They had stopped asking when we were going back to Boston. I was evasive enough for long enough, and they took it for granted that we would be staying in Greensboro. Emmet wanted to know when the ice cream store would open.

I remember that day I finally heard once again from Merrill. I made the familiar trek to the Greensboro Free, signed in and sat down at the computer. When I saw his message, a bolt of joy went through me. He had seen mine, he had written back, he was there. *Catherine,* he wrote, and I could hear the heavy sighing, the weight of his breath as it had always been. *Somehow lost your email, and couldn't reply. Then it turned up, so am sending this now. Am so pleased to hear you've done this. As you know, I am in my seventies. Somehow I'm not writing any more, maybe I have said everything. I had hoped you would write again. Do write when you can.*

The mild-mannered gentleman at the next computer terminal could not have failed to notice that tears were coursing down my face. I wiped them away with my hand, and suddenly felt as young as a student, able to do anything. Merrill wanted me to think of him, to write to him again.

> I am so happy, so tremendously happy to hear from you. You will certainly begin to write some poems again. It is just a pause.

I sounded moronic, idiotic. But it was either those platitudes or something like, Let me pour out upon you one thousand years of exile; rescue me by any conveyance of your choosing, and I shall be waiting. Even Merrill, unfazed by anything I had ever said, could be daunted by this. Among the e-mail messages from the Land's End Shop at Sears or the latest promotion from LL Bean, the name of John Merrill. Oh, Mr. Merrill, do you remember

Sobre Los Angeles, because I still, even now, think about it a lot. *I don't want to force it,* he replied after a few days. *There may be nothing there.*

Emmet; 2005

Someone said to me that Madina's magically perfect life came to an abrupt end when I brought Emmet home. I hoped it was not so, but I knew that Madina was shocked by the squalling bundle of angry boy. For years, Madina had dressed up to go off and get a baby in Kazakhstan; little did she imagine that Emmet would be the one.

For several years, we had lived in our tiny rooftop apartment in Cambridge, strolling out to the corner pizza restaurant, to the park, to the library. Everything Madina said was doted on, attended to and acted upon immediately; her every doodle was cooed over. Peaceful and happy, Madina would lounge in the corner, setting up her elaborate set of Barbie furniture. Every trip to the store meant another trinket or treat. As people pointed out to us, as we walked down the street, we were always deep in conversation. I carried her home from the Red Line stop until she was very big and tall, her legs dangling down unceremoniously as we went.

In those early days, I was still a good citizen at the law school, attending lunches, trying to make conversation with colleagues I met in the hallway. I continued to memorize all the vast, disjointed material on cases and courts and doctrines; I could never hold onto it, my mind kept tossing it overboard as fast as I could learn it. Away, away! I kept calling, but trunksful of it kept on appearing.

I told Madina that some day we would be somewhere

nicer, more beautiful, but maybe she could not imagine anything nicer.

At night I smelled her hair. She was still such a small child then. I could fix everything that was wrong. I could make all sad thoughts disappear.

There was tenure to go through, a more elaborate process than in Dublin; professors slipping in and out of my classroom, taking notes, calls from the Dean to tell me how I was doing. I couldn't have been what anyone really wanted; I had no links and no longings towards the world of courts and judges, no ambition to head out in small planes and give talks to law professors about recent developments in trade jurisprudence. And yet, I had to stay calm, rational, as organized as I could manage to be—and I was terribly disorganized by nature. Madina watched her Pocohantas movie and cried when John Smith sailed away.

It wasn't as if we hadn't discussed it often enough, Madina and I. We had talked about a new baby brother or sister, we had dreamed up all kinds of babies, and Madina had always dressed up joyfully to go get them. *I'm back,* she would cry out after a brief disappearance into the bedroom, holding up a tightly wrapped bundle.

A baby might have been one thing; what she couldn't have imagined was the two year old the size of a six month old, who could barely walk, but stood and pointed at plastic things on shelves and all kinds of kitchen objects, shouting and wailing *Uh, uh, uh,* and stamping his feet. Poor Madina, the peaceful river that was her life was gone, and gone forever.

I guess a few eyebrows were raised when I decided to head off and adopt another child. Up for tenure, single, and getting another? They might have said. Whatever they were saying, it was something along those lines. To have children with a man in the picture erased the impression of it being discretionary. Rather, in that scenario, it appeared as a force of nature, automatically excused. But to voluntarily take on not one, but two, deserved no sympathy, no assistance, no encouragement. Certainly Gramma did all she could to dissuade me; no break from teaching to accommodate the new child was suggested.

My e-mail to the Dean had been cryptic. *I've decided it would be a good thing for my family to have one more child,* or some such understatement, *therefore I will be heading off to Central Asia in the very near future.*

His unembellished reply was the equivalent of, Well, good luck.

I left for Kazakhstan directly from Madina's end of school year concert. All the other parents were smiling and relaxed; I sat in the audience sobbing, unable to look at Madina's little face, earnest but distracted, worried.

That's the recipe . . . for joy! her class sang, words we had practiced many times.

After the concert, Madina and I held onto each other in the midst of all the students and visitors, terrified, crying. I had never been apart from her in nearly five years. A pink pillow of trust had grown over her old wounds. But I was going away now. I was leaving her. I had promised her I wouldn't and now I was going away.

We had known, yet we'd had no idea. I was leaving, off into the void, to see things she wouldn't see, to find a baby brother or sister she did not know. She would be cared for by Una and the babysitter Una had for Hughie. I was going, and that was all Madina knew.

Madina's perfect world came to an abrupt end, and I was in a Lufthansa plane on my way to Frankfurt and Almaty.

What with one thing and another, it took nearly two days to arrive in the provincial city where I would visit the baby house. A tiny plane that sounded like a vacuum cleaner with wings took me from Almaty, with its great mountains and boulevards, north and west over the steppe, where I could look down and see rivers curling across the brown grasslands.

I arrived in the evening. Madina seemed so far away, and I fought against my instinct to watch over her every minute, to know where she was, what she was doing, whether she was happy.

They put me up in someone's apartment, rented out to foreigners like me from time to time at the going hotel rate. It had been recently done over in blue and grey, with a wide low bed, a blank and forbidding living room, and an airless sun porch. The bedroom looked out over one of the main streets of the town. I watched policemen in wide brimmed Russian-style hats flagging down motorists; what for I wasn't sure.

The orphanage looked more or less as Madina's had, except that this one was outside the city by a good bit, sitting back in a large field, surrounded by a concrete wall and locked away behind an iron gate. The building was flat roofed, two storied, with big windows that opened out in the summer. There were miniature dachas on the grounds outside, along with a rusty slide and a couple of curved objects, apparently meant for children to climb on.

As must always be the case with orphanages, there was from the very first step inside the door a smell of vast quantities of boiled vegetables, of endlessly stewed potatoes and cabbage and beets. I saw the inevitable ladies in white coats, some in cooks' hats, some in nurses' headgear, walking noiselessly along the corridors.

The dusty, oppressive heat had come early that year, or so I was told. But because it was still May, the children had to wear jackets and hats when they came out into the sunshine, blinking and quiet. They walked in a hesitant line around the grounds, holding hands.

In the first few days, the orphanage director, a learned, charming doctor, had me meet a number of toddler boys. There were many of them, of varied ages and sizes. With each, I tried to imagine how he would be with Madina; would she love him, would these little boys seem so grown up that Madina would not think it at all like the little baby she had dreamed of carrying in under her arm. But because there were so many toddler boys, I wanted to bring one home with me. Perhaps people were afraid to adopt them, afraid of some problems that would come later, afraid of the future. Each played on the floor of the director's office, thrilled at the array of cars and blocks she kept in a stash on her shelf.

I began to panic; how would I do the right thing, bring home the right brother for Madina, how would I not be afraid myself, an unknown toddler boy in tow. It took me five minutes to decide that I would like to be Emmet's mother; not because I heard songs or saw stars, but because he was so lively, so painfully small, and so eager.

One of the nurses placed him on my lap. *He is the smallest child for his age in the baby home*, she said. He looked like an infant, but was in fact turning two years old. He turned his face to look at me; I cannot say he smiled exactly, but the look was friendly. Then he reached out to grab for a set of rings and blocks on the director's desk, pulling them apart as quickly as he could, as if fearful someone would take them away.

Would you like to spend more time with him? asked the director.

Yes, I said. *I would indeed.*

There were weeks of visiting the orphanage, sitting with Emmet (not yet called Emmet) in a small room, building up block towers that he would then whack down with his hand. He knew that I had yogurt and cheerios in my bag, and he would race to me, tugging at the bags to get me to hand these over before we did anything else. Unlike Madina, who had plunked her bottom down on my lap and refused to move when I went to see her in the orphanage, Emmet wanted things—toy cars, books with doggie and kitty fur on them for touching, spoons, cups, pencils. He wanted everything.

I would have him touch my face before he got to have his cheerios, and he would take his hand and whisk it once perfunctorily down my cheek, then reach out for the bag of cereal. He didn't really hug, or care for a hug. He was glad to see me when I came; his face would open up in a smile, as if he were practicing this new skill. He was shaky on his legs, no doubt because he had learned to walk very late, or so they told me. And also unlike Madina, instead of entering a world with me right away, he was in his own world of anxiety about getting things; getting food, getting blocks, getting the little yellow school bus I had brought him.

When we walked around the grounds of the orphanage, he made a beeline to the gate and watched the cars pass by on the road, pointing. Once some men had parked a broken-down Lada in the driveway, and he couldn't wait to get over to put his hands on the metal, run them up and down the chrome, the bumper.

When I phoned Madina from a public calling center, she was in tears, in bits, weeping into the phone and asking me when I would come back. I sent her photos of Emmet on the computer; she said she had seen him and he looked cute, but she wanted me to come home.

Heat bore down on the open plazas. The stores were quiet. In some restaurants, they only turned the lights on when customers came in. The days were amazingly long. I watched so much Russian television, I began to believe I could understand it. I felt the huge spaces and distances of the Russian-speaking world, a unifying set of accent sounds, even in this far flung place. The old native language had not come creeping back like grasses or small trees with the republic's independence. Rather, Russian was used almost all the time, even for the most personal conversations.

Each day had an endless, undifferentiated quality. I visited Emmet in the morning, then returned to the apartment to make lunch and read Jane Austen. By evening, I was barricaded in behind the metal door of the apartment, with no hope of leaving until the driver arrived in the morning.

The little boys and girls of the orphanage were allowed to take off their caps and sweaters on June the first. They stared at us as they took their little walks around the grounds.

I carried Emmet, and sometimes he fell asleep as I walked. They brought him a morning snack of a half banana, and he stuffed it unceremoniously into his mouth at one go. He still smiled his big, open-mouthed smile when I arrived in the morning. After three weeks, they allowed me to go to court to ask to be his mother.

I would like to have a Kazakh brother for my daughter, I told the judge, a very fashionable woman with bright clothes and jewelry.

Does he look like your daughter? she asked, knowing of course that he did not. In the end, she said that I could adopt Emmet; they gave me flowers and hugged me. I was terrified, as I had been when I adopted Madina. I took Emmet around in the car to get his paperwork. He liked everywhere we went; he grabbed everything and, being Emmet, wanted everything.

At the end of those four long weeks, I went back to Boston. I would have to return to Almaty two weeks later, but it was worth the trip to go see Madina again. The plane was scheduled to leave, as often happens in that part of the world, at the ungodly hour of one a.m. I sat for hours in the airport, watching the ladies walk past in high heels, the shops still open at that hour, willing to sell you a toy camel or yurt. We passed over Russia, maybe over Turkey, and on to Germany. When at last I reached Boston, I found a Madina I had never known before; gaunt, sad, mistrustful. They told me that she had lain for hours in her bed, tossing a tennis ball from one hand to the other. She had eaten huge amounts of candy, sneaking it into bed with her and hiding under the covers. No amount of reassurance would induce her to forgive me.

The summer had begun. I dashed into my office, writing furiously, expanding the footnotes in an article, looking things up. I would have to travel back to get Emmet soon, leaving Madina again. I would have to think about classes that would start in August.

Madina asked what little Emmet was like; would he love her, was he cute? I took her on outings, to Boston's Public Gardens, to the aquarium. She dressed up in her best clothes and posed for pictures. Oh, Madina, a messier, noisier life was about to begin.

The what's- new- in- fiction rack; 2007

You know, I pointed out to Sasha, *a lot of this recent fiction is really trashy. It relies on gimmicks; drug busts, sudden deaths, revelations of the most obvious sort.*

I don't think he knew exactly what I meant.

I always moved from shelf to shelf with hope, picking up one book with a lovely title after another (the titles were good), enticing colors, beautiful scenery. A foot in a shoe, the beach in the background. But on closer inspection they all seemed the same. The shorter ones began with someone finding out something shocking—cancer diagnosis, husband's infidelity. Then life turned around, new discoveries were made. Another sort was the barn burner with three generations of a Tennessee family, rich backwoods Americana, no thanks. Worst of all, the mysterious but dense yarn, full of characters with opaque and monotonous motivations, nothing more at the end than at the beginning.

Maybe I was making excuses, but all my life I had simply reread the same novels; poems as well. To the Lighthouse, Anna Karenina, Jude the Obscure. Few deviations, and most of them unhappy ones. No recommendation for newer books had ever satisfied. Things that looked good in the bookshop often proved to be intolerably lightweight. Pretty writing with nothing inside, or ugly writing with too much inside. Conceits that had hidden political meanings, or glorified the globalization jetset.

I preferred hanging out with Hemingway and his two cold, crisp bottles of wine for lunch.

I wondered what Calvin Pini thought about all this. He had useful views on these matters.

I wasn't sure if Sasha wrote in Russian or not; he clearly wished to be a writer and stacked up as much of these courses as his parents would allow. In the end, he would probably become an investment banker.

How funny to think of Joyce and the tradition of talking, of which I was somehow a part, up against the Japanese wall of silence. Self-defeating or self-punishing; I thought of Kido and the cosmetic gift bags to be given out at his concerts.

As for that whole thing, even Calvin wouldn't know what to say.

Kitty cat; 2007

Given that things with Calvin seemed to have ended with the introduction of a kitten, as well as the fact that Aunt Olive had had a more or less wild, and ferociously unfriendly, cat, and also that I had not grown up with cats, you would think I would not have been keen on the idea. But Madina and Emmet bugged me about it day and night, begging on their knees for a little cat they could love and take care of. On that last point, I had serious doubts. Nonetheless, always seized with anxiety whenever the prospect of making them happy loomed, I gave in, and off to the Waterbury animal shelter we went.

We saw long lines of cats in small cages; grey and orange and brown, big and small. Most were just sleeping, curled up in knots of boredom and despair. We asked the staff to take out several of them so that we could see them in action in the little "play room." My own favorites were two enormous couch potato tomcats, who eagerly rolled over to be patted as soon as the kids starting cooing at them.

In the end, it was mainly Madina who prevailed, though Emmet agreed with her choice, a petite white cat with random grey markings called Princess. Stunned with love and joy, they took turns holding her; she returned their stunned look, but allowed herself to be carried away by us. She didn't seem quite as keen on me, and actually tried to bite me once. She was what I would call medium friendly and certainly on the fretful side.

The kids would hear no criticism of Princess; she was perfect, wonderful, charming, endlessly amusing. Her every action was commented on and praised. Every mouthful of food she took was noticed. Cat toys were purchased at unconscionable prices, feathers and strings flying. Princess was the transition from winter to spring, the certainty that we would be staying, the confidence that even we could offer shelter and safety to a fellow creature.

I could hear Emmet calling *Pincess, Pincess*, whenever they could not find her, which was often. More than once, we were afraid she had somehow got out the front door—something we would never allow—and we walked the grounds of the house, anxiously beating on a food can and calling her name. As we drove up to the house in the evening, Madina would say, *I can't wait to see Princess!*

I guess Princess liked us well enough; I understood dogs much better, I admit. She certainly knew when it was time for food; she pounced on my feet in the middle of the night, she had her routine. Let an insect appear in a corner and she went rigid staring at it, intent, determined, an almost fanatical gleam in her eye. She did not sit on laps, and did not stay put for long. Yet she was always in the shadows nearby, tracking us with some subtlety, waiting, watching.

I saw the kids tummy down on the beds staring back at her, talking in low, secretive voices. Emmet calmed himself long enough to pat her gently on the head and, amazingly, she seemed to welcome his approach.

Princess was better than cartoons, better than bickering. They would hold up pieces of clothing that had the telltale white fur across it; Princess had been sleeping there! With great howls, they protested my view that Princess was not in fact the brightest light bulb, but I also found myself chatting with her, especially after the kids had gone to sleep.

One evening, I found a note that they had left, after much conspiratorial whispering, on my desk: *Can we get one more cat or a dog to be frends with Princess?*

She had an awful kind of meow, had Princess; it sounded more like Waa than meow, and her face came apart in a kind of sad bleating, *Waa.*

It was certainly strange that, at my age, I could be so pleased with myself for having performed the simple act of getting my children a cat.

Almaty; 2005

It was a dark night when I arrived in Almaty for the second trip. I was to pick up Emmet, who was now my son, get his new passport and other paperwork, and bring him home one week later. This time, it will not be a long trip, I had promised Madina, who was rigid with trepidation.

Even on the drive in from the Almaty airport in the dark, I could tell how hot it must be in the day. The air was heavy and humid; there were small, half lit businesses in low buildings along the road. Young men stood on street corners. Then billboards and car dealerships, and on into the main part of the city.

I knew that Emmet had been taken by care takers to a hotel room and that I would find him there. I was increasingly apprehensive as I passed by the noisy casino on the ground floor of the hotel, and through the cavernous lobby. Onto the elevator, down the long corridor. And there, in a crib low to the ground, slept little Emmet, small as a peanut, busy with his dreams. They left me alone with him; he was legally mine now, and I waited until he opened his eyes and looked into mine.

It seemed he remembered me, but I couldn't be sure. I had hoped for a more touching reunion, but right away he was up and on his feet, hands outstretched to get out and move about and look into bags.

And thus we spent an entire week in a hot hotel room on the seventh or eighth floor, nothing to do but run water in the tub, and walk lazily out and around the little park nearby, and back in again. The sun beat down mercilessly. Emmet fussed. Time stood still.

The plane would leave at the same ungodly hour,

two or three a.m., or whenever they got around to calling it. I got Emmet ready early, dressed in the clothes I had brought from home. He hardly looked at me, but ran about the hotel lobby, climbing on chairs and trying to knock over lamps. I put a little white hat on his head, which he in turn pulled off each time and threw to the floor.

As had happened with Madina, something changed utterly once we checked in our bags and entered the waiting room for passengers who would be on the flight out. Emmet settled in according to some instinct that, yes, this was it. He took his little cars and trucks and, tiny as he was, began shooting them across the broad shiny floor, then chasing them with glee. He stayed within a reasonable orbit, not straying too far, but neither paying me much attention. Once on the plane, he seemed content, and gobbled up the whole of my cheese omlette. For much of the flight, he slept in a restless, shallow sleep, twisting and turning. By the time we entered Frankfurt airport—old, crowded and uncomfortable though it was then—Emmet was my boy.

There were not many places to go, so we hung out at the McDonald's, of all venues. There was a little playground, with colored balls on the floor that the children could slip and slide on. Emmet rolled around happily, grabbing the balls and throwing himself back and forth. In the waiting room for Boston, he managed to amuse everyone, running back and forth, checking out sights and noises, climbing under feet and over barriers.

People watching him did not know what to make of him; he was small enough to be an infant, but with the flitting energy and action packed agenda of a much older child. His teeny white ankles and feet stuck out comically from the baggy blue trousers that had once been Hughie's. It was on the second flight that all hell broke loose.

Emmet screamed, simply screamed his lungs out, for several hours. It began when he refused to be strapped in his seat, and nothing I could do would make him stop. His face was red, his eyes closed tight. He didn't seem to hear my voice, and wouldn't so much as look at me.

I walked him up and down, but there was no comfort for him in it. He screamed when we landed and went on screaming, if somewhat more quietly, as we entered the cool dark space of Boston airport. There was no one to meet us, as I had not asked anyone to come.

I remembered arriving with Madina years back, late at night. Sven came rushing up to greet us and she had stuck out her arms for him to take her, perhaps on the theory that she had used up all I could possibly offer.

This time, we were on our own. It was an ordinary summer afternoon in Boston. Emmet's paperwork did not take long; the official looked it over, and sent us on our way. I collected my bags and pushed Emmet along in a stroller. At last, he settled down and stopped crying. He began to look around and I thought I even saw a smile.

I remembered arguing with the cab driver about the best way back to Cambridge. At last, we drove up to the green house where Madina and I had lived in the attic apartment for several years, but would now be leaving.

Emmet had fallen asleep. As I stepped out of the cab, I saw what a tiny child he was, sound asleep, not knowing where he was or why, but somehow going with it.

Book VII

Spring, 2007

There was something I didn't like about Merrill's Collected Poems coming out. I wouldn't have said so, but in my mind it was linked with his message about not writing any more. It was a heavy book, beige and brown like early autumn leaves. I preferred slim volumes of poetry when they were first published—quirky and setting out a marker for a certain moment in time. Those thin volumes would date themselves over the years, like kitchen wallpaper and bedroom colors.

As Leo Ferré said, maybe without meaning it, *Avec le temps, on n'aime plus.* Leo Ferré always pleased me, I loved the way he stood on stage and faced the audience, in unabashed anguish. I wished I could have met him, but of course, he was gone long before.

I should have gone to France; that old debate with myself again. Probably all cultures toss up, genetically speaking, a roughly similar proportion of those like me, but some cultures lionize and others punish. I guess I've made that point sufficiently. Self-punishing romantic as I always was, maybe it made perfect sense that I chose Japan. I slotted right in. And Kido was the greatest of the Japanese romantics, the most in need of salvation. And we know how that worked out.

As for Kido's wife, well, her blog made sense in a way. Having been kept in a box for so long, and facing sixty years old, she decided to write anything that came into her head—pedicures, perfume, who she ran into back stage and what compliments they gave her. What the hell. I understood that.

Here I was, the adventuress, and my own timidity amazed me. Waiting, watching, a mad woman in a repetitious, noisy conversation with myself. Patient as Job, wacky as Ophelia.

Still, I was not completely out of my mind. I had seen enough to know that I was not especially lucky, or fortunate, or whatever you want to call it. It was sinful to say that; terrible things had not happened, and in that sense I was better off than the vast majority of humankind. On the other hand, compared to the mediocrities I saw everywhere, I had not enjoyed what one thinks of in the crass sense as success. I lacked the cliché gene. I was stubborn. I resisted.

Timid and lyrical, stubborn and afraid, I was Emily Dickinson.

I could live ten years or more on a single gesture, and that was hardly a good, certainly not a useful, quality to have.

I had imagined it would morph into something else, but morph it did not. I waited, and still it did not morph. It was time to break the news to myself.

It came to me at last just why I had spent so much time in Japan, what the link was. For both the Japanese and for me, there was a sense of never being able to possess what was there before us to possess. For them, it would mean trying to buy all the beautiful things of the world. For me, it led to that never-ending, bitter internal dialogue; better put, a dramatic soliloquoy heard only by myself.

Maybe I had misheard Leo Ferré. Maybe it was *On aime de plus.* Or *On aime plus.* Which if either was grammatical; my French was rusty. My Japanese was rusty.

It was always like that. I could teach the kids basic Spanish, French, Japanese, even German or Mandarin—but everything was rusty, unusable in real life. I wasn't sure how I would even do with a lunch menu in the various languages. And music; I could teach basic piano and music theory. I would have a go at Algebra I equations and the life cycle of the grey fox. Not ballroom dancing; not yet, anyway.

I could do a little of everything. What a waste it seemed at times.

On these days I had to myself, with the kids at daycare and school, I opened the windows that looked down over into the town. I listened to whatever music I wanted, medicine taken too late.

Sometimes I had to remind myself exactly where I was; there had been too many motifs, and I would come to, as if out of a trance, wondering exactly where I had arrived this time. We had yet to unpack all our boxes. I wasn't sure if we would take the house for one more year; the landlord was lackadaisical and I had always been hesitant to face such issues.

I wasn't far from Saint Theo's and, of course, from Merrill. It occurred to me one afternoon that I could quite easily go see him, talk to him. I could look him in the face again; he still existed. I hadn't changed so terribly much; I didn't look that bad, surely. He had mentioned that back surgery, how unlike him that sounded. I could go find him after that, we could meet in his office, with

John Donne and Randall Jarrell and Mark Strand on the shelves.

I wouldn't be restored, nothing could do that. But there would be magic in his office, and he would touch me on the head and something of the past would be brought back to life.

It was only a sentence or two, but he had wanted me to write to him, wanted to see my name on the e-mail message. I had been asked for something. It was a feeling I had grown very unused to. In the summer, I would visit a Saint Theo's that still, incredibly, existed.

Cambridge; 2005

The very day after I brought Emmet home, we moved to a different apartment, a larger one on the first floor, trading in our cramped third floor walk up. Constantly afraid that Emmet would fall down the stairs or otherwise hurt himself during the move, I had to watch both of them like a hawk, carrying boxes, lifting, tossing, arranging. On one of the last trips out, I asked Madina to run back up and grab something I had forgotten, and Madina said her first big no.

No, she said, sitting there and looking at the ground. *No.*

I had never seen her look like that, helpful little bird as she had been.

Please, Madina, it would so help me, I said, hot, desperate for someone to swoop in and make things easier.

She shook her head again and looked the other way. And so began Madina's new life.

Whereas Emmet adored her from the first moment.

He gazed at her, imitated her words and gestures. *Dina!* He would call out when she was not with us, longing, supplicating. Later, when he could say more, he would cry, *Dina, where is you?* He opened his eyes on Cambridge and there was Madina, standing over him, sizing him up.

Well, he doesn't look Kazakh to me, she said.

His face was red with heat and from all the tears he had shed. He looked around and began to make strange noises, *Uh, uh, uh,* rolling over and grabbing all the bright objects he could hold.

Geesh, he's big, she said. *Not a baby.*

Within a week, Emmet was in a daycare near my office in the law school. Unlike Madina, when he first walked into the place, he looked around, delighted, and took off after the balls, blocks and water table. If he could have talked, he would have said something like, Wow, this is the coolest orphanage I ever saw! His favorite activity quickly became collecting rocks and washing them at the water table. They gave him an empty box to keep them in and let him carry them everywhere he went. He played peek a boo behind the director's chair, raced up and down the playground on the roof, pushed play grocery carts, and never stopped moving. He despised naptime and it was only then that he pulled a cranky face and stamped his foot at the teachers.

People had told me that with another child, it is not a matter of one plus one equals two, but rather some exponential increase in demand that has to be lived through to be believed. The in and out of the car, the strapping and unstrapping, the food rejected, the poo in the bathtub, the spills, the cuts, the tears, the moods. Emmet also had a deep suspicion that he would not get enough, not get his fair share, and his good nature turned to angry vigilance whenever popsicles or candy were being doled out. He got over his love of bananas after downing seven of them in a row; he never looked at them again.

I brought him into Boston on the train with me; just as Madina had loved the stroller, Emmet hated it, squirming and struggling to be let free to run. At the train station, either the escalator or the elevator would be out of order, and I would end up carrying Emmet, stroller and all, up dirty old concrete steps, buffeted by all the twentysomething folks on their way to work. In the office, I worked on my footnotes, writing and writing with one eye on the tenure process. No one mentioned a leave; I never asked. I was afraid that it might interfere with tenure, I guess. I had to stop people from looking at me, discussing me, having meetings to evaluate me. How old was I, for God's sake? She did what, I imagine they said to each other, she took on another child?

When school started in the fall, Emmet and Madina posed for photos outside our house. By then at least, they were smiling and holding hands. True, we had had fifteen fights before getting out the door, but they ended up smiling. I read all the therapeutic parenting guides, did hug times and time ins and beyond consequences. To get them to sleep, I tried tough love and standing in the bedroom doorway, reassuring words and refusal to talk after I'd said goodnight, one book, two songs, two books, one song, no song. I put Madina in with Emmet, Emmet alone, Mommy with one, Mommy with both.

At Christmas time, I had to buy enough to make bliss for two instead of one; cranes and garbage trucks along with American Girl skateboards and Patriot the Foal.

On snowy mornings, I pushed Emmet's stroller

through the drifts as best I could; Cambridge wasn't great on shoveling sidewalks. The trains were delayed. I assuaged Emmet with lollipops.

Mommy, why did you leave me to go get Emmet? Madina asked regularly, never forgetting, especially at night before she went to sleep.

So you could have a brother, and because it's fun to have one more child, I would answer. There was some enormous well of grief, something that had happened that she could never explain. *Isn't it nice, having one more? Like a team.*

I still love you the same as I did, I told her. She began to revert to her toddler voice. *Sing me song!* she would command, kicking her legs under the covers. *Get me drink!*

By the time I got tenure in March, I knew that I was being condemned to teach law forever, that there would never be any escape, no return to poetry readings and secret meetings in shadowy restaurants.

Catherine, good news, the Dean said on the telephone. *A positive vote, good support, a positive result for you and for the law school.* It was a strange kind of language.

Thanks, Dean. I won't let this change anything, I said, moronically, as if taking on his point of view, unable to retain my own. *My best to everyone. I do appreciate it.*

I had done it again, jumped through all the hoops, one by one, day after tedious day, walking my classes, unwilling though they were, through the most impenetrable sections of treaties, agreements, statutes.

Congratulations, Catherine.

Thanks again, Dean.

And how are those kids? It was the obligatory reference.

Fine, fine, they are just fine.

Summer of your life; 2006

What was it about that particular summer, I wonder. I had been through it all many times before, the boom and bust of feeling, the sand buckets, towels, the urge to reach water or mountains, the feeling of conquest and resolution. Dear friends, lovers, well-wishers, By the time you read this, I shall be well on my way towards the heart of summer. Do think of me from time to time.

It was less believable this time, maybe that was it. Nothing at all would happen, I saw that, realized it completely.

Summer would be a short burst of urges, like a cup of iced coffee, quickly downed and scarcely remembered. It went by not only quickly, but brutally, mockingly.

And then August came. The birds went quiet; the dog days came. I left the office and went out onto the streets of Boston. People were hanging about, squinting against the bright light, dejected. I had to begin thinking about law again, MOU's and protocols, who could take an action, against whom could the action be taken, had such an action ever been taken, and if taken successfully, reversed, and to what extent reversed or remanded, referenced, partially overturned, what time limit, subject matter limit, limits of joinder, rejoinder, rejection, presumption of all facts favorable towards him, you, rejection of all arguments not raised by the date in question, incomprehensible chart pointing sideways, up, down, return to sender.

Why that summer in particular, I'm not sure. I didn't complete a little collection of poems, didn't finish a film script. I guessed that it had been fifteen years or so since Kido had written a song really worth listening to, but then he didn't have to any more. He could repackage the old ones as Ansé's Best, Ansé's Silver Best, Only the Best, With Gratitude Best, Retrospectives Best, and so on, without any apparent sense of repetition.

As for love, I remembered the phrase, wherever it was originally from, that *love is short and forgetting is so long.*

As the time grew closer and I saw colleagues scurrying around the halls of the law school, I would pull the same old face, *You know, trying to get something done.* Get something done, a vile phrase, *Oh, just trying to finish things up.* I have a deadline. A deadline, I have a deadline. Meaning someone wants something from you; a point of pride.

Daddy had an old joke about the weather in Vermont, that it was just winter and the Fourth of July, but it fit with this other sense of the desperate shortness of the summer. Had I finished up the poems, even, I would probably have ended up publishing the collection myself, and selling about five copies. The rest would be piled up in a corner years later, and I would tell people, Oh it was a good experience. I don't regret it. Piaf, c'est moi, *Hymne a l'amour.*

It was as if I had done all I could do, done it as many times as I had it in me to do. Enough with the teaching, the yammering, the explications. Enough with the WTO, the lunches where names of judges were dropped and where, you know, that self of mine went draining away.

Simply put, I would die if I tried to do it again. Something terrible would happen.

I hadn't in fact been trying to finish something up that summer; rather, I was waiting for the announcement that someone had arrived to save me, to open the gates of the tower and let me go free. But as in other summers, such a person never appeared, and, more painfully, the scenario seemed far less plausible.

In Gramma's world, summer was the time of dying; the scent of carnations at a Watertown funeral parlor in the evening, the whispered tones of a wake. Everyone except Daddy had died in summer, everyone she knew. I fought mightily against that notion, struggled to prove that summer was instead my magic time, my zone of perfection.

Gramma said some funny things that summer. One morning, the nurse's aide in her assisted living had to wake her; she never overslept, but that morning she was hard to wake. Gramma opened her eyes and said to the aide, *Yes, dear, I guess I was dead, but I didn't know it.*

That summer didn't deliver for me, not a thing. Not a moment of the usual hope, not even the usual boom and bust of expectation and disappointment. The whole thing refused to get off the ground at all.

I couldn't deliver the perfect essence of summer to Emmet and Madina either; just the usual visits to the pool, the week away, camps and air-conditioned restaurants. That August was my mortal enemy.

Funny how I still remembered Miles Bradford; how funny he was. His old words from that letter written at Alma's, that it was *Up up up or downhill all the way.* I saw again what he meant.

The invitations to the law school's Welcome Back Lunch came out. This was a bad sign. The net was closing around me. The grading committee would be meeting to decide whether to go for a mandatory curve; the Dean would be commenting on whether it was likely we would move up a fraction of a tier in the national rankings. But most of all, there were the law books to open again, like vials of poison I had kept under lock and key.

I was allergic to law offices and even the clothes worn by lawyers; the facial expressions, the gestures, the manner of closing a cell phone.

At her worst moments, Gramma had a way of looking around the room and saying, *Won't somebody help? Can't somebody do something?* I had heard this so many times, I usually responded by saying that no one could take away old age and that we would just have to soldier on as we were.

I did understand her, though; I did see what she meant.

I had my intro lectures done; the concepts, the promises of riches and rewards to come. I would not tell them that law was a trap, an absurdity, that most of it made no sense except from the point of view of preventing things from changing in a way that you would touch or taste. The pages upon pages of indigestible notions; fog across a lost world; the dark forest.

Summer as it had been once, me in my white dress, standing on the train platform at Ochanomizu in an unthinkably distant time; or in Ireland on a June night that refused to get dark.

Like Gramma, except that embarrassment kept me from asking, Can't somebody do something? But you promised, you said, I thought, but, but.

And we started back teaching in August. August! The warmest, laziest, stickiest month, like the old age of summer, designed to force us to let go even our wish to hold onto summer. August. Into the classroom, out with the jurisprudence. Only people with no feelings could imagine, could devise, such a thing.

I had always anticipated ending up like Nina in *The Seagull*, but at least that would have been the right sort of failure. But that was merely a lament, gather ye rosebuds and all that, I wish I wish I wish in vain, et cetera. It was something much deeper, darker, a feeling unto death.

I would leave, or I would die, somehow death would come stalking me for bad faith.

In the Victorian novels, the ladies feared that at thirty the bloom was off the rose, but fifty, what was that all about. And forgetting is so long.

They assigned me a classroom that I didn't like. That was always the case; I had to adjust.

There's a feng shui problem here, I joked to the students. Not one of them smiled, let alone laughed.

I feel like I am talking to the air, I went on. Silence. *Isn't it great, being back in August? I mean, who needs summer?* No one smiled or laughed or looked me in the eye. They wanted to see a smart businessman or gal, wellfitting suit, confident and predictable, indifferent to the season, fond of good restaurants, briefcase full of impeccable paper.

I considered different jokes, references to just arriving back from Saint Tropez; knowing they wouldn't laugh even then. It depended on how reckless I was feeling.

How was your summer, Catherine? The other law professors asked me. *How are those kids doing?*

They are well, nutty as they come, but fine overall, I would say. It was my way, our way of responding, that extra dimension of self-deprecation. I couldn't help it, it was impossible for me to speak in any other way.

I don't know how you do it, they would say. *How on earth do you do it?*

Well, I don't, I would say, and they also failed to laugh. What did that mean? What wasn't she doing?

I could imagine my colleagues saying, *The students really value real world examples. Too bad she doesn't seem to offer those the way Larry did.* But can you imagine, really, me offering anyone examples of anything from the *real world*?

I dreamed of getting the children away from the city, to a place where a long rambling garden provided endless delights, nooks and crannies, sloping into old growth perennials and contented trees. Gramma's brother had died in his thirties. He had contracted TB as a sailor and was put in a sanitorium with no view at all. She told me how he looked out the window and saw green hills and sheep. *It's so beautiful out there, can you see it?* he had asked her. She had looked out and, of course, it was nothing much, just a car park and a busy road beyond. *I can see it right out there, a lovely green hill.*

It was a common trait of Catholics, the vision thing. To those other denominations, well, You take earth, then, and we'll have heaven.

I may sound spoiled, but I wasn't spoiled. I didn't want much, didn't even need much. Just please, I thought, do not make me do this again. No more. What's the worst that can happen? You take earth, I'll take heaven.

Greensboro; 2006

It had been harder than ever to leave the Tisdale house that last summer vacation. I felt like a refugee as I closed the screen door and walked across the lawn, my arms full of plastic beach items, draped over with bags.

I wish it was our house, I said to Una.

Well, we never make anything happen, Una replied. She had shut down as we left the house. She was in revenge mode for the passivity and acceptance of Gramma and Daddy, their failure to struggle against fate.

We could, I said meekly.

It is what it is, she said, ending the conversation, angry in turn at me, Sven, Gramma, Daddy and various unnamed forces pulling us relentlessly in the unworldly direction.

On this trip, we had made our usual rounds; Stowe, Hyde Park with its cemetery full of Daddy's old friends, Wolcott with its unchanged gaggle of riverside houses and churches.

Not another cemetery, Madina complained, throwing herself against the back of the car seat.

When we were little, we amused ourselves in the back seat, I said. *Coloring books, looking out the window, playing games with the license plates.*

Ahh, ahhh, Madina sighed. But it was perfectly true. Somehow or other, Una and I had sat for hours without a word of complaining, watching the little rivers that followed the roads in Vermont, waiting for the familiar sights.

On these holidays, Una railed against a bad weather forecast, throwing up her hands and looking around as if to say, Okay, who's the culprit? It was some moral failing; had we just tried that bit harder, we would have earned better weather. Other people didn't get crappy forecasts like this; *just* my luck, damn it all, rain for most of the week!

What was the word we had used in college, Calvin Pini

and I: lastness, I think it was. That trip to Greensboro had the whiff of lastness.

Just when; 2007

I never liked those e-mails with someone's name in the subject line. As with telegrams edged in black, you knew immediately that the news would not be good. When I saw the message that said simply "John Merrill" in the subject line, it was a stunning, terrible moment.

It had been forwarded to me from the English Department at Saint Theo's and read:

> We wanted you all to know that our friend John Merrill suffered a heart attack three days ago. As most of you know, he went in for a long-planned back surgery at the end of the academic year. The surgery went well; he was awake and talking to friends and family. Sadly, soon after, he had the heart attack. He has not regained consciousness. He is strong, and we are hopeful that he will pull through. His family has asked that he have no visitors at this time. Your prayers are most welcome. We will keep you posted.

I cried through dinner and cried myself to sleep. He hadn't been conscious for days; there was no telling if he was still there or not.

I prayed that he would live, that I could go to Saint Theo's and see him, to have him tell me again that I had the power of words, a power that had once wowed him and that guaranteed he would never forget me. *You are not banished, Catherine,* he had written, even in those dark seasons when the rain fell in Dublin day after day, even then.

Then just recently, he had wanted me to write to him. He had asked me to. He had told me about not writing any more, and said he didn't want to be Robert Frost.

I began to phone people I'd known at Saint Theo's. I kept asking what the doctors thought; never mind this talk about Merrill not being out of the woods yet. Suddenly practical, and God knows I had no belief in doctors, I wanted to know if he was coming out of the woods at all. I forwarded the message to Calvin marked Urgent. He wrote back, *I'm sorry, how awful.*

> Calvin, I heard from someone up at Saint T's that Merrill's wife (remember the knitter?) left him some years ago. Even at his age, he married again. Did you know all this?

What I didn't write to Calvin was God, if I had known, I could have thrown my hat in the ring. I could have done it, stranger things have happened. They told me that this second marriage had been good for him, kept him from being morose.

It would have been a bit weird, but I could have. We loved each other, after all, surely we did.

The next day, and the next, the e-mails came at intervals, saying that Merrill was hanging on, but that there was no change in his condition.

I phoned the college and asked if there was a chance he would recover; whether of all the mid-western revelries and streams alive with fish and garden scenes, seasonal obsessions, anything remained. They were carrying out tests now, I was told.

I continued to wait. And as I feared, the news from the tests was not good. They let him go, and John Merrill was no more.

Everything I heard and saw made me cry, cry for John Merrill, Mr. Merrill, first and last to smile on my gifts, arbiter of words, wiser than anyone. Sometimes lush and generous with his own words, and sometimes terse, with only one or two to spare.

> Calvin, I forward below info on memorial service. Will you come? More than anyone, I would like to see you. Please come. I so want to see you.

Mommy, just stop talking about that person if it makes you sad, Madina said. They were utterly fed up with my tears. She crossed her arms in a pout, Emmet standing loyally next to her. If I put on sad music, she snapped it off in a huff. *Stop, Mommy, stop, we don't like it,* she said.

I really scrambled to recover myself, I tried. There was an unpleasant blankness about things. I was frightened. I had gone to John Merrill at the very beginning, before my later conceit and self-absorption, to verify the thing about the words.

I tap out sentences on my fingers, I had told him. He didn't laugh, or even comment. He looked at me, and he sighed. This meant something to him; he knew. And it wasn't even just that. It was much more than that.

The green gardens were blank, the vistas blank. There wasn't much left, and absolutely nothing of that long standing.

I could have thrown my hat in the ring. I could have gone to see him now and again. I could have offered to be with him. It was a mad, zany thought, but at least it would have been fun.

I'm sorry, Una said when I told her. She remembered Merrill from years past. *That's really unfortunate.*

But from Emmet and Madina, there was no mercy at all. No music for me, no time on the porch, no crying.

It wasn't exactly grief; I had hardly seen him in recent years, after all. Rather, it was a sense of pointlessness, a coldness, that blank quality that undid even my memories. No one around me remembered what I remembered. It felt old, tired, a giving up beyond the giving up I thought I had already done.

You could go in the blink of an eye from charming, desirable, wonderful, to unknown, frumpy, anonymous. The point was who was watching, thinking, remembering the movie with you in it. Who was aware of you there in the world, your walking and moving and even your sleep. Who was curious about you, who wanted to sit and eat with you while the night sky settled in beyond your shoulder.

Beware, I thought, he warned you of bad endings. He warned mostly of happy ones; the clichés of togetherness, *It's all our'n,* as he'd put it, while making us laugh in the writing seminar. There were the trite but unhappy endings as well, though not as easy to recognize or pillory.

Still, on waking in the morning, there was that knowledge of not being able to head out, find him if I needed to, elicit from him a sign of knowing, a sigh, a word.

Calvin didn't answer my last message. Apart from him, there was no one to tell. Well, Una had some idea, but not as much as Calvin Pini did. He had been in the writing classes with me, back in the days when I was so important, was sought after and serenaded. For you, Calvin had written to me, who could raise small birds to a whisper.

But there was nothing much I wanted to say to Una. When she called, I just repeated, *I'm really unhappy about Merrill, I can't believe he's gone.*

She wasn't terrible about it. She actually sympathized to some degree.

At the end of one telephone conversation, just as we were about to hang up, she told me, *Gramma said a funny thing. I told her that it was really hard for you that Merrill had died. Oh, isn't it time for her to get over that, Gramma said. He was a married man with a family, for God's sake. Why is she carrying on over a married man?*

Greensboro; 2006

Like a homing pigeon that particular August, I was driving north. I left the law school, got the kids, packed as much as I could, and drove north. When we got to Vermont, at that place that always lived in my mind, the place where the river divided New Hampshire from Vermont, the place Daddy always told us to stop and listen, that it was Vermont, completely different, Madina asked me why we were going back up again. Did Una tell us to meet her there? I told her no, that I had decided we needed to go one more time, that I needed to see the fields as they were being made ready for the harvest.

Like a homing pigeon. I kept going north.

The fields had changed their look, from high summer to anticipating the fall. Madina kept asking, *Are we really going back to Vermont, Mommy? Why? Did we forget something?*

I liked that idea; it appealed to me. Yes, I forgot something and we are going back to get it. The locals in Greensboro, had they noticed or cared, would have said to themselves, Thought we just got rid of that crew—what are they doing back?

From Concord, New Hampshire on I knew every twist and turn in the road, into Vermont and the leisurely way the highways rose and fell, everyone speeding up to glide on the down slopes, saving on gas. These were Daddy's roads; if he was wandering anywhere, it was on these near-empty Vermont highways.

We dere yet? Emmet kept asking, bored and restless after his initial surprise. He was probably wondering if this meant he could choose yet another prize at Willey's or the Shaw's General Store in Stowe.

As I drove, I was faintly aware that I would never have to think through all those legal puzzles again; shared competence, exclusive competence, preliminary references, interim relief. I would never have to, I would never be allowed. It was vaguely euphoric, as if emptying out the contents of a big suitcase as we traveled along, watching the clothes go flowing off into the fields out the back window.

Somewhere in Central Vermont, a song from *Astral Weeks* came on the radio.

Like a homing pigeon, I continued; Hyde Park, Morrisville, past the old road to the dump, past the field where Daddy and his cousin used to lie in the grass watching the train to Walcott pass.

That summer had been the worst of all, the worst ever. When the Fourth of July came, I shuddered in fear; I would have to face them again. I would have to stand up and bring my mind into line with the cases, statutes, the meaning of a semicolon, be it implicit *and* or *or*, the grounds of decision, the questions as to whether a court had ever in the past deviated from, or hinted at, such a point, and I would have my usual reaction, I don't know the hell, ask a lawyer. For several weeks, I worked at staying jovial, enjoying the summer mornings and the long summer evenings. Then August came like the Grim Reaper, and a grey cloud descended over my head. I couldn't do it again. I couldn't face it. I might never be the lovely girl on the station platform at Ochanomizu, but I couldn't face this sort of August again.

I started my classes, I did. I don't think I attended the welcome back lunch, though I've blocked it out and can't be sure. *Yes,* I asked the students, *Why waste time until Labor Day?* No one laughed. The intense heat outside, the withering leaves; the air-conditioned interior, the bing of the elevator.

I either had to leave, or die. There was no way around it. I just couldn't do it anymore.

Students wanting advice on what the next journal symposium topic would be left waiting. Professor Darcy will reschedule all appointments for a much, much later time.

I would have disappointed them in any case; I would have been off the beam, my mind on something else altogether. Professor Darcy, inimitable Consultant to the Government of Nowhere, on the topic of how to avoid the end of all things.

No one would miss me. If I had died, no doubt they would have stepped right over me. One of those e-mails would have made the circuit, with Professor Darcy in the heading.

And so, goodbye. Exactly like a homing pigeon, I flew north, not quite to Canada, but decidedly north.

Saint Theo's; 2007

The memorial service was set for a Saturday afternoon of high summer; a classic summer day of hot wind and pale grass bent flat along the hillsides. It might have prefigured rain, or maybe not, the leaves were turned inside out, silver green, the cows lying in the cool spaces near water.

I left the kids with Emmet's babysitter and promised to be back by late evening. I felt as if I had John Merrill in the front seat of the car with me; it was a once-off thing, he would never ride there again. But this one day, having left Emmet and Madina in Greensboro, I could have Merrill with me. Come along for a ride in my mother's old Buick, I thought. It feels like the old days.

I walked across the campus at Saint Theo's. It was ghostly; a deserted feeling, high summer. Little had changed in thirty years, only a new building here and there.

I went and sat on one of the benches that faced the chapel. I watched people arrive in ones and twos, small groups. All the women, like me, were wearing sleeveless black; items pulled from the back of the closet, awaiting a summer wedding, an evening one, put to different use today.

It was high summer, the real thing.

I thought I recognized people from Merrill's family. I sat on the bench, early, alone, looking out at Saint Theo's and feeling quite as if I'd never left. If someone had told me I was a senior doing my final papers, I would easily have believed it.

I sat there alone, in the warm wind. With a kind of

terrible desire, I wanted Calvin Pini to appear, to park his car and saunter over to me, to say something cynical and sad. I wanted to see Calvin, to talk about Merrill with him.

In the chapel, familiar to me from years past, even from my brother Jack's wedding a zillion years ago, I saw people enter in couples and small groups. It was the younger women who came in alone, with hair swept up and black mourning garb, sad and silent.

I saw professors I'd had in class more than thirty years previous, still energetic and completely recognizable; most did not in any case recognize me. I was tempted several times to lift my hand and wave my fingers to them, but did not. Instead, I sat rigid and grieving in the pew I had chosen, midway down the church.

From somewhere, appropriately in the heat and waves of quiet and swoon of midsummer came the sounds of the song *Gracias a la vida.*

I wondered if Merrill had chosen that himself for the occasion. I knew he would not mind me asking. He was not into reverence. It had the feel of too much resignation, though, and I wasn't sure he would be that even-handed about it all. Thanks for everything, it's been great.

I so, so wanted Calvin Pini to arrive.

I kept seeing people I hadn't seen in decades enter the chapel; the same, except for white hair. I imagined Calvin bursting out of the old dorm building, charging along, calling to Louis. There were dogs everywhere in those days. If I could catch up to Calvin, I might avoid every stupid thing I later did.

Merrill had wanted me to write to him; he had hunted around for my e-mail address; he had found it and written saying, I thought I would hear from you. He had asked. That and ten cents, as Una was fond of saying. But he had. And now there was no one to care about that, no one to tell.

I looked in the distance, to the visitor parking. Right up until the service began, I thought Calvin might arrive. Inside the chapel, I looked around for him, maybe smiling ironically in the corner, dressed casually but with a touch of summer charm. We would talk about Merrill.

I felt beautiful in my summer black sleeveless. I swayed between disbelief and disbelief. This was not good; this was final. He was lost to me. The part of my life that had begun with Merrill was over.

At the reception that followed, some of them looked at me as if I'd appeared out of a fog, a haze, a creature of the distant past they had assumed was far away, pursuing some obscure goal, and well outside the orbit of Saint Theo's. Then on recognizing me at last, *Catherine! Of course! I knew your father. What are you doing? Where are you now?*

The artists and the English professors, still the same, genial, kind, warm in a way that most of the world has turned its back on. They looked puzzled to hear that I was teaching a course at Stannard State. Stannard; it must have sounded mundane and local to them, given the hype that had attended my time at Saint Theo's.

Merrill's brother looked eerily like him, a nearly identical face, though I overheard him sheepishly admitting that, unlike his brother, he was no poet. Seeing his brother made me crave Merrill, crave his return, and for a moment I wondered if there was some kind of magic that could resurrect him.

Calvin; 2007

I could have let it go, but I persisted anyway. I had always been persistent, stubborn. I wrote to tell him how I had expected him right up to the time I left, thought that against the odds he might appear.

I told him about who I'd seen, what they looked like now. About Merrill's family and who had read at the service, the aging poets who had appeared and gone sadly down the aisle. *There is no one who could understand how I feel about Merrill but you*, I wrote to him. Whether this would be welcome news or not, I didn't know.

When he replied, it was very short. *I like the Mercedes Sosa version of* Gracias a la vida. *Do you know it?* he wrote, and included a link to YouTube.

But this did not stop me. At this point, I wanted to know, was he on my side or not.

> I wish you could have seen that bench outside the chapel before the memorial service. Besides you, there is no one else who could possibly understand about Merrill. I can't help but ask you, do you care that he's gone?

It was a dare of sorts, I guess. There he was in his bookshop, surrounded by antique editions of *Treasure Island* and *Moby-Dick*—he had always dreamed of a navy blue sea—and I persisted in asking him, raising the stakes as his silence persisted in turn. Do you care, Calvin Pini, do you wish to return, do you wish to remember?

Several days passed. I wrote again, just one word.

Well?

When Calvin wrote back, it was brief and certainly to the point. He said:

I don't live in the past like you.

And so that was that. I replied that I would not be writing to him again, not about the past, not about anything, and I didn't. I could be as stubborn in leaving as in seeking out. I liked those dramatic scenes in novels and plays where one person tells another, From this time forward, I will treat you as if dead to me. I know no such person as you.

I don't live in the past like you, wrote Calvin Pini to me. Well, fine, then. I would live there by myself.

Endings

Una didn't exactly share my delight at the prospect of the Stannard teaching gig.

It could get a little weird, isolating. I don't really like to think of you stuck there.

I generally protested, defending Stannard against charges of strangeness or being too out of the way.

Anyway, see how it goes. You don't have to decide anything.

This was one of Una's grand themes. Get all the facts, put off a final decision until later.

Keep your eyes open; there might be something better to apply for.

Una enforced this by falling silent for a few seconds whenever I mentioned Stannard. Then, as if to cut the discussion short, she would add something like, *Well, whatever. See how it goes.*

But I didn't want to see how it went. That was the whole point. I didn't want to wait and see and look around and pack my suitcase and wonder and hope. It was a simple bargain I was going for now, a fair exchange, one that in its own way felt like a great luxury. I could arrive home with the kids on a fall evening, and not fear anything, not agonize over anything.

Given what I had recently felt for Merrill, it was hard to be sure I had really given up; I was devious, I had my own silent agenda, but it was close.

Gramma had an early autumn birthday. I was trying to make her laugh and said, *Well, not long before your birthday comes round again, Gramma. You're heading for ninety five.*

Don't mention it to me! she said. *How I wish God would give it to someone who would enjoy it!*

As for Greensboro, I know there were other endings that would sound much better. For instance, one snowy afternoon, I would run into Miles Bradford in front of Willey's, realizing in a coup de grâce that he had not died after all. I would be wearing a long blue coat with a faux fur collar, just as it had been then. We would pick up where we left off, driving about the Vermont roads just as we had so many years before. But of course, that did not happen.

Or as in an O. Henry story, a letter from Vincenzo the water engineer would be delivered, dated 1989. Since I moved so often, it had gone astray, but managed to reach me these many years later. *Marry me, as you should and must,* it would say, an awkward translation by the writer himself, *Come and live with me forever at Lago di Como.*

As for Kido, I was so annoyed at him that I refused to imagine an ending of this kind for him. In any case, it would have been too painful.

Emmet had already decided that he would grow up to be a rich man and live in a very big house. He liked limousines, the longer the better. We had a joke that Mommy would one of these days meet a Greek millionaire.

Lally like that, he said earnestly.

But what if he was strict, Emmet? I asked. *He might not be all that nice.*

What do then? Emmet asked, worrying as he always did, his eyes full of concern.

Then, Emmet, Mommy would say to that man, Leave your money and go.

Emmet found this tremendously funny; he laughed and laughed.

It was fitting that Merrill had warned me, warned the class really, but I remembered it as a personal caution: Beware of ending the story with lovers arm in arm, overlooking a big valley and saying, *It's all our'n.*

My wardrobe was limited in a familiar way: dark cardigan, white shirt, black pants. My hair style hadn't changed in several decades. Still eyeliner and a dash of lipstick every morning, not sure for whom. The same gestures, incredibly repetitious as I had always been, the same happiness on greeting the early morning, like I was getting it over on others that I was up and they were not.

Madina was moody in the morning. Emmet was crabby. I for my part was the same silently scheming, disciplined and undeviating self I had always been. Only now I didn't have to make flow charts, nor sign in at law faculty meetings, nor account for what a particular Court of Appeals had held on any given topic. Caspian Lake changed color with each new morning. I had no wish to read new things, except in the rarest of cases. Mostly, I reread everything I had ever liked.

A big box of books I had in storage at Park Baun arrived, musty but forgiving, emerging like old pals.

> Once upon a time and a very good time it was there was a moocow coming down along the road and this moocow that was coming down along the road met a nicens little boy named baby tuckoo....

There was something to it, this verbal thing, the thing about words, coming out of the tall grass near Park Baun and Turlough, the near mad thing with words, the fire leaping.

The turfcoloured water of the bath at Clongowes.

Turlough, just up the road from the dreary little slip of a town where Parnell had caught his last cold and then died from it. Stephen Dedalus feared the old fellows living in rural areas, red-rimmed watery eyes, standing at the half door. It wasn't that kind I feared at all.

If Madina was born to ride a horse across the steppe, then I was born a fire leaper and as that would go to my grave. Funny to have chosen Japan, the utterly silent world. Funnier yet to imagine myself in law, stylized, frozen, not even as lively as science because it was simply made up, created to be rigid and threatening.

But now, I could read all the same books, with only a few spaces allotted for newly discovered European romantics, stumbled upon at the Stars and Moon

Bookshop. I read *Room With a View*, and was convinced, once again, agreed by the end to love George Emerson, body and soul. I read *Eva Trout* and rented the strange musty house named Cathay, hard by the sea, told some fibs, hid my true self and surreptitiously sought out a few soulmates. It was all in a day's work.

I hadn't sold the house at Park Baun; there was the question of who would want it, but beyond that, still it was mine. I thought now and then of trying to sell it, but then did nothing. The cold stars would appear up above it, the house might feel aggrieved at being left behind after all the fuss. When I thought about it, I could feel the silence in which it waited; I could imagine the fox in his hole, emerging at nightfall to laugh softly in the neglected grass. And then there were the badgers that came out only at night and were never seen by people, not even in car headlights.

You are off-narrative today.

I thought of jokes like this, and there wasn't a lot I could do with them. *Ha ha,* Madina would say, *Funny not.*

But I didn't have to sit through meetings, listening as each participant lined up his best and most sonorous self promotion; letting fly anecdotes about when he was in-house counsel, or confidant to the AG, or finalist in an important dean's search.

I didn't have to convince a new roomful of students that I was big, tall, and important, despite indications to the contrary: my oft-washed jacket and odd mane of hair.

Emmet's English had improved dramatically, no question. One night as he was drifting to sleep, he opened his eyes, their shallow lids invisible in the dark room.

Mommy ruled by fear?

Where had he heard this, I wondered, *Star Wars*? *Princess Diaries*? Madina's influence was immense, but it didn't sound like her style of thinking.

Am I ruled by fear, do you mean? Why do you ask?

Lally is, at night, with bad dreams.

Was it Camus or one of those other existentialist guys so morbidly popular in the seventies, who invented a character who didn't want to die, so made his life longer by waiting in cinema lines. When he got to the front of the line, he would return again to the end, just to make things so tedious that time itself would last longer. I think I had managed something like that; if things went to plan, I wouldn't have to regret or expect or dread the baton of one season being passed off to the next.

Good or evil angels,
I don't know which,
hurled you into my soul

It was repetitious, my taste, the same old fragments of Alberti, but this time seen on the reverse journey.

At moments, it seemed that things might have gone any number of ways; but it was the fact that they didn't that was compelling. They didn't go that way; there were no genuine surprises, despite the fact that I was continually surprised at how things did not go according to my waking designs. Despite all the places, it came down to a pretty familiar map. In some mysterious way, I had made it come out just like this. A clumsy compromise, the bargain I kept thinking about as I took the Buick and drove away from Boston. But that's not quite right, either. I could have been convinced along the way. I might have done otherwise.

I probably never fooled anyone, not for a moment. My manner was that of a school girl, a Catholic school girl in a hand-me-down blue uniform, blue belt twisted into a rope around my waist, in love with my Holy Name shoes; or in the alternative, like a peasant educated in secret under a hedge, books piled haphazardly next to the open fireplace. Aloneness was my *eau de cologne*, that inexplicable aloneness that should have entranced or repelled, but in the law school made them all simply write me off without mental comment.

I sent Una a YouTube link to that famous scene from the movie *A Man and a Woman*, the scene with the car at the seaside, Ba da da, na na na, na na na na na; the woman is on the beach with the kids and the race car driver sees them from afar; he flashes the lights, then gets in the car and drives towards them. He gets out and runs at full tilt; she runs towards him, the kids run towards him and they spin and spin with the grey expanse of sea and the overcast French sky behind them.

Wow, she wrote back a day later, *great. Where did you find it?*

Una could be receptive when caught in the right mood.

What was I good for; or more nicely put, what was I good at; another way of saying, where the hell did all this come from? But I was good at something. This put me in mind of Daddy, who when making one of his more risqué jokes would say, *You're a good girl, honey; only problem is, there's no demand for them.* This, of course, struck me quite differently twenty or thirty years on.

In the Galway pubs way back when, I would stand at attention when the band struck up *Soldiers Are We* at the end of the night, frowning my strongest frown of disapproval at those who just sat there nursing a beer. I could plunk myself down in the kitchen of cousin Mary's tiny mobile house on an early summer's evening, light up a cigarette, the late sun oblique and blindingly gold on the hill across the way. I could do all of that. I was a genius at it, it was so easy. Devoted, stubborn, unchanging, obsessive, peasant with a stack of books, tossing the undrunk tea out the door into the back garden. Saint Patrick's prayer of devotion, I bind to myself today.

One major trouble was, there was no demand for it.

And despite its pleasures, I still couldn't say, *That* is where you'll find me.

Dear darling John Merrill, on whom I poured out elaborate affection *in absentia*, need not have worried about a badly conceived ending. I had the opposite of the Midas touch; there was no ending, and the best I could pull off was thanks to the few measures of courage I had left in the barrel. I could, you know, escape.

No winning lottery tickets, Greek millionaires, handsome vets, out of the blue murders, identity theft, barn fires, an award winning organic jam business or a hit show in community theatre. Kido had once said I was pure, and so I was. *Kimi wa pyuua da yo.* It was meant, I suppose, to contrast with either himself or the world he lived in.

I would have asked Kido to think of Astrud Gilberto singing *If it takes forever.*

One humid night in Tokyo, under a dark canopy of trees, we said goodbye. I could go on and on, but let's just put it this way: think Astrud singing that song.

In the meantime, here I was, the rented house overlooking the lake, two little doves almost asleep, balancing my checkbook. On Monday, I would drive over to Stannard to re-read and map out *Shayō, The Setting Sun.*

It gets colder quickly in September. I close the front window, against the wishes of Princess, the cat. It crosses my mind that, damn, I wish I'd done Mediterranean studies.

As stories go, it was funny, really, at least some of it. Funny, or something a little harder to identify. *Say it's so, compañera, marinera, say it's so.* No story, no fragment of music, was too grandiose for me, though look what came of it.

When I was little, I would come running home when the other kids were mean to me; a mean comment or a cross look would probably do it. Gramma would crouch down and say, *Don't you cry, they aren't worth one of you tears, not one of your tears.* Gramma had her good side.

Calvin Pini and I had a joke, a very good joke. We liked the poet Mark Strand back then, liked him enormously. From Strand we got a line, *Yes, I am tired, Yes, I want to keep reading.* I think it continued *I say yes to everything,* or something like that. Strand referred to . . . *a black line that would bind us or keep us apart.*

I am still laughing at things Miles Bradford said, more than thirty years later.

I often see Nuala looking at me, smiling and showing her gums. *Which do you like best, Cat?* she is asking.

CPSIA information can be obtained at www.ICGtesting.com
Printed in the USA
LVOW06s0325231115

463622LV00003B/3/P